I AM DEATH

Seven days after being abducted, the body of a twenty-year-old woman is found. Detective Robert Hunter is assigned the case and almost immediately a second body turns up. Hunter knows he has to be quick, for he is chasing a monster.

THE CALLER

Be careful before answering your next call. It could be the beginning of a nightmare, as Robert Hunter discovers as he chases a killer who stalks victims on social media.

GALLERY OF THE DEAD

Robert Hunter arrives at one of the most shocking crime scenes he has ever attended. Soon, he joins forces with the FBI to track down a serial killer who sees murder as more than just killing – it's an art form.

HUNTING EVIL

Lucien Folter, the most dangerous serial killer the FBI has ever known, has just escaped. Now, he's hunting for Detective Robert Hunter – and he's going to make him pay . . .

CHRIS CARTER
WRITTEN IN BLOOD

**SIMON &
SCHUSTER**

London · New York · Sydney · Toronto · New Delhi

First published in Great Britain by Simon & Schuster UK Ltd, 2020

This paperback edition published 2021

Copyright © Chris Carter, 2020

The right of Chris Carter to be identified as author of this work has been
asserted in accordance with the Copyright, Designs and Patents Act, 1988.

3 5 7 9 10 8 6 4 2

Simon & Schuster UK Ltd
1st Floor
222 Gray's Inn Road
London WC1X 8HB

Simon & Schuster Australia, Sydney
Simon & Schuster India, New Delhi

www.simonandschuster.co.uk
www.simonandschuster.com.au
www.simonandschuster.co.in

A CIP catalogue record for this book is available from the British Library

Paperback ISBN: 978-1-4711-7960-0
Export Paperback ISBN: 978-1-4711-9843-4
eBook ISBN: 978-1-4711-7959-4
Audio ISBN: 978-1-4711-8975-3

Printed and bound in Great Britain by CPI Group (UK) Ltd, Croydon, CR0 4YY

MIX
Paper from
responsible sources
FSC® C020471

Dedication

Initially, this book was supposed to be dedicated in loving memory of my partner, Kara Louise Irvine, who left this world in September 2019, taking with her all of my heart, but since then, the whole world has received a wake-up call.

So much has changed for so many of us.

With that in mind, I would like to dedicate this novel not only to Kara, but in loving memory of everyone who unfortunately has lost their battle against COVID-19. We weren't prepared.

To everyone else – that battle carries on, so please stay safe.

The loneliest moment in someone's life is when they're seeing their entire world crumble before their eyes, and all they can do is watch.

One

There were exactly three weeks until Christmas Day. To Angela Wood, that Saturday officially marked the beginning of what she called 'high season'. Shopping malls, main streets, even tiny corner shops would already be covered in fake snow, flashing lights and colorful decorations, all of them heaving with people eager to spend, searching for those perfect gifts. It was the one time of the year when, with a shrug, most people would turn a blind eye to the state of their finances and say to themselves, 'Oh, what the hell, it's Christmas' – and with that they would dig deep and go beyond their means, spending more, sometimes a hell of a lot more than their bank accounts would've allowed them to.

To Angela, 'high season' meant happy people with fat wallets in their pockets and handbags, because as Christmas approached, for a limited period, real cash tended to make a comeback. In this day and age, on any given day, most denizens of Los Angeles carried no cash with them, not even small change – everything was touch-and-go – from buying a single pack of gum from a corner store to spending an absolute fortune on Rodeo Drive. No cash, no mess, no fuss. The era of electronic purchases had well and truly arrived. Not that it mattered that much to any salesperson or shop owner anyway. But Angela was no salesperson. She was no business owner either. What she was, was a master pickpocket and, as such, touch-and-go didn't really work for her. Sure, she could and did make use of credit cards and smartphones when she got them, but in her world, cash was king, and that was why 'high season' always put a smile on her face.

This year Angela decided to start her high season by paying a visit to a cozy shopping street in Tujunga Village.

Located near Ventura Boulevard in Studio City, Tujunga Avenue was nestled between the neighborhoods of Colfax Meadows and Woodbridge Park. 'The Village' was the trendy block-long stretch where one would find a very diverse and charming variety of shops, boutiques, restaurants, bars and cafés. Not surprisingly, The Village attracted a significant number of shoppers all year round, especially over the weekends. During 'high season', that number would multiply exponentially, flooding the street with an ocean of happy people and their loaded wallets.

Whenever possible, Angela preferred to work at night, which was another reason why she loved the festive season so much. To accommodate the heavy number of customers, most shops stayed open later than usual throughout the month of December. Knowing that, Angela got to Tujunga Village just as the sun was beginning to dip behind the horizon, and as she approached The Village from the Woodbridge side she was pleased to see that the number of shoppers crowding the street seemed to have doubled, compared to just a year ago.

'Oh, I so love Christmas season,' Angela said to herself, as she cracked her knuckles against the palms of her hands before slipping on a pair of very thin, red leather gloves.

With the sun just about to bid a final goodnight to the City of Angels, the temperature on the streets had slipped down to eight degrees Celsius, not bad for a winter night where Angela was from, but in a city where the heat and the sun were considered honorary residents, eight degrees was more than enough to cause any proud Angeleno to search their wardrobes for the thickest and warmest coat they could find. For someone like Angela, thick winter coats were a blessing in disguise, because most people made good use of their outside pockets. Such coats offered a thicker layer of insulation between the person's body and those outside pockets, which meant that one didn't even need to be a proficient pickpocket to be able to relieve a victim of their possessions. In a crowded environment, where bumping into another person on the street or inside a store was certainly excusable, picking somebody's pocket became an even easier task. To a highly skilled expert like Angela, a congested Tujunga Village where eighty percent of people were wearing thick coats was like a free gift shop.

'Let's do this,' Angela said as she joined the crowd, her eyes like a hawk's searching for prey.

Before she had even made it halfway down the block-long stretch, Angela had already snatched three wallets. It could easily have been more, a lot more, but during 'high season' Angela had no reason to 'pick-blind' – snatch a wallet without having a good idea of what she was getting.

Her approach was simple and uncomplicated – observe as a customer paid for an item either in store or on the streets. The advantage of that simplistic approach was two-fold:

One – Angela could easily identify who was carrying cash and who wasn't. Two – she could see where the target had placed their wallet – coat pocket, jacket pocket, handbag, etc. With that done, all that was left for Angela to do was tail the target and wait for the right moment to strike, and she never rushed. This time around, it took her only fifteen minutes to get to what Angela called 'checking time'.

Angela never allowed greed to take over. Not anymore. The one time she did, it had been her downfall, costing her a short stint in jail, a place she swore she'd never go back to. Since then, she would only pick a maximum of three wallets at a time, before checking them for cash and credit cards. If she had made enough, she would call it a day. If not, she would dispose of the wallets before going back to the streets for a second round.

After lifting her third wallet, Angela needed a safe place to check the contents of her pickings. Tucked away just behind the historic and always busy Vitello's restaurant, right at the heart of Tujunga Village, was the Rendition Room – a 1930s-themed, speakeasy cocktail bar, the restroom of which would be perfect for what Angela needed to do

Angela had been to the Rendition Room a couple of times before, but she had never seen that place so busy. In the ladies' restroom, she had to wait in line for over five minutes before she could use one of the cubicles. Once in there, she checked the wallets for how much cash they had, and she couldn't be any happier.

Six hundred and eighty-seven bucks for less than fifteen minutes' work, she thought to herself, as she hid most of the cash inside her bra. *Not bad for day one.*

For a split second, she considered going back out onto The

Village for a second round. 'There's so much more out there,' 'Reckless Angela' tried to whisper in her ear. 'You could make one month's picking in one night.'

But 'Sensible Angela' was right there too and, in a heartbeat, she slapped that idea back into oblivion.

'We're done here, Angela. You know much better than this. Instead of doing the dumb thing, why don't you go celebrate and have a drink? After all, you're in a cocktail bar.'

Angela did know much better than that. Since doing jail time, she never argued with reason anymore.

Before exiting the cubicle, and since she was done for the night, Angela first removed the black wig she had on, then her dark contact lenses, and put them away.

Out in the busy bar area, it took her several minutes to finally get served. After skimming through the cocktail menu, Angela decided to go with a classic – the sidecar. Tablewise, she got lucky pretty quickly. Just as she turned away from the bar with her drink, a small, circular, stand-up table vacated just a few feet from her. Angela quickly stepped up to it.

As she sipped her cocktail, her eyes began scanning the crowd. Not that she was reconsidering her decision to call it a night. To Angela, scanning people around her, no matter where she was, had become second nature ... a reflex ... a force of habit. It was something she did without even realizing that she was doing it. Within twenty seconds, she had singled out three of the easiest pickings she had ever seen.

Four tables to her right – two forty-something men. Both positively tipsy. The one wearing glasses had placed his wallet in his jacket pocket and then placed the folded jacket on the empty stool to his right, wallet pocket facing up.

Three tables in front of her – two twenty-something women

sipping margaritas. The one with her back to Angela had her unzipped handbag hanging from the back of her chair.

Next table along to her right – a tall gentleman whose attention was cemented onto his cellphone. He had placed a very elegant leather bag on the floor, several inches away from his feet. Angela hadn't seen the contents of the bag, but she was willing to bet that it would be something valuable.

People have absolutely no clue, Angela thought, as she shook her head ever so slightly. *It's like they never learn*.

As Angela's attention moved back from the bag on the floor to the man and his cellphone, an older gentleman, probably in his mid-sixties, approached the man. Angela could hear their conversation.

'Excuse me,' the older gentleman said. He was carrying a whisky tumbler. 'Do you mind if I rest my drink on your table? It's quite busy tonight.'

The tall man did not break eye contact with his phone.

'I'd rather you didn't.'

Angela frowned at the man's reply, as if she'd heard it wrong.

The older gentleman was clearly taken aback, too.

'I'll just use a tiny corner of the table,' the older gentleman tried again. 'Just to rest my drink. I won't bother you.'

'Well, you're already bothering me,' the tall man said back, finally locking eyes with the older gentleman. 'Go find somewhere else to rest your drink, old-timer. This table is taken.'

Angela's eyes widened as she stared at the tall man in disbelief. *What a total dickhead*, she thought.

Lost for words, the old man stood still for a moment, not really knowing what to do.

'I said fuck off, old man,' the tall man said, his voice firm.

Shocked, the old man turned and walked away.

Angela was just about to offer her table to the older man when 'Reckless Angela' whispered in her ear.

'That guy with the phone is a total and utter dick, Angie. You could teach him a lesson.'

Angela's eyes went back to the man's leather bag on the floor. The tall man's attention returned to his cellphone.

Angela finished her drink and rounded her table to the other side. She was now standing just behind the tall man. She grabbed her cellphone and brought it to her ear so she would look inconspicuous. As she began her fake phone conversation, her right foot moved out just enough to reach the tip of his leather bag's shoulder strap on the floor.

The man was ferociously typing something into his cellphone.

As Angela fake-talked on the phone, she rotated her body away from the man and took two steps in that direction. She stretched her neck and looked around the place, as if searching for someone else inside the cocktail bar. As she did, her right foot stealthily dragged the man's leather bag along with her.

The man was way too occupied with his cellphone to notice his bag moving an extra two feet away from him, but if he had, with the place so busy, Angela could easily just give him the excuse that her foot had got tangled in the shoulder strap by chance, that was all, a simple mistake.

Angela took another step; another bag-drag, and then Lady Luck smiled at her. A few tables in the opposite direction, someone knocked a tray of drinks to the floor. The loud noise of glasses and bottles breaking attracted a multitude of eyes, including the tall man's. By the time his attention returned to his phone, just a few seconds later, Angela was already exiting the Rendition Room with the man's leather bag hidden inside her coat. Five minutes after that, she was on board the 237 bus, heading home.

Angela was dying to look inside the bag, but despite getting a seat at the back of the bus, she resisted the urge. She didn't want any prying eyes checking the contents as well.

From Tujunga Village, it took her a little over forty-five minutes to get home, a small one-bedroom apartment on the south end of Colfax Avenue. As soon as she closed the door behind her, she kicked off her shoes and took a seat on her bed. Legs crossed, yoga style, Angela placed the leather bag in front of her and finally unzipped it open.

Disappointment.

Maybe it was due to the size and shape of the bag, or maybe it was because of how much it weighed, but Angela was almost certain that it would contain something like a laptop or a tablet. It didn't. The only item inside the bag was an eight-by-eleven-inch black, leather-bound journal, which was surprisingly heavy.

'Wow, so instead of a laptop, I get a notebook? Awesome.'

Angela laughed at her misfortune, glad that the only reason she had snatched that leather bag had been to teach that dickhead from the bar a lesson.

'What a rude motherfucker,' she said with a shake of the head. 'I hope that this book is important to you.'

Instinctively, she flipped the book open and carelessly leafed through the pages. The first thing she noticed was that the pages were packed with neat, dense handwriting. Not all the pages contained words. A few of them had been filled with crude drawings and sketches, which Angela didn't pay much attention to. Some had Polaroid photos stapled onto them. As her eyes came to rest on the first photograph she came across, her heart skipped a beat.

She flipped to another page … another Polaroid photo. This time, her heart pretty much stopped beating. With shaky hands she lifted up the photo to see if there was anything written at the back of it, or on the page behind the photo. There was nothing.

'What the fuck?' Those words dribbled out of Angela's lips and, reflexively, her eyes moved to the words on the page, directly beneath the photo. A few lines were all that she could manage before her entire body started shaking.

'Oh God! What the fuck have you done, Angie? What the fuck have you done?'

Two

The LAPD's Ultra Violent Crimes Unit's office was located at the far end of the Robbery Homicide Division's floor, inside the famous Police Administration Building, in downtown Los Angeles. Detective Robert Hunter, who was the head of the UVC Unit, had just returned from his lunch break when the phone on his desk rang.

He answered it after the second ring. 'Detective Hunter, Ultra Violent Crimes Unit.'

'*Robert, it's Susan,*' the caller announced. '*Do you have a minute?*'

Dr. Susan Slater was one of the best lead forensics agents California had to offer. She had worked closely with the UVC Unit in a number of cases.

'Of course, Doc,' Hunter replied. 'Is there something wrong?'

'*I'm not sure,*' Dr. Slater said before a brief pause. '*There might be.*'

Intrigued, Hunter readjusted his position on his seat. 'OK, I'm listening.' His eyes moved to the diary on his desk and he instinctively flipped back a few pages, just to be one hundred percent sure that the UVC Unit wasn't waiting on any forensics test results.

He was right.

'*This is a funny story,*' Dr. Slater began. '*This morning, as I was leaving my house to come to the lab, I checked my mailbox, as I do every morning. Besides the usual weekend junk mail, I found a regular office-size envelope. The envelope had my name in large letters across the front of it, but that was about it.*'

'What do you mean?' Hunter asked.

'*It didn't have my home address, Robert,*' the doctor explained. '*Just my name. There was no stamp, no US postal service mark, and no return address either.*'

'Which means that it was hand-delivered.'

'*Exactly,*' Dr. Slater agreed.

'Have you opened it yet?'

'*I have, but obviously, after all the necessary precautions. What I was presented with, was a book.*'

'OK?' Hunter frowned at the phone.

'*Well, to be more specific ... it's some kind of journal, really.*'

'What sort of journal?'

There was another brief pause.

'*The kind of journal that I think you and Carlos need to come have a look at.*'

Three

Hunter's long-term partner at the Ultra Violent Crimes Unit was Detective Carlos Garcia. They shared the same office space – a claustrophobic 22-square-meter concrete box with a single window, two desks and not much else, but it was still a completely separate enclosure from the rest of the Robbery Homicide Division floor, which, if nothing else, kept prying eyes and the endless buzzing of voices locked out.

While Hunter was on the phone to Dr. Slater, Garcia was seated at his desk, going over some electronic paperwork.

'Want to take a ride to the FSD Criminalistics Lab?' Hunter asked him, as soon as he disconnected from the call, already reaching for his jacket.

The FSD Criminalistics Lab, part of the LAPD's Forensics Science Division (FSD), was comprised of eight specialized unit laboratories, which provided support services to investigations conducted by the various departments of the LAPD. Most of those labs operated out of the Hertzberg-Davis Forensic Science Center, located inside the campus of the California State University in Alhambra, in the western San Gabriel Valley region of Los Angeles.

'The Criminalistics Lab?' Garcia asked, his eyes narrowing at his partner. 'Do we have a result pending?'

'No,' Hunter replied, before quickly recounting the conversation he'd just had with Dr. Slater.

'A notebook?'

'That's what she said,' Hunter confirmed.

'And the Doc gave you nothing more?' Garcia got up, also reaching for his jacket.

'Just that we needed to have a look at it.'

'Yeah, of course I'm in,' Garcia said. 'I've always been a sucker for suspense.'

Four

In city traffic, on a Monday afternoon, it took Hunter and Garcia around twenty-eight minutes to cover the almost six miles between the Police Administration Building on West 1st Street, and the California State University in Alhambra. After parking in the area reserved for law enforcement officers, the two detectives made their way to the Hertzberg-Davis Forensic Science Center – an impressive five-story building, situated in the southwestern quadrant of the university campus. Once they cleared reception, Hunter and Garcia took the stairs up to the second floor, where the Trace Analysis Unit lab was located and where Dr. Slater had told Hunter to meet her.

'Are you looking forward to the ball tomorrow?' Garcia asked, as they cleared the first flight of stairs.

'You mean the LAPD Christmas Ball?' Hunter replied, his facial expression totally lacking excitement. 'Are you?'

'Yeah.' Garcia, on the other hand, looked genuinely thrilled. 'I've got my Zombie-Santa outfit and all.'

'Zombie-Santa?' Hunter's lips stretched into a thin line. 'Really?'

'Hell, yeah! Those parties are so boring. Need to inject a little bit of fun into them.'

'And a Zombie-Santa outfit is your idea of how to inject fun into a party?' Hunter asked.

'You're just jealous cause you can't wear a costume,' Garcia countered. 'You and Captain Blake are at the mayor's table, aren't you?'

Hunter nodded as he rolled his eyes. 'That will be a ton of fun.'

Garcia chuckled. 'Yeah, I bet.'

The Trace Analysis Unit was one of the eight units that comprised the FSD Criminalistics Lab. Its main function, as the name suggested, was to perform analyses on trace evidence that might have occurred as a result of physical contact between suspect and victim during a violent crime. It also analyzed any traces of materials, organic or not, that might have been found at a crime scene.

At the lab double doors, which were kept locked at all times, Hunter pressed the buzzer and waited. A couple of seconds later, the doors unlocked with a subdued hiss.

The lab, which was easily the size of the entire Robbery Homicide Division's floor, was chilled to a couple of degrees below comfortable, but was still relatively warm compared to the temperature on the streets. Several forensics agents, all of them in long white lab coats, were busy at different workstations. Soothing classical music played at very low volume in the background.

'Over here, guys.'

Both detectives heard Dr. Slater call, as the doors slowly closed behind them.

The doctor was sitting in front of an inverted microscope, not that far from where Hunter and Garcia were standing.

In her mid-thirties, Dr. Susan Slater was five-foot seven,

with a slim, toned body, high cheekbones and a delicate nose. Her long blonde hair was pulled back into a disheveled bun at the top of her head. Her makeup was subtle and brought out the light blue of her eyes.

'Thanks for coming over so quickly,' she said as she greeted both detectives with a simple head nod.

'Well, you really hooked us with that mysterious phone call,' Garcia said with a smile. 'So what is it that you got?'

'Exactly what I told Robert over the phone,' Dr. Slater replied. Her voice was soft and jovial, but also full of knowledge and experience. 'Someone hand-delivered a package to my mailbox over the weekend – probably late last night or in the early hours of this morning. The envelope alone grabbed my attention.'

'Why?' Garcia asked. 'What was wrong with it?'

'No address or stamp, to start with. Just my name. No return address either.' She indicated a large, see-through evidence bag that was on the worktop by the inverted microscope in front of her. Inside the evidence bag they could all see a brown envelope. Across the front of it, handwritten in large black capital letters, was her name – Susan Slater.

'May I?' Hunter asked, indicating the evidence bag.

'Be my guest.'

Hunter picked it up so he and Garcia could study the envelope inside it.

'I'm guessing you've tested it for prints already?' Garcia asked.

Dr. Slater nodded. 'None other than mine.'

'The handwriting?' Hunter this time.

'All capitals and nothing special about it. The pen used was a cheap marker pen with a fine tip. No point in trying to trace the ink to any specific brand, as the result would most certainly lead us to the kind of marker pen that is stocked by all major supermarkets.'

Hunter nodded, as he put down the evidence bag. 'And you mentioned something about a notebook?'

'Yes,' Dr. Slater said, pointing toward the back of the lab. 'And that's where the plot really thickens. Come, let me show you.'

Hunter and Garcia followed her past a group of forensics agents, all too absorbed in what they were doing to even acknowledge the two detectives. As they reached one of two separate enclosures at the far end of the lab floor, they waited while Dr. Slater entered an eight-digit code into a metal keypad on the door handle.

The enclosure was about twenty-six feet long by twenty wide. Inside it, on three separate worktops, sat five computer screens and six different microscopes – two laser-scanning, two stereo, one inverted and one laser confocal. The temperature inside the new room dropped another degree or two when compared to the rest of the lab. Dr. Slater guided Hunter and Garcia to an empty worktop to the left of the door.

'This morning,' she explained, 'when I checked my mailbox and picked up the envelope, I came this close to opening it right there and then.' She indicated with her thumb and forefinger. 'I couldn't remember ordering anything over the Internet, but I've been known to order stuff and completely forget about it, especially if it takes over three days to arrive. Also, sometimes, either the FSD or some other forensics lab around the country will send me unsolicited samples, material, whatever, simply because . . .' She shrugged. 'They do stuff like that. Anyway, I was about to rip the envelope open when my brain decided to wake up. No one from the FSD, or any other forensics lab around the country, would hand-deliver an unsolicited package to my door. If they did, it would be because it was something quite urgent and they would ring the bell and deliver it to me, not drop it in my mailbox. With that in mind, I brought it straight here and this morning the package went through three different scanners – regular X-ray, which revealed that the contents were a notebook; explosive detection, which came back negative; and poisonous or hazardous substances, which also came back negative. So, after feeling like a complete idiot for being too paranoid and wasting government resources, I finally opened the package.' She indicated another evidence bag that was on the worktop directly behind her. Inside it was a leather-bound notebook. 'And that right there is what I got. Don't forget to glove up before opening the evidence bag.'

From a dispenser mounted onto the wall by the door, Hunter and Garcia each picked up a pair of blue latex gloves and put them on.

With the notebook still inside the evidence bag, the first thing that both detectives noticed was that the book's black leather cover was thicker than you would expect on a notebook. There was no design, no inscription, no carvings, no marks of any kind to either the front or the back cover.

The second thing they both noticed was that the journal weighed relatively more than a regular notebook, even though it only seemed to be about one hundred and twenty pages long, maybe a little more. When looked at from a side angle, it was obvious that the pages didn't sit smoothly between the two covers. Most of them were warped, which indicated that either those pages had gotten wet, or they had something stuck onto them, or both.

Hunter and Garcia repositioned themselves around the workstation before Hunter pulled the notebook out of the see-through plastic bag. He then placed it on the worktop and flipped it open to the first page.

Contrary to what one would expect from a personal diary or a journal, it didn't open with an owner's information page. Nothing on the flipside of the front cover either. No name, no address, no cellphone number, no email . . . nothing.

Hunter and Garcia quickly checked the first page.

The entry also differed from that of a regular diary in the sense that there was no date or any other sort of time stamp at the top or anywhere else on the page. There were also no page breaks and no paragraphs, just word after word, forming line after line in a seemingly interminable block of text, but the entry writer had at least made use of punctuation, which, if nothing else, helped to separate his thoughts and make the text less confusing.

The handwriting throughout the whole book was cursive and relatively neat, all in black ink. Any mistakes were dealt with via a single line across the wrong word or phrase – no White-Out, no erasing, no scratching . . . no mess. There was no yellowing of the pages or its edges either, which immediately indicated that the diary couldn't have been that old. Despite the pages being unlined, Hunter was impressed with how straight the writer had kept the text.

Garcia was just about ready to start flipping through pages in the journal when Hunter placed a hand on his right arm, stopping him. His eyes had moved to the first line on the page and he had started reading it.

Her name was Elizabeth Gibbs, born 22nd October 1994. Not that I care at all about their names, who they were, or any other aspect of their lives. After so many, they become nothing more than meaningless faces lost in darkness. One will morph into another ... which will morph into another ... and so on. The cycle never ends. My memory isn't so good anymore. I forget things. I forget a lot of things, and it's just getting worse. That's one of the reasons why I decided to keep this journal. The second is for security. I should've started these records a while ago, when I first heard the voices, but that's water under the bridge and the journal is here now. I did try remembering facts ... details from past events, but my memory isn't so good anymore and it won't be getting any better, only worse. Once again, the voices were very specific about the subject. Female. Minimum height: five-foot seven. Hair: black – long – straight. Eyes: dark. Weight: no heavier than 165 pounds. Ethnicity: white. It took me only a few days to find her. It wasn't hard. After tailing the subject around town, an opportunity to take her finally showed itself. Date and time: February 3rd 2018 – 19:30. Location: Albertsons' parking lot, Rosecrans Avenue, La Mirada. Photo: Same night, a few hours after abduction.

Hunter turned the page. There was nothing written on the reverse of it. The writer had decided to use only the front of each diary page. The next one along started with a gap of about three inches – roughly fifteen lines. Two tiny holes right at the top of the page indicated that something had been stapled to it. On the right, closer to the page's edge there was a smear of what looked like blood. Hunter's eyes moved to Dr. Slater.

'There was a photo?' he asked.

'There was indeed,' she replied, as she walked over to a different worktop to pick up yet another evidence bag before handing it to Hunter. Inside it there was an instax-mini Polaroid-style photograph – sixty-two millimeters long by forty-two wide. It showed a woman in her mid-twenties. Her long, straight black hair fell loosely over her shoulders. The look in her dark eyes mirrored the expression on her face – total and utter terror. Tears had come and gone, dragging most of her mascara and eyeliner with them, creating a crisscross of watery black lines all the way down to her chin. The light-red lipstick she had worn that night was smeared over her lips and across her face. The collar and shoulders of the pale-blue blouse she had on were wet with perspiration. The photo had been taken against a cinderblock wall.

'They have all been bagged,' Dr. Slater added. 'Ready to be taken for analysis,'

'They?' Garcia asked, his eyes moving from the photo to the doctor.

She nodded as she breathed in. 'There were a total of sixteen photos stapled to that journal. Sixteen different "subjects".'

Hunter and Garcia had both noticed the small pile of evidence bags on the worktop directly behind Dr. Slater, but had assumed that those were evidence belonging to different cases.

'How about this smear at the bottom of the page here?' Hunter asked. 'Is this blood?'

'It is,' Dr. Slater confirmed. 'Every single photo I retrieved from that notebook came accompanied by a similar blood smear. The logical conclusion is that the blood belongs to the subject in the photo. I've swabbed that specific one you're look-ing at and the swab has already been sent to the DNA Unit for testing.' She crossed her arms in front of her chest. 'But please, carry on reading. The really good part is just a few lines ahead.'

Hunter placed the evidence bag down on the worktop next to the journal before allowing his attention to return to the writing, which re-started directly after the gap. On this page, there was a sketch showing a rectangular box. Underneath it, the word 'wood' had been written. Every dimension to the box panels, including the lid, were clearly noted.

Unlike the last subject, which turned out to be a terribly messy affair, the preparation and delivery of this one was relatively simple. No blood. No torture. No humiliation. No degradation. I heard the voices loud and clear – 'You need to bury her alive.'

Five

Hunter paused. His concerned stare returned to the Polaroid photo inside the evidence bag before moving once again to Dr. Slater.

'Is this for real?' Garcia asked, a skeptical expression on his face. 'Are you sure that this isn't a hoax?'

'Well,' the doctor began. 'That's why I called you guys. I wouldn't like to waste your time, so I took the liberty of checking her name and photo against the Missing Persons database.' Her eyebrows arched as she reached into her lab-coat pocket. 'Elizabeth Gibbs,' she read from the printout in her hand. 'Born October 22nd, 1994, right here in Los Angeles. Resident of La Mirada. She was reported missing on February 4th, 2018, by her boyfriend, Phillip Miller, with whom she shared a house not that far from the location cited in that book – the Albertsons parking lot on Rosecrans Avenue. Her car, a white Nissan Sentra, was found abandoned by the Sheriff's Department at that exact location. Nothing was found in her car – no prints, no clues. Elizabeth Gibbs has also never been found. She's still listed as missing.' Dr. Slater returned the printout to her pocket. 'If you missed that, the date matches the entry in that journal.'

'Yeah, I got that,' Hunter said. His brow was creased in thought.

'Does that printout mention the name of the detective assigned to the case?' Garcia asked.

Out came the printout again. 'Detective Henrique Gomez,' she informed them. 'LAPD Missing Persons Unit. Do you know him?'

Hunter and Garcia both shook their heads.

'As you might expect,' Dr. Slater continued. 'Miss Gibbs's boyfriend came under heavy scrutiny, but his alibi was solid.'

Garcia scratched his forehead uncomfortably as he breathed out. 'I'm starting to get a severe case of déjà vu here.' His eyes widened at Hunter. 'Another notebook describing victims and how they were murdered?'

Hunter knew that his partner was making a reference to Lucien Folter – without a doubt the most dangerous and delusional serial killer they had ever chased – but thanks to their team effort, Lucien's new permanent address was the United States Federal Supermax prison in Florence, Colorado.

'This isn't the same thing, Carlos,' he came back.

'I'm not saying it is,' Garcia agreed. 'All I'm saying is that a notebook describing victims and how they were murdered brings back some pretty awful memories.'

'What are you guys talking about?' Dr. Slater asked, curiosity all over her face. 'What memories?'

'It's an old case we worked on,' Hunter replied, but left it at that. His attention reverted back to the notebook on the worktop so he could finish reading the rest of the entry.

Building the box where the subject lay was easy. The voices gave me no specifications when it came to the container itself, so I was free to do as I liked. A few solid planks of wood and a bag of nails was all it took. There was no point in making the inside of the container comfortable. The technical side of the request took me a whole day to finally get it all working, but in the end everything ran smoothly and without glitches. The subject was never retrieved from its resting place – 34°15'16.9"N 118°14'52.4"W.

Garcia's jaw dropped open. 'Is that what I think it is?'

Hunter felt a surge of adrenaline rush though him. The writer had ended the entry with longitude and latitude coordinates.

'I think so,' he replied.

Both detectives looked back at Dr. Slater, who nodded almost apologetically.

'Call me curious, but I couldn't wait. I entered those coordinates onto a web map application.'

'And?' Garcia asked, eagerly.

'And what I got was a somewhat remote location by a cluster of trees near some hills, about a mile into Deukmejian Wilderness Park, in Glendale. Though the location is somewhat remote,' the doctor added, 'it's certainly accessible.'

For a moment, the room went completely silent.

Garcia saw the look on Hunter's face and spoke first.

'OK.' He nodded at his partner. 'I know that look, Robert. I know what you're thinking, but before we take this to Captain Blake asking for a green light for a digging expedition, don't you think that we should at least wait for the DNA results from that blood smear? Elizabeth Gibbs's DNA will be on file with the Missing Persons Unit. If there's a match then I'm sure we'll get a "go ahead", but if we go up to the captain right now with nothing more than matching dates on a suspicious notebook, she'll red-light us. You know she will, especially with all these budget cuts that the department's been getting.'

'We also have the Polaroid photos,' Dr. Slater offered.

'Still,' Garcia argued. 'That won't be enough to get Captain Blake to approve an excavating expedition somewhere in the woods. Not with the pressure she's under because of these budget cuts. Those come at a high cost. We'd need to get an entire crew over to that location with a digger, lights, power generators, the works. The Captain will need more than matching dates and Polaroids.'

'Yes, you're right,' Hunter agreed. 'But DNA analysis can take a while. You know that. Even with an urgent request.' He checked his watch.

Once again, Garcia recognized the look on his partner's face.

'You cannot be serious,' he said, looking at Hunter sideways.

'It's coming up to two o'clock now,' Hunter came back. 'We can probably make it up there for about three, three-thirty at the latest. That'll give us about one to one and a half hours of sunlight today, but if needed, we can go back tomorrow.'

Garcia's disbelief increased. 'Have you lost your mind? The Doc just told us that those coordinates point to a location somewhere inside Deukmejian. You've been there before, right? It's rugged terrain, Robert. Rocky in places, hard ground in others . . .' He shrugged. 'You probably know this, but by hand and in "optimum soil", it takes an experienced gravedigger around six hours to dig a six-foot grave. How much experience do you have with a shovel?'

'A little,' Hunter replied.

'Which is also known as – not enough,' Garcia came back.

'Well, me neither. It will probably take the two of us a full day of solid work to dig a grave. We'll be up there for the rest of today, all of tonight and probably the whole of tomorrow as well. We need a pro digging team, Robert.'

'You're right, and I appreciate your argument,' Hunter said. 'But there are a couple of things that you're forgetting.'

'Really? Like what?'

'It might not be optimum soil up there,' Hunter began. 'But we won't be digging untouched ground. We'll be re-digging pre-disturbed soil, which makes the job considerably easier. And we've been to a few sites where the perpetrator had dug a makeshift grave to hide a body, or remains of such, remember?'

'Yes, of course I do.'

'Then you'll also remember that those graves were all shallow graves. Not once have we encountered any that were deeper than two, three feet at a push, and that fact repeats itself across the board for the exact same reason you've just mentioned – it takes an experienced gravedigger around six hours to dig a six-foot grave by hand in optimum soil. An inexperienced digger, in rugged terrain?' Hunter shook his head. 'It would take him a full day, if not longer.'

Garcia scratched the underside of his chin.

'If he was digging in his backyard then maybe,' Hunter continued. 'But we're talking about a public park here. Yes, there are several very secluded areas up there, but it's still a public park. No one would risk spending a full day digging a grave to hide a body in a public park. A few hours, sure, but not a full day. I'd be very surprised if we need to dig any deeper than two and a half feet.'

Garcia couldn't argue with his partner's logic.

'Where are we going to get shovels and everything else we need?' he asked.

Hunter looked at Dr. Slater.

'We've got them,' she said, nodding at Hunter. 'We've got a couple of vans downstairs loaded with digging equipment. You can borrow whatever you need.'

Garcia threw his head back and closed his eyes. This battle was already lost.

Six

From one of the forensics vans parked at the back of the Hertzberg-Davis Forensic Science Center, Hunter and Garcia borrowed a couple of shovels, two heavy-duty pickaxes, two pairs of thick gardening gloves, two crowbars and two double-bulb headlamp units.

With everything loaded into the trunk of his car, Garcia entered the coordinates cited in the notebook into his satnav system.

The park itself occupied a rugged 709-acre site in the foothills of the San Gabriel Mountains at the northernmost extremity of Glendale. Though the park included a few isolated streamside woodlands, it was predominantly chaparral and sage scrub, not to mention all the rocks and hills.

'Definitely not the best of terrains for digging,' Garcia said, as they finally reached Dunsmore Canyon Trail, the road that took them through the park.

'That's for sure,' Hunter agreed. 'But there are several pretty secluded areas off the main trail, some of them small woodlands with softer soil, and those are scattered all throughout the park. I have no doubt that was why this place was chosen.'

Garcia tilted his head to one side ever so slightly in a 'maybe' gesture.

'If this craziness turns out to be real, Robert,' he said. 'If somebody did actually deliver that ...' Garcia paused for a second, trying to choose his words. '... "Diary of Death" to Dr. Slater, then I've got two questions swimming around in my head.'

'Who delivered that package to her mailbox?' Hunter beat him to the punch. He was thinking about the same thing.

'That's definitely question number one,' Garcia agreed. 'Was it the person who made those entries to that notebook? In that case – the killer himself. Was it someone who was working with the killer and decided to jump ship? Was it some pour soul who came across that diary somewhere? Who?'

Hunter's stare focused on the flora outside his window.

'And then there's prize question number two,' Garcia continued. 'Why deliver it to the Doc?'

'I'm not sure,' Hunter finally replied, not wanting to speculate.

'Well, I can think of only two possible scenarios,' Garcia proceeded. 'Either, for some reason, whoever delivered that notebook to her mailbox really wants her to be involved in whatever madness this might turn out to be, or the person knows her. Maybe the person in question doesn't know her personally,' Garcia admitted. 'Maybe they only know what the Doc does for a living – this person could've seen the Doc on TV, on an interview. He or she could've attended one of her lectures, or read one of her papers or studies ... I don't know.' He checked his satnav again. They were almost there. 'But the person probably somehow knows that she is a great forensic scientist and that she's part of the LAPD FSD. If that person wanted the notebook to be looked at and examined straight away, dropping it in her mailbox would certainly do the job a lot faster than sending it over to the LAPD or the FBI.'

'That's true,' Hunter agreed. 'But what bothers me is – why deliver it to her house? Why not send it to the FSD Criminalistics Lab? If the person wanted Susan to look at that notebook ASAP, all they needed to do was address the package to her and write the word "urgent" on it. That would've done the trick. Why was it delivered to her house?'

Still on Dunsmore Canyon Trail, Garcia geared down. On his screen, the checkered flag that marked the destination was off-road directly to their left, about thirty-five yards into the chaparral. There was no turning, no road or track that would lead them there. The only way to get to the location shown on the satnav's screen was to leave the car by the side of the road and carry on the rest of the way on foot – and even then, there was no visible footpath. They would have to create their own trail through the shrubs and the heavy rocky terrain.

And that was exactly what they did.

In places the vegetation was so dense that both detectives were forced to use their shovels as improvised machetes. Though their eyes searched the ground as they walked, neither Hunter nor Garcia were really expecting to find any real signs of anyone having been through there before. First: whoever had written that entry could've used a number of different paths to reach the location shown on Garcia's screen. Second: the date mentioned in the entry took them back to over two years ago. Any marks or signs that might've been left behind would've been completely erased by the elements by now.

It wasn't exactly what Angelenos would consider a warm day. The weak sun above their heads made it a very comfortable fourteen degrees Celsius, but still, the rough terrain coupled with the heavy tools they were carrying was already making them sweat.

'According to this thing,' Garcia said, wiping his forehead and nodding at his smartphone, 'the spot we're looking for should be just past these trees here.' He indicated a cluster of trees just ahead of them.

They circled around the trees to get to the other side.

'This is supposed to be it,' Garcia said, checking his smartphone screen and looking around the area they were in. 'Please excuse my ignorance on this subject, but how accurate are these longitude and latitude coordinates?'

'That really depends on two main factors,' Hunter explained. 'The position on the Earth's surface or, more specifically, the latitude at which the measurement took place, and the data referenced to represent the Earth.'

Garcia stared back at his partner, blank-faced. 'And for those of us who do not speak nerd, what does that mean?'

Hunter smiled. 'Sorry. Well, in short, the more numbers you have to the right of the decimal point, the more accurate the location. It can be accurate down to a fraction of an inch if a person so wishes.'

'Decimal point?' Garcia queried, checking the coordinates that he had entered into his map application – 34°15'16.9"N 118°14'52.4"W. 'Shit, there's only one number to the right of the decimal point here. So this position is probably just a rough ballpark.'

'Not that decimal point,' Hunter came back. 'It has to be converted into longitude and latitude decimal form.'

Garcia paused. 'Do you know how to do that?'

'We don't have to. The application you're using on your

phone has already done it for you, I'm sure. It should be either next to, or directly under the coordinates you entered into the search box.'

Garcia checked his phone again. Hunter was right. Directly under the coordinates that Garcia had entered into the map application were two different numbers: 34.254694 and -18.247889.

'OK,' Garcia said. 'So we have a figure with six numbers to the right of the decimal point here.'

Hunter nodded. 'That will probably guide us to the location with inch-perfect precision.'

Garcia looked at the ground they were standing on. There wasn't much vegetation, just turf and a few loose rocks. 'So this is it, really. We are on it.'

Hunter dropped the pickax and the headlamp he was carrying. 'I guess we better start digging then.' He readied the shovel in his hands.

Garcia put the pickax and the crowbar to one side and used his shovel to push the loose rocks out of the way.

The ground was hard, but wasn't as solid as it looked or as they expected it to be. It had been patted down, which indicated that it had been disturbed before.

Hunter and Garcia dug side by side. Even with the soil being a lot softer than they had expected, the work was laborious and progressed slowly.

'I told you this wouldn't be as easy as you thought it would,' Garcia said, checking the sky. They hadn't been digging for very long and the sun was already about to disappear behind the horizon. 'It's getting dark, and we forgot to bring water.'

Both of their shirts were drenched in sweat.

'Yes,' Hunter agreed. 'That was a mistake. My mouth is as dry as a bag of roasted peanuts.' He paused and reached for his head-lamp. 'Look, let's carry on for another half an hour. If we don't get anything, then in the morning we take it to the captain and see if we can get clearance for a digging expedition with what we have.'

'Fine,' Garcia said with a nod. 'But if she declines, you're going to come back here tomorrow and carry on anyway, aren't you?'

'Probably,' Hunter admitted.

Garcia shook his head as he picked up his headlamp. 'Half an hour – that's all.'

'You can time it,' Hunter said, switching his headlamp on.

'I will,' Garcia replied, setting the timer in his smartphone for thirty minutes and showing it to Hunter, who nodded and began digging again.

Garcia turned on his headlamp and also went back to work.

They didn't need another half an hour. Twelve minutes later, Hunter's shovel hit something that produced an odd sound – solid, but hollow at the same time.

Both detectives stopped dead.

'Whatever that is,' Garcia said, '. . . it's not soil.'

Hunter used the tip of his shovel to scrape away some dirt, before going down on his knees to use his hands.

'Solid wood,' he said, using his knuckles to knock against the new surface he had found.

Hunter got back on his feet and, though visibility had deteriorated due to a moonless night sky, their headlamps were powerful enough to allow them to carry on shoveling for another hour, until they had revealed the top of a rectangular wooden box that looked to be about two feet wide by six feet in length. The wood used was light in color and very sturdy. The killer had used twelve nails to seal the box shut.

'Shall I call it in?' Garcia asked, putting down his shovel. 'We're going to need a full lineup here – forensics, a digging team, lights, everything. This entire area will need to be dug for other graves.'

'We need to open this first,' Hunter said, nodding at the wooden box.

'Don't you think it's better to wait for forensics and reinforcements? They'll be able to pull this whole casket out of the ground, and they'll be much better equipped to preserve whatever needs to be preserved when that lid comes off.'

'Agreed,' Hunter said. 'But all we've done here is find a box in the ground, Carlos. This isn't an LAPD investigation. Not yet. For all we know, this box could be full of marshmallows. For us to call it in, we need a body.'

Garcia blew into the palms of his hands, which were by then red-raw and hurting like crazy. He wanted to argue with Hunter, but he knew that his partner was right.

'All we need to do here,' Hunter said, 'is use the crowbars to remove the nails and pry open the lid.'

Lifting the nails from the lid wasn't as easy as they hoped it would be. Whoever had nailed that lid shut had used heavy-duty round wire nails that were two inches long. It would've been easier to use the crowbars to smash open the lid instead of extracting the nails, but they wanted to keep the casket as intact as they possibly could.

Being extra careful to keep the wood from even chipping was a painstaking job and it took Hunter and Garcia almost twenty-five minutes to extract all twelve nails. As the final one came off, the two detectives looked at each other, their foreheads wet with sweat, their faces smeared with dirt. With their headlamps on, they looked like a pair of coalminers.

'You grab that end,' Hunter said, 'and I'll grab this one. We lift it together.'

They got down to their knees again and reached for the lid, which was about an inch thick, weighing somewhere in the region of twelve to fifteen pounds. The whole box looked to have been built with solid planks of wood that had been cut to size, all of them about an inch thick.

Doing their best to keep the lid as level as possible to try to avoid any dirt slipping into the box, they carefully lifted it up and to one side until they were finally able to see what lay inside the makeshift casket.

'OK.' Garcia spoke first, after several silent seconds. 'I sure as hell wasn't expecting this.'

Seven

'What the hell?' Dr. Slater gasped, as the extra-bright beam from her flashlight illuminated the open casket inside the shallow grave by her feet. She had driven up to the park ahead of the forensics circus that was about to descend on them.

Lying inside the makeshift casket, still in the very early stages of decomposition, was a female body. Her eyes, nose and lips were completely gone, leaving her skull with three ominous black holes and two lines of exposed stained teeth, but a fair amount of dried skin and muscle tissue was still attached to her skeleton.

The state of the body didn't surprise Hunter, Garcia or Dr. Slater, as they all knew that without a coffin, in ordinary soil, an unembalmed adult body buried six feet under would take somewhere between eight and twelve years to fully decompose to a skeleton. Placed inside a coffin, the timeframe for the body's decomposition would be considerably longer, depending on the type of wood used. Since the body Hunter and Garcia had uncovered had been placed inside a sturdy wooden box that had been tightly sealed and buried in a two-foot-deep shallow grave just over two years ago, its slow decomposition matched the expectation. No, what had surprised everyone had been the wedding dress.

'Her killer dressed her up in a wedding dress?' Dr. Slater asked. 'Why?'

She wasn't really expecting an answer. Hunter and Garcia both knew that.

'Was there any mention of a wedding dress in that notebook?' Hunter asked.

Dr. Slater angled her head to one side, shrugging. 'I haven't read much further than what the two of you have. We are running behind in so many cases, I just couldn't find the time, but up to the point I got, there was no mention of it.'

'Is the notebook still back in the lab?' Garcia asked.

'Not in the one you were in earlier today,' she replied. 'I sent it over to the DNA lab for testing, together with all the Polaroid photos.'

The FSD Serology/DNA lab was the only FSD specialized unit lab that did not operate out of Cal State Alhambra. It was located four and a half miles away in the C. Erwin Piper Technical Center in Downtown Los Angeles, not that far from the Police Administration Building.

'But out of pure interest,' Dr. Slater admitted, 'I did photograph the first few pages so I could read them later.'

'Can you send those photos over to the UVC Unit ASAP?' Hunter asked.

'Of course,' she confirmed.

'But now that we're sure that the book isn't a hoax,' Garcia said, 'we're going to need the entire notebook photographed.'

'No problem,' Dr. Slater replied. 'I'll get in touch with the DNA lab tomorrow and ask someone to photograph all the pages.' She allowed her attention to return to the body in the casket. A few seconds later, she frowned. 'Wait a second. Something else isn't quite right with this picture.'

Hunter nodded. He and Garcia had already discussed it while waiting for the doctor.

'You found her in this position?' she asked.

'We haven't touched a thing, Doc,' Garcia confirmed.

The body was lying on its back, in a traditional burial position – legs extended, arms by the side of the torso, bent at the elbows with the fingers interlaced and the hands resting on the body's stomach. Her long black hair was sprawled around her head like a fan.

'But according to the notebook,' Dr. Slater said, her stare moving between the two detectives, 'the victim was buried alive.'

Hunter nodded once.

'So how come she's in such a tranquil position, right?' Garcia asked. 'Once she woke up inside a dark box, it would've taken her just a few seconds to realize that it had been nailed shut. From then on, panic would've taken over. She would've kicked, punched, scratched, screamed, head-butted . . . anything to try to free herself. She should've been in any other position but that one. And then there's the hair. It perfectly frames her face, as if she was posing for a photograph.'

'And she did fight,' Hunter confirmed, indicating the lid that they had carefully rested against a tree a few feet behind them. 'On the inside of the lid there are plenty of scratch marks, some blood and a few embedded fingernails. She fought all she could.'

Dr. Slater shifted her flashlight beam toward the trees and the lid, but she stayed where she was. She would get a chance to better examine the lid back in the lab.

'The second problem with this picture,' Hunter carried on, 'is that the dress should've been at least torn in places and certainly dirty.' He nodded at the body in the grave. 'Look at it. It seems almost pristine.'

The penny finally dropped for Dr. Slater.

'Jesus!' She gasped. 'So whoever buried her alive waited for her to die, then came back here, dug her up, reopened the casket, dressed her up in that wedding dress, posed her perfectly, and then buried her again?'

'That's the assumption,' Hunter agreed.

Dr. Slater breathed out heavily. She wanted to ask 'why' again, but right then, no one but the killer would really be able to answer that question. Instead, she looked around the area they were in.

'This is a relatively large area,' she said. 'Do you think that there might be any more graves around?'

'Right now it's anyone's guess,' Hunter replied. 'But I would hold back on a full search excavation operation for now. We have the book,' he explained. 'Since whoever wrote those entries gave us the exact coordinates to her . . .' he indicated the body on the ground. 'It stands to reason that he would've also noted down the coordinates for any other subsequent graves he might've dug, here or elsewhere.'

'Fair point,' the doctor agreed. Right then, her phone rang in her pocket. 'Excuse me for a second.' She turned away from the grave and took the call.

'*Doc.*' It was Kenneth Morgan, a senior forensics agent who worked with Dr. Slater at the FSD. '*We're here. Parked just behind your car. So how do we get to this place?*'

'Stay there. I'll come and get you.'

Due to the harsh vegetation and the unforgiving hilly and rocky terrain, vehicle access to that particular spot inside the park was downright impossible. No forensics van or police car would be able to get through. They needed to park on Dunsmore Canyon Trail and carry everything in by hand, including lights, excavation equipment and power generators. It was nearly eleven thirty in the evening when the full forensics circus was finally able to be lit up.

'Getting a crane up here is out of the question,' Dr. Slater informed Hunter and Garcia. 'We'll have to re-seal the box, to avoid dirt falling into it, and dig the whole thing out by hand.'

Both detectives had guessed that that would be the case.

'While we were waiting for you,' Hunter said, 'Carlos and I looked around the area for any traces of anyone being here. This is such an isolated spot that if we'd found anything – a cigarette butt, a piece of gum, a candy wrapper, a discarded bottle of water, whatever – there was a good chance that it would've come from whoever dug that grave. Whoever that person is, it looks like he spent a considerable amount of time up here, especially if he came back to dig her up and then bury her again.'

'Did you find anything?'

'Not a thing,' Garcia replied. 'But I'm sure that we weren't nearly thorough enough. It's pitch-black up here and all we had were these headlamps.'

'Don't worry,' Dr. Slater assured them. 'If this monster has left anything behind, we'll find it.'

The forensics photographer moved past them and began photographing the body inside the coffin.

'This is going to be slow and boring work,' Dr. Slater said to Hunter and Garcia. 'We'll be here for hours. You guys should go home. I'm sure it's way past the end of your shift. If we uncover anything else, I'll let you know straight away.'

'I'll stay for a little while,' Hunter said, before turning to face his partner. 'But you go home, Carlos. Say hi to Anna for me. I'll see you at headquarters tomorrow.'

Garcia was about to leave when the photographer snapped another picture and something inside the coffin caught his eye. Something that seemed to be attached to the right corner by the body's head. Something that her fanned hair had been hiding.

'Detectives,' he called, putting down his camera. 'Maybe you want to come and have a look at this.'

Hunter, Garcia and Dr. Slater moved closer, crouching down by the grave. Kenneth Morgan joined them a second later.

'Right there.' The photographer carefully moved some of the hair out of the way and indicated a small, black, rectangular box, about the size of an eight-pin Lego brick.

'Let me have a look,' Morgan said, grabbing a brand-new pair of latex gloves. He moved closer still and reached for it, but the tiny black box didn't budge. 'It's not coming out,' he announced. 'I think it's glued to the wood.'

'What the hell is it?' Dr. Slater asked.

'I'm not entirely sure,' Morgan replied, angling his body over the coffin to try to get a better look at it. That was when he noticed the tiny, round lens on its face. He paused and looked back at Dr. Slater, his eyes full of surprise.

'I think this is a camera, Doc. A streaming camera. Whoever did this didn't just bury this poor woman alive. He watched her die.'

Eight

Tuesday, December 8th

Barbara Blake, the captain of LAPD's Robbery Homicide Division, had spent the best part of her morning in yet another budget meeting. Once the meeting was over, she dropped a file on her desk and went straight into Hunter and Garcia's office.

'OK,' she said, as she closed the door behind her. Her long dark hair was tied back into a slick ponytail, revealing shiny silver earrings dangling from tiny lobes. She wore a dark blue pencil skirt suit. Her jacket was undone, showing a silk white blouse underneath. 'What's this file that was on my desk this morning? A "murder diary"? A shallow grave up in Deukmejian? A woman who was buried alive? What the hell?' Both of her palms faced up.

Hunter ran the captain through the whole story.

'So where is this diary now?' she asked when Hunter was done.

'With the FSD DNA lab,' Garcia replied. 'But we should be getting photographs of every page sometime today.'

'And who's the woman . . . the victim, do we know?'

'We still need to wait for DNA confirmation to be one

hundred percent sure,' Hunter replied, indicating the photos that were taken by the forensics photographer that were already pinned to the photo board.

The captain's stare moved to it for a brief second, while Hunter reached for a notepad on his desk.

'But I will be very surprised if the DNA test doesn't confirm the information in the diary,' he said.

'The diary describes her abduction?' Captain Blake asked.

'Not the method,' Garcia replied. 'Just the location.'

'Whom did the case belong to in Missing Persons?' the captain asked.

'Detective Henrique Gomez,' Hunter replied.

'I know Gomez.' The captain nodded. 'Have you spoken to him yet?'

'We did, this morning,' Garcia confirmed. 'But given the amount of cases Missing Persons have to deal with on a daily basis, and taking into account that Miss Gibbs's disappearance happened over two years ago, it's no surprise that Detective Gomez barely remembers the case. All the info we got came from the case file he handed us and, from what we gathered, the case died a death within weeks.'

Captain Blake's eyebrows arched.

'Missing Persons interviewed everyone they could,' Hunter explained. 'The boyfriend, the family, friends, work colleagues, gym members, Albertsons employees who were working on the night that she went missing ... everyone they could think of, and they got absolutely nothing. Every path led to a dead end. Her car didn't give them anything either. Officially the case was still open until now. Miss Gibbs was still listed as "missing" according to the MP database, but because every avenue they pursued led them to a complete standstill, unofficially, Missing Persons had classed Miss Gibbs as a "runaway".'

'Well, not anymore,' Captain Blake said. 'There was no CCTV on the parking lot?' She sounded surprised.

'None around the spot where she parked that night,' Hunter revealed. 'The place in question, on Rosecrans Avenue, is a huge open complex where you'll find restaurants, bars, banks, supermarkets, drugstores . . . there's even a six-screen cinema. The parking lot alone, which doesn't change a parking fee, covers an area equivalent to one city block, with *eleven* entry and exit points. It's accessible via three different main roads – Rosecrans Avenue on its north side, La Mirada Boulevard on its west side and Adelfa Drive on the east.'

'Our guy,' Garcia jumped in again, 'the person who took Miss Gibbs, is no amateur. According to his entry in the note-book, he tailed his target for four days before an opportunity to take her presented itself. That alone shows patience and determination, not to mention knowhow.'

The captain's stare returned to the photo board. She had read about the wedding dress in the file Hunter had left on her desk that morning, but seeing it, even if only in a photograph, made it completely real.

'And he buried her in a wedding dress?' she asked, her frown revealing how incredulous that sounded to her.

'Reburied,' Hunter corrected his captain, and proceeded to explain their conclusion.

'Jesus! Why?'

'At this point, only the killer knows,' Hunter said. 'But maybe the voices told him to.'

Captain Blake's head jerked back slightly and she almost smiled at Hunter. 'Voices?'

'In his entry,' Hunter explained. 'The little that we read, the perp mentions "voices". He says that he should've started the journal a while ago, when he first heard them. He then states that the voices had asked for a very specific type of subject, or victim – certain type of hair, height, eye-colour . . . everything. We haven't read more than just about a page and a half of the journal, but from that entry alone, it seems that he does what he does because voices tell him to. Maybe that's why he went back to her grave, dug her up, dressed her in a wedding dress and buried her again.'

'So we're talking about someone who's highly delusional.' Captain Blake didn't phrase it as a question.

Hunter replied with a half nod, half side-angling of the head. 'If he's hearing voices in his head, he's certainly schizophrenic. Delusions and hallucinations are simply symptoms of such mental illness, but everyone is different, Captain. Not everyone with schizophrenia will experience every symptom.'

'Well,' Garcia said, nodding at Hunter. 'It sounds like this one does.'

'And what's this I've read about a streaming camera placed inside the coffin?' Captain Blake shook her head once again.

'It's true,' Garcia confirmed.

'Will a camera stream images when placed underground?' the captain asked. 'How?'

'We were also unsure of how that could happen,' Garcia explained. 'And that's why this morning we talked to Michelle Kelly. She's the head of the FBI Cyber Crime Division.'

'Yes,' Captain Blake nodded. 'I remember her. She worked with you two in a couple of cases, didn't she?'

'That's right.'

'And what did she say?'

'She told us that it all depends on two things,' Hunter explained. 'The strength of the signal and how deep underground we were talking about. When I told her that it was a shallow grave two feet deep, she laughed. She said that from that depth, even without a full-strength signal, one could easily stream images and make phone calls. The images might not stream smoothly, but they would stream.'

'So for him to have a signal, he would've needed a cellphone provider?' Captain Blake concluded.

'Yes,' Garcia agreed.

'Can't that be traced?'

'Perhaps.' Hunter spoke this time. 'We're looking into it.'

Garcia walked over to the coffee machine in the corner and poured himself a cup before offering one to his captain.

She declined. Hunter already had one on his desk.

'So the perp we're dealing with here not only hears voices in his head,' Captain Blake added, 'and acts according to what they tell him to do, but he also seems to have a PhD in sadism, because it wasn't enough for him to just bury this woman alive. He had to sit and watch the whole thing – the desperate panic, the struggle, the fight – all the way until her death.'

'And I wouldn't be surprised if he did all that from his living room,' Garcia suggested. 'While eating some popcorn and playing with himself.'

Captain Blake looked at him in disgust. 'I thank you for that.'

All that Garcia had done was state something that all three of them knew to be true – around ninety to ninety-five percent of all serial murders in the USA had their basis in some sort of sexual gratification. The vast majority of serial killers killed because something about the murder act – the violence, the victim's fear, the suffering, the pleading, the torturing, the power over the victim, death itself – something aroused them like nothing else could.

Garcia shrugged. 'We all know the statistics, Captain. Why would this guy be any different?'

'Yes, I *do* know the statistics, Carlos,' Captain Blake agreed. 'But I could've done without the mental image.' She turned to face Hunter. 'How many entries are there in this "diary"?'

'We're not sure. But Dr. Slater retrieved sixteen Polaroid photos from the book,' Hunter told her. 'Sixteen different "subjects". This guy has been active for years, Captain. Though the first entry in the diary takes us back to just over two years ago, in that entry there is mention of previous victims. No names. Just that there had been previous victims. And as I mentioned, the perp wrote that he should've started those records a while ago, when he first heard the voices.'

Captain Blake breathed out and used her thumb and forefinger to massage her temples. 'So what's the next move then?'

'As I said,' Hunter explained, 'the diary is now being analyzed and tested by the FSD DNA lab, but since the book appears to be a "private" diary that somehow managed to find its way to Dr. Slater . . . ' He shrugged. 'Maybe the owner lost it. Maybe somebody stole it. We don't know, but at the moment it doesn't look like the owner parted with that book on purpose. With that in mind, there's hope that whoever wrote those entries wasn't as careful as he should've been when it comes to fingerprints, DNA, even the entries themselves.'

'So you believe there's a good chance the FSD might come up with something,' Captain Blake said.

'That's the hope,' Garcia confirmed. 'Either a fingerprint, a DNA sample, or maybe even a compromising entry where he reveals more than he should. Like I've said before, we should be getting photographs of every page any minute now.'

'So for now we wait,' the captain concluded.

'Yes,' Hunter agreed. 'We also need to break the news to Miss Gibbs's parents and probably her boyfriend, as soon as we get DNA confirmation on the body.'

Captain Blake understood very well that that was one of the worst jobs a homicide detective had to take on. She was about to say something when the phone on Hunter's desk rang.

'Detective Hunter, UVC Unit.'

'*Robert, it's Susan,*' Dr. Slater said. '*I'm glad that I've got you at your desk.*'

'Hold on, Doc, let me switch the call to speakerphone. Carlos and Captain Blake are here.' Hunter pressed a button on his desk phone before returning the handset to its cradle. 'Go ahead.'

'*I'm at the DNA Lab,*' Dr. Slater told them. '*And like I've said, I'm glad that I caught you in the office this early because I'm about to send you something.*'

Everyone in that room moved a little closer to the phone on Hunter's desk.

'Not the page photographs?' Garcia asked.

'*No, not yet, and though those will follow shortly, this is something much better. I'm emailing it to you right now.*'

Nine

It took less than three seconds for Dr. Slater's email to come through. As soon as it appeared on Hunter's inbox tray, he double-clicked it to open.

As a subject, the email showed the official number that had now been assigned to the case. Its body contained a five-word message – 'Have a look at this' – followed by a rectangular blue box, indicating that there was an image attachment – 00001.jpg.

Hunter clicked the attachment.

'We've got a fingerprint?' Garcia asked, as soon as the image opened on Hunter's screen.

'*This didn't come from one of the pages in the diary,*' Dr. Slater clarified. '*We're still analyzing those. This came from one of the Polaroid photographs – one of the "subjects". It was lifted from the bottom right-hand corner – front and back – thumb at the front, forefinger at the back. And it's not a full print. It's a partial one – about seventy-five percent of the thumb print and fifty percent of the forefinger.*'

'Seventy-five percent?' Captain Blake this time. 'That should be good enough for a search against IAFIS.'

'If there is a match in IAFIS.' The comment came from

Garcia. 'Then yes, a seventy-five percent partial print should be good enough to identify it.'

'*If* there is a match,' Hunter said, being cautious as always.

'*There is,*' Dr. Slater confirmed.

Everyone inside the UVC Unit's office frowned at the phone on Hunter's desk.

'What do you mean, Doc?' Garcia asked.

'*I'm sorry about that,*' the doctor replied. '*Once again, curiosity took over and I took the liberty of checking. Since what we've got is only a partial fingerprint, it took IAFIS a little longer than usual to find a match, but the real surprise is ... it's not a "he" ... it's a "she".*'

Ten

There was a time when matching a fingerprint to any already stored into IAFIS – Integrated Automated Fingerprint Identification System – would take days, sometimes weeks. Matching a partial fingerprint, even if 'partial' meant seventy-five percent or more, was almost impossible, but those days are long gone. Today, from their own smartphones, any detective or forensics agent could run a search against the millions of entries stored into IAFIS and a result would come back in seconds. Partial fingerprints would take a little longer.

Hunter didn't doubt Dr. Slater, but he had to run his own search against the IAFIS database just to be thorough. Once he'd downloaded the partial fingerprint image he had received and fed it into IAFIS, it took the database just a little over four minutes to find a match. As the arrest file filled Hunter's computer screen, Garcia and Captain Blake repositioned themselves behind his chair to have a better look.

The large mugshot on the top left-hand corner of the screen showed a young white woman, staring straight at the camera and holding the traditional 'arrest information' placard. The look in her eyes was intriguing, to say the least – focused and careless in equal measures. Her buttery blonde hair, although a little disheveled, showed signs that it had once been styled into a side-swept, classic bob. The shape of her face sat midway between a heart and a diamond, with thin lips, almond-shaped eyes that were hazel-blue in color, and a small button nose. Her makeup was a little odd – light on the eyes and lips, but quite heavy on the cheekbones and eyebrows. Not a very flattering look.

'Angela Wood,' Captain Blake read from the placard the woman was holding. 'Twenty-one years old.' Her attention, together with Hunter and Garcia's, moved to the information on the arrest sheet and they all read it in silence.

Miss Wood was from Pocatello, Idaho. She had moved to Los Angeles when she was only seventeen years old and got arrested a year later – pickpocketing in Santa Monica Beach. She was caught with six different wallets and four different smartphones. Judge Connor sentenced her to 120 days in jail for her crime. According to the arrest sheet, she lived some-where in Studio City.

Captain Blake paused, straightened her body and looked at her detectives.

'This doesn't really read like the rap sheet of a serial killer with over sixteen heinous murders under her belt, does it?'

'She's not our killer, Captain,' Garcia said. 'But if her fin-gerprints were on one of the victim's Polaroid photos, it means that sometime, probably in the four years that she's been living in LA, she came into contact with the person we're after.'

'Doc,' Hunter called.

Dr. Slater had stayed on the phone while they'd run their own IAFIS search.

'*Yes, I'm still here.*'

'Have all the Polaroids been dusted for prints,' Hunter asked. 'Or just the one from which you retrieved this fingerprint?'

'*The photos have all been dusted and analyzed,*' the doctor confirmed. '*The pages in the diary, not yet.*'

'And is her fingerprint on all the Polaroids?'

'*No,*' Doctor Slater surprised everyone. '*Only one out of the sixteen.*'

'Which photo is it?' Hunter asked. 'Is it the one from the victim we found last night? The first entry in the diary?'

'*No, it's not. I don't really know who the person on the photo is. I haven't checked it against the diary, but the photo is of a boy who looks to be ...*' She paused as if weighing her conclusion. '*... seventeen ... eighteen, maybe.*'

'Can you do us a favor, Doc?' Hunter asked. 'Can you expedite all those photos to us?'

'*Of course. The pages from the journal will follow later today.*'

'Thank you.' Hunter disconnected from the call and immediately put a call to his research team, asking them to compile a file on Angela Wood. He put the phone down and checked his watch – 11:38 a.m. 'Want to take a drive to Studio City?' he asked Garcia.

'I thought you'd never ask,' Garcia replied, reaching for his jacket.

Eleven

Colfax Avenue, located north of San Fernando Valley, on the other side of Hollywood Hills, was a three-mile-long straight avenue that led from North Hollywood to Studio City, which was the address that Hunter and Garcia had obtained from Angela Wood's arrest sheet. The building in question was a pale-fronted, three-story-high structure, directly across the road from a medium-sized independent supermarket and liquor store called 'The Village Market'.

'I think this is it,' Garcia said, as he slowed down to check the number on the building.

'That's the one, all right,' Hunter said, reading from his notes. 'Apartment 309.'

Garcia pulled up onto a street parking space just past the building. As they took the short flight of stairs that led up to the entrance lobby, they got lucky. The postman had just finished delivering the mail to the building's postboxes. As he was leaving, he saw Hunter and Garcia coming up the stairs and held the entrance door open for them. That would allow them to go straight up to apartment 309, instead of having to ring the intercom.

Being arrested is a very unpleasant experience, so it's no

surprise that people who have spent any sort of time in jail, people with a rap sheet, tend to be very reluctant to talk to cops, even if they have nothing to hide. Knowing that, the less warning Hunter and Garcia gave Angela Wood that they were coming, the better.

'Hold on a sec,' Garcia said. 'Let me go check the back of the building for a fire escape.' He shrugged at Hunter. 'You never know how spooked people might get once you flash a detective's badge at them.'

Hunter waited while Garcia quickly rounded the building. He was back in less than thirty seconds.

'Nope,' he said with a headshake. 'No fire escape.'

They took the stairs up to the third floor, which dropped them at the beginning of a short and brightly lit corridor with five doors on each side. Apartment 309 was the last door on the right. Hunter gave it three hard knocks and they waited.

Twenty seconds went by with no reply.

Hunter knocked again and he and Garcia moved their ears a little closer to the door.

This time they heard some noise coming from inside, but they still had to wait another fifteen seconds for a reply.

'Who is it?' a tired, probably just-out-of-bed female voice called from behind the door.

Before Hunter could reply, Garcia stopped him with a gesture and pointed to the door, indicating that it had no peephole. He then took over.

'It's the postman,' he said in a firm voice. 'I have a letter for a Miss Angela Wood that requires a signature.'

'A letter?' The female voice took a somewhat skeptical and defensive tone.

'That's correct, ma'am,' Garcia confirmed. 'It's from . . .' He looked at Hunter with a question in his eyes.

'Pocatello, Idaho,' Hunter mouthed the words. He remembered her birthplace from her rap sheet.

'Pocatello, in Idaho,' Garcia called out.

The next ten seconds went by in complete silence. Clearly, Angela Wood wasn't expecting any mail from her hometown.

'Ummm ...' she finally called from behind the door. 'Give me just a minute, I need to put on some clothes. I was in the shower.' Her tone was still skeptical.

Hunter and Garcia once again moved closer to the door to try to hear what was going on inside. They heard what sounded like someone urgently hurrying around.

They moved their ears closer still – that was when they heard an odd squeaking noise, as if something was being dragged on unoiled wheels.

Hunter looked at his partner.

'Window,' he said.

'Window?' Garcia questioned. 'We're on the third floor and there's no fire escape. Is she nuts?'

Without waiting for a reply, Garcia took off down the corridor in the direction of the stairs.

Hunter turned toward the door and knocked again. The postman trick obviously hadn't worked. 'Miss Wood, this is the LAPD, please open the door.'

Three seconds – no reply.

He knocked again. 'Miss Wood, please open the door. This is the LAPD. We need to talk to you.'

Nothing.

'Miss Wood, this is your last warning. If you don't open the door, I'll be forced to kick it in.'

Another three seconds. Still nothing.

Hunter took a step back from the door and sent the heel of

his right boot flying against the door handle. The loud noise of his kick echoed down the corridor, the door shook, but it remained locked. Hunter hit it again, putting more power into his kick.

Almost, but not quite.

Once again, with everything he had.

This time the doorframe cracked and split, sending the door flying back and wood splinters flying in the air. Hunter immediately stepped inside to find Angela Wood with a backpack strapped to her, sitting at the window ledge, her legs hanging outside.

'Wait!' he shouted, standing at the door to her apartment, his hands coming up in a surrender gesture. 'What are you doing? We just want to talk to you. Nothing else.'

'Yeah, right.' She grabbed the ledge with both hands, ready to push herself off.

'Please don't,' Hunter pleaded, keeping his distance so he wouldn't come across as a threat. 'Miss Wood, please listen to me. That's a very bad idea,' he said in the calmest voice he could muster. 'The drop from that window to the ground below is around forty-five feet, maybe a little more. If you're lucky, and that's saying something, you'll end up with a broken leg. Probably two. Probably exposed fractures. We're talking wheelchairs and crutches for at least the next six to nine months. I'm sure you don't want that.' Hunter sensed Angela's hesitation. 'Listen, we're not here to take you in. I give you my word. We really just want to talk to you. We need your help. Please, come back inside.'

Angela peeked over her right shoulder back at Hunter. To her, the man standing at her door sounded sincere, but she had been fooled before and she wasn't about to take any chances.

'What the hell is going on here?' A half-surprised, half-concerned voice called from just a few feet behind Hunter.

Hunter turned to find a 250-pound bald-headed man standing in the corridor just outside the door to Angela Wood's apartment. He was menacingly holding a baseball bat. Clearly a neighbor who had heard the commotion and was trying to help.

'It's all right, sir,' Hunter said, flashing the man his badge. 'I'm a detective with the LAPD. Everything is under control here. Please put down the bat and go back to your apartment.'

The man relaxed his grip on the bat and angled his head to have a better look at Hunter's badge. All of a sudden, the man's eyes widened in surprise and shock at something he saw just past Hunter's shoulder.

'Jesus!' he gasped.

Hunter immediately spun around.

There was nobody at the window anymore. Angela Wood was gone.

Hunter looked back at the man, who shrugged at him.

'She jumped.'

Twelve

Garcia got to the end of the corridor and, instead of running down the stairs, he leaped over the entire first flight. As his feet touched the landing, he heard a loud thumping noise echo through the hallway he had just come from. He figured that was Hunter trying to break into Angela Wood's apartment.

Garcia turned the corner and once again leaped down the next flight of stairs ... and the next ... and the next ... all the way down to the ground floor.

An old and clearly fragile lady was closing the entry door behind her just as Garcia hit the lobby landing. She hadn't seen the detective until he jumped right in front of her.

'Oh dear Lord!' the lady cried in a weak voice, dropping her cane before taking a step back and placing a hand over her heart. Her mouth opened in a gasp that was half fright, half panic. A split second later, she looked like she was having difficulty breathing. Her legs weakened under her, forcing the old lady to lean against the glass door behind her for support.

Garcia saw her already pale face lose even more color and immediately moved to her.

'I'm so terribly sorry,' he said, gently placing his hands on both of her shoulders to comfort her. The old lady seemed to be more bone than flesh. 'I didn't mean to startle you.'

She looked back at him with unfocused eyes, still struggling to breathe.

Garcia was unsure of what to do. He needed to run. He needed to get to the back of that building before something unthinkable happened, and this situation wasn't helping. He tried to calm the old lady down.

'Just breathe,' he said in a steady voice. 'Nice and slowly. Don't try to rush it.' He began breathing in a sturdy rhythm to demonstrate, while at the same time softly placing two fingers over her wrist to assess her pulse – faster than it should've been, but not life-threateningly so. 'I am so sorry,' Garcia tried again, before explaining. 'I'm a police officer with the LAPD . . . and I need to get going.' The urgency in his voice brought some focus back into the old lady's eyes. 'Just keep on breathing, nice and slowly like you're doing now, and you'll be all right.' He picked up her cane and placed it in her right hand before moving her away from the door and shooting past her like a bullet.

Five seconds later he'd made it to the back of the building, just in time to see Angela Wood leap from a third-floor window.

Thirteen

Angela Wood wasn't exactly what psychiatrists would call 'textbook suicidal', at least not anymore, but there was a time when the idea of ending her life was all she could think of. And she had tried – more than once – taking herself as close to death as anyone could possibly come without finally crossing over. That time had started around five years ago, when she was only sixteen years old.

At that young age, and for a whole year, Angela had struggled desperately with depression, every day isolating herself more and more from everyone and anyone around her, while allowing sadness, emptiness, guilt and a never-ending feeling of worthlessness to suffocate her from the inside. Self-harming became a common, albeit well-hidden occurrence and drugs, prescription or otherwise, became the gospel that she lived by ... but Angela hadn't always been that way.

Throughout her entire childhood and part of her teenage years, Angela had been a smiling, positive girl, full of life. The problems and arguments she'd had with her parents while young weren't that dissimilar from the problems and arguments most kids faced while growing up. In school, she got along well enough with her teachers, had excellent grades, and her friends considered her to be a fun, easy-going person. The change came just a week after her sixteenth birthday, the consequence of a terrible tragedy – the death of her younger brother, Shawn.

Shawn's passing sent Angela into a dark and soul-crushing downward spiral, which very quickly swirled out of her control. Truth be told, if Angela hadn't left her family and the city of Pocatello when she had, chances were that her parents would've lost a second child by now.

As crazy and as improbable as it may sound, it had been the move into the City of Angels that had somehow rescued Angela from what could easily be considered 'the mouth of the abyss'. But the war hadn't been won yet.

The sadness, emptiness and the feeling of worthlessness hadn't completely dissipated. Not a day would go by that she didn't desperately miss her younger brother, and she wouldn't argue that some days were undoubtedly a lot harder than others. But somehow, a little light had finally found its way into the darkness that had lived inside her for so many years, and little by little Angela had begun to climb back out. She didn't self-harm as much, drugs had practically become a thing of the past and she hadn't thought about joining her brother in over three years.

The leap from her window to the ground below hadn't been a throwback to those dark days. It had been a planned escape. She had practiced the move countless times, but this had been the first time that she'd had to do it for real.

Actually, the leap wasn't really from her window to the ground below, but from her window to the reinforced rainwater drainpipe that ran almost all the way from the building's roof down to the ground. By pure chance, the drainpipe was affixed to the building's exterior wall, just about a foot and a half from Angela's window. It being reinforced meant that it could easily hold Angela's weight, which had never gone beyond 135lb, together with the light contents of a small backpack.

As Hunter's attention was diverted from her to her neighbor, who was standing in the corridor directly behind him, Angela used the heels of her feet to push against the wall just beneath her window ledge, throwing herself to her left, in the direction of the drainpipe. It was an easy leap.

Angela grabbed the pipe with both hands, also clamping it with her thighs. Her knees scraped against the building wall, but it was nothing that she couldn't handle.

The easiest way to get down to the ground below was to slide down the pipe, but it had to be done in three quick stages, as the thick metal rings that had been used to fix the pipe to the wall wouldn't allow a smooth, firefighter-like slide. But Angela had practiced it enough times to know exactly how to do it. Less than four seconds after leaping from her window, her feet were touching the ground down below. With a proud smile on her lips, she looked up at her open window before quickly turning on her heels to start her run ... but that didn't go half as well as she would have expected.

As Angela began turning, her movement was interrupted by Garcia, who was standing right behind her.

'That was cute,' he said, slapping his handcuffs around Angela's right wrist before she could even blink. 'Do you take bookings for birthday parties?'

Angela looked back at the detective in total surprise. 'How the hell did you get down here so fast?'

Garcia smiled. 'What, do you think you're the only one with tricks?' In a lightning-fast movement, he rotated his body to position himself just behind Angela. As he did, he reached for her left wrist and quickly cuffed it to her right one. 'Ta-da,' he said in a fanfare voice.

'Let me go, you jerk.' Angela tugged at the handcuffs. 'I haven't done anything.'

'Is she all right?' The question came from Hunter, whose entire torso now hung out of Angela's apartment window above them.

'We're good here,' Garcia replied, giving Hunter a thumbs up.

Hunter nodded. 'Great. I think I'll use the stairs, though.'

As Garcia escorted Angela toward the front of the building, the look in her eyes was cold fury, pure and simple.

Fourteen

In the basement of the Police Administration Building, Angela had been sitting alone inside one of the interrogation rooms for almost half an hour. Her hands were cuffed together by a foot-long chain that ran through a loop at the center of the metal table in front of her. The table and the chair she was sitting on were both bolted to the floor.

Leaving a suspect waiting in an interrogation room, typically in cuffs, was a very well-known psychological technique used by the police. The advantage of it was two-fold:

One – the waiting tended to heighten the suspect's apprehension. It unnerved them. A nervous and anxious suspect was much more prone to make mistakes and contradict themselves, if they were lying during the interrogation. Leaving the suspect cuffed restricted their movements, but most importantly, it put forward the idea that the police already considered that person to be guilty of something, which also served to amplify the suspect's anxiety.

Advantage number two was that, despite the suspect having been left alone, the police would, without a doubt, have eyes and ears in that interrogation room. Someone, either through a two-way mirror or via CCTV cameras, would be studying the suspect's movements, reactions and facial expressions. That someone would usually be the interrogating detective or a trained psychologist. The microphones inside the room would also have been turned on. Sometimes the cops got lucky and the suspect, when left alone for any significant amount of time, would say something to himself. Guilty and nervous suspects tended to rehearse what to say.

The interrogation room that Angela was in did have a two-way mirror – a very large one to the right of where she was sitting. At the other side of it, Hunter and Garcia had been attentively observing Angela from the start and they were both impressed by how calm she had been.

As soon as Angela was left by herself, she slouched on her chair as best as she could, taking into account that her hands were cuffed to the tabletop, rested her head against the chair's backrest, closed her eyes and practically went to sleep. No angry jerking of the cuffs. No swearing at the police officer. No neck or shoulder movement to relax her muscles. No looking around the room anxiously. No impatient shaking of the legs. Nothing. No signs of being nervous whatsoever. In fact, Angela looked like she was about to doze off when Hunter and Garcia finally opened the door and stepped inside.

'How are you doing?' Hunter asked, as he approached the table and placed a plastic cup full of water in front of her. 'My name is Detective Robert Hunter and this is Detective Carlos Garcia.'

Angela wore all black: jeans, a T-shirt, and a hoodie that carried a metal band's name across its front that was practically unreadable. On her feet she wore running sneakers. Her back-pack had been confiscated and searched. They found over one thousand dollars in cash, a cellphone and a change of clothes.

'How am I doing?' Angela asked rhetorically, in a voice that carried more irritation than anger. Her gaze kept moving from one detective to the other. 'I'm bored and pretty pissed off, that's how I'm doing. I've been sitting here for God knows how long, chained to this table like an animal, and I still don't know what I'm doing here.'

Hunter and Garcia had given Angela the 'Deluxe' silent treatment on their way to the PAB.

'No one has told me squat so far,' she continued, the intensity of her stare giving both detectives a new tan. 'Am I under arrest for something here? Because if I am, you guys fucked up, big time. I was not read my rights, I was not given my phone call, I was not informed of the reason why I was being arrested and I've been treated like a smelly stray dog since I got here. And then there's the door to my apartment, which was kicked in.' She chuckled. 'Oh man, am I going to have your asses for this.'

Hunter waited until Angela was done ranting.

'Would you prefer coffee rather than water?' he asked in an amicable tone, as he uncuffed her hands. Before doing so, he placed the paper folder he had with him on the table. In small black letters across the front of it was the name 'Angela Wood'. As Hunter freed Angela's hands, he saw her quickly peek at it with concerned eyes.

'No,' she replied, massaging her wrists and sitting up on her chair. 'I'd rather you tell me what the hell this is all about. Am I under arrest for something?'

Hunter picked up the folder and he and Garcia sat down across the table from her.

'Should you be?' Garcia asked.

She glared at him. 'Should I be what ... under arrest? No, why should I?'

Garcia crossed his right leg over his left. 'I don't know. You tell us.'

Angela regarded the two detectives in front of her for a few seconds before allowing her lips to break into a confident smile. Her teeth were perfectly aligned and completely stain-free.

'Oh, I see what you're doing here,' she said, assuming a much more relaxed position on her chair. 'That's why there's been no move from either of you to record this interview, isn't it? Because you've got nothing on me.'

Both detectives stayed silent.

'So since you've got nothing on me, what you decided to do was use the most basic of psychological techniques to try to get me to slip up.' She laughed. 'The silent treatment in the car, leaving me waiting in here for over twenty minutes, the file with my name on it on the table . . . all of it.'

She's pretty savvy, Hunter thought. His and Garcia's poker faces, nonetheless, didn't change.

'Where did you learn that?' Angela continued. '*Psychology for Dummies?*' She shook her head sarcastically. 'Well, you're not doing a very good job here, Detective . . . ?'

'Garcia.'

'Maybe the two of you should try reading some other psychology books too, Detective Garcia.'

The 'lone waiting' trick wasn't the only reason Hunter and Garcia had taken half an hour to join Angela. They'd been waiting for her file.

Interrogation rule number one: know as much in advance as you possibly can about the suspect.

'I haven't read *Psychology for Dummies*,' Garcia admitted. 'Have you?' The question was directed at Hunter.

'No,' Hunter replied. 'I can't say I have.'

'Do you recommend it?' Garcia asked Angela.

She laughed. 'For you? Yes. It might help you polish your technique.'

Hunter nodded his agreement before flipping open the paper folder and skimming through the first page of her file. Not that he needed to do so. He had already read the entire document while in the observation room. The file was only five pages long.

Angela tried her best to read the man across the table from her, but Hunter's facial expression gave nothing away.

'So,' she asked. 'Are you going to tell me the truth about what I'm doing here, or are you going to lie like before?'

Hunter looked at Angela quizzically.

'Back in my place, remember?' She pulled a face and her voice took on a mocking tone. 'We're not here to take you in. I give you my word. We really just want to talk to you. We need your help.' Her tone went back to normal. 'What a crock of shit.'

Hunter was surprised that, even under pressure, Angela had remembered what he had told her back in her apartment word-for-word.

'But do you know what the funny thing is?' Angela asked. 'For some reason, I almost believed you.'

'I apologize for the lack of information,' Hunter said. 'You're right. We should've been more forthcoming with it.'

Slowly, Angela's lips stretched into another amused smile. 'Oh wow, just look at you, backpedaling like a champ. Is that because you now know that you've fucked up and I can sue your ass for this, or is this just another trick from your arsenal of bullshit tricks?'

'It's not a trick,' Hunter told her.

From the folder in his hands, Hunter retrieved an evidence bag containing a Polaroid photo and placed it on the table in front of Angela.

'This is why you're here.'

Angela's eyes moved to it and the smile vanished.

The Polaroid was a portrait photo of a boy who looked to be around seventeen years old. His blond hair was longish, skater/grunge rock style. His pale blue eyes were puffy, the white in them more reddish than white, indicating that he'd been crying for some time. His expression was the definition of fear.

'Can you tell us who this is?' Garcia asked.

Angela's attention stayed on the photo. Her lips stayed sealed.

'Did you take this photo?' Garcia tried a different approach.

'No.' Angela's reply had been a reflex rather than a conscious answer. Garcia's question had clearly rattled her.

'Do you know who took this photo?' he pushed. 'Were you present at the time?'

'No.' Again, another reflex answer. This time, fear came through in her tone.

'That's funny,' Garcia added, giving Angela no time to elaborate. 'Because we found your fingerprints all over it.'

A huge knot tightened inside Angela's throat. She had made a mistake. She had made a terrible mistake.

Angela had delivered that horrible book to Dr. Slater's postbox in the very early hours of Sunday morning. Before doing so, she had wiped down the book cover and the edges of every page she had touched, she was very certain of that, but it looked like in her rush and desperation to get rid of that notebook, she had somehow forgotten about the photo she had touched ... the boy. Thinking back, she couldn't remember wiping it clean, and that had obviously been how they had managed to track her down so quickly. She had stupidly given them her own fingerprint. In silence, she cursed herself for her mistake.

It took Angela several seconds to be able to drag her stare away from the photo and back to Hunter. Fear had no doubt crept into her eyes. If the LAPD had found her prints on a photo inside that sick book, of course they would think that she was somehow implicated with it.

When Garcia told her that her fingerprints had been found on that photo, he and Hunter saw the color drain from her face.

'So,' Garcia continued. 'If you didn't take this photo and you weren't present when it was taken either, can you please explain to us why your prints were the only prints that were found on it?'

Angela's gut was telling her to tell Hunter and Garcia the truth – that she had no idea who the boy in that photo was . . . that she had nothing to do with that photo or that book – but she knew much better than that. She knew that the 'truth' didn't matter. What mattered was what she could prove. Not to mention that she had no way of telling them the truth without revealing that she was a professional pickpocket. Not a great move when you're locked in a room with two detectives inside the LAPD headquarters.

This time Angela went with reason instead of impulse.

'Am I under arrest here?' she asked. 'Because if I am, I'd like to exercise my right to my phone call.' The look in her eyes was defiant.

'No,' Garcia finally replied. He wanted to add "not yet", but he decided to keep that detail out for the time being.

'Then I'm free to go, right?' Her stare moved from Garcia to Hunter. 'So I guess that's what I'll do, right about now.'

Angela got to her feet.

'One last question, if I may?' Hunter said.

Angela crossed her arms over her chest.

'The boy in the photo,' Hunter said, nodding at the Polaroid. 'Does he remind you of your brother?'

Fifteen

Angela Wood had always been as bright as they came. At the end of her sophomore year, her teachers were so impressed with her grades that they decided to put her through a battery of tests and exams to see if she was good enough to skip a whole year in school. To no one's surprise, she aced them all, which culminated in Angela bypassing all the juniors and becoming a senior at the age of fifteen.

The summer her brother died, Angela had just turned sixteen. She had also just graduated from high school and, for the time being, she was really enjoying being able to sleep in on weekdays. That morning, though, she didn't manage to sleep in as much as she would've liked to. At around 7:30 a.m., she was hastily woken up by a thunderclap so powerful she could feel her bed shake.

Despite officially being the second week of summer, when the temperatures in Pocatello could get up to as high as thirty-one degrees Celsius, that Thursday had been an ugly day from the start, with frightening dark clouds, severely strong winds and blindingly bright lightning. The thunder that had woken Angela up was the first in a series, announcing the torrential rain that was gaining momentum just over the horizon. And rain it did. For hours on end.

That afternoon, since leaving the house was completely out of the question, Angela spent it with her favorite pastime – books. She loved reading and even during the school year, despite all the exams and homework, she would still get through at least seven to ten books a month. Her brother Shawn, who was only eleven at the time, spent the day in front of the TV, playing video games.

The rain, which had started pelting down just after nine in the morning, finally let off at around three in the afternoon. Outside, the streets and roads looked like flowing rivers, as the city's drainage system struggled to cope with the sheer volume of water that had descended over the town – one month's rain in just a little over six hours – but as a crack of blue light finally slit through the tired, gray sky, it looked like the flood was over at last.

'It stopped,' Shawn had said, looking out the window. 'It's finally stopped.'

'Thank God for that,' Angela had replied. 'A little longer and we would've needed life vests.'

'Maybe some people do,' Shawn had said. 'We live up a hill, remember? Maybe some houses got flooded.'

'Maybe.' Angela had accepted it, without too much concern.

Shawn kept staring out the window for a while. 'I'm hungry,' he had said.

'Why are you telling me? Go check the fridge.'

'I did, earlier, we don't have anything. You're not hungry?'

'Not particularly, no. Anyway, Mom and Dad will be home from work soon and we'll have dinner, so chill out.'

'It's almost three-thirty,' Shawn had said, pointing

to the clock on their living room wall. 'Mom and Dad won't be home until around six, maybe even later with all this rain out there. Dinner won't be until gone seven. I'll starve by then.'

'Oh my God, you're so dramatic,' Angela had said. She was getting annoyed by the interruptions to her reading. 'Have a banana or something. We've got plenty of those.'

Shawn had replied with a disgusted face. 'I hate bananas. You know that.'

'OK, so go make yourself a peanut butter and jelly sandwich then. Do whatever you like. Just stop bothering me.'

'I would if we had any bread or jelly, but we're out of both. How long haven't you been in the kitchen, Angie?'

'Well, what do you want me to do, Shawn? Turn myself into some food for you?'

'No, but we could take a walk to the store and get some. You must be bored of reading by now. You've been reading all day long.'

'Are you bored of playing video games?'

'No.'

'There's your answer. And I'm not going out in this rain. I'm not a fish.'

'It's not raining anymore.' Shawn had walked back to the window. 'And look, the black clouds are going away.'

Angela didn't look.

'C'mon, Angie, please, I'm hungry and the store is just down the road. Fifteen minutes and we're there and back. You can go back to your book then.'

'I'm not going out,' Angela had told Shawn in a firm voice. 'You can forget that idea.'

'OK, so give me some money and I'll go.'

As they were leaving for work that morning, Angela's mother had been very clear in her instructions.

'It looks like we're going to get a hell of a lot of rain today, Angie,' she had said, as she frowned at the dark morning sky. 'So whatever you do, don't go out.'

'Nope,' Angela had told her brother. 'Mom told me not to allow you to go out by yourself.'

'Oh, c'mon, Angie, I'm not going to the skate park or anything. I'm going to the store to get some bread and jelly, that's it. I'll be back in ten minutes.'

'You said fifteen a second ago.'

'That was if you were coming. I walk and run faster than you.'

'You wish.'

'For real, Angie, I'll be back in ten minutes. I just want to go get some food.'

Angela knew her brother well. She knew that if she didn't go to the store with him, or allow him to go by himself, he wouldn't shut up. She would never be able to get to the end of the chapter she was on, and she was getting to the big reveal of the story.

'C'mon, Angie. Please, please, please—'

'Fine,' Angela had blurted out with irritation. 'But I'm not going with you. Here's ten bucks, get some bread and some jelly ... strawberry ... and bring me back my change. And you better be back here in ten minutes, Shawn, you hear? Ten minutes.'

'No sweat.' He took the money before grabbing his coat. 'Ten minutes and I'll be back. You can time me.'

'Oh, I will.'

But Shawn never came back.

Five weeks later, his mutilated body was found on the outskirts of the city, by the banks of the Portneuf River.

Despite all the efforts by the police, the Sheriff's Department and the FBI, his killer had never been caught.

Sixteen

'The boy in the photo,' Hunter asked. 'He reminds you of your brother, doesn't he?'

The UVC Unit research team had added a newspaper clipping about Shawn Wood's murder to the file they had compiled on Angela. The clipping – a five-year-old article taken from the *Idaho State Journal* – came with a portrait photograph of an eleven-year-old Shawn. Though the article did report on the discovery and identification of Shawn's body, the newspaper had chosen not to publish any photos taken at the banks of the Portneuf River, for obvious reasons.

The Polaroid on the table showed a boy who looked to be around sixteen – the same age that Shawn would've been if he were still alive. But the age match was not the only similarity. Both Shawn and the boy in the Polaroid had similar color hair, similar color eyes, similar skin tone and similar face shape.

Angela's reply to Hunter's question was to look away. She found a neutral spot on the cement floor and focused her stare onto it. Her arms were still crossed over her chest.

Hunter gave her a moment.

'It wasn't a trick, Angela,' he finally said. 'Our

intentions really weren't to bring you in. All we wanted was to talk to you.'

Angela's eyes didn't leave the floor.

'The book is real,' Hunter informed her.

That was the game changer. Angela's frightened stare crawled back to Hunter, but this time it brought something else with it – a question that she didn't seem to have the strength to ask.

Hunter picked up on it. 'Yes,' he said with a nod. 'The murders described in those pages . . . they're all real. The people in those photographs . . .' His gaze moved to the photo on the table for just an instant before resettling on Angela. 'They're all gone.'

Tears welled up in Angela's eyes.

It was time to strike.

Neither Hunter nor Garcia liked resorting to cheap tricks to get a person to talk, but certain tricks, when done properly, tended to bypass several hurdles at once. Given the head-start that this killer already had on them, both detectives were prepared to do what was necessary.

'The truth is,' Hunter began, 'we don't really believe that you are directly linked to that book, or any of those murders.'

He saw Angela flinch at his words, which indicated that she had picked up on his slight emphasis of the word 'directly'. If Hunter got it right, in her mind, that would be translated into – 'but we still believe that you are *somehow* linked to it'.

'The problem is,' Garcia said, taking over, 'what we believe doesn't really matter. What matters is what can be proved and right now, the only thing that we can prove is that the fingerprints found on this photo belong to you.' He paused for effect.

'The other fact that really isn't helping your case here is that you ran. Guilty people tend to run.' Another pause. This one, a little longer. 'But we're not unreasonable people. We've heard you when you told us that you weren't the one who took this picture, nor were you present at the time. We want to believe you, Angela, we really do, but you need to help us get there. You need to give us something.'

'If what you're saying is true,' Hunter jumped in, 'then it can only mean that at some point, probably very recently, you came into contact with the owner of that book, and if you did, you need to tell us.'

It didn't take an expert to see the mental turmoil that Angela was going through.

Garcia was the one who delivered the final blow.

'Is he, or was he, your boyfriend? Is that the connection you have with him?'

'What? No,' Angela cried out, her voice unsteady. 'I don't have a connection with him.'

'But you know who he is.' Garcia phrased it as a statement rather than a question.

'No, I have no idea who he is.' Her voice was rough with unshed tears. 'I don't. That's the truth.'

Angie, both Angelas whispered in her ear. *For the love of Christ, stop talking right now. Ask for your phone call, call a lawyer and don't say another word until they get here.*

Angela took a moment to compose herself. 'I think I really need to call a lawyer now, if you don't mind.'

Hunter had been observing Angela all along. Once he had read her file, he began piecing together a possible scenario of what might've happened – how her prints got onto that one photo but none of the others. Now, after watching her reactions to what they were throwing at her, that scenario began making a lot of sense. All he needed was to fill in a few blanks.

'Is that because you need to take the Fifth?' Hunter asked.

The Fifth Amendment to the constitution of the United States of America contained several provisions relating to criminal law, including the one made famous by so many celebrities and Hollywood films, which was the right to refuse to answer any questions in order to avoid incriminating oneself.

Angela locked eyes with Hunter once again. 'Not for the reasons that you're probably thinking.'

'Would you like me to tell you what I'm thinking?'

No reply.

Time to put the theory to the test, Hunter thought.

'The reason why we were able to match your fingerprints to the ones lifted from this photo,' he began, his tone of voice non-aggressive and nonjudgmental, 'is because your prints are on file. The reason why they are on file, is because you've been arrested before.' He lifted the dossier he had in his hands to emphasize his point. 'Pickpocketing. That was three years ago.' It was Hunter's turn to pause and fix Angela down with a firm stare. 'Sure, you might've gone straight since then, but the one thousand dollars in cash that we found inside your backpack, together with your attempt to run when we knocked at your door, and now your desire to take the fifth – according to you, not for the most obvious reasons – tells me that pickpocketing still plays a pretty big part in your life.'

Angela looked away from Hunter's stare.

'So this is my theory,' Hunter continued. 'The reason why you came across that book and this photo is because without really knowing what you were doing, you stole it from the owner, didn't you?'

Angela stayed silent, but Hunter knew that he was on the right path.

'The reason why we've got that book now,' he carried on. 'It's because the boy in this photo reminded you of Shawn, didn't he? And that prompted you to do the right thing and get it to the authorities.' He gave her a couple of seconds. 'So how am I doing so far?'

Angela didn't look up, but Hunter saw a muscle tighten around her jaw. He could tell that he was starting to win her over. He reached for his credentials and placed them on the table.

'Detective Garcia and I are with Homicide Special. We're part of a specialized unit called the Ultra Violent Crimes Unit.' He indicated his credentials. 'What I'm trying to tell you here, Angela, is that we don't care about the "stealing" part. We're not here to arrest you for pickpocketing. You have my word on that.'

Angela slowly shifted her weight from one foot to the other.

'Earlier,' Hunter said, 'you mentioned the fact that there was no move from either of us to record this interview. That's because the truth is, we've never believed you were a suspect.' He shook his head. 'It takes a special kind of person, a special kind of evil, to be able to do any of the things described in that book. And you're not it, Angela. Trust me. We've met those kinds of people before.'

Angela finally sat back down, reached for the water on the table and took a healthy sip. Just like back at her apartment, she sensed sincerity in the words coming from the detective in front of her.

'I'm not sure how much of that journal you read before you decided to place it in Dr. Slater's mailbox,' Hunter pushed. 'But whoever wrote those entries won't stop just because he had his diary stolen. That's not how his brain works.'

Angela fidgeted. She was getting jittery, a clear sign that her defenses had been breached. With that, Garcia decided that it was time to appeal to the emotional and painful memories that he was sure Angela carried with her like heavy luggage.

'This guy is going to keep on killing, Angela,' he said. 'He's going to keep on abducting people ... some of them young boys, just like your brother, Shawn.'

Angela closed her eyes, as tears began running down her cheeks.

'He's going to carry on doing whatever he pleases with them, before murdering them and dumping their bodies somewhere isolated. And that's why we need your help, Angela ... because you've met him. You know who he is.'

Angela's eyes shot open again.

'No, I don't.' The words flew out of her lips. 'I have no idea who he is.' She turned and addressed Hunter. 'Whatever I tell you here, you promise that it won't be used to incriminate me?'

'I promise.' Hunter replied. 'You have my word.'

Visibly more nervous now, Angela breathed in deeply. 'Your theory is pretty much on the money,' she told Hunter. 'Yes, I stole a bag from someone, which contained that book. I didn't know what I was stealing, and the worst of it all is that I didn't even steal it for profit. I did it to teach the guy a lesson.'

Both Hunter and Garcia frowned at that comment, but neither interrupted her.

'And yes,' she continued, 'the boy in this photo resembles my brother, but you're wrong if you think that I needed this to remind me of Shawn.' She nodded at the photo on the table. 'I think about him every – single – day.'

Tears returned to her eyes.

'You stole the bag to teach the guy a lesson?' Garcia finally asked. 'How so?'

Angela wiped the tears from her eyes before finishing her glass of water.

'*Well, now that you've started,*' the Angelas whispered in her ear. '*You might as well tell them everything.*'

Seventeen

Angela gave Hunter and Garcia a short description of the events that had taken place that Saturday evening. The emphasis, of course, was on what had happened inside the Rendition Room cocktail bar and how she came to be in possession of that diary.

Hunter and Garcia listened without interrupting. When she was done, Hunter was the first to put a question forward.

'So you never got to see his face?'

'Not really,' Angela replied. 'His back was toward me and he had a hood pulled over his head. Even as he was being a dick . . .' She paused and lifted her hand, indicating that she was sorry for her choice of words. 'Even as he was being rude toward the older man, he didn't lift his head or break eye contact with his phone. He spoke sort of sideways and over his shoulder, like this.' Angela demonstrated by slightly turning her head to the right. 'From where I was, there was no way I could see his face.'

'How about height, or body shape? Age bracket? Anything distinctive?'

'He was about your height,' Angela said, nodding at Hunter. 'And just as strong too. Maybe even a little more.'

'By "as strong",' Garcia jumped in, 'do you mean well built or big?'

'He definitely wasn't fat, if that's what you're asking,' Angela said. 'Even from the back and with a hoodie on I could tell that he was in good shape . . . muscly, not fat. Age wise . . .' She shrugged as she thought about it. 'I would say that he was in his late thirties or very early forties, no older.'

'How about his voice?' Hunter again. 'Anything that stood out, like an accent or something?'

'I didn't pick up on one, but then again, there was music playing and I wasn't paying full attention to it, but his tone was powerful . . . strong, you know? As if he was used to talking to people that way, like giving them orders or something.'

'I'd like to go back to something you mentioned earlier,' Garcia said. 'You said that you went into the Rendition Room because you wanted to check the wallets you had picked that night, is that right?'

Angela nodded, defiantly. 'I don't get greedy anymore. I boost two, maybe three wallets max before checking them for cash and credit cards. If I've made enough, I call it a day. If not, I'll dispose of the wallets before going back for a second round. If the wallet contains only cash and credit cards, I keep those and throw the wallet in the trash. If the wallet contains any personal documents, like driver's license, work credentials, ID cards, whatever, I mail them back to their owners.'

That made both detectives frown.

'You mail them back?' Hunter asked.

Angela scratched the back of her head. 'Look, I know the kind of headache that replacing personal documents can be. Most replacements will cost money too. I've already taken that person's money and credit cards. There's no need for me to also kick them while they're down, right?'

Garcia chuckled while looking at Hunter. 'What do you know? A thief with morals.'

'I'm assuming there were no personal documents inside this bag you mentioned,' Hunter said.

'No, nothing, just that book.'

'Please tell me that you still have the bag,' Garcia said, leaning forward and placing his elbows on the table.

Angela looked away.

'Really? What did you do with it?'

'I threw it away.'

'You've got to be joking.' Garcia's hand moved to his forehead. 'That bag probably contained fingerprints, DNA, fibers . . . everything.'

Angela glared at Garcia. 'What did you want me to do with it, keep it? It's not like I was expecting you guys to come knocking on my door looking for evidence. Do you think that I left my prints on this photo on purpose? You're lucky that I even decided to post that book. I could've very easily thrown everything away and be done with it.'

'Oh yes, I forgot,' Garcia came back. 'A thief with morals.'

'Was there anything else inside the bag?' Hunter asked, interrupting the argument.

'No, nothing else. Just the book.'

'Maybe we can still retrieve the bag,' Garcia said, not wanting to give up. 'When and where did you throw it away?'

'You can't,' Angela replied. 'It's gone.'

'Why? What did you really do with it?'

'I threw it away, but garbage collection day on my street is Monday morning – yesterday. I watched as they emptied the building dumpsters into the garbage truck and crushed everything. The bag is gone, trust me.'

Garcia didn't look too convinced by Angela's story.

'Wait a second,' he said. 'You told us that you mail the wallets back to their owners, right? But the journal wasn't mailed to Dr. Slater.' He looked at Hunter as if he had figured out the flaw in Angela's story. 'It was hand-delivered.'

'Yeah, so?'

'So, question one – how did you know where she lived or who she was? Two – why deliver it to a forensics doctor when you could've sent it directly to the LAPD?'

Angela went quiet again.

'You're lying, aren't you?' Garcia challenged. 'Your entire story is one huge pile of bullshit.'

Angela looked like she was trying to figure out what to say.

'Do you know what I think?' Garcia continued, his voice calm. 'I think that you know very well who the owner of that diary is. I think that you used to be his girlfriend, or lover, or whatever you want to call it. I think that he got tired of you and probably left you high and dry ... maybe swapped you for someone else and that really pissed you off, so as an act of revenge, you stole his diary and came up with this bogus story.'

'You can't be serious,' Angela said in disbelief.

'Oh, I'm very serious. And I wouldn't be surprised if you helped him with some, if not all of the murders in that journal.'

'Are you crazy?' Angela's scared eyes flipped to Hunter. 'Is he crazy?'

'My version makes a lot more sense than yours,' Garcia countered.

'Your version is delusional,' Angela refuted. 'You know I don't even have to be here.'

'Really? So prove me wrong. How did you know where Dr. Susan Slater lived, or even who she is? And why did you deliver the journal to her mailbox when you could've sent it directly to the LAPD or even the FBI?'

Angela knew that she should stop talking. This was looking horribly bad for her.

'A thief with morals,' she finally replied, using Garcia's words.

'You stole her purse,' Hunter said, Angela's story finally making sense to him.

'What?' Garcia asked again, this time addressing Hunter.

'You don't remember?' Hunter asked.

'Remember what?' Garcia's brow creased.

'About a month ago,' Hunter clarified. 'We were at that triple homicide crime scene in Encino. Susan was the lead forensics agent.'

'Yeah, I remember it, what about it?'

'Actually,' Hunter said, as he revisited the scene in his memory. 'Maybe you weren't in the room at the time. Anyway, Susan told me that she'd had her purse stolen from her bag a couple of nights before while out with some friends.'

Garcia shook his head. 'No, I don't remember that at all.'

Hunter looked at Angela. 'That was you.'

Angela shrugged, as if she weren't to blame. 'She left her bag unzipped and unattended, hanging from the back of her chair. She might as well have put a sign on it saying "please take me".'

'Her purse,' Hunter concluded, 'was one of those you've returned to the owner.'

Angela nodded. 'She kept everything in her purse – driver's license, LAPD and lab credentials, medical ID, security card, everything. I'd never picked a cop before, so as soon as I saw all her documents and IDs, I sort of panicked a little.'

'So you mailed it all back to her.'

'Everything,' Angela confirmed. 'Credit cards, cash, documents, purse . . . everything. I didn't keep any of it.'

'So what?' Garcia questioned. 'Are you trying to tell me that you keep a record of everyone in this city who you have returned their wallets or purses to?'

'No, I don't,' Angela replied in the same tone Garcia had used. 'But I've got a very good memory. For some reason I'm able to remember things very easily. In this case, like I said, she was the first cop I've ever picked.'

'She's not a cop,' Garcia cut her short.

'Yes, but she works for the Forensics Science and Technical Division,' Angela argued. 'Which is part of the Criminalistics section of the LAPD.'

Garcia's skeptical stare intensified.

Angela read it. 'I told you that I remember things very easily. Anyway . . .' preferring to talk to Hunter, she turned to address him. 'I had no problems remembering her home address.'

'So why didn't you mail it?' Garcia wasn't cutting Angela any slack. 'Why did you decide to hand-deliver it?'

'Spur of the moment decision,' Angela angled her head slightly to the right as she replied.

'I'm not buying that,' Garcia said.

'That's good, because I'm not selling it. It's the truth.' Once again, she addressed Hunter. 'Yes, if Shawn was alive today, he would probably look very similar to this guy.' She indicated the photo on the table. 'And . . .'

This time Angela was unable to fight back the tears. She turned and looked away from both detectives.

Garcia looked like he was about to say something, but Hunter stopped him with a subtle hand gesture.

'Give her some time,' he mouthed.

Eighteen

Angela hadn't lied when she told Hunter that she didn't need that Polaroid to remind her of her brother. She really did think of him every day, but the resemblance between Shawn and the guy in the photo did stir something inside of her in a way that she wasn't expecting.

'Could I please have another glass of water?' she finally said, after wiping the tears from her face.

'Of course,' Hunter replied before getting up and exiting the room. Less than thirty seconds later, he was back with an icy-cold metal jug of water. He refilled her plastic cup, placed the jug on the table and sat back down.

Angela reached for the cup and drank half of it down in three big gulps. Her hands were shaking.

'It's my fault.' Those words escaped her lips as a choked whisper, but still loud enough for both detectives to hear them.

'What is?' Garcia asked.

Hunter immediately signaled to him again – a very subtle headshake.

'I shouldn't have allowed him to leave the house that day,'

she said. Her gaze had fallen to a random spot on the floor. Her catatonic eyes, glassed over by tears, had practically stopped blinking.

Angela wasn't staring at the floor. Hunter knew that. To her, the floor didn't exist. The room didn't exist. Hunter and Garcia didn't exist. Her memory had whisked her back to the day that Shawn had gone missing. Instead of interrupting her with questions, which would only serve to break her out of her trance-like state and dissipate the memory, the best option was to allow her emotions to talk.

'Mom told me not to.' Angela swallowed a lump of tears, as her nose started to run.

Hunter quickly reached into his jacket pocket for a packet of tissues and placed it on the table in front of her.

'I was too lazy,' Angela continued in a voice so filled with emotion it didn't sound like her own. 'Too lazy to get off my ass and go with him. That's what I should've done. Instead, I just let him go on his own . . . and he never came back.'

From this, Hunter began getting a real idea of what had happened that fateful day, just over six years ago.

Neither detective had had time to properly research the story of Shawn Wood's disappearance and murder. They didn't really know what had happened on the day that he went missing or what sort of efforts were put into the investigation. Their entire knowledge of the case had come exclusively from the six-year-old article taken from the *Idaho State Journal* that their research team had added to Angela's file.

'He was eleven years old,' Angela said, as she reached for the packet of tissues. 'Eleven . . . and that monster . . .' She shook her head, unable to put words to her feelings.

The article they had read didn't really describe in any detail the circumstances of Shawn's murder. It only mentioned that the body had been savagely mutilated.

'That bastard took everything from my little brother,' Angela said, after drinking the rest of her water. 'His dignity . . . his innocence . . . his life.'

Tears streamed down her cheeks.

'He took Shawn from all of our lives . . . mine . . . my mom's . . . my dad's. It destroyed our family.'

Hunter could practically feel Angela's pain right at that moment. He knew from experience that the loneliest moment in someone's life was when they were witnessing their whole world crumble before their eyes, and all they could do was watch.

She used another tissue before finally lifting her head to look at both detectives again.

'Regardless of that guy looking like Shawn.' She indicated the photo on the table. 'He is someone's son. Probably someone's brother too.' Angela paused to wipe her nose and take in a lungful of air. 'But no, this photo didn't remind me of Shawn. What it reminded me of was that that fucking psychopath was never caught. It reminded me that he's still out there, probably still doing what he did to my little brother to other kids. This photo and that book reminded me that he isn't the only one. They reminded me that this fucked-up world is full of fucked-up people just like him – predators, evil itself.' She locked eyes with Hunter. 'My first thought was to send that book to the LAPD, but what guarantees did I have that it would've been taken seriously? I might pick people's pockets, but I'm not stupid. I know that you guys receive a ridiculous amount of calls, letters, packages, emails, whatever . . . about all kinds of bogus shit. I am sure that if I had sent that book to the LAPD, someone would've decided that it was no priority and put it to one side. Maybe someone would have had a look at it, or maybe not. Maybe it would've been considered a hoax without any of it ever being checked and the whole thing would've been thrown in the trash.'

Hunter's eyes stayed on Angela, but he could practically feel Garcia's stare moving to him. Her assessment of what could've happened was not a fantasy.

'That was when I remembered the doctor that I had picked several weeks back,' Angela told them. 'A doctor with the Forensics Science and Technical Division of the LAPD.' She refilled her cup with water. 'If ever there was someone who could bypass the red tape and check if that book was real, she was it. I figured that unlike the LAPD, the Forensics Division didn't get a substantial amount of bogus mail, if any at all. Choosing to hand-deliver the book instead of posting it was a tactical decision.'

'Tactical?' Garcia queried.

'All I did was put myself in her shoes,' Angela explained. 'If I had received a package with only my name on it – no address, no stamps and no return address – it would've tickled my curiosity a lot more than a regular package, because I knew that that package had to have been hand-delivered . . . *to my door.*' She straightened herself up on her chair. 'The fact that I'm sitting in here with you guys two days after I delivered that book is clear evidence that my logic worked, isn't it?'

Hunter nodded. 'It worked.'

Garcia agreed. 'I have one more question, though.'

Angela pulled a face.

'Whoever made all those entries to that journal,' Garcia said, disregarding Angela's attitude, 'doesn't come across as stupid. On the contrary. We haven't had time to check all the entries yet, but the one we did check was executed with military precision. Nothing was left behind – no prints, no DNA, no fibers, no mistakes.' He gave Angela a few seconds to process what he was saying. 'What I'm getting at here is: someone like that doesn't sound like the kind of person that would be easily fooled by a regular pickpocket. But you're telling us that just like that.' Garcia snapped his fingers. 'No difficulty at all, you were able to relieve this person of probably his most prized possession. His murder journal. The one thing that could bring him down. The one thing that could put an end to his years-long murder spree and his freedom.' Garcia angled his head from left to right a few times, as if he were weighing the alternatives. 'A little hard to believe, don't you think?'

This time, Angela didn't disagree. 'Sure. The difference is – I'm not it.'

'You're not it?' Garcia asked. 'It what?'

'A regular pickpocket.' The look Angela gave Garcia was full of confidence. 'You said that someone like that doesn't sound like the kind of person that would be easily fooled by a regular street pickpocket, right? Well, I'm not one of those. I'm the best there is.'

Garcia, on the other hand, looked full of doubt. 'You are the best pickpocket there is?'

Angela nodded. 'For real.'

Garcia sat back on his chair, brought a hand to his chin and began scratching the underside of it. A couple of seconds later he looked at Hunter.

'Now we have no other alternative,' he said. 'We're going to have to do this.'

Angela frowned at both of them. 'Do what?'

Nineteen

There were no windows down in the interrogation room. Air was supplied by an archaic ventilation system that didn't seem to be working too well. Consequently, the air inside the room was rapidly becoming heavy and stale. Despite the low temperatures outside, beads of sweat were starting to form on the foreheads of all three occupants. Angela used a tissue to wipe hers.

'Do what?' she asked again, her stare playing tennis between the two detectives.

Garcia stood up and walked over to his left, pausing about four feet from the large two-way mirror on the wall.

'Do what you said you're the best at,' he finally replied before reaching into his inside jacket pocket and retrieving his wallet. 'Here's my wallet.' He held it up to show it to Angela. 'I want you to take it from me.' He returned it to his right inside pocket.

Angela's eyebrows moved up almost an inch. 'Are you serious?'

'I'm very serious. You just told us that you're the best there is at this. I want to see it. I want to see the master at work.'

'That's not how it works,' Angela came back, her tone now a little unsure.

'What do you mean – "not how it works"? You're either good at this or you're lying.'

'People are not exactly expecting to have their wallets stolen from them when they are out on the streets,' Angela explained. 'And that's where the big difference is. Their attentions are elsewhere, not on their wallets or on their pockets, which is our biggest trump card. You, on the other hand, are not only expecting your wallet to be taken, but you also know when and by whom. No matter how much you try to pretend, as soon as I approach you, you will subconsciously be on alert and start concentrating on your wallet, which kills the element of surprise, and that's eighty percent of the game.'

'Well, why don't you give it your best shot, anyway? I want to see how skillful you are. Even if I'm expecting it to happen, I'm sure that I'll be able to appreciate your technique ... if it's good enough, that is.'

'It won't work,' Angela insisted.

'Give it a try,' said Garcia.

Angela knew that she had no way out of this one. She breathed out in frustration.

'All right.'

She got to her feet and walked over to the two-way mirror, pausing about seven feet in front of Garcia. They faced each other as if they were about to have a duel, Old West style.

Hunter repositioned his chair and made himself comfortable. He had a front-row seat to the show.

Angela quickly explained how she first observed people to identify where they had stored their wallets or purses.

'Great,' Garcia said back, as he tapped his torso, just under his right pectoral muscle. 'So let's say that you just saw me put my wallet in my inside jacket pocket, like you did. How would you go about taking it from me?' He used his hands to urge her toward him. 'C'mon, show me.'

Angela glanced at Hunter, who looked like he was also very interested in seeing her technique. She shook her head to indicate that she believed the whole scenario was pointless.

'All right,' she began. 'Let's do this slowly, so I can show you how it all works.'

'That's fine by me,' Garcia said.

'I'm glad to hear it,' Angela continued. 'As I'm sure both of you know, the most used approach is to walk in the direction of your target and bump into them.' She approached Garcia. 'We always bump into the subject at the opposite side from the target object. So if I know that your wallet is in this pocket.' She used her left hand to tap the detective on the right side of his torso, right where his wallet was. 'I would bump you on this side.' She showed him. 'If I know that your wallet is in this pocket, for example.' With her right hand, she tapped Garcia's left outside jacket pocket. 'I would bump you on this side, but I'm sure you already knew that too, right?'

Garcia nodded, sarcastically.

She walked back to her original position, about seven feet in front of Garcia. 'All right, so let me show you what I do. Your attention is on anything else, but on me, OK? On a busy street, you won't even notice that I'm coming toward you.'

'OK.'

Angela walked forward until she was almost upon Garcia and then she stopped. 'The reason for the bump is to distract the person and to give me an excuse to place my hands on my target. Like this.'

Angela rammed her left shoulder against Garcia's left shoulder just hard enough to make him turn to face her.

'Oh, I'm so sorry,' she said, looking Garcia in the eye. At the same time, both of her hands moved to him. Her right was placed on his left arm and her left on his torso, just about the exact position where his inside jacket pocket was located.

Hunter's eyes followed Angela's hands.

'Now here's the thing,' she said to Garcia. 'Pickpocketing is very much like a magic trick, in the sense that for it to work, it mainly depends on one thing – misdirection.' With her right hand, Angela tapped Garcia's left arm twice. 'And our biggest advantage when it comes to misdirection, is the fact that the human body's nervous system is very easily distracted ... very easy to fool. What I mean by that is, it tends to pay attention, or concentrate on only *one* point at a time. The point where the contact is stronger.'

Garcia pulled a 'you're not telling me anything new here' face.

'Which means that since I am touching your body at two different locations at once ...' Angela demonstrated by once again using her right hand to tap Garcia's left arm, while at the same time, her left hand tapped just under his right pectoral muscle. 'I can control where your nervous system will concentrate its attention by applying more strength or pressure to wherever I want. Like this.'

She tapped his left arm one more time. This time, just a little harder.

'You felt that, right?'

'Of course.' His stare jumped to his left arm and her hand.

'That would be the misdirection,' Angela explained. 'By tapping or touching this or that side of your body with a little more strength than the other, I bring your attention to that location.' Her eyes then slowly moved across to her left hand.

Garcia's eyes followed.

'While my other hand would be executing the trick.' Very slowly, she moved her left hand into Garcia's jacket and into his inside breast pocket to take his wallet. 'Like so.'

Garcia watched the move in silence. 'Yes, but I felt that. You wouldn't get away with this. I would've stopped you before you'd gotten two feet away from me.'

Angela took her hands off Garcia. 'We were doing this in super-slow-motion. Of course you're going to feel it. But remember when I said that for pickpocketing to work, it mainly depends on misdirection.'

Garcia nodded.

'There's one more factor that comes into play. And that is speed. The whole thing will be over in three, four seconds max. Too fast for you to notice.'

Garcia looked back at Angela in a way that told her that he was still waiting for her to convince him.

'OK, so let's do it again, this time in real time.'

She returned to her starting position – facing the detective seven paces ahead of him.

'Ready?' she asked.

'As much as I'll ever be.'

They walked toward each other. Quick shoulder bump.

'Oh, I'm so sorry,' Angela said, her hands moving to Garcia's torso, her eyes holding his stare. 'Are you OK?'

'I'm fine.'

Three seconds and she was gone, stopping a couple of feet behind Garcia.

Garcia didn't look back at her. His left hand moved to his inside jacket pocket and he shook his head.

'My wallet is still in my pocket.' As Garcia said those

words, he saw the smile on Hunter's face. 'What are you smiling about?'

'Your wallet is still in your pocket,' Hunter replied. 'But
your cellphone and your badge are gone.'

Garcia checked his jacket inside pocket, left side – no phone.
He checked his belt – no badge. He turned around to look at
Angela. She had his phone in her right hand and his badge
in her left.

'Shit!' Garcia said. 'I didn't feel any of that.'

'I could've taken your firearm as well,' she said, with a
head tilt. 'But I figured that if I had done that, your partner . . .' She nodded at Hunter. '. . . would've probably shot me
where I stood.'

Hunter nodded back.

'But I've unclipped your holster.'

Garcia checked his weapon shoulder holster, which secured
his Wilson Combat Tactical .45 pistol to the right side of his
body, just a couple of inches under his arm. The security clip
that held his gun in place was undone. He never left it undone.

'She's good,' Hunter said, giving Angela an approving nod.

'I'm the best,' Angela corrected him before handing Garcia
back his cellphone and badge.

Hunter got to his feet. 'OK, that settles it for me. Let's go.'

'Where are we going?' Garcia asked.

'To the Rendition Room in Tujunga Village. That's where
you were when you boosted the bag, right?'

Angela nodded.

'I'm sure they have CCTV cameras in that place,' Hunter
said. 'Most bars do. Who knows, we might get lucky. Also,
there's a chance that the bag owner went to ask at the bar or
talk to the management once he realized his bag was missing.

Ms. Wood might've not seen his face, but maybe someone else did.'

'That's a good point,' Garcia said, clipping his badge back onto his belt.

'You say "Ms. Wood" and I start looking for my mother,' Angela said. 'You can call me Angela.' She shrugged. 'Or Angie. So am I free to go?'

'Unfortunately not,' Hunter said. 'I'd like you to stay with us for a while longer, just until we confirm your entire story.'

'You're kidding?'

'Why?' Garcia asked. 'Are we going to make you late for work? Some more wallets you need to steal?'

'Oh,' Angela said, a cheeky smile on her lips. 'Look who's a sore loser. Did I hurt your pride?'

Garcia shook his head. 'I'm not sore, or a loser. And my pride is intact.'

'Don't be too harsh on yourself,' Angela tried to comfort him. 'I really am the best. The only reason why your partner saw me taking your phone and your badge was because of this set-up situation. He was specifically looking for it. In a street environment, no one sees or feels me doing anything.'

'May I suggest we get going,' Hunter said, bringing the confrontation to an end and ushering everyone out of the muggy and uncomfortable interrogation room.

Twenty

Once again, Garcia drove. This time, the silence wasn't intentional. No one really had anything to say. Every now and then, through the rearview mirror, Hunter would check on Angela in the backseat. She sat with her arms crossed in front of her and her stare fixed outside her window. At a glance, she looked calm and in control, but every so often she would bite her bottom lip and her eyes would wander a little aimlessly for a second or two. When they did, they looked troubled and full of sorrow.

Traffic was moderate and it took them thirty-two minutes to cover the fourteen miles between the PAB and the Rendition Room cocktail lounge.

Normally, the lounge would only open its doors to the public at 5:00 p.m., but with just over two weeks until Christmas and the streets heaving with eager shoppers, the management had decided that during the month of December they would add a few more coffee-based cocktails to their list and open from lunchtime, a decision that seemed to be paying off.

At just a few minutes past three in the afternoon, the place was pretty busy, with every table taken. All that was left were three scattered seats at the long, dark-wood bar counter.

Hunter paused as he, Garcia and Angela stepped into the atmospherically lit and beautifully decorated 1930s speakeasy-style lounge. Ragtime played through several mini-speakers that had been strategically positioned throughout the place, filling the large room with a contagiously cheerful vibe.

'Can you show me where you were?' Hunter asked Angela.

'Right over there,' she replied, indicating a small table just a few feet from the bar. The table was taken by two men, who were leisurely sipping from bottles of beer.

'And the man?' Garcia this time.

'He was at the next table over.' She indicated the table just ahead of the one she had pointed out.

Hunter studied the location of the tables in relation to the floor area before checking around for CCTV cameras. He saw three of them, all standard ceiling cameras encased in dark glass. The first one was positioned at the bar, directly above the cash register, which was in an almost direct line with the tables that Angela had showed them. The second CCTV camera was to their left, close to the doors to the bathrooms. The final one had been placed by the lounge's entrance.

'Was he facing the bar?' Hunter asked.

'No. Neither of us was. We were both looking the other way.'

Hunter nodded before approaching the bar at its quieter end, on the far right, just by a door with a placard that read 'Staff Only'. Garcia and Angela stood right behind him as he signaled one of the three bartenders.

'Hello,' the young barman said, immediately placing three round drink coasters on the bar in front of the new customers. 'What can I get for you folks today?'

Hunter discreetly showed the young man his credentials. 'I'm Detective Robert Hunter with the LAPD. This is Detective Carlos Garcia.'

Garcia did the same.

The bartender studied them for a couple of seconds before looking back at Hunter curiously.

'Were you, by any chance, working here this past Saturday,' Hunter asked. 'Evening shift?'

'No, I wasn't. I was off the entire weekend, but Ricardo, the manager, was.' His head tilted right to indicate the bartender closest to the cash register – a tall and slender man with side-parted hair and a perfectly trimmed pencil moustache.

'Ricky,' the young bartender called before motioning the manager to come closer.

'How can I help?' Ricardo asked, as he joined the group. He looked to be at least a decade older than the first bartender.

Once again, Hunter began by discreetly showing the manager his credentials and introducing himself.

Ricardo took his time studying them. 'Is there some sort of a problem?'

'No, no problem at all,' Hunter replied in a comforting tone. 'We're just trying to identify, and hopefully find, a customer that we know came into your establishment this past Saturday. Apparently he took that table right over there, and that was around . . .' Hunter looked at Angela.

'Five-thirty,' she said with a head shuffle.

'We believe that he had his bag stolen from him while he was in here.' Hunter took over again. 'Does that ring any bells? Did anyone come to you, or any of the bartenders, complaining about a stolen bag on Saturday evening?'

The bar manager frowned at Hunter. 'So today you're after the man who had his bag stolen, rather than the bag itself, or the person who took the bag?'

Ricardo's words intrigued everyone.

'I'm not sure I follow,' Hunter said.

'The officer who was here on Sunday,' Ricardo explained, 'was concerned only with finding the person who took the bag – the thief – which, I must admit, is the more logical approach. But you are asking about the victim.' He shook his head, as if confused. 'Didn't he come to you, the police, to report that his bag was stolen?'

'You had an officer here on Sunday asking about the stolen bag?' Hunter asked.

'Yes, that's right.'

'Was that a plain-clothes officer?' Garcia this time. 'A detective like us, or a uniformed one?'

'Full uniform,' Ricardo confirmed. 'I'm talking LAPD cap and the standard-issue sunglasses. Even in this light.' His right index finger pointed up, toward the ceiling. 'He kept them on the whole time.'

Hunter peeked at Garcia. 'Did you talk to him yourself on Sunday?'

'Yes.'

'Did he give you a name, a phone number, any way that you could contact him in case of any information?'

'No, he didn't.'

'Did he tell you which precinct he was from?' Garcia asked.

Ricardo thought about it for a moment. 'If he did, I can't remember.'

Angela was beginning to look quite lost.

'On Saturday evening,' Hunter asked, 'the night that the bag was stolen, did the owner of the bag approach you or any of your bartenders once he realized that his bag was gone?'

'No,' Ricardo replied. 'Not at all. There were no incidents that evening.'

'Are you sure?' Garcia pushed. 'Don't you need to ask the bartenders?'

'Positive.' Ricardo looked almost offended. 'If any of our customers come to any of our bartenders to report a theft from inside the Rendition Room, they have to bring it to the manager on duty. I was the manager on duty on Saturday evening. There were no incidents.'

'Going back to the officer that spoke to you on Sunday,' Hunter said. 'Could you run us through what he said? The more you can remember, the better.'

Ricardo was unable to hide his confusion. 'Now I am the one who doesn't follow. What is going on?'

A few more people had just entered the Rendition Room and approached the bar.

'Maybe it would be better if we could talk somewhere a little more private,' Hunter suggested. 'Is that possible?'

Ricardo hesitated for a moment before checking his watch. 'This place gets quite busy at this time of the year, as you can see.'

'We really won't take too much of your time,' Hunter insisted. 'This is very important.'

Ricardo ran a hand over his mouth before looking at his two other bartenders. 'Mick, George, hold the floor for a bit, will you? I'll be right back.'

Both bartenders nodded.

'OK,' Ricardo said, indicating the 'Staff Only' door. 'Please follow me.'

Twenty-One

The 'Staff Only' office that Ricardo guided Hunter, Garcia and Angela into was small and cluttered, with crates of beer and boxes full of spirits just about everywhere. The walls were once white, but time had taken its toll and they were now a dirty beige.

'Please excuse the mess,' Ricardo said, clearing a couple of boxes full of vodka bottles from two wooden chairs that sat in front of a small desk with a computer. 'Sorry, I only have two chairs in here.'

'We don't need the chairs,' Hunter said.

Ricardo nodded, leaned back against the edge of the desk and folded his arms in front of his chest. Classic defensive posture.

'There's a chance that the man who came to talk to you on Sunday,' Hunter began, 'wasn't really an LAPD officer.'

The confusion in Ricardo's eyes deepened. 'Really? But why would he do that?'

'That's why we need to know what was said during the conversation,' Hunter replied.

'And with as much detail as possible,' Garcia added.

Hunter noticed the manager's hands tighten their grip on his crossed arms ever so slightly.

'I don't want to be rude here, or anything,' Ricardo said. 'But could I have a look at your IDs again?'

Hunter was already half expecting that move. In short, what he and Garcia were doing was trying to discredit someone who probably looked completely legit as a police officer, uniform and all. More legit than Hunter and Garcia looked at that particular moment.

'Of course,' Hunter replied, handing Ricardo his detective ID. Garcia followed suit.

'How about her?' Ricardo asked, gesturing toward Angela.

'She's not an officer,' Garcia said, telling a quick white lie to avoid even more explanations. 'She's a civilian "ride along".'

Ricardo didn't look too convinced, but there wasn't much he could say. The credentials that Hunter and Garcia had handed him looked authentic, not that he would really be able to identify a fake. He studied them for several long seconds before returning them to both detectives.

'Are we good?' Garcia asked.

'Yes, sure.'

'So,' Hunter asked again, 'can you now please run us through what this "officer" told you on Sunday?'

Ricardo shrugged, as he gently shook his head. 'There wasn't that much conversation, to be honest.'

'What do you mean?' Garcia asked.

'The officer came to me, explained what had happened the night before – the theft of a bag – indicated the table, just like you did, and asked if he could have a look at the CCTV camera footage from the night in question.'

'So there *is* CCTV footage?' Garcia asked. 'The cameras in the lounge are real.'

'Yes, of course.'

Hunter and Garcia had both seen too many fake CCTV cameras in too many different establishments to ever assume anything anymore.

'And this "officer" did check the footage?' Hunter asked.

'Yes. I brought him in here and he used this computer. It didn't take him long. He was in and out in about ... fifteen minutes.'

'Did you stay with him?' Garcia again. 'Or did you leave him in here by himself?'

'I showed him the CCTV app then just left him to it,' Ricardo replied. 'The floor was way too busy on Sunday afternoon for me to babysit a police officer.' He paused for a second. 'At least that's what I thought he was.'

'Do you mind if we have a look at the footage?' Hunter asked.

'Sure, be my guest,' Ricardo said, rounding the desk to face the computer monitor. 'Hang on a sec ... Any particular camera you'd like to have a look at first?' Ricardo asked after a moment.

'Let's start with the one on the ceiling right above the cash register,' Hunter said.

'No point,' Ricardo told him. 'That camera is trained directly on the register itself.' His hands moved up in a 'what can I do?' gesture, before explaining. 'In the past year, we had to let three people go due to stealing.'

'OK,' Hunter said. 'So let's go with the one closest to the bathrooms.'

'Sure.' Two mouse clicks. 'You want to look at the footage from this past Saturday, right? December 5th.'

'That's correct.'

Another click.

'And you said that the time you're looking at is around five-thirty?'

'Actually,' Hunter said, 'let's go all the way back to five in the afternoon.'

'Sure, no problem.' Another two clicks. Ricardo then paused and frowned at the screen. 'OK, this is weird.'

'What is?' Angela asked, her voice a little anxious. Her concern was that the camera would show her boosting the bag.

Hunter, who already had a pretty good idea of what Ricardo was referring to, checked the timeframe clock on the top right-hand corner of the screen. He was right.

'A huge segment of the footage is missing,' Ricardo informed them, as he indicated the clock. 'From around two in the afternoon on Saturday all the way to six in the evening. Look at this.' He slowed the footage down to 'frame by frame' speed. As the clock reached 14:00:00, it suddenly jumped to 18:00:00. 'The whole chunk is gone.'

'Recycling bin?' Hunter suggested.

Another mouse click.

'It's been emptied,' Ricardo said.

Angela seemed relieved, but Hunter scratched his forehead.

'Let me check the other camera,' Ricardo said. 'The one by the entry door.'

Neither Hunter nor Garcia said anything, but they both knew that the exercise would be pointless.

'It's also gone,' Ricardo announced after a couple more clicks. 'The exact same four hours.'

'No surprise there,' Garcia commented.

Ricardo looked back at the detectives, intrigued.

'There's a chance that our IT forensics unit will be able to retrieve something from your hard drive,' Hunter explained. 'Which means that we'll need that hard drive.'

Ricardo took a much more defensive position.

'I'm sorry, but for that you'll need a warrant. I can't just hand over the lounge's computer like that. I'm just the manager here, not the owner.'

Hunter was quick to calm him down. 'Yes, we understand. We'll get you the warrant. I wasn't suggesting that we take the computer right now. Maybe that won't even be necessary, I'm not sure, but meanwhile, I'd suggest that you get in touch with the owners and maybe start making a copy of whatever other documents you have on that hard drive.'

'Jesus!' Ricardo gasped, running his thumb and index finger over his moustache. 'All of that because of a stolen bag? What the hell was in that bag?'

'You really don't want to know,' Angela said, as she reached for the door.

Twenty-Two

It had rained while Hunter, Garcia and Angela were inside the Rendition Room – one of those famous LA 'flash downpours'. Puddles reflected the scale of the rain, but the sky would confuse anyone. There wasn't a single dark cloud in sight. The sun was already back out, trying its best to produce some warmth, but the rain had chilled the afternoon air and filled it with humidity.

As they stepped outside, all three of them quickly zipped up their coats. Despite the rain and the fact that it was a Tuesday afternoon, the streets were heavy with shoppers.

'So am I free to go now?' Angela asked. 'I can walk home from here or jump in a bus. It's just a short ride.'

'Not that simple,' Garcia replied.

'Why not?' Her eyes pleaded. 'There's nothing else I can do to help you. This is it. This is all I know, and you just had confirmation that I'm telling the truth, didn't you? Why else would that dude come back here dressed as a cop, check the CCTV footage for the exact time I told you I was here and then delete it, if not to hide his identity? The cameras obviously picked up his face.'

'Maybe his wasn't the only face the cameras captured,'

Hunter said. His gaze kept on running up and down the street, as if he were looking for someone. 'And I'm sure that that was what he was really after.'

Angela's features knotted in doubt. 'I'm not really with you here.'

'Do you think you would recognize him if you saw him again?' Hunter asked. 'Like on the streets, or something?'

Angela chuckled. 'Were you listening when I told you what happened? I never got to see his face. He had a hood on and he never really lifted his eyes from his cellphone. He could bump into me right now and I wouldn't know it was him. I'm telling you, there really is nothing else I can do to help you find him. Just let me go . . . please.'

Hunter checked his phone. Still no email from Dr. Slater.

'We need to get back to the PAB,' he informed Angela. 'There's still a little bit of paperwork to be done. After that, you're free to go.'

'More paperwork? Are you kidding?' Angela threw her hands up in the air, annoyed. 'You don't need me there for that. Can't you guys do that on your own?'

'How about your backpack?' Garcia asked.

Angela had forgotten about the fact that her backpack was still back at the PAB, but what was really bothering her was the feeling that Hunter was trying to dodge explaining what he meant.

'Sure,' she finally agreed. 'Let's go back to the PA whatever, but first you have to stop ducking the question.' She stopped Hunter with a pissed-off look. 'What did you mean when you said that maybe the man's face wasn't the only face the CCTV cameras captured?'

Hunter walked back to Angela. His gaze stopped wandering

the streets and he locked eyes with her. His eyebrows came up ever so faintly.

The penny dropped.

'My face?'

'Would it really surprise you,' he asked, 'that whoever the owner of that journal is, he wants it back?'

Angela's lips drew a tight line when she remembered that she had already taken off her wig and her contact lenses when she boosted the man's leather bag.

'From his point of view,' Hunter continued, 'the only way he can do that is by finding you first. That's the main reason why he came back here for the CCTV footage.'

A few seconds went by as Angela's brain processed everything. Then, her stare returned to Hunter. 'Is that why you keep looking up and down the street?'

Hunter stayed quiet.

'It is, isn't it?' It was Angela's turn to quickly scan the crowd of shoppers. 'That's why you've asked me if I would be able to recognize him if I saw him again. You think that he might be staking this place out on the off-chance that I come back here?'

'If he has managed to get a clear image of your face from the CCTV footage,' Garcia jumped in, 'then that would be a pretty logical move on his part, don't you think?'

'Jesus Christ!' Angela gasped, as she pulled her hoodie over her head as far as it would go.

All of a sudden, going back to the PAB sounded like a great idea.

Twenty-Three

The idea of staking out the Rendition Room had occurred to the man. He knew that thieves, particularly pickpockets, tended to stick to the same areas, busy areas, which they knew were lucrative. If the person who had taken his bag was really a professional pickpocket, which the man believed was the case, then that person probably wouldn't go back to the Rendition Room so soon – too risky to hit the same establishment in such a short period of time – but there was a fair chance that the thief would be working other bars or shops in Tujunga Village, especially over the Christmas season when the movement of people increased exponentially. Knowing that, staking Tujunga Village wasn't such a bad idea, but first the man needed to identify the little weasel who had taken his bag. His only chance of doing that was if the CCTV cameras inside the Rendition Room had captured the thief's face.

Posing as a cop had been a great move. People were much more inclined to cooperate if they believed that they were talking to a law enforcement official. Once the bar manager showed the man to his office and left him alone to check the CCTV footage, he was free to do as he pleased.

The man wasn't really worried about his face showing up

in any of the recordings. That was something he was always extremely careful about – never going anywhere without his aviator sunglasses and his hood up over his head. True, he had taken off his sunglasses inside the Rendition Room that Saturday evening, but not before identifying the position of all three CCTV cameras. Once at his table, he had positioned himself facing east, away from all three cameras. His biggest mistake that night, he knew, had been placing his leather bag on the floor, by his feet.

Since the man had started writing his diary, he kept it with him at all times, taking the book with him wherever he went – a mixture of paranoia and fear of needing to write something down and forgetting what it was if he didn't do it straight away. That night, as he placed his bag on the table inside The Rendition Room, he almost knocked his glass over. That prompted him to place the bag on the floor. A big, big mistake.

Since, on Saturday, the man had positioned himself facing away from all three cameras, he was concerned with the possibility that the thief, whoever he or she might be, also did the same. In their line of work, they couldn't really afford not to be cautious. If that had been the case, then the man would be stuck. He would have no other way of identifying who had taken his bag.

The man didn't check any of the CCTV camera footage while inside the manager's office. That would've taken way too long. Instead, he copied the recordings of all three cameras onto a flash drive, including the footage from the camera over the cash register, and deleted it.

Back at his place, the man connected the flash drive to his computer and began scanning what he had. First up was the camera that was positioned by the lounge's entrance. Instead of scanning the footage from the beginning, he started from the time he had arrived – around five twenty-five in the afternoon – because he first needed to identify the thief, and it didn't take him long. Just after he had told that old man who had asked to share his table to get lost, he noticed that the woman who was occupying the table just behind his finished her drink but didn't leave immediately. Instead, she took out her cellphone and made a call, or at least pretended to make one. Oddly, the woman could've made the call from where she was standing, but she instead moved around to the other side of her table, a lot closer to where his bag was.

Her phone conversation lasted less than a minute and though the camera angle wasn't wide enough to show what was happening at floor level, the man was sure that she was using her foot to slowly drag his bag away from him and closer to her.

She was good, the man had to give her that. No panic, no awkward body movement, nothing suspicious whatsoever – just someone having a perfectly normal conversation on her phone.

Then something unexpected happened, because all of a sudden everyone looked right, including him.

At his computer, he paused the footage and thought about it for a moment.

'Oh, that's right,' he said as he remembered. There had been a loud crashing noise. A waiter had dropped a tray of drinks by the other end of the bar. Once the man resumed the footage, he saw that in a flash, the woman thief recognized the opportunity and reached down to take the bag. By the time he had returned his attention to his cellphone, she had already rounded her table and left the bar.

The man couldn't help smiling at how calm and smooth the woman had been. There was no question that she was a pro.

The problem he had was that not once during that whole footage segment did the woman look up, not even as she was exiting the lounge, which meant that he didn't have a clear shot of her face. But at least he now knew who to search for.

The man rewound the footage back to about five in the afternoon and began again. It wasn't until around five-thirty that he saw the woman entering the Rendition Room lounge. He had to rewind and watch that segment of the footage a few times to make sure, because she looked different. When she entered the bar, she had short black hair, instead of a blonde, side-swept bob. What gave her away was the coat she wore.

'There you are,' the man said, nodding at his screen. His voice was dry and husky, as if his vocal cords had somehow been scarred. 'C'mon, glance up. Say hello to the camera. All I need is one look.'

But he wasn't so lucky. Keeping her head down, the woman entered the lounge, zigzagged through the crowded bar area and moved straight toward the other end of the room. The line of vision of the camera above the entrance didn't reach that far, so the man couldn't quite see where she went, but it looked like she had aimed for the bathrooms. She stayed in there for quite a while – almost fifteen minutes. Once she resurfaced, she moved to the bar, ordered a drink and took the table that had vacated just behind her, right next to the one that the man was occupying.

Still no clear shot of her face.

'C'mon, baby, look up. Let me have a look at that pretty face of yours.'

Still no luck. Time to check the footage from the other camera – the one positioned by the doors to the bathrooms.

This time it all moved a lot faster, as the man knew the exact time frame to look for – five-thirty in the afternoon.

From this new camera angle the man saw the woman zigzag the crowd and push open the door to the lady's bathroom, all the while keeping her head down.

The man began losing hope. If the woman was a regular, someone who was used to boosting bags and wallets from inside the Rendition Room, then it was only logical that she knew the locations of the ceiling cameras. That could've been why she never looked up or positioned herself in a direct angle to any of them.

'Last chance saloon,' the man said without much optimism, as he fast-forwarded the footage. At around 5:47 p.m. the woman reappeared and that was when Lady Luck finally smiled on him. As the thief pulled the door open and stepped outside the washroom, her head angled slightly left and up for a very brief moment.

The man immediately stopped the footage before rewinding it frame by frame.

'Bingo!' he said as he came upon a frame that showed all of her facial features. 'There you are.' A bright smile graced his lips. 'So nice to finally meet you.'

The man took a snapshot of that particular frame before opening it in a professional image editor. After cleaning and sharpening the image as best as he could, he saved it to his desktop. Now all he needed to do was find her, and he had a pretty good idea of where to start.

Twenty-Four

It was nearly a quarter to five when Hunter, Garcia and Angela got back to the PAB. Before signing her out, Hunter retrieved her backpack from the holdings office and handed it back to her.

Angela unzipped it to check its contents. Inside it she found her cellphone and the change of clothes she had packed when trying to flee her apartment.

'It's still there,' Hunter said. 'The cash is in the outside pocket.'

Angela checked the pocket. It was all there. Every dollar. She looked back at him, surprised.

'We can't prove that the money doesn't belong to you,' Hunter explained. 'If we did confiscate the money, it would just sit in the holdings office until the end of time, because we'd have no way of finding out who to return it to.'

Angela zipped up her backpack and swung it over her right shoulder.

'The LAPD will send someone to fix your front door,' Hunter said, consulting his watch. 'But unfortunately it probably won't be today.'

'You better,' Angela said in return. 'Or else my landlord will have my ass.'

'Do you have somewhere else you can stay?'

Angela detected real concern in Hunter's voice.

'I'll be fine. I'll find a way to lock my door for tonight, but you guys really better get that fixed.'

'We will,' Hunter reassured her. 'I have your cellphone number in case I need to contact you anyway.' He handed her a card. 'My cell number is on the back, in case you need to get in touch with me.'

Angela regarded Hunter for a beat. The concern was still in his voice, but it went deeper than just a busted door. She didn't take the card.

'This isn't just about my front door, is it? You're concerned about this guy.' She took another moment studying the detective before her. 'You're worried about that CCTV camera footage, aren't you? You're worried that whoever this guy is, he might now have an image of my face.'

Angela was quick on the uptake, Hunter couldn't deny that. 'I am, yes.'

'Well, so am I,' Angela accepted. 'But let me ask you something – what's the population of Los Angeles?'

Hunter already knew where Angela was going with this.

'Over four million,' he replied.

'Exactly, so now *he* has a problem.'

'I know,' Hunter took over. 'Even if he now knows what you look like, he still needs to somehow find out who you are. And in a city with over four million people, that's not an easy thing to do when all you have is a photograph.'

'There's hope for you yet,' Angela said with a cheery smile. 'Look, his only point of reference when it comes to finding me is Tujunga Village. You know that.' She pointed a finger at Hunter. 'That's why you were so worried earlier on when we were standing outside the Rendition Room, isn't it? Looking up and down the street? Because you thought that he might've been staking the place out in the hope that I would go back.' Angela didn't wait for a reply. 'So the answer is simple – I'll stay the fuck away from Tujunga Village from now on.'

'That's definitely a good move,' Hunter agreed.

Angela regarded Hunter for another moment. 'But you still look worried.'

'Of course I'm worried,' Hunter explained. 'As a detective running an investigation, I have to consider every possible scenario. We don't even know if your face does or does not appear on the CCTV footage from the Rendition Room. If it does and the owner of that journal now knows what you look like, then the possibility of him somehow finding you, however small, does exist, and if that possibility exists then you need to stay vigilant at all times. Staying away from Tujunga Village is a great move, but not the only one. Be alert, be on the lookout.' Hunter was still holding out his card for Angela. 'This guy is not your average, run-of-the-mill criminal.'

Angela still didn't reach for the card.

'Look,' Hunter said. 'I've spent my entire professional life studying and chasing murderers like the owner of that journal.'

'You mean serial killers.'

'Yes,' Hunter agreed. 'Serial killers. Very few are as prolific as the man you saw on Saturday evening. The reason for that is because most of them will inevitably make a mistake one time or another.'

'So then all you have to do is wait for this guy to make a mistake and we'll be fine,' Angela said lightly.

'That's the problem.' Hunter's tone, on the other hand, was deadly serious. 'Whoever he is, he's been doing this for years.

The book you stole is proof of that. He's claimed at least sixteen victims so far and we didn't even have a clue he existed two days ago. What that translates into is that in all these years he's been active, he's never made a mistake.' He paused so the significance of what he was trying to tell Angela could sink in.

'So what are you really saying?'

'All I want is for you to understand that whoever this guy is, he's careful, he's methodical, he's thorough, and he seems to be very ingenious. Him turning up at the Rendition Room dressed as a cop, so he could access the CCTV recordings before doing away with them, is just an obvious example of how resourceful and determined this guy can be.'

Angela moved her backpack from one shoulder to the other.

'It would be a big mistake on our part,' Hunter continued, 'for us to underestimate such a person.' He once again offered Angela his card. 'All I want is for you to be careful and if you get suspicious about anything, whatever it is, don't hesitate – give me a call.'

This time Angela took the card. As she turned and walked away, Hunter's cellphone vibrated inside his jacket pocket – two quick bursts – announcing that he had just received a new email. He quickly checked it – Dr. Slater had finally sent them the photographs of all the pages in the journal.

Twenty-Five

As soon as Hunter got back to his desk, he opened the email he had received from Dr. Slater. The file contained one hundred and twenty images, each matching a page in the journal. To avoid confusion, the forensics agent who had taken the photographs had, at Dr. Slater's request, re-matched all the Polaroid photos to their respective pages, keeping them in the exact order that they appeared in the book. Hunter downloaded the attached zip file.

Garcia, who had been copied in on the email, did the same.

Hunter poured two cups of coffee for himself and his partner before opening the first image, titled 'page 1'. All images had been exported in high resolution, which made them very easy to read.

Despite having already read the first couple of pages back at the FSD lab, Hunter started from the beginning again. The rest of the entry described how the killer had put together the box in which Elizabeth Gibbs had been buried. After that, it explained how easy it had been to drug her with common crushed sleeping pills before placing her inside the makeshift box and sealing it shut.

The entry mentioned nothing about the small camera they

had found inside the box, but it went on to describe how hard she had fought once she'd been buried alive, clawing at the lid, punching it, kicking it, even biting it at times before finally losing all her hope and strength.

According to the entry, it had taken Elizabeth Gibbs almost twenty-four hours to run out of oxygen and finally suffocate. Her last couple of hours were spent crying and praying, instead of fighting. The entry ended with a surprise, though.

Just like with all previous subjects, this one also cried and begged for her life when I came for her. They all ask the same questions – Why? Why me? Why are you doing this to me? What have I ever done to you? It's intriguing to observe a subject as they realize that they ARE going to die and that there's absolutely nothing that they can do to stop it. Some will offer me their bodies. Tell me that I can do whatever I want to them, as long as I set them free afterwards. Some will tell me that they can pleasure me in ways I didn't even know possible. Some will try to appeal to my humane side and tell me stories. Stories about their lives and how much they have already suffered in life. Some will tell me about their families ... their parents ... their brothers and sisters ... their partners ... even their pets. This subject was no different. She told me about her childhood and how she was systematically raped by her father-in-law for three years when she was just a kid. She told me how much he'd hurt her – physically and psychologically. She told me that her father-in-law tore her inside and because of that she would never be able to have children of her own. She told me how much that knowledge broke her ... how close she had come to ending her life more than once, and that the only reason why she had never succeeded had been because of her best friend, who had become her boyfriend, and was now her fiancé. She told me that they were set to get married in eight months' time. I've heard all different types of stories from all different types of subjects and I don't blame them. People will try whatever they can to save their lives. That's human nature. For some reason, this subject's story stayed with me. Maybe it was the look in her eyes ... maybe it was the deep pain in her voice, or maybe it was because she reminded me of someone I knew a long time ago. I don't know, but I decided that I would give her a gift. I decided that in eight months' time – on the day that she was supposed to get married – I would dress her in a wedding dress.

Hunter stopped reading and looked up from his computer screen. As if on cue, so did Garcia.

'Did you get to the part about the wedding dress?' he asked.

'Yes,' Hunter replied.

'Is that his idea of being merciful?' Garcia continued. 'To dress her in a wedding dress on the day that she was supposed to get married?'

'I don't know ... maybe.'

'Well, he calls it a gift. Can you believe that crap?' He quoted. '"But I decided that I would give her a gift". This guy is clearly deranged, don't you think? He went back to dig her up, eight months after he'd buried her, to dress her up in a wedding dress ... but for what? Just so he can feel good about himself? Did he do it to lessen his guilt?'

Hunter didn't reply.

Garcia still wasn't finished.

'Can you imagine the patience?' he carried on. 'The perseverance? The body wouldn't be in perfect condition. That much we know. Decay would already have started to some degree, but still, he extracted her, soft body and all, probably undressed her from her old clothes.' He paused and lifted a hand. 'I'm guessing that he buried her with clothes originally. Then dressed her up again in a wedding dress.' Garcia shook his head as he considered the scenario. 'And he probably also cleaned the inside of the coffin as well. There was no mess, remember?'

Hunter nodded.

'If those aren't the actions of a deranged mind, then I don't know what is.'

'The best we can do is to carry on reading,' Hunter said.

'Sure,' Garcia agreed. 'But I need a bathroom break first.' He got up and left the office.

Hunter moved on to the images titled 'page 7' and 'page 8' – the second journal entry. The next 'subject'.

The Polaroid photo that corresponded to the entry was the same photo that Dr. Slater had sent them earlier that morning – the boy with longish blond hair and pale blue eyes that had reminded Angela of her brother.

Hunter sipped his coffee and went back to the text. Once again, the entry contained no drawings or sketches, no page breaks, no paragraphs ... just word after word, forming line after line in a solid block of text.

The voices are back. I heard them late last night. To be honest, I wasn't expecting to hear them so soon. It's only been twenty-two days since the last subject, but it seems to me that the voices are getting hungrier ... greedier ... and the sadism and humiliation are definitely back. Once again, the voices came to me with a very specific request – this time Male. Age: No older than eighteen and no younger than fifteen. Minimum height: five-foot six. Hair: natural blond (not dyed – very important), no specific length. Eyes: blue, any shade, but blue and only blue – not green, not brown ... 'BLUE'. Weight: not important. Ethnicity: white. I first believed that finding the target would've been a simple task, after all this is Los Angeles, the city where blondes seem to grow on trees, but as it turns out, and I should've known this from experience, most people aren't really what they appear to be. Apparently, in this city, one in every five blonde women and one in every three blond men isn't a natural blonde. Roaming the streets for an easy target, one that wouldn't really be missed by anyone, was a pointless effort. It appears that there are no homeless white boys with blond hair and blue eyes anywhere in this city. The age bracket also made things a little harder – fifteen to eighteen years old – high school age. It took me a few days to select three possible targets. It took me twelve days (four consecutive days observing each of them) to pick the winner – Cory Snyder – a sixteen-year-old boy from Lakewood, Southeast LA. It took another four days of constant staking out before the perfect opportunity to take him finally presented itself. Date and time: March 25th 2018 – around 01:45. Location: Centralia Street, Lakewood. The subject was making his way back home from a party he had attended. The subject being highly intoxicated and high on weed made the abduction relatively easy. Photo: Late next day, after the subject had sobered up.

Garcia came back to the office and took a seat at his desk. As he did, Hunter paused to have a look at the Polaroid once again, and his heart was filled with intense sadness. The psychological effect of humanizing a victim (putting a name to a face, identifying where the victim came from, and so on) was indeed a powerful one.

Hunter minimized the image on his screen and called up the Missing Persons database. The result came back in under five seconds.

Cory Snyder was born on 10 July 2001 in Los Angeles. Like the diary entry indicated, he was a resident of Lakewood, a very diverse neighborhood in Southeast LA. Cory was an only child and lived with his mother, Ms. Linda Flynn, who had reported him missing on 25 March 2018, after he failed to return home from a party at a friend's house less than a mile away from his home. Cory's parents were divorced, had been so since Cory was five years old. His father, Mr. Martin Snyder, lived in Palo Alto, California. Cory's address, according to the Missing Persons report, was 5941 Elsa Street, CA 90712. Cory Snyder was still listed as missing. The investigation was still marked as open.

Hunter quickly called up a map application on his computer and checked the boy's address. Elsa Street was a short residential street just off of Centralia Street, the street mentioned in the diary as the location for the abduction. It seemed like Cory Snyder was just minutes away from home when he was taken.

Hunter went back to the Missing Persons report and checked the name of the assigned detective – Winston Bradley. He knew

Detective Bradley. The UVC Unit had been called in to take over a couple of his Missing Persons investigations after they'd been escalated to homicide.

Hunter went back to the image and continued reading.

Like I've said, sadism and humiliation are definitely back on the menu, because the instructions from the voices were simple – 'Flagellation. The boy is to be stripped naked and tied up – his arms are to be stretched out above his head, with his wrists shackled together. He is to receive 25 lashes to his back and 25 lashes to his front every single day until death. The lashes are to be applied with a leather bullwhip. I want to see how long . . . how many days a pretty white boy can survive. The boy is to be hydrated and fed once a day, no more. He's not to pass from hunger or dehydration. He must perish from the lashes. The wounds are not to be attended to. Any bleeding is not to be stopped.' The instructions were followed exactly as the voices requested – 50 lashes every day – 25 to his back and 25 to his front. At night the subject was given food and water. My accuracy with the bullwhip wasn't great to start with. It did get better the more I used it, but despite aiming solely for the front and back of the torso, several of the lashes were wrongly delivered to the back and front of the legs, the groin region, the neck and the face. It didn't take long for it to become a very bloody and messy affair. The tip of a bullwhip can slice through human skin and muscle tissue with tremendous ease. Despite my initial inaccuracy, every single lash I administered violently ruptured the subject's flesh, creating the sort of deep lacerations that would bring terror into the

*heart of any medic. With every lash, blood gashed out of
the fresh wound like a camel's spit, misting the air with
a dark crimson cloud. Also, due to my inaccuracy, after
the first few lashes, many of the subsequent whip blows
hit directly over an existing wound, either cutting across
it or deepening the lesion almost to the bone. At times,
entire chunks of flesh flew up before dropping to the
ground. Understandably, throughout his ordeal, the subject passed out innumerable times, during which I would
stop and wait for him to naturally regain consciousness
before continuing from where I had left off. In answer
to the voices' question – and to my surprise – the subject
lasted a total of 241 lashes. The subject perished on the
fifth day.*

Twenty-Six

'Jesus!' Garcia gasped from his desk, as if he and Hunter were reading in synchronicity. 'Have you read the second entry yet? The second victim?'

'I'm just getting to the end of it now,' Hunter replied, lifting his hand at his partner to signal that he was almost there. That was when he realized that the hairs on his arms were standing on end and his heart was beating faster than minutes earlier.

I saw no point in placing the subject inside a casket. Decomposition works much faster when the body is in direct contact with soil. Let the earth take what was left of him. 34°11'48.1"N 118°17'38.3"W.

Hunter minimized the page image and quickly brought back his map application. After entering the longitude and latitude coordinates into the search box, the map on his screen navigated to Burbank, an incorporated city twelve miles northwest of downtown Los Angeles; more specifically, it zoomed in on another isolated cluster of trees by Skyline Mountain Way, not that far from Deer Canyon.

As Hunter studied the map, the rush of adrenaline that inundated his veins made his hands shake.

Garcia pushed his chair away from his desk and got to his feet. 'He whipped the boy until he died?' His tone was half disbelief, half anger. 'What the actual fuck?' He began pacing in front of his desk. 'And all because a voice in his head told him to?' He shook his head in total disgust. 'This is sick . . . and completely fucking nuts.'

Hunter also pushed his chair away from his desk, but stayed seated, the expression on his face thoughtful and solemn at the same time.

Garcia checked his watch – 5:51 p.m.

'So what do you want to do?' he asked, quickly studying the map application that he too had opened on his computer screen. 'Do you want to take a trip to Burbank and engage in another digging expedition?'

In December, the average sunset time in LA was around 4:45 p.m.

'If we start now,' Hunter said, with a shake of the head, 'we won't be done before ten, maybe even midnight.'

Garcia breathed out in relief. He wasn't too keen on spending another evening shoveling soil.

'This is also now an official investigation,' Hunter added.

Garcia smiled. 'Which means that we can put in a request for a professional digging operation to start first thing in the morning. We don't need to do any of it ourselves.'

Hunter agreed with a simple head gesture. 'I will put in a request for a new digging crew for tomorrow morning, first thing.'

After a couple of phone calls, Hunter pulled himself back to his desk and once again maximized the page images.

Garcia noticed the way that Hunter was pinching his bottom lip, something that he did when deep in thought.

'Something wrong?' Garcia asked.

'This is just ... odd,' Hunter replied, his stare glued to his computer screen.

'Odd is a massive understatement, Robert,' Garcia disagreed. 'This guy is well and truly fucked up.'

'I'm not talking about the perpetrator,' Hunter said. 'I'm talking about the voices he hears.'

'What?' Garcia queried. 'Why? What about them?'

'Contrary to what a lot of people might believe,' Hunter began, 'schizophrenics aren't usually violent. Only a very small number of people struggling with such illness may become violent, and eight out of ten times, that violence is directed toward themselves, not others. The cases where someone who suffers from schizophrenia will turn violent against someone else, driven by voices inside their heads, are very few and far between.'

'Yes,' Garcia interrupted Hunter. 'But they do exist and this is clearly one of those cases.'

'Oh, I'm not arguing that,' Hunter agreed. 'What I'm getting at is that the voices that people with schizophrenia hear don't normally come from a total disconnect to their lives. They usually have firm roots in real-life events experienced by that person, especially when the voices are commanding the subject to be violent toward others.'

Garcia's eyes squinted just a little, as he scratched his chin. 'Could you simplify that some? I'm not quite sure what you're trying to say.'

'The orders from the voices,' Hunter tried to clarify. 'The tremendous specificity of it – age, height, hair color, eye color, ethnicity ... everything, not to mention the orders regarding the punishment – specific number of lashes to the front and the back of the victim and so on.' Hunter paused and looked at his partner. 'Now let me put this to you – pretend that we know nothing about this killer ... that we don't have his diary ... If we turned up at a crime scene and this was what we found – a white boy of seventeen years of age, blond hair, blue eyes. Stripped naked – tied up with his arms above his head, who had been whipped to death ... What would be the first thing to come to your mind?'

Garcia stopped his pacing and locked eyes with Hunter.

'Straight off the bat,' Hunter insisted. 'What would be your first intuition about the scene?'

Garcia squared his shoulders. 'That the perpetrator had a huge beef with the victim and wanted to punish him. That would justify the torture ... the flagellation.'

'Right,' Hunter accepted it. 'So now let's move this up a step. Let's say that we just found the perpetrator's diary and we now know that there's no personal connection whatsoever between the killer and the victim. So the initial huge-beef theory is out.'

'All right.'

'But we still have the same victim and the same torturous crime scene – the flagellation of a young man.' Hunter sat back on his chair. 'So, now that we know there was no personal connection between the victim and the killer, what new conclusions would spring to mind?'

Garcia leaned against the edge of his desk, considering Hunter's question. 'That the perpetrator's beef wasn't specific to an individual,' he finally replied. 'But generic ... to a certain group or type of individuals.'

Hunter pointed his right index finger at Garcia, indicating

that he had hit the nail on the head. 'Exactly. That group or type of individual being . . . young, white, blond-haired and blue-eyed, right?'

Garcia nodded.

'Which sounds like . . .?'

'A very racist grudge,' Garcia said, starting to jump on board with Hunter.

'Right again,' Hunter confirmed. 'And this will take us back to what I was saying earlier – that the voices that people who suffer from schizophrenia hear don't normally come from a total disconnect to their lives. They usually have firm roots in real-life events experienced by that person, especially when the voices are commanding the subject to be violent toward others.'

'So what you're suggesting here is,' Garcia concluded, 'that sometime in this killer's life, presumably when he was young, he was either abused, or hurt, or humiliated, or whatever, by a young, white, blond-haired, blue-eyed boy of around seventeen years of age, and that that trauma manifested itself in the form of schizophrenic voices inside his head. Voices that are now commanding him not only to find someone who resembles the kid who traumatized him, but to also torture, mutilate and kill the boy.'

'That is one of the possibilities,' Hunter agreed. 'A strong one.'

Garcia's face was a picture of confusion. 'A strong one? What's another?'

Hunter knew that that question was coming. 'You're correct about some sort of very traumatic experience involving our killer and a young, white, blond-haired, blue-eyed boy of around seventeen years of age, but the actions you've mentioned – abused, hurt, humiliated, or whatever – might've not happened directly against our killer.'

Garcia brought two closed fists to his head before quickly moving his hands away, while at the same time spreading his fingers and making an 'explosion' sound.

'My head just blew up, Robert. What the hell are you talking about?'

'Traumas can occur in a variety of ways, Carlos,' Hunter clarified. 'Yes, they mainly come from acts experienced by the traumatized party, but they may also come from something they saw, or read, or heard.'

Garcia became pensive.

'Maybe the abuse, the hurt, the humiliation,' Hunter continued, 'wasn't experienced directly by our killer, but it was something he either saw, or heard, or read about. Maybe the person who was hurt was a family member ... a brother, or a sister, or his mother, his father, or a close friend, or whatever. Maybe it was no one he really knew, but a story that he read or heard and the awful details stayed in his subconscious.' Hunter's palms turned to face the ceiling. 'At this point there's no telling exactly how our killer was traumatized by the figure of a young, white, blond-haired, blue-eyed boy, but from what we know now ...' He pointed at his computer screen. 'The most logical psychological diagnosis, like we've concluded, would be that our killer *has* suffered a terrible trauma where somehow a boy that matches that description is to blame.'

Garcia folded his arms in front of his chest, as his forehead creased with thought.

'Hold on a second there,' he said.

From Garcia's facial expression alone, Hunter already knew what was coming next.

'If this is true for the second victim mentioned in the diary,' Garcia asked. 'Then wouldn't it also be true for the first one?

Because correct me if I'm wrong, but according to his diary, the reason why he buried Elizabeth Gibbs alive was because voices told him to do so.'

Hunter nodded. 'And now we're back to the point where I said that this whole thing sounded off. The voices he hears ... something doesn't seem to add up here.'

As Hunter's attention returned to his screen and the diary entries, Garcia's cellphone rang on his desk. It was Anna, his wife.

'Hey, baby,' Garcia said, bringing the phone to his ear. 'How's it going?'

'*Where are you?*' Anna asked, her tone not quite annoyed, but close. '*Are you coming to pick me up or what?*'

It took about half a second for the wrecking ball to hit Garcia.

'Oh damn!' His eyebrows arched, as his eyes moved to Hunter, who frowned at him. 'The Christmas Ball.'

Those three words were meant for Hunter just as much as they were for Anna.

'*Don't tell me that you've forgotten?*' This time, her annoyance was crystal clear.

Hunter immediately sat back on his chair and threw his head back. Both of his hands shot to his head before he checked his watch – 18:09. 'Fuck,' he whispered under his breath.

At that exact moment, the door to their office was pushed open to reveal a very stylishly dressed Captain Blake.

'What the hell are you two still doing here?' Her uncompromising stare bounced between both of her detectives. 'You guys should be at the Globe by now.'

'I'm on my way, baby. Sit tight.' Garcia ended the call and reached for his jacket. 'I'm leaving, I'm leaving,' he said, as he squeezed past Captain Blake and shot across the detective's office like a bullet.

The captain leaned against the doorframe.

'Please tell me that you're going to wear a goddamn suit, Robert. We'll be sitting at the same table as the Mayor of Los Angeles and the Governor of California.'

Hunter got to his feet, grabbing his jacket. 'Yes, of course. I'll be wearing my very best suit.' He too quickly squeezed past his captain. 'I'll see you at the Globe.'

Hunter only had one suit.

Twenty-Seven

Angela took one last drag of her cigarette before flipping the dying butt into a puddle. She wasn't really a smoker. In fact, she hated the awful taste that lingered in her mouth after she'd finished a cigarette, but a few years back she had discovered that nicotine had an almost magical way of calming her down and taking the edge off. To Angela, cigarettes were like a bad-tasting medicine – something that she went back to when her nerves got the best of her. That had been her eighth cigarette since she'd left the Police Administration Building that afternoon.

'This guy is careful,' Hunter had said, his words still ringing in her ears. 'He's methodical, he's thorough. It would be a big mistake if we were to underestimate such a person.'

Angela unwrapped a stick of gum and placed it in her mouth.

This was not what she had in mind. All she wanted to do was teach that jerk a lesson for being rude to an old man. How could that have ended up with a serial killer trying to track her down? How totally crazy was that?

Angela returned the pack of gum to her pocket and entered the liquor store, located just across the road from her apartment building.

After leaving the PAB late that afternoon, Angela had gone back to her apartment, but once there, she didn't know what to do with herself. First, she paced her living room for over an hour, one million thoughts falling over themselves inside her head. When her four walls became too much to bear and the urge for a cigarette too strong to resist, she grabbed a coat, some cash, came up with a quick fix for her front door and aimlessly took to the streets. She smoked two cigarettes and walked for about twenty minutes until she reached a green area, several blocks west from where she lived. At that time on an early Tuesday evening, there weren't that many people around. Angela found a bench by a small pond, lit up another cigarette and allowed her thoughts to wander.

There's no way this guy can find me, Angela thought. The calming effect from the nicotine was taking control of her nerves. *How could he find me in a city as large as LA when all he's got is a photograph. And he might not even have a photograph. I don't remember looking up at all while at the Rendition Room. Maybe the cameras never caught my face, and even if they did and this guy does have an image of me, what's he going to do with it? Go around the streets asking people?*

Angela laughed. The life of a pickpocket was a lonely one – no real friends, no romantic relationships, nothing, so asking around, even with a photo of her, would yield no results. She was very sure of that. The only person who she had properly gotten close to had been about four years ago, when she had just arrived in LA, and he was long gone.

As Angela finished another cigarette, a new thought came into her head, a thought that made her shiver. Maybe there was a way in which the man could find her. Dizzy K.

Every professional pickpocket, in any major city around the world, has a 'fence' – the middleman who takes the stolen goods off of the thieves' hands before passing them on, usually to people inside organized crime. Angela always kept the money from the wallets she boosted, but she had no real use for all the credit cards and cellphones she stole. Instead of throwing them away, she sold them to a heavily tattooed, mixed-race man in his early thirties who went by the pseudonym of Dizzy K.

Dizzy K ran his business out of Vermont Knolls, a rough and dangerous neighborhood in South LA.

He's methodical, he's thorough, and he seems to be very ingenious. Hunter's words echoed inside her head again.

If this guy really were as clever and as ingenious as that detective painted him to be, then he would know about fences. If he knew about fences, it wouldn't take him long to do the math. What if he started asking around with a photo of Angela? What if he managed to track down Dizzy K?

Angie, stop overthinking things. This is Los Angeles, how many fences do you think exist in this city? ... Probably thousands. Do you really think that this guy, clever or not, ingenious or not, will manage to go around asking every fence in LA? And then there's the small issue of some dude walking around the Los Angeles underworld, asking questions, trying to identify someone in a photo. How well do you think that that is going to go down?

Angela had a couple more cigarettes before deciding that she needed a drink. Actually, she needed a whole bottle. The only thing she had at home was a half full bottle of white wine and that just wouldn't do. Tonight she needed something a lot stronger.

At the liquor store, Angela decided to go with a bottle of Bulleit bourbon. She also got a large bottle of cola, just in case. She had one last cigarette before making her way back to her apartment. At the entrance lobby, she checked her postbox – nothing except a menu for a new pizza joint about a block away called 'Pizza 2 Your Door'.

'Actually,' she thought as she took the stairs up to the third floor. 'I could do with a pizza.'

She scanned the menu. They had all the traditional ones, plus a few crazy options.

'Banana, cheese, sugar and cinnamon?' Angela read out loud. 'Cheese, ham, pineapple and peaches? What sort of evil pizza joint is this?'

All of a sudden, as she took the last flight of stairs to the third floor, she felt an odd tingle start somewhere deep in her stomach. Something just didn't feel right. She paused at the last step and looked down the corridor ... at her door stood a tall and well-built figure, wearing a long black coat with its hood pulled over his head, seemingly studying the damage to her doorframe and lock.

The first thought that popped into Angela's head was that the man was from the LAPD and he was there to fix her door.

That thought lasted less than a breath, immediately substituted by a much darker one.

Angela froze.

She didn't know if she made any noise or not, but for whatever reason, the man at her door looked up at the right moment and he and Angela locked eyes for a fraction of a second.

The man straightened his body.

Angela let go of the pizza menu and the bottle of bourbon,

which shattered as it hit the floor, and in a flash, turned around and ran.

A split second later, she heard his heavy footsteps coming after her.

Twenty-Eight

Just like Garcia had done that same morning, Angela didn't actually run down the stairs; she leaped down them like a terrified frog – her mouth bone dry, her palms clammy. As she reached the landing halfway between floors two and one, she heard the man's boots land heavily on a landing not that far above her. He was following her example – leaping over the stairs instead of running down them.

Angela's head-start was three, four seconds at best, but the man was much taller than her, which meant that he had longer legs and, therefore, longer strides. If she didn't think of something fast, the man would be upon her in a matter of seconds.

Angela jumped the next three flights of stairs like a champion hurdler, every fiber in her body pumped with adrenaline. She hit the ground-floor landing and in a blink of an eye she was at the lobby door. She had no idea of how she thought of it so quickly, but the lock at the building's entry door was one of those that had an internal lock switch. When engaged, the key cylinder would lock in place and the key simply wouldn't turn. A person coming into the building would be stuck outside, but all someone who was trying to get out had to do was disengage the switch on the inside of the door.

As Angela pulled the door open, she quickly flipped the switch to 'lock'. She knew that she wasn't locking the man in. Her trick was meant to buy her a few very valuable seconds. And it worked.

Angela slammed the lobby door closed and took off toward Colfax Avenue, her heart now smashing against the inside walls of her chest like a wrecking ball. Two seconds later, she heard someone trying and failing to pull the door open behind her. As much as she wanted to, she didn't look back. That would've cost her time. Time she didn't have. As she sprinted away, she heard the man desperately tugging at the door, trying to pull it open by sheer brute force.

That little trick cost the man ten seconds, more than enough time for Angela to get to Colfax Avenue and cross over to the other side, but now what? Keep on running down the road? Rush back into the liquor store and ask someone for help? Try to hide somewhere? What?

Think, Angie, think.

But luck didn't seem to have abandoned Angela quite yet. On Colfax Avenue, just a few yards ahead of her, a cab had just pulled up to drop someone. The passenger paid the driver, opened the door and stepped out onto the sidewalk. Angela got to the cab just as the passenger was about to close the back door.

'I'll take it. Thank you.' The words came out of her mouth in a rush as she threw herself into the backseat of the yellow and blue Crown Vic and slammed the door shut, a move that not only startled the driver at the wheel, but severely displeased him.

'What are you doing, crazy woman?' he said, swinging around to look at her, his eyes wide open.

'Please, sir,' Angela pleaded in a shaky voice, also swinging around on the backseat to search for the man. He had just crossed to their side of Colfax Avenue. 'My ex-husband wants to beat me up again. Please, sir, just go ... please. Last time he broke both of my arms.'

The quiver in Angela's tone was a clear indication that she was holding back tears.

'What?' the driver asked, confused. His eyes left Angela and moved to his rearview mirror. He saw a tall and burly figure in a long black coat fast approaching his cab.

'Please, just drive.' Angela begged, turning to face the driver. Her heart was beating in her throat.

The driver locked eyes with her for just a flash. In them, he saw nothing but panic.

The man was less than three feet from the cab.

The driver faced forward and put the car in gear.

The man reached for the backseat door.

The driver stepped on the gas. The Crown Vic's tires screeched loudly against the asphalt and the car shot forward with a jerk.

The man's fingertips grazed the cab's backdoor handle, but he wasn't able to grab hold of it in time. In anger, he sent a heavy kick toward the cab. The steel toe tip of his boot almost connected with the right rear light, missing it by a hair's breadth.

Angela swerved on the backseat to look behind her once again. The man was standing on the sidewalk, watching the cab distance itself from him.

Twenty-Nine

'What the hell is wrong with him?' the cab driver asked, using the rearview mirror to fix Angela with a stare that was part fright, part anger and part surprise.

Angela breathed out in relief. Only then did she realize how much her whole body was shivering.

'He's a very violent man,' she replied, slumping back on the rear seat.

'And very big,' the driver added. 'You should go to the police.'

Angela wasn't listening anymore. Her thoughts were in turmoil. *How is this even possible? How the fuck did he find me so fast? He knew where I lived.*

'Hey, lady?' the driver called again, this time waving at her through the mirror.

Angela looked up to meet his eyes. She was so lost in reflection that she didn't even notice that he had asked her the same question three times.

'Sorry?' she said with a slight shake of the head. 'What did you say?'

'Where to?' the driver asked for the fourth time. 'Where would you like me to drive you to? Do you want to go to the police?'

Angela turned to look behind them one last time. They were too far away now for her to be able to spot the man. 'I'm not sure.' Her voice was still unsteady.

The driver took Ventura Freeway underpass, staying on Colfax Avenue. 'Well, you have to give me a destination, lady, unless you just want me to drive around.' He shrugged and indicated the meter. 'It's your money, but if you want to go to the cops, North Hollywood Police Station isn't that far from here.'

Angela's thoughts slowly began to unfog.

'My cellphone number is on the back,' the detective had said, as he handed her his card. 'In case you need to get in touch with me.'

'Hold on a second,' she told the driver, reaching into her front-right jeans pocket. All she found was the money she had brought with her, about fifty bucks. Front-left pocket – her packet of gum. Back pockets: left one – nothing. Right one – her cellphone. Hoodie pockets – her cigarettes and a lighter. No card. 'Fuck,' she cursed under her breath once she remembered that she had left Hunter's card on the kitchen counter back in her apartment. 'Fuck, fuck, fuck.'

The driver was still waiting.

Angela could ask him to drop her at the Police Administration Building in downtown LA, but she was sure that neither of the two detectives she had spoken to that afternoon would still be there. She would have to speak to an officer at the reception desk. After explaining that she had lost the detective's card, the officer would ask her to take a seat. Since he wouldn't be able to disclose Detective Hunter's personal cellphone, he would have to try to get in contact with him at that time in the evening. Angela could be sitting at the PAB for hours.

'Shit!' She tried to think.

Maybe she could call Matteo, an Italian guy with whom she had gone out on two dates with, several months ago. He lived in Toluca Terrace, not that far from where they were. She still had his phone number in her cellphone.

Are you nuts? she thought to herself. *Have you forgotten what kind of man he is? In that case, let me remind you – he's a dick and a bully. Are you really prepared to owe him a favor?*

And he's a bad fuck to boot. You go to his place and you know that you're going to have to sleep with him, right? Are you prepared to endure that pencil dick?

Angela shook her head, banishing the thought.

'So what's it gonna be, lady?' the cab driver insisted. 'Do you want me to drop you off at North Hollywood Police Station?'

'Umm . . .' Angela looked out the window to see if she recognized where they were. The driver had just turned right on West Magnolia Boulevard. 'No,' she replied. 'I've been there before and there isn't much that they can do.' She checked the meter – $21.25. 'Actually, I have a friend who lives just around the corner,' she lied. 'So you can drop me right here, if that's OK.'

'You're the boss.' The driver pulled up by a Target. 'Are you sure you gonna be OK, lady?'

Angela paid the driver. 'Yes, I'll be fine, thank you.'

As the cab drove off, Angela zipped up her hoodie against the cold wind and looked around.

'So what now?' she asked herself.

As Angela tried to think, her cellphone rang in her back pocket. She reached for it and checked the display screen: 'unknown number'.

She took the call.

'Hello?'

'*Angela?*' a rasping male voice asked. Angela didn't recognize it.

'Yes.'

'*You've got something that belongs to me.*'

Angela's breath caught in her throat and she felt her heart go from resting rate to supersonic in less than a second.

'*And I want it back.*' The man's voice sounded calm and controlled, not angry.

How can this be happening? Angela thought. *How does he know my name? How come he has my cellphone number?*

'*Have you heard what I've said?*'

No reply.

'*I know you're there, Angela. I can hear your breathing.*' He paused for a heartbeat. '*If you want to continue doing that – breathing, I mean – I suggest you answer me. Where's my diary?*'

Angela could feel her legs starting to weaken under her.

'*Is it in your apartment?*'

Angela wanted to reply, but she was so scared, her vocal cords failed to produce even a measly 'no'.

'*Let me make this easier for you, Angela. I'm standing in your living room right now, staring at your three-seater sofa with the ugly leopard-print throw.*'

Angela's heart played hopscotch for a second. She couldn't believe that the man had gone back to her apartment and broken in.

'*Tell me where my diary is and I won't make a mess, I'll just take it and you won't ever hear from me again.*'

Angela had no idea of what to do. She thought about calling the police and reporting a break-in in progress, but she didn't expect the man to just sit there and wait. It would take the cops at least eight to ten minutes to respond to her call and the man had probably anticipated such a move from her anyway. She drew strength from every corner of her body to finally be able to speak.

'It's not in my apartment.' Her voice was so weak, it was barely audible.

The man went completely silent for a moment.

'*So where is it then? Do you have it with you?*'

'No . . .'

The man waited.

'I don't have it. I don't have it anymore.' Angela leaned against a wall for support.

A long pause this time, as if the man was waiting for Angela to develop on what she'd just said.

'I . . .' Her voice faltered. 'I sent it to the police.'

'*I wouldn't really recommend lying to me.*' Even after Angela's revelation, the man's voice lost none of its composure. Mentioning the police didn't seem to faze him at all.

'I'm not.' Angela's voice, on the other hand, was strangled by tears. 'I . . . got scared and sent it to the cops.'

'*Can you get it back?*'

The question surprised Angela. The man didn't really sound concerned that the LAPD had his diary. 'Get it back?' She shook her head at the Los Angeles night. 'No, I don't think so.'

'*You don't think so, or you know so?*'

Angela allowed her back to slowly slide down against the wall until she was sitting on the ground, her legs bent at the knees.

'I know so. I can't get it back. I can't.'

Several silent seconds went by.

'*In that case,*' the man said at last. '*May I suggest that you enjoy the little time you have left on this earth, Angela. And trust me – you really don't have that long left.*'

The line went dead.

Thirty

Wednesday, December 9th

It was almost 1:00 a.m. when Hunter managed to finally get away from the Ball. If it had been up to him, he would've left a lot earlier; he was dying to get back to the killer's diary and the rest of the entries, but Captain Blake was adamant that he was not to leave the ball before Governor Gordon had given his speech, which was scheduled for midnight. Speech done, Hunter still had to sit for another twenty minutes or so before the captain at last gave him the all-clear.

Next year, he thought, as he got back into his car and turned on the engine, *I'm definitely joining the Santa group.*

The Santa group was a band of ten police officers and detectives that dressed up as Santa and walked around the ball handing out silly gifts and cards, some of them as pranks. Garcia had joined the group this year and his 'Zombie Santa' outfit had been the talk of the ball. If not for Garcia, Hunter truly believed that he could've died of boredom.

At that time of night, the drive from the Globe Theatre in Downtown LA to Huntington Park took Hunter twenty-eight minutes. Once home, he changed into something more comfortable, poured himself a double dose of Kilchoman Sanaig single-malt scotch whisky and took a seat at the small dining table in his living room that doubled as a desk. He switched on his laptop and called up his email application. Hunter couldn't wait to get back to the diary entries, but as his attention settled on his computer screen, he felt his eyelids become heavy and his concentration wander.

Hunter had been an insomniac for most of his life and, as he left the ball, he had fully expected to experience another sleep-less night. All the telltale signs were in place – the unresolved thoughts, the frustration, the avalanche of questions he had no answers to – everything he needed to keep his brain working at top speed without a sliver of a chance for some rest. Knowing that, Hunter was more than prepared for it, but one thing that he had also learned very early on was that though it didn't happen often, occasionally, without any warning, insomnia would take a break and simply leave him be.

Hunter had barely touched his whisky, so he knew straight away that the heavy eyelids and his wandering concentration wasn't the alcohol talking. He sat back, closed his eyes and allowed his body to relax. Within seconds, he had identified it for what it really was – pure and simple exhaustion. His body was begging him to go to sleep.

Hunter's life of insomnia had taught him many things, and the most important of them all was to never turn his back on such a request. In the rare occasions when insomnia allowed him to go to sleep easily, Hunter would grab at it with everything he had. He powered down his laptop, drained his whisky tumbler and went to bed.

Thirty-One

Wednesday, December 9th

The longitude and latitude coordinates linked to the second burial site took Hunter to an isolated dirt road that led up to Deer Canyon in the Verdugo Mountain Range.

The excavation operation was set to begin at 07:30 sharp, but due to how difficult the actual location was to access from Skyline Mountain Way, everything was running late . . . very late.

Garcia was talking to a forensics agent when he saw Hunter park next to one of the two FSD vans by the side of the road.

'It's going to take them at least an hour just to get all the equipment from the vans to the actual site,' Garcia told Hunter, as he stepped out of his old Buick LeSabre.

Hunter nodded. 'What time did you get here?'

'A few minutes ago,' Garcia replied. 'I was just asking the forensics agent if they had already started when you arrived.'

'What time did you leave last night?'

Garcia chuckled. 'This morning, you mean.' He gave Hunter a shake of the head. 'Not that long after you. Around one-thirty, I think.' That was when he noticed something unusual. 'You look ... rested,' he said, his tone a little uncertain.

'I am,' Hunter agreed and simply left it at that. He looked around and saw the agent that Garcia had been talking to disappear behind some thick bushes to the right of the dirt road. He checked his smartphone. According to the map application, the burial site was around fifteen to seventeen yards off-road and into the chaparral. Hunter nodded at one of the FSD vans. 'Let's give them a hand with the equipment.'

As he and Garcia reached inside the van, Hunter's cell-phone rang in his pocket. The call was coming from the Police Administration Building. Hunter took the call and listened for about ten seconds.

'What?' he said. 'She's there?'

Garcia looked at his partner, intrigued. 'What's going on, Robert?'

Hunter gestured for Garcia to give him a minute. 'Yes, sure,' he said into the mouthpiece. 'Tell her that I'm calling her back right now.' He disconnected from the call.

Garcia asked the same question again, this time with a simple look instead of words.

'Angela is at the PAB,' Hunter said, searching his phone contacts for her number.

'Right now?'

Hunter nodded.

'Why? What happened?'

'We're just about to find out.'

Hunter found the number and made the call. Angela answered it almost before her phone started ringing.

'Angela, it's Detective Robert Hunter. I just got a call saying that you are at the PA ...' He listened for just a beat. 'Whoa,

whoa ... hold on. Take a breath and start at the beginning again. What happened?

...

'When was that?'

...

'Why didn't you ...?' Hunter paused, knowing that the 'whys' and 'ifs' didn't matter anymore. 'OK, stay exactly where you are. I'm on my way. Don't go anywhere, you hear me? I'll be with you in about half an hour. Stay put.' He ended the call.

'What the hell was all that about?' Garcia asked.

Hunter quickly explained the little that Angela had told him.

'This freak went to her apartment?' Garcia's eyes grew to the size of two quarters. 'How the hell did he—'

'Carlos,' Hunter cut him short. 'All I know is what she told me over the phone, which wasn't much, but I'm going to go pick her up right now. You stay here with the digging team. That way we can keep each other updated.'

Garcia nodded and watched as Hunter jumped back into his car and drove away.

Thirty-Two

Hunter wasn't far off with his time assessment, because it took him just under twenty-nine minutes to get to the Police Administration Building. In the building's underground garage, he parked at one of the reserved spaces and ran up the stairs to the main entry lobby. As he got there, he spotted Angela straight away, sitting at the large waiting area to the right of the reception counter. She was wearing the same outfit she had worn the day before. Her arms were crossed, defensively. Her eyes were half shut, with her head slumped back against the chair's backrest. She was clearly struggling to stay awake.

'Angela,' Hunter called, as he approached the young woman.

The sound of his voice, though not threatening, startled her, making her jump on her seat. She looked up at him and blinked a couple of times to do away with the stupor of tiredness. That was when Hunter noticed how exhausted she looked – the white of her eyes were strawberry red and the circles under them made it look like Goth makeup gone wrong.

'Are you all right?' Hunter asked.

It took her eyes a second to be able to focus properly on

the detective in front of her. She gave him a not very convincing nod.

'Physically I'm fine,' she explained. 'Just tired. I haven't slept at all, I've been sitting up for most of the night.' She stretched her arms above her head. 'Emotionally, I'm pretty screwed up.'

'Have you been here all night?'

Angela shook her head while she cleaned some crust from her eyes. 'I couldn't go back to my apartment and I couldn't think of anywhere else that would be open all night other than Denny's diner, so I've been sitting inside the one in North Hollywood since about one o'clock this morning.'

'Why didn't you call me?' Hunter asked.

Angela explained about leaving his card back at her apartment.

'Why didn't you come here and do what you did this morning – ask the officer at reception to get hold of me?'

Angela shrugged dismissively. She was way too tired to go into any more details.

Hunter didn't push. 'Would you like some coffee?'

'No, thank you,' Angela replied. 'That's all I could afford to drink at Denny's – coffee and water. I'm all coffeed out.'

'Are you hungry? Do you want me to get you some breakfast?'

'No, I'm OK, thank you. I had enough for an order of pancakes before heading here.'

'OK,' Hunter said, extending a hand to help Angela up. 'Why don't we go up to my office and you can tell me exactly what happened last night?' They took the elevator to the fifth floor.

'Nice,' Angela said sarcastically, as soon as she and Hunter entered the small and crammed office. 'Two of you work in this shoebox?'

Probably due to how tired she was, her attention settled on how crammed the room was, instead of the photos that had been pinned to the pictures board.

Hunter quickly rotated it around, before pulling Garcia's chair from behind his desk so Angela could have a seat.

'This place is so crowded,' she said, adding insult to injury. 'You probably need to step outside just to change your mind.'

'We can go somewhere else if you like. We can use the same room we used yesterday.'

'No.' Angela lifted her hands in acceptance. 'This is fine. I just needed to make a joke about it.' She took a seat.

'So what actually happened last night?' Hunter asked, leaning against the edge of his desk. 'Start from the beginning, please.'

Angela rubbed her eyes once again, before telling Hunter everything that had happened from when she had decided to go out for a cigarette.

Hunter listened without interrupting her.

'How?' she asked at the end of her account. 'How in God's fucked-up world has this psycho managed to find out where I live? And how the hell did he get hold of my cellphone number?'

Those questions also worried Hunter because it proved that whoever this killer was, he was a lot more resourceful than they had given him credit for. All Hunter could offer in reply was a shake of the head.

'I don't know, but you saw him this time?'

'For the briefest of moments,' Angela replied. 'He was at one end of the corridor and I was at the other ... and then I was running. If you're looking for a description, I've got none. All I can tell you is that he's fast. And big.'

'How about the phone call? You've said that "unknown number" showed up on your display screen, right?'

'That's right.'

'Do you mind if I have a look at your phone?'

Angela unlocked her smartphone and passed it over to Hunter.

'Was his the last call you received prior to mine?' he asked.

'Yep.'

Hunter checked the recent-call list. The unknown number call had come in at 9:39 p.m. last night.

'Give me a second.' He reached for the phone on his desk and called Shannon Hatcher, the leader of the UVC Unit research team. He didn't hold out much hope, but he gave her Angela's phone number and asked her to try to find out anything she could about that call.

'You've said that during the call he told you that he was inside your apartment?' Hunter asked, handing Angela her cellphone back.

'Are you surprised?' Angela volleyed back. 'My front door doesn't have a lock, thanks to you.'

'I apologize again for that. I take it that you haven't been back there since.'

Angela replied with a snort and a shrug. 'Sorry, but I'm not that brave.'

'It's not about being brave, Angela. It's about being smart, and that was definitely the smart thing to do.'

Once again, Hunter reached for the phone on his desk. This time he called the forensics unit and requested that a team be sent to Angela's apartment ASAP. If this killer had been inside her flat searching for his diary, then chances were that he had left some sort of forensics evidence behind. That's the magic of forensics. Every person leaves a trail, wherever they go. They're just unaware that they are doing it.

Despite the UVC Unit having unofficial priority over most other LAPD units or divisions, forensics told Hunter that they had no agents available at that time. Every agent on duty was attending a crime scene somewhere in LA. Availability would depend on how long those agents would take to process those scenes.

Hunter knew there was nothing that he could do to speed up that process. When it came to law enforcement in the USA, the lack of personnel due to budget cuts was a very real problem just about everywhere.

'I'm going to go check out your apartment,' Hunter told Angela. 'You're welcome to come along, or if you prefer you can stay here.'

'There's no way that I'm waiting around,' Angela said, getting to her feet. 'I'm definitely coming with you.'

Thirty-Three

'Wow,' Angela said, as Hunter held the passenger door to his car open for her. 'This is one hell of a rust bucket, if I've ever seen one.'

Hunter was used to such comments. His Buick LeSabre was well over twenty years old. Its original silver paintwork had long ago bleached into something that resembled a sort of psychedelic-style, tie-dye pattern. The inside smelled of old, sun-beaten leather, courtesy of the once raven-black leather seats, but Hunter kept it clean – no food wrappers on the floor or seats, no old coffee cups on the dashboard, no half-eaten donuts anywhere.

As they joined Santa Ana Freeway heading northwest, Hunter placed a call to Garcia.

'Carlos, how is it going over there?'

'*Slow,*' Garcia replied. '*But all the equipment is finally in place and they are just about to start digging. How about you? How is Angela?*'

Hunter gave him a quick update. 'I'm on my way to her place right now, but forensics won't be there until much later, if they can actually manage it today.'

'*All right. Keep me posted.*'

Five seconds after Hunter disconnected from his call to Garcia, his phone rang on his dashboard. It was Dr. Carolyn Hove, the Chief Medical Examiner for the Los Angeles County Department of Coroner.

Hunter took the call, but this time he used a Bluetooth earpiece instead of his car speakers. 'Good morning, Doc.'

'*Robert, this is just a quick call to let you know that I've just finished autopsying the female body that we received yesterday. The one linked to the investigation that you are heading. Case file . . .*' The doctor gave Hunter the fifteen-digit file number.

She was referring to Elizabeth Gibbs's body. Hunter knew that, but it was common practice all over the country among anyone who dealt directly with homicide victims, especially the ones with a heavy workload like Dr. Hove, to stick to case numbers rather than names. The less personal they got, the less their emotions came into play.

'*Despite being buried for over two years,*' the doctor continued, '*most of the body's internal organs were still in a good enough condition for me to be able to at least perform a partial post-mortem examination.*'

'OK, and has it given you anything out of the ordinary?'

'*Not really. Nothing that you weren't probably already expecting.*'

Hunter heard the sound of pages being turned.

'*Death occurred due to lack of oxygen – cerebral hypoxia from suffocation. Though I was able to examine the body's internal organs, unfortunately, due to the deterioration of the epidermis and muscle tissue, I couldn't one hundred percent determine if there was any physical torture or not, but it doesn't appear so.*'

Hunter stayed quiet, but he was sure that Dr. Hove was right – Elizabeth Gibbs hadn't been tortured. If she had, the killer would have mentioned it in his diary, just like he'd mentioned his torturing of Cory Snyder.

'How about sexual assault?' Hunter asked. From the corner of his eye, he saw Angela looking at him.

'*Impossible to tell after two years inside a box.*' Dr. Hove replied. '*Even with a well-sealed coffin like your report suggests. Like I've said, due to the deterioration of the epidermis, no flesh bruises can be correctly identified. Internally, the body shows no signs of forced penetration, but they very rarely do, unless the perpetrator makes a specific point of using some sort of abrasive object that would leave internal scars.*'

'OK,' Hunter said, nodding at the road in front of him.

Some more pages turning.

'*There isn't much else I can tell you, Robert,*' Dr. Hove concluded.

'Thanks, Doc.' Hunter veered right onto El Camino Real. 'Unfortunately it looks like I'll be sending you quite a few more bodies linked to the same investigation. Carlos and Dr. Slater's forensics team are digging another one up as we speak. The problem that we might have is that it appears that these bodies will all be unique.'

'*They always are, Robert.*'

'Not in the way that you're thinking, Doc,' Hunter leveled with her. 'Though we're talking about a single perpetrator, the MO seems to completely differ from crime to crime. They might be digging up another body. But unlike the one you've just autopsied, this one wasn't buried alive.'

'*Well,*' Dr. Hove said back, '*whatever you get, I'll be waiting for it.*'

Hunter thanked the doctor and disconnected from the call. Twenty-five minutes later, they arrived at Angela's apartment building on Colfax Avenue. As they reached the landing on the third floor, Hunter turned and addressed Angela.

'Wait here. Let me go in first.' He drew his weapon.

Angela's head jerked back.

'Are you serious right now? Do you really think that this psycho will be sitting inside my apartment, waiting for me?'

'No, I don't, but it's better to be safe than sorry, don't you think?'

Angela watched as Hunter walked down the corridor and paused at her door before carefully pushing it open.

Inside, the lights were off, but the curtains on both living room windows had been drawn back, allowing plenty of light to bathe the medium-sized room.

Weapon ready, and moving as quietly as possible, Hunter stepped into the apartment.

Knowing that the killer had been in there blindly searching for his diary, Hunter was fully expecting to find the place trashed, with upturned furniture, smashed objects and the floor littered with household debris, but in that first room he saw none of it.

To his right there was an old, blue-fabric, two-seater sofa. A severely worn leopard-print throw had been nicely folded and placed at one end of it. Behind the sofa there was a tall bookcase, which held a few colorful jars and boxes, potted plants, several paperbacks and four picture frames. If any of it had been disturbed, Hunter wasn't able to tell.

On the square, glass coffee table in front of the sofa, there were two scented candles and a TV remote control. The television itself sat on a unit that matched the bookcase, across the room from it.

Hunter took two steps to his right and angled his body to check behind the sofa – nothing – no broken objects on the floor either. There was nowhere else in that room where a person could hide, so Hunter stealthily moved on to the kitchen, which was to the right of the TV. In there, once again, he encountered no mess other than a few dirty dishes in the sink and a couple of pans on the stove. The cupboards under the sink were too small for someone who was around six foot to hide inside. Still, operating on pure instinct, Hunter checked them all.

Once he exited the kitchen, he crossed the living room to the other side and entered Angela's bedroom. Contrary to the rest of the apartment, this room did seem a little messy, with an unmade bed and several items of clothing thrown carelessly on the floor and on the bed. A few hung from a full-length mirror that sat by a two-door, wooden wardrobe. Both wardrobe doors had been left open, exposing a small collection of T-shirts, blouses, hoodies, and trousers – mostly black. On the wardrobe's top shelf, Hunter saw a see-through plastic bag containing a few different wigs. He didn't need to disturb any of the wardrobe items to know that there was no one hiding behind them. Four pairs of shoes untidily occupied the floor between the full-length mirror and the wall to the left of it. To the right of the wardrobe, there was a small dressing table with a three-way folding mirror. A multitude of makeup items and bracelets were scattered all over the tabletop.

From where Hunter was standing – several feet away from the bed – he bent down to check under it. There was nothing there but a large red suitcase.

Angela's bedroom was an en-suite, with the bathroom located to the right of the bed. Its door was ajar, but not enough for Hunter to be able to see inside. It took him five noiseless steps to get to it. With his back against the wall to the left of the door, he used his left hand to carefully push it open. The hinges were old but not rusty. The door opened without a squeak.

Hunter took a deep breath and in one quick movement, rotated his body into the small bathroom – his gun searching for a target.

A faint smell of mold and mildew attacked his nose.

Hunter looked left – nothing.

Right – nothing.

That was when, from the corner of his eye, he caught some sort of movement reflected on the rectangular mirror above the washbasin to his left.

His heart froze.

A split second later, he heard a noise come from directly behind him.

Thirty-Four

It all happened faster than a pin drop.

Hunter's eye caught a shadow of movement coming from his left, but he knew that the movement wasn't coming from inside the bathroom. There simply wasn't enough space between Hunter and the sink for someone to hide. The shadowy movement coming from his left, he knew, was a reflection. In a flash, Hunter's heart tripled its rhythm inside his chest. All of his senses heightened, as extra blood was pumped to every corner of his body.

Survival instinct kicked in. His eyes found the target and his finger tightened on the trigger.

'Jesus Christ!' Angela yelled, jumping back, blood draining from her face.

Hunter's eyes widened in total surprise and his finger immediately eased from the trigger. For a moment neither of them were able to speak. All they could do was look at each other with semi-terrified eyes.

'Have you lost your mind?' Hunter finally asked, lowering his weapon. 'Do you have some sort of death wish or something?'

'Me?' Angela challenged back.

'Yes, you. Didn't I tell you to wait outside until I gave you the all-clear to come in?'

'Well,' Angela shrugged Hunter's irritation off. 'You were taking way too long.'

Hunter breathed out, waiting for his nerves to calm down. 'So you knew that there was an armed cop inside your apartment, looking for a killer who could be hiding anywhere in here, and still you decided to sneak up on me like that.'

'I didn't really sneak up on you. I simply came in here to try to find out what the hold-up was all about. It's not a very big apartment, you know?'

Hunter shook his head. 'I almost blew your face off.'

'Yeah,' Angela said, still making light of what had just happened. 'But you didn't, so let's just ...' She paused mid-sentence, allowing her stare to move straight past Hunter and refocus on the shower curtain behind him. Her eyes narrowed and her forehead creased, while she angled her body to the right just a touch.

Hunter saw the look in Angela's eyes and his muscles tightened. Instantly he turned around, his weapon ready once again, his finger back on the trigger, but Angela wasn't looking at an intruder. It took Hunter another fraction of a second to realize that. She was looking at something that she could see through the gap in the curtain.

Hunter angled his body to match her line of vision. That was when he finally saw it too.

Thirty-Five

It took the forensics excavation team up in Burbank almost four hours of solid digging before they finally came across what they were looking for. The body had been buried a little deeper than the one that Hunter and Garcia had unearthed back in Deukmejian Wilderness Park two nights ago.

'Doctor,' Miguel Rodriguez, one of the four agents who'd been working with a shovel, called with a hand gesture. 'I think we've got something here.'

Dr. Slater and Garcia moved closer.

Miguel put down his shovel and grabbed a brush before going down on his knees to carefully dust a patch of earth measuring about two square feet. Several seconds later, he uncovered a piece of heavy-duty plastic, black in color.

'It seems to be wrapped around something,' he announced, as he retrieved a medical scalpel from his equipment bag, before cautiously tearing an opening in the plastic. It exposed the lower end of a tibia, with very little flesh or muscle tissue attached to it.

'This is human, all right,' Miguel said, using the scalpel to tear some more of the plastic away. This time it revealed an ankle bone, which was still attached to the tibia.

Garcia stayed with the excavation expedition until Cory Snyder's entire body had been unearthed and moved into a forensics van, ready to be transported to the Hertzberg-Davis Forensic Science Center. The operation took longer than expected because the body had been buried whole, as opposed to having been dismembered. Doctor Slater wanted to keep it that way for the examination, which meant uncovering the entire body first before extracting it from the ground.

'I'm not sure if we'll be able to reveal that much more in the lab,' Dr. Slater told Garcia, as he was getting into his car. 'We already know the cause of death and just by looking at the bone development out here, I can tell that the victim was still in his teenage years, which matches the information we got from the diary.'

'Whatever help you can give us, Doc, it will be very much appreciated,' Garcia said in return.

On his way back to the Police Administration Building, Garcia called Hunter and was surprised to hear that he was still at Angela Wood's apartment on Colfax Avenue. Instead of asking for more details about what was going on, Garcia took a detour and headed that way.

Thirty-Six

In the afternoon, a crime scene forensics team, consisting of two field agents, was finally dispatched to Angela Wood's apartment. Since this was a latent crime scene – no body – there was no need for a forensics doctor to attend or for the LAPD to implement full scene-containment protocol. Garcia got there not that long after forensics had arrived.

In the living room, one of the agents was dusting for prints. Garcia greeted him with a nod and quickly checked the kitchen before moving over to the bedroom, where he saw Angela sitting on her bed with her back against the headboard. Her head was buried in her arms, which were hugging her knees.

'Are you OK?' Garcia asked, pausing at the door, his tone concerned.

Angela slowly lifted her head to meet the detective's eyes, revealing how pinkish hers were. Garcia couldn't tell if she'd been crying, or if they looked that way from lack of sleep, but he did identify something else in them. Something he'd seen plenty of times before – fear.

'Carlos,' Hunter called from inside the en-suite bathroom. 'In here.'

Without saying a word, Angela buried her head back in her arms.

Garcia adjusted his ponytail and stepped into the bathroom. As he did, he paused. 'What the hell?'

Hunter was standing to his left, by the sink. The toilet was to his right. Directly in front of Garcia was a small shower stall, where the curtains had been drawn back all the way. Standing inside the enclosure, on the acrylic shower plate, was the second forensics agent. He was carefully examining the white tile wall at the back of the shower.

Garcia glanced at Hunter with troubled eyes.

'It's from him,' Hunter confirmed with a nod, answering Garcia's silent question. 'When I got here,' he explained, 'I was expecting to find the place completely trashed. He was looking for his diary ... but nothing seems to have been disturbed. It looks like our guy didn't touch a thing, except for a lipstick from Angela's dressing table.'

Garcia's stare returned to the tiled wall.

The forensics agent who had started dusting the wall for prints stepped out of the way so Garcia could read the full message.

He didn't need to be a graphologist to see that the handwriting was identical to the one in the diary.

The girl is already dead. You can't protect her. You can't save her. She will pay for what she's done, but there's still time to save yourself. Give me back my diary. Cease and desist and I'll forget that this whole thing has happened. Don't, and your fate will be worse than hers.

Garcia read the message twice over before looking back at Hunter.

'Is this psycho threatening us?'

'It looks that way,' Hunter replied.

Garcia shook his head, trying to make sense of it all. Now he understood why Angela looked so perturbed.

'I'm guessing Angela has read this,' he said.

Hunter nodded. 'She didn't wait for me to give her the all-clear before coming in here.'

He never would've allowed her to read it.

'So what's next now?' Garcia asked, his attention back on the message.

'We need to get Angela to a safe house,' Hunter replied. 'I've already called Captain Blake with the request.'

The LAPD kept several secret locations in and around Los Angeles, which were mainly used for victim and witness protection.

'This ...' Garcia said, pointing at the message. 'This takes some guts. Threatening not only Angela, but also the detectives investigating the case?' Another disbelieving shake of the head. 'Who the hell is this guy? Don Corleone?'

'He's someone with tremendous self-control,' Hunter said.

'Self-control?'

The forensics agent dusting the wall also looked back at Hunter, intrigued.

'From what I understand,' Hunter clarified, 'when the per-petrator called Angela, he was in here. He was standing inside her apartment. In the call, he asked her to tell him where she had hidden the diary.'

'And Angela told him that it wasn't here,' Garcia said. 'I know, you told me.'

'That's right. She told him that she had handed it over to the police. Now let me ask you a couple of questions.' Hunter lifted his right index finger to emphasize his point. 'If you were him and you've put yourself through the risk of coming here . . . the risk of exposing yourself just to retrieve your diary and then you were told that it wasn't here . . . that you had put yourself through all that risk for absolutely nothing and that the diary had been handed over to the police. First question, would you really believe that?'

Garcia grimaced. 'No, probably not.'

The forensics agent agreed with Garcia by shaking his head.

'Neither would I,' Hunter confirmed. 'So my most logical move would be to—'

'Search the place.' Garcia beat Hunter to the punch.

Hunter agreed again. 'We've seen places that have been searched by perpetrators before. Have you checked the living room, the kitchen and the bedroom?'

Garcia nodded. 'Nothing trashed.'

'Which suggests that he either searched this apartment with the utmost concern for keeping everything exactly the way he found it, or he did believe Angela and decided not to search the place at all.'

Garcia finally saw Hunter's logic.

'But that's not all,' Hunter carried on. 'So let's say that he believed Angela when she told him that his diary wasn't here and that it had been handed over to the police. If that were you, how would you feel?'

'Very fucking pissed off.' The reply came from the forensics agent, not Garcia.

'So would I,' Hunter agreed.

It was the agent's turn to catch up with Hunter's line of thought.

'Out of pure frustration and anger,' he said as a follow-up, 'he should've trashed the place anyway. I don't really know the details of what's going on, but from the scenario you've just described,' he nodded at Hunter, 'most people would've trashed the place just to let out their anger.'

'Nevertheless,' Hunter added. 'There's no mess ... nothing broken. The killer found out that his diary is now in the hands of the LAPD. That means the end of a secret that he's been keeping for years. It means that just like that.' Hunter snapped his fingers. 'He went from being a ghost – a very prolific and cautious serial killer, who no one even knew existed – to someone now wanted by the police. The kind of self-control one must possess to be able to keep the sort of anger that he must've felt locked inside ... to simply shrug something like this off with nothing more than a threatening message written in lipstick?' Hunter addressed the forensics agent. 'All that he's shown here is incredible discipline, self-control and self-assurance, because just like you've said ...' He nodded at Garcia before once again indicating the message on the wall. 'He's confident enough to give the LAPD an ultimatum. That's something you don't see often.'

Right then, Hunter's cellphone rang inside his jacket pocket. It was Captain Blake. She gave him the address to the safe house he'd requested and explained that different teams of two LAPD special officers would be on rotation and at Angela's side 24/7. When Hunter disconnected from the call, he turned to face the forensics agent.

'The message has already been photographed, right?' he asked.

'It has,' the agent confirmed.

'Could you do me a favor? When you're done here, could you please wipe the whole thing off the wall?'

'Sure. No problem.'

'I'm going to ask Angela to pack a bag,' Hunter informed Garcia. 'Then I'll take her to the safe house.'

'OK,' Garcia nodded. 'I'll head back to the PAB to file all the paperwork on the digging operation. I'll be in the office until late, so if you need anything, let me know.'

As Garcia left the building, he never noticed the tall man, smoking a cigarette, who was standing across the road from Angela's apartment building. The man watched Garcia get into his Honda Civic and drive away. He used his smartphone to photograph the car, making sure that he had gotten the license plate. About forty minutes later, the man watched as Hunter and Angela exited the building and got into Hunter's Buick. Angela had a bag slung over her shoulder.

'Going somewhere, Angela?' the man whispered to himself, while once again discreetly photographing everything. 'And you must be the one who's got my diary. Detective ... Hunter,' he said, checking the name on the card he had taken from Angela's apartment. 'Robert Hunter. Nice to make your acquaintance.'

Thirty-Seven

The address that Captain Blake had given Hunter over the phone took him to the city of Calabasas, just north of Malibu. The city was best known for being the gateway to the Santa Monica Mountains recreation area.

As Hunter drove past Encino Golf Course, Angela reached inside her backpack for her cellphone and her headphones.

'Do you stream music from the Internet, or do you have it saved to your phone?' Hunter asked, as Angela slotted the first ear bud into her ear.

'I stream it,' she replied.

'I'm sorry,' Hunter said, placing a hand on Angela's arm to stop her from slotting the second ear bud into her ear. 'But unfortunately you won't be able to do that.'

Angela's face screwed up into an unhappy ball. 'Why not?'

'Because, like I've said before, we're not sure of what this guy is really capable of, but he's clearly very clued-up and very resourceful. Taking into account that he's now got your phone number, it's not too much of a leap to imagine that he could also, somehow, have access to a GPS tracker, or something similar.'

Angela pondered over Hunter's words. 'GPS tracking can't

be that simple. Not to track a phone that's not registered to you. If it were, every goddamn jealous husband ... wife ... or whatever would be doing it. The world would be in chaos.'

'You're right. It isn't,' Hunter agreed. 'There's a lot of technology involved, but I'm not taking any chances.'

'So you're telling me that I can't use my phone at all? For however long this thing lasts?'

'You can use the phone,' Hunter replied, aware of Angela's frustration. 'But not your SIM card. In fact, I think it would be better if you switched off your phone right now.'

'You're joking, right?'

Hunter's head angled slightly to the right. 'I'm afraid not.'

'Oh, that's just great,' Angela said, pulling her ear buds from her ears and slouching back on her seat. She switched off her phone and showed it to Hunter. 'There you go, it's off, see?'

Hunter acknowledged it with a head gesture, but unfortunately that wasn't enough. 'I'll need you to hand me your SIM card as well.'

'No way,' Angela's lips crooked a smile. 'Now you have to be joking.'

'It's for your own protection, Angela, and if you really just want to use your phone to stream some music, I can get you a tablet by tomorrow.'

'Do they have a Wi-Fi connection wherever it is that we're going?'

'I'm pretty sure they will do.'

Angela shook her head, still clearly annoyed. 'This whole thing feels like a joke already.' She opened the glove compartment and began searching for something that she could use to extract her SIM card. It took her just a few seconds to come by a paperclip. She bent it out of shape and inserted one of its ends into the SIM card release aperture. 'Here,' she said, handing Hunter the tiny piece of plastic. 'Happy now?'

Hunter ignored her comment as he placed the SIM card inside his jacket pocket. 'Do you want me to get you a tablet?'

'Can you get one tonight?'

'I doubt it, but I can try. If not, I'll get you one by tomorrow.'

Angela pulled a face and slouched back into the passenger's seat. Her attention shifted to the world outside her window and it stayed there for the next hour.

'Wait a second,' she finally said, looking at Hunter with doubt in her eyes. 'We've driven down this road before. I recognize that house.' She indicated the sharp-lined, modern-architectured house they'd just driven past.

'Yes, we have,' Hunter admitted.

'Are we lost?'

'No. I'm just following protocol.'

'In case we're being followed?' Surprise peppered Angela's tone. Immediately she turned around in her seat to look at the road behind them.

'Yes,' Hunter accepted. 'In case we were being followed, but you can relax. We're not.'

'How can you be sure?'

'Because I've been checking for any tails since we left your apartment. We've been driving for over an hour now. If we were being tailed, I would've spotted it.'

'You're very sure of yourself. What if you've made a mistake?'

'I haven't. Trust me. This is not my first time doing this.'

The conviction in Hunter's voice persuaded Angela to drop the argument, but every minute or so after that she would either check the passenger's side-view mirror or turn around in her seat to look behind them.

Almost two hours after leaving Angela's apartment in Studio City, Hunter finally parked his car on the driveway of a small, but very elegant Mexican-style, green-fronted house, at the very end of a nondescript, cul-de-sac.

'Here we are,' he said, as he switched off his engine.

With critical eyes, Angela studied the house for a moment.

There was a neat and compact front yard, where a couple of lemon trees took center stage. The bright-red front door contrasted nicely with the avocado-green walls and the terracotta roof, giving the entire structure a very pleasant and somewhat calming feel.

'How long will I have to stay here?' she asked.

'I'm not going to lie to you, Angela,' Hunter replied. 'I'm not sure. Hopefully not long, but at the moment I can't really give you a timeframe.'

'Great,' she said, just about to open the passenger door.

'Just a sec.' Hunter stopped her, nodding at the two men sitting inside a black Cadillac ATS that was parked across the road from the house.

Angela's stare followed Hunter's nod and apprehension clouded her eyes.

'Who are they?' she asked.

'They are LAPD SIS,' Hunter replied. 'They're here for your protection and they are the best at what they do, but before we take you inside, we need to check the house.'

The LAPD Special Investigation Section was an elite, tactical surveillance squad, famous for being masters in disguise and stealth. Every SIS officer was also an expert in close-quarters combat, as well as a distinguished marksman.

'Check the house?' Angela frowned. 'I thought this was supposed to be a safe house.'

'It is,' Hunter reassured her. 'But we have a protocol to follow. It won't take long.'

As Hunter stepped out of his car, so did the two SIS officers. They displayed their credentials and introduced themselves as James Martin and Darnel Jordan.

Martin was about six-foot one, with short black hair and two-day stubble. His heavy-lidded eyes gave him a rather menacing look, while his long face, dimpled chin and hazel eyes were quite charming.

Jordan was a six-foot two African-American, with the physique of a heavyweight champion. His arms looked like legs and his legs like tree trunks. His voice was deep and velvety. If he ever decided to leave law enforcement, he could easily make a living as a documentary narrator or a voice over.

Jordan waited outside by the car, while Hunter and Martin went in to check the house.

The living room was large and bright with old ceiling beams and exposed brickwork. A large red corner sofa sat next to a half-empty bookcase and two matching armchairs. Opposite the sofa was a wall-mounted TV set. The kitchen was a modern mix of chrome and glass, offset by a four-seater wood dining table. In there, large double doors gave access to a pleasant grassy backyard, which was secluded from prying eyes by a cluster of very tall trees. There were two bedrooms in the house, both very decent in size, accessed via a short hallway at the north end of the living room. In the master bedroom there was a double bed, a tall wardrobe and an old chair. The second bedroom was equipped with two single beds, one wardrobe and not much else. The bathroom, also quite spacious and tiled in white and blue, was at the end of the hallway.

While Hunter checked the inside of the house, Martin checked the backyard.

'All clear out here,' Martin said, as he met Hunter back in the kitchen.

Outside, Hunter introduced Angela to Martin and Jordan. She barely looked up at the two SIS agents.

While Martin and Jordan went to get their surveillance equipment from the trunk of the ATS, Hunter took Angela into the house.

'You get the big room,' he said, showing her the master bedroom.

Angela hadn't paid much attention to any of the rooms in the house. She simply threw her backpack on the floor and slumped into bed.

'There isn't much food in the house,' Hunter said, standing by the bedroom door. 'I'm going to pop to the store to get a few things. What would you like?'

'Whatever,' Angela replied. She had linked her fingers behind her head and was just lying there, staring at the white ceiling above her bed.

'We can order a pizza or whatever else you like.'

Angela's reply was a dismissive shrug.

Hunter scratched his nose. 'Angela, I know that this isn't an ideal situation. I know that you don't want to be here. None of us do, but unfortunately it's the predicament that we now find ourselves in. We can't escape it and we can't circumvent it. Trust me, I've been here before. The best thing to do in this case is to just get on with it in the best way we can.' He shrugged. 'Everything in this house is covered by the government. You can request anything you like at the expense of the LAPD – cake, pizza, chicken, salads, shakes . . . whatever – so my suggestion to you is – go nuts.'

'How about some beers and a few bottles of wine?' Angela's gaze finally moved from the ceiling to Hunter.

Hunter's lips drew a thin line. 'I can possibly get you one can of beer, but that will be all.'

'And why is that?'

'Because you won't get drunk on a single can of beer.'

'Well, I've got nothing better to do tonight. I can't even listen to my music, can I?'

'There's a TV in the living room,' Hunter retorted. 'And a radio in the kitchen. You can bring the radio in here if you like. I'll grab you a couple of books and some magazines from the store as well.'

'Why can't I have a drink?' Angela asked. 'I'm not going to get drunk, drunk – like falling-down drunk. I never do that anyway, but a little drink might help me fall asleep.'

'For one, it's protocol,' Hunter replied. 'But the practicality of it is that you need to have your wits about you at all times, in case we need to get you out of the house fast.'

Angela's eyes widened. 'Are you for real? I just got here.'

'I'm not saying that that is what's going to happen, Angela, but it's our job to try to cover every possible scenario, and that scenario does exist.' Hunter paused and checked his watch. 'So, what would you like me to get you other than a can of beer?'

'Whatever. I don't have much of an appetite anyway.'

But you will, Hunter thought. 'OK. I'll pick you up some snacks. If later you feel like ordering a pizza or anything, just ask either James or Darnel and they'll order it for you. For drinks, other than your beer, do you prefer soda, juice, or something else?'

'I don't care.'

Hunter could see that Angela would not make this easy.

All of a sudden Angela's brow creased and her eyes narrowed into two tight slits. She quickly moved from a lying down position to a sitting one.

'You've said that whatever I order will be at the LAPD's expense, right?'

'It sure will.'

'Can I get some cigarettes? Is that allowed?'

Hunter considered the request for a couple of seconds. 'I don't see why not.'

'Awesome.' A flake of excitement found its way into Angela's tone of voice. 'Can I get ten packs, please?'

'Ten?' Hunter clearly wasn't expecting that.

'I smoke a lot,' Angela lied. 'And just a minute ago you told me to go nuts. This is me going nuts.'

Hunter didn't want to carry on arguing. 'Fine, ten packs it is. Any brand in particular?'

'Marlboro Smooth, please.'

In the living room, Hunter told the two SIS agents, who had just finished installing their surveillance equipment, that he was doing a quick grocery run for Angela and asked them if they needed anything. Both agents declined.

Outside, Hunter jumped back into his car and backed out of the driveway. He had driven past a cluster of stores, not that far from where the safe house was located, which included a large Walmart. In there, he grabbed a selection of snacks, a couple of TV dinners, a large bottle of soda, two bottles of juice, two bottles of water, a can of beer and Angela's cigarettes. The trip took him around twenty-five minutes.

As he parked back on the driveway of the safe house, his cellphone rang inside his jacket pocket – 'unknown number'.

'Detective Hunter,' he said, bringing the phone to his ear. 'UVC Unit.'

'*Hello, Detective Hunter.*' The male voice at the other end of the line was dry, husky and monotone.

Hunter didn't recognize it.

'*You've got something that belongs to me.*' There was a short, but very anxious pause. '*I need it back.*'

Thirty-Eight

This killer certainly had balls. Hunter had to give him that.

Immediately, Hunter tapped the icon for the 'phone call recording' application he had installed on his cellphone.

'*Did you hear me, Detective Hunter?*' the caller asked. '*I need my diary back.*'

The caller's voice sounded authentic to Hunter. He detected no analog or digital pitch shifter, no distortion and no effort from the caller to naturally soften or deepen his tone.

'Yes, I heard you,' Hunter finally replied, his tone composed. 'Sure, you can have it back. Just drop by the Police Administration Building any time and I'll hand it back to you, how does that sound?'

'*I'm afraid that won't be possible, Detective.*' Another short pause. '*What is possible and what you "will" do, is follow my instructions on how to get it back to me. You do that and only the girl dies. You don't . . . then I'll be coming for you too.*'

Hunter blinked.

Had the caller really just made a direct threat on his life?

Hunter wasn't just astonished by how confident and fearless the caller sounded, he was intrigued. He had to hear what the man had to say.

'Follow your instructions?' Hunter asked. No sarcasm in his voice.

'*That's correct.*'

'OK,' Hunter said, sitting back on the driver's seat. 'So how would you like me to get your diary back to you? What are the instructions that you would like me to follow?'

'*When you have the diary in your possession,*' the caller replied without missing a beat, '*I'll be in touch again with the instructions.*'

'What makes you think that I don't have the diary with me right now?' Hunter asked.

'*Because I'm not stupid, Detective.*' The caller had no desire or need to explain himself. '*I'll give you until seventeen hundred hours tomorrow to have the diary with you. Keep your phone by your side.*'

Hunter's eyebrow arched, but before he had a chance to say anything back, the line went dead.

Out of habit more than hope, Hunter immediately placed a call to the LAPD's Technical Investigation Division and asked them if they had a location for the last call made to his cellphone. It took them less than thirty seconds to come back with the answer that Hunter was expecting.

'*Sorry, Detective, the caller has used a pre-paid phone with either no GPS chip, or a disabled one.*'

For the next minute or so, Hunter sat completely still at the driver's seat of his Buick, his brain going back over every word the caller had said to him.

'Everything OK?' Jordan asked, as he exited the house and approached Hunter's car, his right hand hidden behind his back.

Hunter knew how good the LAPD SIS really was. They had, no doubt, already installed surveillance cameras at the front and back of the house. They would've seen and heard Hunter's car approaching way before Hunter had had a chance to park on the driveway.

Hunter opened his door and stepped out of the car, his concerned gaze searching up and down their dead-end road, as doubts began clouding his thoughts.

Yes, Hunter had followed counter-tailing protocol from the moment they'd left Angela's apartment. In fact, he had used a combination of counter-tailing techniques, stretching a forty-five-minute ride into a two-hour trip. Throughout the drive, he'd checked his mirrors every minute or so. If someone had been tailing them, especially for such a long ride, he would've spotted it. He always did.

Instinct and experience told Hunter that he had nothing to fear, but the timing of the call, together with the fact that the caller had sounded so calm and collected, planted a seed of doubt in Hunter's mind. *What if he had made a mistake? What if the killer had been watching Angela's apartment building all day long, just waiting for the LAPD to turn up, because he knew that they would turn up?* If that had been the case ... if the killer had witnessed Hunter and Angela as they left for the safe house ... what was there to stop him from tailing them?

Hunter's counter-tailing measures – that was what.

'Detective,' Jordan asked again. 'Is everything OK?' Instinctively, the SIS agent followed Hunter's worried gaze as the LAPD detective checked the entrance to their street. 'Do you think that you might've been followed? Do you think that this safe house might've been compromised?'

Still with his gaze firm at the top of the street, Hunter slowly shook his head.

'No,' he said decisively.

'The threat to the woman in there,' Jordan asked. 'Are we talking about a single individual here, or an organization?'

Hunter knew why the question was asked. A great number of protection details that the LAPD SIS was assigned to tended to involve witnesses relating to organized crime.

'All the evidence we've gathered so far points to a single individual,' Hunter replied.

Jordan had never met Hunter until that night, but he had certainly heard of the success rate and reputation of the Ultra Violent Crimes Unit. Detective Hunter wasn't a man known for making many mistakes.

'It's your call, Detective,' Jordan said after a long instant. 'Your decision, but if you have any doubts that this location is still safe, then you need to call it in and we'll need to take the witness to a brand new safe house. You know we can't risk it.'

Mentally, Hunter tried his best to revisit the entire journey from Angela's apartment to the safe house. Not only did he believe that he had not been followed, but not once throughout the entire trip had he even felt worried. Not once did he clock a suspect vehicle behind them. Not once did he see the same vehicle twice. Of that he was absolutely sure.

'No,' he said with even more conviction than before. 'The safe house hasn't been compromised. We stay.'

Thirty-Nine

Angela was still lying on her bed, vacantly staring at the ceiling, when Hunter paused at her bedroom door.

'Are you hungry yet?' he asked, leaning against the doorframe.

'No, not really, but I could do with a cigarette and a beer.'

Her attention finally hopped from the ceiling down to Hunter. He was holding a ten-pack carton of cigarettes in his right hand and a can of beer in his left.

'I suspected that you'd be going for these first.'

Angela swung her feet off the bed to come to a sitting position by its edge. 'Can I smoke in here?'

'I'm afraid not, but there's a small backyard.' Hunter's head tilted to his left. 'Through the kitchen. It's completely secluded by a wall of tall trees. No one can look in, or out.'

Angela walked over to Hunter, who handed her the cigarettes and the can of beer. 'I can go outside then?'

'Sure, as long as you don't do it unaccompanied.'

'Right.' Angela took out a cigarette pack before throwing the rest of the carton onto the bed. 'Do I need a babysitter to go pee as well?'

'Angela.' Hunter halted her as she tried to go past him. He

had never been one to lecture people, but he needed Angela to remain calm and focused. 'I understand your annoyance and that you're now facing a lack of privacy that you simply aren't used to, but you need to check your attitude.'

The strict tone of Hunter's words took Angela by surprise. She took a step back and glared at him.

'Like I said earlier – I understand this is difficult but you need to remember that we're here to protect you. This icy-cold attitude of yours is understandable,' he continued. 'It's your coping mechanism trying to cover for how scared or angry you are, but do you know what? It's OK to be scared. It's OK to be angry. No one here is going to judge you. We're all here to help you. Please understand that.'

The glare disappeared from Angela's eyes, giving way to some internal turmoil.

'I'm sorry,' she finally said after a long pause. Her voice was a little unsteady, but genuine. 'I do know that you – all of you – are here to protect me from my own stupid mistake.' She matched eyes with Hunter once again. Hers were glassy with tears. 'You're right. The attitude is my own way of hiding how scared I am . . . how angry I am with myself.' Her voice croaked in her throat. 'Since what happened with my brother, to keep myself from falling into an abyss, this is the only way my brain has figured out how to deal with fear and pain and anger.' She looked away again. 'The truth is – I'm scared all the time. I'm in pain all the time. Inside me there's nothing but sadness, pain and loneliness.'

Angela's tears finally broke through her defenses and began streaming down her cheeks.

Hunter didn't say anything to try to comfort her. He understood that sometimes the best comfort, the best release, was to allow the fear and the anger inside to pour out. Instead of words, Hunter offered her a tissue.

What Angela didn't know – what she would never know – was that, for different reasons, Hunter felt exactly the same inside.

'Damn,' Angela said as she dabbed the tissue against her cheeks. 'I could really do with that cigarette right about now.'

Hunter walked with her.

Outside in the backyard, they sat at the edge of the wood decking that led from the kitchen door to a small grassy area. Angela lit up a cigarette and breathed in its smoke as if it would save her life. As she exhaled through her nose, she offered Hunter one. He declined. She cracked open the can of beer and took a healthy sip.

'I should've asked for vodka,' she said, an honest smile parting her lips.

Hunter smiled with her.

'Here,' she said, offering him the can. 'Have some.'

'I'm OK, thank you,' Hunter declined again.

'C'mon,' Angela insisted. 'I know that you're on duty, but a single sip won't get you drunk, plus, it's horrible drinking alone.'

'That's very true,' Hunter agreed, looking up at a starry sky. He said nothing else.

'Really?' Angela asked. 'Not even a sip?'

Hunter remained silent.

'Fine . . . more for me.'

Hunter could see that her coping mechanism was clearly starting to kick back in again. She had another mouthful of beer and took another long drag of her cigarette. Hunter watched the smoke dance into the night breeze for a moment.

'There's something I need to ask you,' he said, the killer's phone call still playing in his head.

'Sure.'

'When you were on the phone to the person who you took the diary from—' Hunter began.

'You mean – the killer who is after me?' Angela interrupted him.

'Yes,' Hunter agreed. 'When you were on the phone to him, you said that when he asked about his diary, you told him that you had handed it to the police.'

'That's right,' Angela confirmed.

'Can you remember if you mentioned anything about dropping that package into Dr. Slater's mailbox? Did you mention the doctor's name at all?'

Angela had another couple more sips of her beer and another drag of her cigarette. 'No, I don't think so.'

Hunter waited an extra second. 'You don't think so, or you know so?'

Her eyes narrowed at him.

'Angela, this is very important.'

As she finished her cigarette, Angela remembered the words on her shower wall – the direct threat the killer had made to Hunter and Garcia. She could feel her core starting to shudder again. 'Do you think that he might go after her?'

Hunter had no reason to lie.

'If you have mentioned her name to him,' he said, 'then I'm sure he will try. The fact that he's now dealing directly with the LAPD doesn't seem to bother him at all. In fact, he seems excited by it. That's why I really need you to think back to exactly what you said to him over the phone. I really need to know if you mentioned her name, or anything about the FSD Criminalistics Lab. Anything at all that could give him a hint that Dr. Slater has seen his diary. Can you recall the conversation in full?'

'I've already told you the whole conversation.'

'I know, but maybe now that you're a little less nervous than before,' Hunter insisted, 'you may be able to recall something that you might've forgotten the first time around.'

Angela lit up another cigarette.

In her head she went over the entire conversation, from the moment she received the killer's call, as she exited the cab, until when he put the phone down on her. She could remember every word.

Hunter waited.

'No,' she finally said, with a firm shake of the head. 'I never said anything about the doctor or the lab. I told him that I had sent the diary to the police. That was when he told me that I would pay for what I'd done.' Her voice was beginning to falter again.

'It's OK, Angela.' Hunter placed a comforting hand on her shoulder. 'You did great.'

An airplane crossed the dark sky above their heads and Angela stared at its blinking lights for a moment.

'Do you mind if I ask you something a little more personal?' Hunter asked, bringing her attention back to him.

'I don't mind you asking,' Angela replied. 'You can ask whatever you like. I'm not the boss of you.'

'But you won't answer it,' Hunter picked up on what Angela was suggesting.

'I didn't say that,' Angela came back. 'I might answer it, or I might not, that will depend on how personal your question is. So please, ask away.'

Hunter smiled at the woman sitting next to him. The fact that Angela seemed to be constantly on the defensive reminded him of himself when he was younger.

'You're clearly a very bright and skillful woman,' Hunter began. 'You're self-assured, you're strong-minded, you don't seem to take shit from anyone—'

'Enough with the flattery,' Angela cut him short. 'What is it that you want to know?'

'How did someone with all those qualities get into something as low-level as pickpocketing?' Hunter finally asked.

Angela studied Hunter, as if she was deciding if she would answer him or not.

'My very first day in LA, actually,' she replied after several silent seconds. 'I was walking the streets completely lost, both physically and mentally. I turned a corner, and as I was walking past a bus stop, I saw this guy lift a woman's wallet from inside her handbag. He was smooth – very – but I saw it, so I couldn't believe that no one else did.' Angela had another long drag of her cigarette. 'I was desperate. I had no money, no place to stay and I was hungry. I also didn't think that I had anything to lose, so I went up to him as he walked away from the bus stop and told him that it had been a nice lift, but if he didn't split the cash from the purse with me, I would tell the cops. There was a cop car parked just across the street.'

'So he split the money with you,' Hunter assumed.

'Nope. First he was shocked. He couldn't believe that he was being hustled by a seventeen-year-old girl from Pocatello, Idaho, but then he smiled and said, "I can do something much better than give you half of the money . . . I can teach you how to do it yourself, so you can keep everything you lift".' Angela shrugged. 'And that was that.' She paused and once again studied Hunter, as if deciding whether or not she should reveal any more. 'We ended up becoming a couple.' Angela looked away as she said those words.

'Obviously, it didn't work out,' Hunter said.

'It did for about a year.' Angela's gaze returned to Hunter. He looked like he was expecting her to go on, but Angela said nothing else.

'So what happened?' Hunter pushed.

'You're a nosey fucker, aren't you?'

Hunter accepted with an apologetic tilt of the head. 'I'm sorry. You're right. It's none of my business.'

Angela laughed, as she put out her cigarette. 'You need to learn how to chill, man. I was just joking. I don't care. I'm a nosey fucker myself.' She sipped her beer. 'Like so many couples,' she explained, 'things started to fizzle out after the honeymoon phase. He wanted to upgrade and I didn't.'

'Upgrade from pickpocketing, you mean?'

'Yep. That's when I said – "not for me". This is just a temporary gig. I'm not going to be a pickpocket all my life.' Angela's tone sounded as if she really wanted to explain herself to Hunter.

'Temporary?' Hunter questioned. 'How long is temporary, because you've been doing this since you got to LA?'

'Don't you start on me with that bullshit.' She pointed a finger at Hunter. 'How easy do you think it is to get a job in this city when you've run away from home, you're depressed, you're hurting, you're in pieces inside, you have no experience of anything except school, you have no home address, and you're broke?'

Hunter shook his head. 'Still—'

'No,' Angela cut him short again. 'There's no "still". I needed to eat, and sleep, and clothe myself, and everything else. I know it isn't right. I know I was brought up better than this, but I am not putting people out of business. I'm not destroying people's lives. I'm not taking away their life savings. Do I look like I'm rich to you?' She didn't give Hunter a chance to reply. 'I just take enough to get by, and that's all. Like I said, I will give this up sooner rather than later, so don't you "still" me.'

Hunter saw no point in pushing for an argument. 'So what happened to the guy?' he asked. 'The one you dated. The one who taught you to pick people's pockets? Did he upgrade?'

Angela chuckled. 'Yeah, we went our separate ways and he did upgrade. A year and a half later, he got busted. He's now at LAC.'

LAC was the acronym used for the California State Prison, Los Angeles County.

Hunter thought about asking if she visited him or not, but quickly gave up on the idea. Instead, it was Angela who surprised him with her next question, especially after her mini-outburst.

'Would you please stay?'

He looked back at her, intrigued.

'I know that those two in there are here to protect me,' Angela explained. 'I know that you've said they are the best at what they do, but I'd feel a lot more at ease if you were around. I don't really know why, but I know that I'll feel safer if you're here.'

Hunter regarded Angela for an instant. Nothing about her expression or body language gave him the impression that she was joking.

'Please,' she asked again, her voice soft. 'Just for tonight.'

Hunter staying the night hadn't been on the cards, but since his phone conversation with the killer – since the seed of doubt that that particular phone call had planted in his mind – he had already decided that, at least for tonight, he would join Martin and Jordan as part of Angela's protection detail.

'Sure,' Hunter nodded. 'I can stay in the living room.'

'Thank you. I really appreciate it.'

Forty

Thursday, December 10th

That night, unlike the previous one, Hunter's insomnia well and truly delivered. Sleep came to him in random waves that didn't last nearly long enough, crashing too quickly against a rough shore of nightmares and doubts. To Hunter, the 'stop-start' was by far the most debilitating type of insomnia there was, because instead of keeping him awake, it would allow him to fall into a temporary deep sleep, tricking not only his brain but his entire body into the illusion that he could relax. Once sleep-numbness was achieved, insomnia would savagely jolt him awake again, only to allow him to fall back asleep several minutes later. That torturous process repeated itself through-out the entire night. Falling asleep was never a problem. Staying asleep was but, broken or not, Hunter still managed to get around three hours of sleep, give or take. Certainly not ideal by most people's standards, but in the greater scheme of things, for a person who faced chronic sleeplessness on an almost daily basis, three hours was definitely not that bad going.

After leaving Angela a note, Hunter left the safe house at 5:15 a.m. Regardless of his insomnia, Hunter had always been an early riser, preferring to get to his office as early as possible, but before making his way to the Police Administration Building, he wanted to drive by his place to grab a shower, a shave, a change of clothes and a decent breakfast, which was Hunter's best trick when it came to getting his brain and body to cope with so few hours of sleep. And he knew exactly what he would cook himself.

For someone who had lived alone for most of his life, Hunter's cooking skills left a lot to be desired, but his protein-filled omelet would give any Michelin-starred chef a run for his money. Garcia had joked a few times that if Hunter ever decided to quit the police force, he could open an omelet-only restaurant. His menu would be simple – one item – 'Robert's amazing protein-filled omelet'.

'You'd get people lining up outside and around the block just to eat this,' Garcia had said, after he'd had Hunter's omelet for the first time. 'I'm serious, Robert. This is some gourmet stuff right here. You could be making a killing out there. At least a lot more than you make as an LAPD detective.'

That had made Hunter smile.

On his way back to his apartment, Hunter remembered that his coffee machine had broken. In Hunter's mind, a healthy breakfast without good coffee was practically a wasted meal.

As he veered off the Santa Monica Freeway and joined South Santa Fe Avenue, Hunter remembered a small organic coffee shop he'd been to a few months back. It was tucked away in a corner of the Arts District, just a stone's throw from where he was, and their coffee was one of the best he'd had in quite some time. He also remembered that, according to the sign on their door, they opened every day at 5:30 a.m., except weekends. His mouth watered. That was all the incentive he needed. Less than a minute later, Hunter parked right outside Urth Caffe on South Hewitt Street.

Inside the shop, two baristas were busy arranging cakes and sandwiches into a large, glass display unit.

Hunter would usually just have a black coffee with his breakfast, but since he had a choice, and a large one at that, he thought that he might as well go for something different. His eyes scanned the menu and as they did, his lips stretched into a smile a couple of times. Some of the choices sounded more like a milkshake than a coffee.

'Unless you like your coffee sickly sweet, I'd stay clear of the Double Cream Vanilla Deluxe.'

The advice came from the person standing directly behind Hunter, and as he heard those words, he froze in place. He not only knew whom that voice belonged to, but those had also been the exact same words that she had said to him the very first time they met, inside a library room at UCLA, almost a year and a half ago.

Still facing the coffee board, Hunter took a silent, deep breath, but it didn't stop his heart from picking up speed inside his chest. A millisecond later, he turned to face the woman standing behind him.

'Hello, Robert,' Tracy Adams said with a subdued smile.

'Tracy?' Hunter said, still a little doubtful that they were actually standing face to face again.

After that initial meeting at UCLA, where the attraction on both sides had been immediate and undeniable, Hunter and Tracy had begun dating, but despite having a lot more feelings for her than he would ever admit, Hunter never allowed romance to properly take off – which, on reflection, had been a good move.

Around six months ago, after a disastrous and terribly tragic turn of events, Hunter and Tracy's relationship had come to a very abrupt end. They hadn't seen or talked to each other since.

Hunter smiled back. There were close to one million things that he wanted to say to Tracy, but right then, all he could come up with was: 'What are you doing here?'

Despite his surprised tone being more than genuine, he felt the need to explain. 'I mean . . . what are you doing in this part of town so early? Have you moved?'

The last time Hunter saw Tracy, she lived in Hollywood, which was about eleven miles west of where they were.

'No,' Tracy replied. 'I still live in West Hollywood. Same old apartment.'

Hunter didn't ask anything else.

'I spent the night at Amber's,' Tracy clarified. 'I'm not sure if you remember her or not.'

Hunter did. Amber was Tracy's best friend.

'She lives just around the corner,' Tracy continued. 'As you know, I'm not usually up at this godforsaken hour, but I have an early class at UCLA that I still have to prepare for. I just stopped by to grab a quick breakfast on my way in.'

Hunter allowed his eyes to do all the smiling. With her black-framed, cat-eye glasses that perfectly suited her heart-shaped face, her green eyes, her heavily tattooed arms and her nose and lip piercings, Tracy Adams had always reminded Hunter of some sort of paradoxical modern 1950s pin-up model, but her bright red hair was a little shorter than Hunter remembered, and its color looked to be a shade lighter, which somehow made her look even more attractive than she did before.

'Are you still in Huntington Park?' Tracy asked.

'I am.'

Tracy chuckled. 'I'm not even going to ask how come *you're* in this part of town this early.'

This time Hunter tried a real smile, but he felt as if the corners of his lips were refusing to comply.

'You look well,' he said. 'I like the new hair. It really suits you.'

Tracy looked surprised by the fact that Hunter had noticed.

'Thank you.' She looked flattered. 'You too. You look ...' She tried, but she had always been a terrible liar and she knew that there was no way she could get one past Hunter. '... You look tired, Robert.'

Hunter gave her a nod. 'It's been a bit crazy of late.'

'Oh c'mon, it can't be that bad.' Tracy checked her watch. 'We've been talking for all of two minutes and your phone hasn't rung yet.'

Hunter smiled again. 'That's true.'

They both went quiet for a very short moment, which was more than enough time to allow awkwardness to come between them.

Not once during their brief relationship had Hunter and Tracy ever found themselves in an awkward silence. On the contrary, from the very first day they met, they felt as comfortable with each other as a couple that had been together all their lives, in silence or otherwise.

'Would you like a suggestion?' Tracy asked, nodding at the coffee board and piercing a much-needed hole through the deafening silence. 'Go for the Caffe Quadra, or the Rude Awakening. Both use extra espresso shots to top up the coffee. They might come in handy.'

Hunter turned and checked the description of the two coffees that Tracy had suggested.

'Both sound nice,' he agreed. 'Rude Awakening sounds stronger, though.'

'It is,' Tracy confirmed.

Hunter ordered a large one. While he waited, Tracy ordered a medium Spanish Latté and a Berry Bowl to go.

'By the way,' she said to Hunter, as the barista got busy with her order. 'I'm moving to the East Coast. A week from today, actually.'

The news caught him completely by surprise.

'Oh, where to?' he asked, doing his best to keep his emotions in check, but as soon as he uttered those words, he realized how personal his question had been. 'I'm so sorry.' He lifted an apologetic hand. 'I didn't mean to pry. You don't need to answer that.'

'It's all right,' Tracy said, handing Hunter another disarming smile. 'If I didn't want you to know, I wouldn't have mentioned it.' She paused for just a second. 'I was approached by Yale. The position I was offered was simply impossible to refuse.'

Initially, Hunter felt a choking sadness grab hold of his heart, but it didn't hold on for long.

'That's fantastic, Tracy.' He was truly happy for her. 'Congratulations. You thoroughly deserve it.'

The barista came back to the counter with Hunter's order. He took it before his gaze met Tracy's one last time. Looking into each other's eyes, they both went silent for another second or two. This time, there was no awkwardness.

'It was very nice seeing you again, Tracy,' Hunter said, hoping that his tone didn't sound half as emotional to her as it did to him.

'You too, Robert,' she said back without any hesitation. 'It really was. I mean that.'

An odd tingle began gaining momentum somewhere deep inside Hunter, but he managed to stop it before it was too late.

'Thanks for the tip,' he said, lifting the large cup of coffee. 'And . . . take care of yourself, OK?'

'I will.'

Tracy wanted to say 'you too' back to Hunter, but she, more than most, understood how pointless those words would sound. She halted him with a stare and said the only thing left to say.

'Goodbye, Robert.'

Hunter couldn't bring himself to say 'goodbye' to Tracy. Not again. Instead, he gave her one last wave from the coffee shop door before walking back to his car, his heart dragging along a few paces behind him.

Forty-One

Hunter's pit stop had taken him a little longer than he had expected, so by the time he finally parked his car at the PAB parking lot, the late-rising winter sun had already breached the horizon line and, like a spider, was slowly climbing up the sides of buildings in central LA.

Up in his office, Hunter wasn't surprised to see Garcia already at his desk. Garcia was also a very early riser and, more often than not, he would get to the UVC Unit office before Hunter.

'I'm just brewing a pot of coffee,' Garcia said, as Hunter got to his desk and fired up his computer. 'It should be ready in a couple of minutes.' He gave Hunter an approving nod. 'Brazilian Supremo Bean – Dark Roast. It doesn't get much nicer than that.'

Having inherited his love of coffee from his Brazilian father, who was a total aficionado, Garcia took his coffee very seriously. The coffee maker in their office was his own, an elegant and shiny piece of equipment that had set him back a little more than what he could afford at the time – but to him, that machine was worth every penny, an opinion clearly shared by Hunter. But a machine alone doesn't count for much. That was why once a week, either Hunter or Garcia would drop by one of the many specialized coffee stores around Downtown LA and pick up a bag of something distinctive.

The smell already filling their office was indeed mouthwatering, but Hunter disregarded it completely, something that didn't happen very often.

'He called me,' he said, which wasn't the reply Garcia was expecting.

'What?' His eyes narrowed. 'Who called you? Brazilian Supremo Bean – Dark Roast?'

Garcia's joke hit a wall. 'The killer,' Hunter clarified. 'The diary owner. He called me last night. Right after I dropped Angela at the safe house.'

Garcia's eyebrows arched in shock. He heard Hunter loud and clear, but his brain was having a hard time processing his words.

'Wait ... how?' A puzzled shake of the head. 'I mean ... how did he know to call *you*? And how the hell did he get your cell number?'

'He obviously found the card I gave Angela when he searched her apartment,' Hunter replied.

'I forgot about that,' Garcia said. 'Anyway, what did he say?'

Hunter reached for his cellphone. 'Here, you can listen to it for yourself.' He connected the phone to his computer speakers for better sound.

As the recording played, Garcia's face morphed from surprise, to doubt, to disbelief.

'Did I hear this right?' Garcia asked once the recording had ended, his tone lacking conviction. 'This sack of shit gave you an ultimatum?'

Hunter sat back in his chair. 'Pretty much.'

'And the deadline is five o'clock today.'

'Deadline for what, coffee?' The question came from Captain Blake, who had reached their office door just in time to hear Garcia's last sentence.

As both detectives looked back at her, it was hard not to notice the worry in their eyes.

'What's going on?' The playful tone in her voice completely vanished.

'You better come in and listen to this, Captain,' Garcia said, motioning her in with a hand gesture.

The captain closed the door behind her and approached Hunter's desk, placing her empty mug on it.

'What am I listening to?'

'The killer's phone call to Robert,' Garcia explained.

'The what?' The lines on her forehead deepened as her eyes widened.

Hunter replayed the recording, by the end of which, Captain Blake was just as stunned as Garcia had been moments earlier. Not only by how fearless the caller seemed to be, but also by how calm and unconcerned he sounded. Calm when considering his demands and the threats that he was so freely dishing out; unconcerned when bearing in mind that he was talking directly to an LAPD Robbery Homicide Detective.

'He's one cocky sonofabitch, I'll give him that,' the captain said, once Hunter had halted the playback.

'He's also a lot more knowledgeable than we're giving him credit for,' Hunter countered.

Captain Blake walked over to the coffee machine and filled up her mug. 'Knowledgeable about what exactly, Robert?'

'The criminal investigative procedure,' Hunter replied. 'I think he understands it, and he understands it well.'

From the pocket of her perfect-fitting black blazer, Captain Blake retrieved a small sweetener dispenser and dropped a single tiny tablet into her coffee. 'And what makes you say that?'

'This phone call, for one,' Hunter said, leaning forward in his chair and placing both elbows on his desk. 'He told me that once I had his diary back in my possession, he would call me to give me instructions on how to deliver it back to him. When I asked him what made him think that I didn't have the diary with me right then, his reply was—'

'Because he wasn't stupid,' Captain Blake cut in. 'Yes, we just heard that, Robert. What's your point?'

'My point is that though that specific reply could be interpreted in various different ways, I get a strong feeling that what he truly meant by it was that he knew that his actual diary – not photocopies of it, not digital scans, not photos, but his actual physical diary – wouldn't have been with me no matter where I was. Not in my car . . . not in my apartment . . . not even here in the Police Administration Building.'

The captain sipped her coffee before allowing her eyes to rest on Garcia for an instant. He seemed just as intrigued as she was. They both looked back at Hunter expectantly. He gladly obliged.

'This killer knows that if the LAPD came into possession of his diary, one of our very first moves would be to hand it to forensics. With page upon page of solid text, Polaroid photographs, blood smears and what-have-you, he also knows that it could be weeks, if not months, before forensics is done analyzing that book. That's why he gave me until five o'clock today to get it back. He knew that it would take me some time to do so.'

Captain Blake reflected over Hunter's theory for an instant.

'When the killer called Angela and asked her about the whereabouts of his diary,' Hunter continued, anticipating his captain's next question, 'she told him that she had sent it to the LAPD. The *L-A-P-D*. She never mentioned anything about the FTD, the FSD, or about dropping it into Dr. Slater's mailbox. I confirmed it with Angela last night.'

Captain Blake had another sip of her coffee. 'If, like you're suggesting, he knew that the LAPD's Forensics and Technical Division had his diary, then why did he call you? Why not skip the middleman and call them directly?'

'Because he wouldn't have gotten past the switchboard,' Hunter replied. 'If he tried calling the FTD without a specific case number, his call would've died there. Clever or not, there's nothing he could've said that would've resulted in him being given a specific name. Even if they wanted to, they wouldn't be able to do so. A complex piece of evidence like his diary would have to be put through an enormous battery of different tests – fingerprints, DNA, graphology, paper analysis. I gave Dr. Slater specific orders that that diary is not to be disassembled, which means that that entire book has to be passed around the different labs. Any number of scientists and technicians will be dealing with it, not a single person. Calling the FTD would've been a waste of time and I'm sure he knew that.'

There was a moment of silence while the captain finished her coffee.

'So we really don't have the diary?' she asked.

'No.' Garcia confirmed it. 'FTD has it. All we have here are scanned photographs of its pages.'

The captain nodded her understanding. 'So what are we going to do in relation to his demand?' She lifted a hand to indicate that she wasn't done yet. 'I know that the textbook thing to do would be to set up some sort of sting operation and wait for his call later this afternoon, but from what you've just told me,' she addressed Hunter, 'I don't suppose that catching him would be as simple as setting up a trap, would it?'

Hunter's palms faced the ceiling and his shoulders came up in a shrug.

'We can try, but I sincerely doubt it'll work.' He indicated his cellphone on his desk. 'You've noticed how calm and confident he sounded throughout the duration of the call, right?'

A nod from Captain Blake.

'Which is probably because he's already thought of the perfect way for Robert to deliver the diary back to him, without him risking being caught,' Garcia suggested.

'I don't doubt he has,' Hunter agreed. 'But his confidence goes a lot deeper than that. It goes way beyond this call.'

'In what way?' Garcia took the question from Captain Blake's lips.

'I've lost track of how many times I've listened to this recording,' Hunter clarified. 'And the feeling I got from his words . . . from his tone of voice . . . was that he wasn't trying to sound confident just for the sake of this particular phone call . . . just because he was talking directly to the LAPD. The feeling I got was that he sounded confident because we don't scare him. I don't mean only the LAPD, I mean any law enforcement agency. He could've been talking to the FBI, the NSA, the ATF, whoever, and he still would've sounded the same. He still wouldn't have been scared. He still would have given them an ultimatum.'

Captain Blake held Hunter's eyes for longer than a heartbeat. In them, she saw an odd sparkle, one that she wasn't exactly a stranger to. Somewhere inside that big brain of his, she knew that Hunter had started putting together some sort of profile of this guy. She pushed.

'And why do you think that is?'

Hunter was finally overwhelmed by the mouthwatering smell of coffee, so he approached the machine and poured himself a large cup.

'It's impossible to tell, Captain. Not without interviewing him.'

'OK, but you can speculate.' She lifted a hand, as she conceded, 'I know that you hate doing that, but please, indulge me here, Robert. I'm just trying to get a little grip on what we're up against. Why do you think this particular nutjob is so confident . . . so fearless?'

Hunter had a sip of his coffee. 'All right, but this is nothing more than pure speculation.'

'I'm OK with that,' Captain Blake agreed.

'OK,' Hunter began. 'One thing that we do know is that he hears voices in his head, which indicates that he's a schizophrenic psychopath. If the voices are commanding him to retrieve his diary, he will do whatever it takes to please them, even if it means disregarding his own safety. Fear, pain, exhaustion, danger, strength, even his psychopathic, narcissistic self-love . . . all of that becomes secondary because the voices and their wishes take precedence over everything. To him, the most important thing would be to not upset the voices.'

Though Hunter's explanation made sense to everyone, Captain Blake got the feeling that he was holding something back.

'All right,' she said. 'But that's not your whole theory, is it? You've got something else? Something that's bothering you.'

Hunter stayed quiet.

'What is it, Robert?' she insisted.

'It's less of a theory and more of a hunch, Captain,' Hunter said, going back to his chair. 'And the only way I can strengthen that hunch is by going through everything Dr. Slater has sent us with a fine-tooth comb. So if you give me some time, I can let you know in a while.'

'Nope,' the captain said with a firm shake of the head. 'I know much better than to disregard these goddamn hunches of yours, Robert. Every time you have one of those, all kinds of hell breaks loose. Tell us now.'

'The captain's got a point,' Garcia said, as he walked back to his computer and loaded up the first few images from the zip file Dr. Slater had sent them. 'What is this hunch of yours?'

Right then, Hunter felt like a kid about to tell his parents that he had seen a unicorn out in their back garden.

'Maybe the strength behind everything he does,' Hunter said, 'comes from the fact that he's used to facing much more frightening opponents than the LAPD. I think that the reason why he understands criminal investigative procedure so well, is because he's been part of it.'

'Hold on a moment here,' Captain Blake paused Hunter. 'You think he's a cop?'

'No,' Hunter replied with a subtle shake of the head. 'Not a regular cop. Not one of us. Someone with a hell of a lot more training.'

Forty-Two

Located near the center of Los Angeles, nestled between the San Fernando Valley and Beverly Hills, was Franklin Canyon Park – 605 acres of chaparral, grasslands, oak woodlands, a three-acre lake, a duck pond, expansive picnic grounds, and over five miles of hiking trails. The lake and pond served as a sanctuary for birds in the Pacific flyway – the major north–south flight path for migratory birds in America, extending from Alaska to Patagonia. It was there, by an isolated cluster of trees at the northwest end of the lake, that the man liked to sit. And sit he did, away from everyone, staring at the water and the birds, lost in his own thoughts, for hours on end.

Despite the park's central location in a city of twelve million souls, its grounds had an almost magical effect. Once you were through the gates, Los Angeles with all its hustle and bustle was completely left behind. It was like being transported to a different world ... a different planet even, and that was why out of so many Los Angeles parks, Franklin Canyon was the man's favorite. On average, he tended to visit it two or three times a week. The tranquility of the surroundings, coupled with the sheer beauty of the lake, its vegetation and diverse birdlife, made him feel as close to being at peace with himself as he would ever be able to.

Officially, the park only opened its doors to the public at 7:00 a.m., but for someone with the man's expertise, breaching the perimeter fence was as easy as breathing. In fact, when possible, he liked getting there before sunrise.

As the sun's first rays illuminated the trees and met the water, it created a hypnotizing sparkling undulation, as if the sun had come to reveal hidden diamonds at the bottom of the lake.

The man finished his pastrami sandwich and had another sip of his coffee. The sun, albeit weak, warmed his skin. In the distance, he could hear a woodpecker beginning his workday. Several different bird species, hidden somewhere in the woodland, were also making themselves heard, greeting the brand-new morning.

Sitting with his back against a tree, the man pulled his knees toward his chest and hugged them. His eyes moved up to the sky just in time for him to see a belted kingfisher circle high above his head and lock its sights on some poor small fish in the shallow waters by the banks of the lake. With its target acquired, the kingfisher dove at it fast and with the utmost precision. Like a guided missile, it splashed into the water, disturbing its sparkling surface, only to re-emerge a second later with the fish securely clasped between its beak. The fish, fighting for dear life, wiggled in desperation, trying its best to break free from the kingfisher's tight grip, but the fish's fight was all in vain. After all, the bird was called 'kingfisher' for a reason. Once it had its victim in its beak, there was nothing else that the prey could do.

As the man watched the kingfisher fly back to a tree branch

not that far away from where he was sitting, he chuckled humorlessly, thinking about the similarities between him and the master fishing bird.

Just like the kingfisher, once the man had taken a subject, the chances of that subject escaping were none, but the similarities didn't end there. Despite how beautiful kingfishers were to look at, with their long, pointy beaks, big heads, large eyes, colorful bodies, small legs and short tails, in the world of ornithology, the kingfisher was considered to be a vicious predator.

It was the brutal and torturous manner in which kingfishers killed their prey that had earned them the reputation of being such cruel killers. Once back at a tree branch, instead of waiting for the fish to die naturally, the kingfisher would savagely slam the fish in its beak against the tree with all its might ... again ... and again ... and again ... until death. In human terms, that was the equivalent to the man slamming a subject's head against a concrete wall nonstop, until the cranium had fractured multiple times and the gray matter inside it had turned to mush.

Life is indeed poetic, the man thought.

The man poured himself another cup of coffee from the thermos he had with him and checked his watch – less than ten hours until he had to call Detective Hunter again.

Though the man would give him a chance to, he wasn't really expecting the LAPD detective to comply. At least not at first. That was why he had already thought of a plan.

He would get his diary back, of that the man had absolutely no doubt. And if he had to kill the detective in the process, so be it – and this time, he wouldn't need the voices to direct him.

Forty-Three

'Someone with a hell of a lot more training than an LAPD cop?' Captain Blake asked Hunter. 'Like who?' The tiny wrinkles around her eyes became more visible as she looked back at her detective. 'Don't tell me that you think this killer could be linked to the FBI.'

Hunter shook his head. 'No, not the FBI either . . . the military.'

Garcia, who was standing to the left of Captain Blake, looked just as surprised as she did.

'Why the military?'

Hunter lifted both of his hands. 'Like I've said – it's just a hunch, but I think that there's a big chance that this killer either is or was with the military.'

'A hunch based on what, Robert?' the captain asked. 'On the fact that he used military time to refer to his five o'clock deadline?'

'That's one factor, yes,' Hunter admitted.

'Many of our schedules use military time notation,' Captain Blake countered. 'You'll also find it in some staff rotas, time-tables, agendas, programs . . . the list is long.'

'Yes,' Hunter agreed. 'In written form, military time is used everywhere, but on average, only people in the military, or with links to the military, use military time when *speaking*.'

Captain Blake hesitated for a moment.

'We might see it written down just about everywhere,' Hunter pushed. 'But most of us won't ever read it as military time notation.'

'Unless he did it on purpose.' Garcia joined the debate. 'With the specific intention of taking you down that path – to make you think that he's got a military background. He certainly seems clever enough for that.'

'But military time isn't the only military associated term he's used. He's also done it in writing.'

He minimized the image on his screen before calling up a new one.

Garcia and Captain Blake repositioned themselves behind his desk.

Hunter addressed Garcia. 'This, you will remember, relates to the second entry in the diary – Cory Snyder.' He indicated on his screen.

Despite my initial inaccuracy, every single lash I administered violently ruptured the subject's flesh, creating the sort of deep lacerations that would bring terror into the heart of any medic.

'Other than in war films and video games,' Hunter asked, 'have you ever heard anyone refer to a doctor as a *medic*, either in conversation or in written form?'

Garcia and Captain Blake stayed silent.

'The word medic is mainly used by military personnel,' Hunter insisted. 'Throughout the diary, there might be other terms that hint at this killer having been, or still being with the military, I'm not sure. We've only had a chance to read two out of the sixteen entries.'

Garcia confirmed it with a nod.

'That's why I want to start at the beginning again,' Hunter continued. 'And go through everything – every page, every word – with an analytical eye. Hopefully, something, somewhere in his diary will give him away.'

Captain Blake, who hadn't read any of the diary entries yet, had kept her attention on Hunter's computer screen.

'All right,' she said in agreement, finally dragging her gaze away from the gruesome text in front of her. 'You two get on with it. Meanwhile, I'll request an SIS and a SWAT team to be on standby for his five o'clock deadline.'

Hunter checked his watch. 'I'll call Dr. Slater to tell her that we need the diary back.'

With another double-take, Captain Blake pinned Hunter down with a stare. 'Whatever sort of instructions you get from this freakshow today ... you're not really considering the idea of having the real diary with you, are you?'

'I might need to, yes,' Hunter replied, already loading new images onto his screen. 'But regardless of what happens today at five o'clock, I do need that diary here with me.'

Captain Blake gave Hunter a couple more seconds, but he gave her nothing more.

'And why is that, Robert?'

Hunter breathed out before resting his right elbow on his desk and locking eyes with his captain.

'For two main reasons. He's going to want some sort of proof that I have it in my hands.'

The corners of Captain Blake's mouth angled downwards as she nodded. 'All right, and what is the second reason?'

Hunter swiveled his chair a few degrees to face Garcia and Captain Blake. 'His almost desperate desire to get his diary back.'

Going on facial expressions alone, Hunter's reply missed the target completely.

'Doesn't that sound a little odd to either of you?' Hunter asked, searching their faces.

Blank.

He clarified.

'This killer obviously knows that by now we would've copied, scanned, photographed every page, every sketch, every Polaroid in that diary. Getting his diary back will not keep us from the information in those pages. It will not prevent us from digging up every single one of his victims. And if his identity is mentioned anywhere in that book, getting it back won't stop us from hunting him down.'

'So it's not the information in those pages that he wants back, it's the diary itself.'

Hunter nodded. 'It has to be. The question is why? The only conclusion I could come to, is that there's got to be something else in that book. Something beyond the words. Something hidden from view. Something that a scan or a photograph would not pick up. Something that maybe even forensics would miss. Why else would he so desperately want that book back?'

Captain Blake felt the hairs on the back of her neck stand on end, but this time, for an entirely different reason.

'Get on the phone to Susan,' she commanded Hunter, as she made for the door. 'Get that diary here ASAP and keep me posted. I'll get on to SIS and SWAT. Let's go get this sonofabitch.'

Forty-Four

Hunter put down the phone, gave the officer standing in front of his desk, Officer Makalsky, his final instructions and immediately returned to the image on his computer screen. He and Garcia, once again, started back at the beginning – page 1 – Elizabeth Gibbs's entry.

Hunter was an extremely fast reader, being able to speed-read with ease, but he purposely slowed his rhythm down considerably. Other than looking for anything else that could lend more credibility to his military theory, Hunter was also searching for something that could be hidden somewhere in that book. The problem he had was that he really had no clue what he was looking for. Should he try reading between the lines for some concealed meaning, or was he looking for something more tangible? Had the killer used some sort of code to hide information? If he had, how would Hunter ever find it?

The answer, he knew, wouldn't come easy, if at all.

Hunter read every full line of text twice – the first time around looking for a possible hidden meaning to the sentence – a play on words or something similar. The second time around his attention moved from word to word and from letter to letter. This time, he was looking for something out of the ordinary. Maybe a word, or even an individual letter that had been somehow stressed – tiny markings under or above it . . . heavier ink . . . anything that could hint at something odd.

By the time Hunter finished reading through Elizabeth Gibbs's entry, he had found nothing that had grabbed his attention – no other hints that could suggest that the killer had a military background and nothing that seemed any more revealing than what they already had. No signs of any code either. The same became true for the second entry – Cory Snyder.

Before moving on to the third entry and a brand-new victim, Hunter got up and poured himself a fresh cup of coffee.

Even though these murders had already been committed and there was nothing that Hunter could've done to stop them, he found himself feeling a little anxious with the thought of moving forward. Every single one of them, he knew, would reveal a new evil . . . a new horror. Every new entry would give him the name and the face of a new victim – poor souls who had been robbed of their life by a sadistic maniac who heard voices in his head. That helpless feeling knotted Hunter's stomach, making him feel sick, but though he couldn't help any of the sixteen victims mentioned in those pages, he would give their families closure, and he would do all he could to prevent this killer from claiming any more lives.

Fresh coffee in hand, Hunter went back to his desk.

The new entry read:

The voices had gone dormant for a while – seventy-eight days to be precise – but they have awakened from their hibernation, coming back at me loud and clear and as hungry as ever. Once again, they had another very specific request – Gender: female. Age: in between twenty-five and twenty-seven. No younger ... no older. Height: five-foot four to five-foot six. Hair: black, straight, long – at least past the shoulders. Eyes: black (very dark brown). Body type: petite – slim. Weight: not an ounce over 130 pounds. Ethnicity: Japanese-American. Personality: shy, introvert. This was the first time that the voices have ever mentioned a preference for a specific personality. Not actually a problem, but that preference will, undoubtedly, delay the subject selection. With all previous subjects, where the requirements were always just physical, selection could be easily done via reconnaissance alone ...

Hunter stopped reading, the veins around his temples tightening with excitement. The word 'reconnaissance', he knew, was often used by military personnel, though not exclusively.

He took note of the word and had a sip of his coffee before going back to the text.

... but with the addition of a specific personality type, reconnaissance alone will not suffice. To be able to discern her personality with any level of confidence, I will have to approach the subject and engage in conversation, probably more than once, something that I would rather not do. 'She needs to be dressed in a traditional Japanese kimono,' was the voices' next request. 'She should also be wearing white socks and traditional wooden geta. No makeup necessary. The color of the kimono is irrelevant.' Despite the unusual level of detail concerning the subject's attire, finding a target wouldn't pose any real problems, except, of course, for the personality issue,

*which, in all honesty, could be circumvented, as there's no
real way in which the voices could discern her personality.*

Hunter paused again, his forehead creasing as his eyes
narrowed. This time, his concern wasn't with any of the
vocabulary used in the entry. 'Circumvented', though not
the most common of words, could not really be considered a
military term. No, it hadn't been a word in the text that had
caused Hunter to stop and frown; it had been the text itself.
The meaning behind it.

Hunter sat back on his chair, crossed his arms over his chest
and stared thoughtfully at his computer screen.

'Everything OK?' Garcia asked, stretching his neck a little
to the left to look past his monitor.

'Umm,' was Hunter's reply, which was delivered together
with a single nod.

Garcia was not convinced. 'I know that face, Robert.
What's up?'

'I'm not really sure.' Hunter tried again. He used his thumb
and forefinger to gently massage his closed eyelids. 'Maybe I'm
just overthinking things – trying too hard to find a way through
to this guy, when really there's nothing here.'

Hunter knew from experience that trying too hard tended
to sabotage the brain. The longer a person tried without success, the more frustrated that person became. Frustration not
only shortened the lifespan of the thought process, but it also
tricked the brain into distorting images, words and sounds,
making you see and hear what wasn't really there and what
hadn't been said.

'OK,' Garcia said back. 'So what do you think you're over-
thinking? Maybe I can help.'

'Maybe,' Hunter agreed. 'But let me carry on until the end of the entry. Maybe things clarify themselves.'

'Sure,' Garcia replied.

Hunter went back to the words on his screen.

But it was when the voices moved on to the kill method that a real problem appeared. 'Dressed in her traditional Geisha outfit,' the voices had said, 'she is to be violently open-handed slapped across the face several times, until blood is running down from her nose and lips. No close-fisted punches. Open-handed slaps only. She's not to be rendered unconscious. With blood on her face, her kimono is to be to be savagely ripped open and the subject raped . . .' That was when I halted the voices. NO. I will NOT rape anyone. If that were their request, they would have to go away again and come back with something else. I WILL NOT RAPE ANYONE.

Hunter stopped reading once again.

'This feels wrong,' he said under his breath. 'This feels all wrong.'

Forty-Five

Despite Hunter keeping his voice to no louder than a whisper, his words traveled the short distance between his desk and Garcia's with ease, reaching his partner's ears loud and clear.

'What's all wrong?' Garcia asked, his tone full of worry.

Hunter didn't reply. Instead, he sat still, his mouth semi-open, his eyes locked onto his computer screen, as he reread the last few lines of text again and again.

'Robert,' Garcia called, a little louder this time. 'What feels all wrong? What did you find?'

Hunter shook his head momentarily, as if trying to shake away a bad dream.

'Whereabouts are you in the text?' he asked.

'About halfway through the third entry,' Garcia replied.

'So we're about even,' Hunter said, gesturing Garcia to come closer. 'Have a look at this.'

Garcia joined Hunter at his desk. 'What am I looking at?'

'Here.' On his screen, Hunter indicated the last piece of text he had read. 'This part, right here.'

Garcia read the section twice, before looking back at Hunter with questioning eyes.

'Nothing strikes you as wrong in this?' Hunter asked.

'The killer declining to go ahead with rape is surprising,' Garcia admitted. 'But I wouldn't exactly call it wrong.'

'Yes, but here's the thing,' Hunter tried to clarify. 'He didn't only decline to go ahead with the rape request. He told the voices to go away and come back with something else.'

Garcia shrugged. 'In a way, that could be seen as a good thing, don't you think?'

'Yes, sure,' Hunter agreed. 'But I'm not talking about that, Carlos. I'm not talking about the rape. I'm talking about the killer halting the voices, and not only telling them that he won't do as he's being told, but also reversing the tide . . . commanding the voices to go away and come back with a different request. From a psychological point of view, when considering schizophrenia, that just wouldn't happen.'

'Well,' Garcia said, quickly angling his head to one side, 'since my knowledge of schizophrenia is pretty basic, I'm going to have to ask you – why not?'

'Schizophrenia is what causes a person to hear voices in their head,' Hunter explained. 'But, as you know, those voices don't really exist. They are created and manifested by that person's own subconscious. The problem lies in the fact that in their heads, those voices sound so real and so different from their own that they really believe that someone, or something, is indeed talking to them. With schizophrenia, there are essentially two distinct types of aural delusions.' Hunter used the fingers on his right hand to count them out. 'One: voices that come with hallucinations, meaning that the person will actually visualize someone, or something, talking to them. The proverbial imaginary friend. And they will look just as real to them as you do to me right now. In those cases, the schizophrenic will inevitably give the imaginary person, or thing, a name – John, Paul, Jenny, The Dragon, Cthulhu ... you get the idea, right?'

Garcia nodded.

'OK,' Hunter carried on, once again gesturing toward his computer screen. 'So because in his entries the killer refers to the voices he hears as simply "the voices", and not by specific names, it led me to believe that our killer fell into the second category of aural delusions – voices alone – no visual hallucinations accompanying them. Those cases tend to be a little more extreme.'

'More extreme?' Garcia questioned. 'Why?'

'Because if a person is hearing voices that they perceive as real, but seeing absolutely no one whatsoever, more often than not, that person will have a tendency to attribute those voices to powerful *non-human* entities – God, the Devil, ghosts, saints, a dead relative ... whatever.' Hunter lifted both hands in surrender, knowing that he was overstretching his explanation. 'Anyway, the voices inside someone's head, in both cases – visual hallucinations or not – are always way too powerful, way too tormenting, way too haunting and certainly way too dominating for a schizophrenic to have any sort of control over them, never mind being able to tell them to go away ... And that's why they're considered schizophrenic.' Hunter paused to give Garcia a moment. 'If this killer is able to halt the voices inside his head whenever he wants, then he has just cured himself of schizophrenia. If you can control the voices, you can control the mental illness.'

Garcia finally saw the logic in Hunter's reasoning.

'And if this killer is able to halt the voices in his head whenever he wants to,' Hunter added, 'why only do it now when he was asked to rape someone? Why didn't he stop them right at the beginning, when the voices first came to him commanding him to kill? Where's the sense in that?'

It was Garcia's turn to shake his head as if trying to dislodge the memory of a bad dream.

'There's something else as well,' Hunter continued, scrolling back on the image on his screen until he got to the desired location. 'Right here.'

Garcia's eyes moved to Hunter's screen and the section of text that he had indicated.

Despite the unusual level of detail concerning the subject's attire, finding a target wouldn't pose any real problems, except, of course, for the personality issue, which, in all honesty, could be circumvented, as there's no real way in which the voices could discern her personality.

'"Circumventing the personality issue"?' Hunter said.

'I think what he means here is that on this occasion the voices could be deceived.'

'Bingo,' Hunter agreed, his eyes widening as he nodded. 'By saying that "there's no real way in which the voices could discern her personality" he's alluding to the fact that, somehow, the voices wouldn't know any better if the victim was an introvert or not, therefore, they could be deceived.' Hunter paused Garcia with a hand gesture. 'Now, how do you deceive something that's a product – a manifestation – of your own thoughts . . . your own subconscious?'

A new penny dropped.

'You can't,' Garcia replied.

'Exactly,' Hunter confirmed. 'It's your own brain. It knows everything you know.'

Garcia took a step back from Hunter's desk and pinched his bottom lip with his thumb and forefinger. 'So what is the conclusion that we can draw from all this? If any.'

Hunter slumped back on his chair, as if he'd just gone ten rounds with a heavyweight champion.

'I'm not one hundred percent sure,' he finally replied. 'But we're only on entry number three out of sixteen. It's too early to start concluding anything just yet. But from a purely psychological point of view, this puts a lot of doubt on this killer suffering from schizophrenia.'

Garcia feared exactly that.

'So how the hell is he hearing voices?' he asked.

Hunter breathed out. 'What if these voices have absolutely nothing to do with a mental illness?'

'I don't get it.'

'What if these are real voices – real people – telling him what to do?'

Garcia's head jerked back. 'What . . .? That's crazy. How . . .? Who would those people be?'

Hunter shrugged. 'I don't know . . . Look, maybe I'm over-thinking things, because this makes very little sense right now.' He pointed at his screen. 'I guess that the best thing to do is to carry on . . .'

Garcia agreed and went back to his desk.

Hunter still had no idea of what he was searching for and, if anything, the more he read, the more questions he had.

If that were their request, they would have to go away again and come back with something else. I WILL NOT RAPE ANYONE. Needless to say that the voices weren't happy, but that's not who I am. I've never raped anyone.

Despite all I've seen. Despite all I've been through. I've never raped anyone – BFOA or otherwise. And I'll be damned if I'm going to start now.

Hunter paused again, his eyes moving back a few words on his screen to settle on the acronym the killer had used – BFOA. With a troubled look in his eyes, he searched his memory for anything that could, even remotely, lend some meaning to it.

Nothing.

Instinctively, Hunter called up his browser and ran a quick Internet search. Most hits came back for Bacterial Foraging Optimization Algorithms.

'That's not it,' Hunter whispered to himself with a shake of the head.

One of the links he got on the returned results page was to an acronym finder.

On that page, he entered the letters 'BFOA' into the 'abbreviation to define' box and clicked the 'Find' button. A blink of an eye later, he had five new definitions listed on a new results page:

> Beller Freibad Open Air (Germany).
> Bull Fights on Acid (band).
> Broward Football Official's Association (Broward County, Florida).
> Birmingham Football Officials Association (Birmingham, Alabama).
> Boao Forum of Asia (Hainan, China).

In the context of the diary entry, none of them made any real sense.

At the top of the acronyms results page, different tabs showed how many results that particular acronym had yielded in relation to specific categories. The results page had defaulted to 'All Definitions', showing the five results Hunter had read. The other 'category tabs' were:

Information Technology – zero results.
Science and Medicine – zero results.
Organizations, Schools, etc. – four results.
Slang, Chat and Pop Culture – one result.
Military and Government – zero results.

Hunter breathed in.

'What the hell does BFOA stand for, do you know?' Garcia asked from his desk.

'That's what I'm trying to find out,' Hunter replied. 'So far, nothing I've found makes any sense in the entry's context.'

'I can't come up with anything either,' Garcia said.

Hunter scratched his nose as he read the sentence on his screen one more time. 'Let's come back to it in a while. I want to get to the end of this new entry first.'

'Agreed,' Garcia said.

I had expected the voices to go away and come back another day. Maybe tomorrow. Maybe the day after, but I was wrong. Despite their disappointment, a brand-new request was voiced by them almost immediately, as if they already had a list of desired subjects in place and they had expected my negative reaction to their original request. The new request was very different not only from the previous one, but from all of them. The level of physical detail, which is usually quite specific, was relatively vague, with most of it left for me to choose, but the major difference between this request and all the previous ones was that the voices didn't request one subject. They requested two.

Forty-Six

Hunter stopped reading again, this time to shrug at thin air. In psychological terms, very little of what he was reading made any real sense. He rubbed his eyes, before picking up the reading from where he'd left off.

They requested two – Gender: Male and Female. Everything else – hair color, eye color, age, height, etc. was irrelevant. What wasn't irrelevant was the status of their relationship. The couple had to be married and they had to have been so for over five years. How long over five years was also irrelevant. Kids: also irrelevant. Straight off the bat and since the voices had left it at my discretion, I decided that I would choose a childless couple. In a city like LA, where traditional family values seem to constantly be going head-to-head with having a successful career, with fewer and fewer professional couples choosing to have children, finding such a couple didn't strike me as being a difficult task. And I was right. All I had to do was visit a few bars and restaurants, and right on the first night of my search, in a restaurant somewhere in Santa Monica, I spotted a young couple sitting

at a window table. Neither seemed to be older than thirty
years of age. She was tall and slim with shoulder-length
auburn hair and magnified brown eyes sitting behind
tortoiseshell glasses. I found her to be neither attractive
nor ugly, just unremarkable. The man sitting with her
was at least three inches taller than his partner, with a
thick beard and a slicked-back haircut. They were both
casually dressed and the wedding bands on their fingers
told me what I needed to know, but what really called my
attention to them at first was the fact that, despite them
sitting at the same table, they might as well have been by
themselves. Their attention, and I mean both of them,
was glued to their cellphones. I observed them for almost
ten minutes and they didn't exchange a single word. In
fact, they didn't exchange a single glance. They smiled,
all right, but not at each other. They smiled at their
screens. I entered the restaurant and took a seat at the
bar, so I could continue observing them. When their food
arrived, they did put their phones down, but not away.
The phones, both of them, were placed on the table, by
their plates. As they ate, their eyes danced between their
food and their cellphones, and even then, the phones
were coming out on top. It was only when they ordered
the check that they actually looked at each other and
exchanged a few words. The man took care of the bill.
She thanked him with a peck on the lips. I followed them
outside and into a cocktail lounge around the corner,
where they seemed to be meeting a few friends. They
stayed for a couple of hours, talking and laughing, but
only with their friends, not between themselves. After
that, I followed them home – an apartment in Wilshire

*Montana. A few days later, Doug and Sharon Hogan
received a visit from a police officer running a routine
survey on home security in their neighborhood. People
can be so gullible. Even in a city like LA, they'll always
open the door to a police officer. Date and time: June
10th 2018 –19.30. Location: apartment 39, number 92,
10th Street, Wilshire Montana in Santa Monica. Photo:
both of them later that same night.*

Hunter took another quick break to call up the Missing Persons
database search application. In the 'search' line he entered the
names the killer had just mentioned. The result came back in
a fraction of a second.

Doug Hogan, a thirty-one-year-old business analyst, and
Sharon Hogan, a twenty-nine-year-old kindergarten teacher,
were reported missing on 19 June 2018, by Sharon's mother,
Mrs. Sandra Carson. After not hearing from her daughter for
several days, which according to Mrs. Carson was unusual, she
tried calling Doug, her son-in-law, but also got no reply. She
then tried both of their workplaces, only to be told that neither
of them had been to work for an entire week. That was when
Mrs. Carson decided to go knocking on their door. With no
reply, she first got in touch with the building's supervisor, who
allowed her into her daughter's apartment. Despite the place
showing no signs of a struggle, Mrs. Carson contacted the
police, saying that she 'just knew' that something wasn't right.
On 19 June she filed an official Missing Persons complaint
with the LAPD. Neither Doug nor Sharon were ever found.
The investigation was still showing as open. The file contained
several photographs – a few individual ones and a couple of the
two of them together.

Hunter closed the Missing Persons database and returned to the diary entry.

When it came to the delivery method, once again, the voices were very clear – the couple was to be stripped naked and chained together, back-to-back. 'They are then to be placed inside a large container, one big enough to accommodate both of them without problems. Then the game begins. They are to be told that one of them is going to die, but the trick is – THEY have to choose which one.' Since I didn't have any sort of container that could comfortably fit two people, I had to improvise. Thankfully, this is LA; a city where having a swimming pool in your backyard is almost a must, but better yet, a city where wildfires have completely destroyed homes and mansions that most people could only dream of ever owning. Places that were now charred, devastated and abandoned. Places that no one wanted anymore. A forty-minute drive around the fire-affected area in Malibu and I could take my pick. I have no idea of what the house I chose had looked like in the past, as it had been completely destroyed by the latest forest fire. I also had no idea who the house had belonged to, but what difference did any of that make, right? Anyway, among the ruins, covered in charred rubble, I found something perfect for the purpose of the delivery method. Something much better than a swimming pool. I found a Jacuzzi big enough for two, maybe even three people.

There was a break in the text, where the killer had added a detailed hand sketch of a teardrop-shaped Jacuzzi, containing specific measurements.

The tub was filled with soot and fire debris, but as luck had it, it carried no structural damage. All it needed was a good cleaning and then I had the perfect container for the task at hand. On Monday, June 11th 2018, I followed the voices' instructions. The subjects were chained together, back-to-back, and thrown into the Jacuzzi. When I asked them to choose which one of them would die that night, what followed wasn't quite what I had expected.

Hunter quickly loaded the next image.

After all the expected crying and the pleading that happens with every subject, the first to finally speak concerning the question I had put to them was the male subject. Maybe I am naïve when it comes to matters of the heart, but I was somehow expecting him to beg me to take his life instead of his wife's. I was expecting him to tell her he loved her so much and that he would rather be dead than to be without her. But what I got was the exact opposite. With tears pouring down his face like a little girl, he began by saying that he had a lot more to live for than his wife did. A lot more to contribute to society than his wife did. In hearing those words, the female subject was so shocked that she did actually stop crying – her bloodshot eyes widening to the size of two casino chips. Completely taken by anger, the female subject uttered the words 'you motherfucker', and back-head-butted her husband. If I had chained them together facing each other, I'm fairly sure that she would've bitten his nose or his lips right off. Maybe that was why the voices asked me to chain them back to back. They were already counting on such a reaction. In my personal opinion, I think that if the female subject had spoken first, she would've asked me to take her life and not her husband's. I'm pretty sure she would have, but after the male subject's outburst, she hit back at him with, 'You fucking spoiled mama's boy, good-for-nothing, cheating asshole. You're so blinded by your own bullshit that you are oblivious to any of the signs that I've been sleeping with three of your so-called friends.' From then on, it turned into carnage, with abuse and overly aggressive back kicks, elbow jerks and back-head-butts being thrown back and forth like confetti during carnival. I observed the two subjects badmouthing and fighting each other for several minutes. It's impressive watching people feed off their emotions, and off the emotions of others, but after a while, it got boring. When the voices told me that they'd also had enough, I gave the two subjects the bad news. Following the instructions of the voices, I had lied to them. They would both die that night, not just one of them. Their argument had been an exercise in futility, but one that had revealed a lot about the two of them and entertained the voices. The revelation that they would both die did quiet both subjects, at least for a few seconds, before the screaming and pleading began again, but it was when they realized how they would die that pure and uncompromising terror took over both of them. I hadn't placed them inside a Jacuzzi just for fun. There was a reason for it. 'The container holding the two subjects,' the voices had said, 'is to be filled either with H_2SO_4 (sulfuric acid), or NaOH (caustic soda).'

Both extremes of the acid/base scale. The choice was left to me. My decision wasn't made based on the fact that base chemicals tend to cause less pain but more damage than acidic ones. When you are covering a subject with enough of either substance to be able to submerge them in it, the pain and the damage will be unbearable and fatal, no matter what is being used. No, my decision was made based on how easy and non-suspicious it would be for me to acquire either of them. It turns out that getting my hands on enough caustic soda to fill a bathtub was considerably easier than getting my hands on the same amount of sulfuric acid. As I poured the first gallon of caustic soda into the tub, I intentionally directed it more toward the male subject, though since they were chained to each other, the female subject got just as much on her as he did on him. The screams were inhuman. Like nothing I've ever heard before, and I've heard plenty. They fought helplessly like insects caught on a spider's web, but the screams and the fighting soon died down. Undiluted caustic soda will do away with the layers of human skin with tremendous ease. Once the skin is gone, that's when the hell really starts. By the end, the Jacuzzi looked like a witch's cauldron. Needless to say that, before they finally perished, both subjects had to endure the sort of pain and agony that not even the Bible talks about. Due to the condition of the bodies, or what was left of them, I decided that the best resting place for their remains, which I had to scoop out of the tub with a shovel, would be the ocean, not the earth. Their remains were dropped into the Pacific approximately 2.2 miles due southwest of Santa Monica beach.

That was the end of the entry.

Hunter sat back in his chair while memories of a past case clouded his mind. He knew exactly what caustic soda could do to a human body. A few years back, he and Garcia were made to watch, via a live Internet broadcast, a very similar death. The killer had placed his victim inside a large, makeshift glass container before filling it with a mixture of water and caustic soda. Even in a diluted composition, the damage and the pain caused were indescribable.

'I've got nothing,' Garcia said, shaking his head in frustration.

It took Hunter's brain a couple of seconds to register Garcia's words. He looked back at his partner with a blank stare.

'B-F-O-A,' Garcia clarified. 'Every definition I've come across for the acronym makes no sense in the context we have – "I've never raped anyone, BFOA or otherwise".'

Hunter had been so taken by what he'd just read that for a moment the acronym conundrum had escaped his mind.

'Hold on a sec,' he said, reaching for his cellphone. After searching his contacts list, he hit the 'call' button.

'Who are you calling?' Garcia asked.

'An old friend,' Hunter replied, as the phone rang once . . . twice . . . three times.

'*Hello,*' a gruff male voice answered at the other end of the line.

'Mr. Wilson?' Hunter asked.

'*Yes, this is he. To whom am I speaking?*'

Despite Wilson recognizing Hunter's voice, who called him at least once a month, the eighty-four-year-old, ex-US Army command sergeant major, always answered the phone in the exact same manner.

What followed was a ritual.

'Mr. Wilson, it's Robert. Robert Hunter.'

'If you lose your strength, you will fail.'

'I cannot fail,' Hunter replied. 'For strength lives within me.'

'You what?' Garcia frowned at his partner. 'What lives within you?'

With a shake of the head, Hunter signaled his partner to ignore what he'd just heard.

At the other end of the line, Hunter's reply was met by a loud guttural laugh. *'I hope it does, Robert. I really hope it does.'*

Command Sergeant Major Adrian Wilson was the father of Scott Wilson, Hunter's first ever partner when he joined the LAPD Robbery Homicide Division. Way over a decade ago, Scott had made Hunter promise him that if anything ever happened to him, Hunter would check on his father from time to time. A year and a half after that promise, Scott lost his life in a boat explosion – an assassination that was made to look like an accident.

Hunter had never forgotten the promise he'd made and since that tragic day, he would either call or drop by Mr. Wilson's house at least once a month. Not that Mr. Wilson needed any looking after. A highly decorated veteran, having fought for the US Army in Vietnam, Lebanon and Nicaragua, Mr. Wilson was, even at eighty-four years of age, an impressive figure – lucid, funny, strong and full of life.

'How are you doing, sir?' Hunter asked.

Even though Hunter had never been in the military, he treated the US Army CSM with the respect he'd earned and deserved.

'Oh well, you know me ... spitting blood, pissing blood, coughing blood, bleeding all over the house.' Despite the joke,

there was an undeniably authoritative tone to every word Mr. Wilson spoke.

'Sorry, sir,' Hunter replied, his tone concerned. 'You're not really pissing blood, are you?'

Garcia cringed from his desk. 'What the hell? Pissing blood what? Who are you talking to?' A split second after he asked that question, his right hand shot up in a stop gesture. 'Actually, I don't want to know. You go ahead and do your thing, Mr. Strength Within.'

On the phone, another guttural laugh from Mr. Wilson. *'No, Robert, of course not. I'm just messing with you. You have to learn how to laugh a little, son.'*

'I need to ask you something, sir.'

The urgency in Hunter's voice caused Mr. Wilson to hesitate at the other end of the line.

'That sounds serious.'

'I just need your help with something.'

'Sure, son, fire away. What would you like to ask?'

'In a military context,' Hunter began, 'does the acronym B-F-O-A have any meaning you can think of?'

In the silence that followed, Hunter could practically hear the gears inside the old man's brain gathering momentum.

'Nothing obvious comes to mind,' Mr. Wilson replied after several thoughtful seconds. *'But this is an old mind, as you know, and my memory misfires a lot nowadays.'* A quick pause. *'Maybe if you give me a little more, son. Where did you hear that? I mean, in which context?'*

'It's a line in a written statement,' Hunter replied.

'And what does that line say?'

'"I've never raped anyone",' Hunter quoted. '"BFOA or otherwise. And I'll be damned if I'm going to start now".'

To Hunter, the new pause that came from Mr. Wilson's end of the line felt as if the old man had held his breath.

'Sir?'

'*Yes, son.*' Mr. Wilson's voice sounded heavy with sorrow. '*I know what BFOA means.*'

Forty-Seven

The man left Franklin Canyon Park about fifteen minutes after it officially opened its gates to the general public. Despite how secluded his favorite spot was, he knew that, come rain or sunshine, trackers, joggers, cyclists and dog walkers would, with their distasteful and annoying colorful clothes, completely spoil the natural beauty of the place, not to mention the noise they brought with them, scaring most of the wildlife into hiding. Now, with a clear mind, the man was ready for what was about to come.

The drive from the park to Santa Clarita, where the man had transformed a deep underground basement into a horror chamber, took him just under an hour.

Inside the disused building, which stood at the edge of some isolated woodland, he descended a set of worn concrete steps one by one. His shadow, cast onto the brick and cement walls by a single fluorescent tube lamp at the top of the stairwell, danced ominously before him with each step he took. The smell at the stairwell was an odd combination of mildew, sour milk and disinfectant, as the man would clean those steps religiously, every week.

The stairs curved right in an angular L-shape, where the

already weak light from the fluorescent lamp at the top lost most of its strength. At the bottom, the man came to a three-foot-wide by seven-foot-tall metal door. Instead of a key, its sophisticated locking mechanism required either a six-digit combination or a thumbprint. The man pressed his right thumb onto the digital reading pad and the door opened with a loud buzz, allowing him to step into a square and empty room, except for a flat workbench pushed against the far wall. A multitude of steel pipes, some thick, some thin, ran across the ceiling in all different directions. The walls were made of solid cinderblock. The man flicked the light switch to his right and a new tube lamp, this time long and nestled between two pipes above his head, struggled to come to life, blinking on and off for several seconds before finally engaging and bathing the room in a dull orange glow.

Directly across the room from where the man was standing was a new metal door, this one heavier than the first. Once again, the locking mechanism required either a six-digit combination or a thumbprint. This time, the man pressed his left thumb onto the digital reading pad and the door clicked open. The room beyond was a little smaller than the one before. It contained a control desk, a couple of chairs and a large computer monitor mounted onto the wall directly above the desk. To the right of the desk there was a tall metal unit filled with electronics and computer equipment. To the left of the desk there was yet another metal door. The door sat so perfectly in its frame that no hinges were visible.

The man flicked on the lights and the eight halogen bulbs on the ceiling immediately sprang to life, burning the room with bright light.

Eight steps took him over to the control desk, where he

pressed a button to switch on the computer monitor. As he did, the screen before him was filled by four different images, each occupying an exact quarter of the screen – two at the top and two at the bottom.

The door to the left of the control desk led to a very long and dark L-shaped corridor. Along that corridor there were five rooms. Four of those were individual containment cells that he had built himself – all of them escape-proof. Each of those cells had a CCTV camera sitting inside a metal mesh box at the center of the ceiling, which could be quickly switched into infrared mode if needed, just like they were right then. The images on the computer screen above the control desk were being broadcast live by those cameras. Only one of the four containment cells was empty.

The man got comfortable on the office chair that faced the monitor and observed the screen for an instant before speaking.

'How are you all doing this morning?' he asked in a murmur, as his eyes jumped from one image to the other. 'Let's take a closer look, shall we?'

The man typed a command into the keyboard on the control desk and the four-way split image on the screen changed into a single one. At the top of the new image, small white letters read – 'cell 1'. He typed a new command – 'cell 2'. And again – 'cell 3'. He spent several minutes going back and forth from one camera to the other, watching the three subjects. The person inside cell one was sitting with her back against the northwest corner of the cell, her thighs pressed against her chest as she hugged them, her head down into her knees. The man didn't have to switch on the microphone inside the cell to know that she was crying. He could see the slight bobbing of her head and shoulders.

The man moved on to the camera inside cell two. The second subject was sitting on the cement bed, his legs crossed under him, his elbows resting on his knees and his hands locked together in a prayer position. The man couldn't tell if he was really praying or not, but he didn't really care. Prayers didn't matter. They never did.

The subject inside cell three seemed to be sleeping. She was lying facing the wall in the fetal position.

The man flipped once again between the three cameras. He had a decision to make – who out of those three would die that day.

The man chuckled, amused with himself.

'Life is indeed unpredictable, isn't it?' he asked, as if he were talking to the three subjects at the same time. 'I bet that none of you ever thought that your fate would be decided by a nursery rhyme.'

The man sat back on his chair as he started singing. 'Eeny, meeny, miny, moe . . .'

Forty-Eight

There was something in the way in which Mr. Wilson spoke that made Hunter hold his breath in anticipation. He waited, but Mr. Wilson went quiet again.

'Sir?' Hunter called. 'Are you still there?'

'Yes, I'm here.' Mr. Wilson coughed to clear his throat. '*Son, one thing that I'd like you to understand is that in times of war, certain things can happen, regardless of orders or whichever bullshit rules-of-engagement and treaties have been signed by stupid politicians in some good-for-nothing international organization. Soldiers aren't machines, son. They're human beings. They're people just like you and I, and just like you and I they are sometimes guided by emotions instead of orders, or even reason. Sometimes our soldiers will act on pure anger, brought upon by an overwhelming feeling of revenge, especially when fighting against certain enemies.*'

'Certain enemies?' Hunter asked.

'*You are a very intelligent person, son, so I know that you'll know this to be true – no country, when at war – when defending its freedom and the lives of its citizens – will one hundred percent stick to these rules. It's impossible, and I'm talking about democratic countries like the USA. Now, there are certain countries on this planet, where the oppression, the torture and the murder of their own citizens is an intrinsic part of their governing system. You know that, right?'* The old man didn't wait for a reply. *'Those countries don't give a rat's ass about any piece of paper trying to dictate how they should fight their wars. To them, international laws don't mean spit, so they fight like they fight, and let me tell you, son, they fight filthy dirty, and they make no distinction between soldiers and civilians. Sometimes, for whatever reason it may be, democratic armies fighting against these enemies may find it valid to give some of their filth back to them.'* Before continuing, Mr. Wilson paused and cleared his throat once again. *'Rape, or sexual violence, is a weapon that's frequently used by these enemies as a means of psychological warfare. They use Psy-Ops in order to humiliate their opponents. You more than anyone can understand how tremendously effective that would be, right, son?'*

Hunter could feel the pain in Mr. Wilson's voice.

'Sometimes,' the old man carried on, *'out of pure anger, our soldiers may see fit to use against them, the same psychological warfare weapons that they have used against us or our allies. Please tell me that you understand that, son?'*

'I do,' Hunter replied. He might've understood the old man's explanation, but it didn't mean that he agreed with it.

'Now, going back to your question.' Mr. Wilson paused again, this time for breath. *'In the context you mentioned, son, B-F-O-A would mean – "By Force Of Arms".'*

Hunter closed his eyes and his lips pressed against one another in a pain-stricken expression.

'What that essentially means is—'

'To achieve something by force and/or the use of weapons.'

Hunter cut Mr. Wilson short. 'In this case – rape under gun-point. I should've figured that one out.'

'*No, son, that's just it. You should not have known that. That particular abbreviation or acronym is never used. The term is always used in full and it's usually used in relation to battles and conflicts. In a personal sense, like in the sentence you've mentioned ... in respect to rape ... it would mean that the person in question did not commit rape even when ordered to.*'

Hunter now clearly understood why the old man had had to explain everything before finally getting to the definition.

Though Hunter had very little doubt of what Mr. Wilson was really alluding to, he didn't want to leave any stone unturned.

'So just to be very clear here, sir,' Hunter said gently. 'The person who has written that sentence ... you would say that the chances of him having been with the military are high.'

'*I would say that there's absolutely no doubt of that whatsoever, son. And this person, whoever he is, has seen combat – and I mean frontline combat.*'

Forty-Nine

Hunter disconnected from the call and, from his facial expression alone, Garcia could tell that he had come across something new. He waited, but Hunter stayed silent, his brain moving information around as fast as it could, trying to slot it into the correct place.

'So who was that on the phone?' Garcia asked. 'And what have we got?'

Nothing.

'Robert?' Garcia called again.

Hunter shook his thoughts away. 'Sorry.'

'Who was that on the phone?'

'Just an old friend who used to be with the military.'

'Used to be?'

'Yes, he's retired now.'

'OK, and what did he tell you? Do we know what BFOA means?'

Hunter kept it simple, giving Garcia just the definition of the acronym and what it actually meant in the context used.

'So you were right,' Garcia said, his tone troubled. 'This killer *is* with the military. That could easily complicate things.'

'*Was* with the military,' Hunter corrected his partner. 'Not *is*.'

'How would you know that?'

'Because it would explain a few things, other than just the terms he used in the diary.'

Hunter couldn't remember the exact words, so he quickly reloaded the image titled 'page 1' onto his computer screen.

'Here,' he said, indicating on the text. 'On the very first page of the diary – Elizabeth Gibbs' entry – the killer talks about his memory not being what it used to be. His exact words were – *My memory isn't so good anymore. I forget things. I forget a lot of things, and it's just getting worse. That's one of the reasons why I decided to keep this journal.*'

'Yes, I remember,' Garcia replied, pushing his chair away from his desk so he could better see Hunter.

'Maybe he'll talk a little more about his loss of memory in the pages that we're still to read,' Hunter explained. 'But judging by these few lines, especially when he mentions that he forgets *a lot of things, and it's just getting worse*, it sounds like his cognitive decline is at least moderate to severe, would you agree?'

Garcia nodded 'It sounds about right.'

'OK,' Hunter continued. 'So most clinicians who deal with cognitive decline, or dementia, use one of two scales to measure a patient's memory deterioration – the Seven Stage Model of Dementia and the Global Deterioration Scale, which is also divided into seven stages. I'm not going to bore you with long clinical explanations, but on both scales, moderately severe cognitive decline falls into stage five.' Hunter used the fingers on his right hand to emphasize his point. 'Which is quite an advanced stage in the progression of dementia and memory loss.'

Once again, Garcia agreed with a nod. 'OK.'

'But Angela told us that the person who she stole the diary from, the person who came after her in her apartment, was in his late thirties or, at a push, very early forties, no older. That's way too young for anyone to be showing signs of stage-five dementia,' Hunter explained. 'That would mean that the onset of the disease would have to have come about in his late twenties, or very early thirties. OK, it's possible,' Hunter accepted it. 'But we would be talking one in a million possibility here.'

Garcia leaned forward on his desk and rested his chin on his knuckles. 'But what if his loss of memory isn't caused by dementia?'

'Exactly.' Hunter's right index finger shot in his partner's direction. 'It probably isn't. My guess is that his memory problem comes from trauma, either blunt, psychological, or a combination of both, and if this killer has really seen frontline combat, the kind of combat where he was ordered to use rape by force of arms as a psychological weapon . . .'

'It probably means that he has not only witnessed, but also taken part in extremely harrowing action,' Garcia concluded.

'I'm sure he has,' Hunter agreed. 'And blunt or psychological trauma could easily have been a consequence of battle and the pressures thereof, not to mention post-traumatic stress disorder, which is practically guaranteed to induce memory loss, among several other problems. Either way, once back in the country after a tour of duty, every serviceman must go through a battery of physical and psychological tests. Memory loss isn't something one can simply hide, regardless of what has caused it. Once that was diagnosed . . .' Hunter's right hand moved across the front of his neck in a cut-throat gesture. ' . . . It would be the end of his military career. Whoever this killer is, he's not an active serviceman anymore.'

'It makes sense,' Garcia agreed, pulling his chair closer to his computer once again.

Hunter cupped his hands together and slowly ran them over his nose and mouth. 'I should've thought of that.'

'Thought of what?'

'PTSD,' Hunter replied. 'War trauma. If we're right about this, it could also explain the voices. It could also explain how he was able to halt them and object to their command. But what if something else is triggering those voices . . . triggering the schizophrenia?'

'Something else?' A crease came between Garcia's eyebrows as they arched. 'Now you're losing me again.'

Hunter got to his feet. 'Veterans who suffer from PTSD,' he clarified, 'can have an episode or a seizure initiated by a number of different factors – a sound, a smell, an image, an object . . . even a face that reminds them of someone can trigger it. If it's something like that that is triggering the voices in our killer's head, it could explain how come he's able to halt them and tell them "no".'

Garcia lifted a hand. 'Hold on. OK, I do get how a loud bang – the sound of a helicopter, the smell of fireworks, or something similar – could trigger an episode. In this case, the voices in our killer's head; but how does that explain him being able to halt them like you've said?'

'Because PTSD episodes triggered by external factors,' Hunter explained, 'are always directly related to a traumatic memory that the subject has lived through. Now imagine if that traumatic memory involves a superior officer, or even just someone who was in charge at the time, ordering our guy to do something he wasn't prepared to do or compromise on – like rape someone, even if "by force of arms".'

The fog began to clear for Garcia. 'So let me see if I've got this right. You're saying that if the voices in our killer's head, which could have been triggered by some external factor – if they are repeating an order that he was given while fighting, an order that he was brave enough at the time to counter, then it's understandable that he could do the same again this time around.'

'Exactly. He did it once. He can do it again.'

Garcia quickly went back to his computer and reloaded the first image in the file that Dr. Slater had sent them.

'So ... if the first victim mentioned in this diary was taken on February 3rd 2018 and we know for sure that there have been other victims before Elizabeth Gibbs, it means that we're looking for someone who is ex-military and who has returned from a tour of duty around what ... 2017? 2016?'

'Maybe even earlier,' Hunter suggested. 'Without knowing how many victims there were prior to Miss Gibbs and the timeframe between victims ...' He simply shook his head as he considered the impossible task.

Garcia looked away for an instant, as if something in the air around them was troubling him.

'You do know that we'll get no help with this, right?' he asked. 'Like you've said, servicemen are put through a battery of tests once they return from a tour of duty. If PTSD or any other psychological problem is diagnosed, the army takes care of them. They have their own doctors, their own psychiatrists, their own psychologists ... you know that. The only way for us to gather any sort of information on any ex-combatant is to approach the army itself.' Garcia chuckled. 'We do that and they won't care if this guy is a serial killer or not. Due to the fact that he's one of their own, we'll have every door slammed shut right in our faces.'

'Yes, I know that,' Hunter replied. 'But we might not need to approach the army. We don't know. We haven't got to the end of his diary yet.'

At that exact moment, a knock came at their office door.

'Come in,' Hunter called, turning to face the door.

Officer Makalsky pushed the door open, walked over to Hunter's desk and handed him the evidence bag containing the diary that he had collected from Dr. Slater.

Hunter waited until the officer had left the room before retrieving a pair of latex gloves from one of his drawers and ripping open the package.

Garcia stood up to get a better line of vision.

Hunter placed the thick, black leather book on his desk but didn't flip it open. Instead, he took a deep breath and stared at the cover.

'I guess the real fun starts now, huh?' Garcia said, nodding ever so gently.

Hunter looked back at him.

'You and I have very different concepts of what fun is.'

Fifty

With the killer's diary in hand, Hunter once again started at the beginning, but this time, instead of concentrating on the words, he turned his attention to the physical pages. He still had no idea of what he was looking for.

Using a magnifying glass and starting with the first page, Hunter carefully checked its outside edges and corners for any markings, impressions, dents, bends, tears ... anything that might seem odd or out of place.

He found nothing.

Next, he tried the internal edge of the page as it curved into the spine of the book. All he found were residues of fingerprint dusting powder. The technicians at the FSD lab had obviously been very thorough.

Despite the killer having used only the front of each page, leaving its reverse completely blank, Hunter checked it with the same determination that he had checked the first page. At the lower, internal edge of it, closer to the book's spine, he did find a couple of tiny dents on the paper, but they were just that – dents on the paper – nothing else.

Before moving on to the next page, the one with the Polaroid of Elizabeth Gibbs stapled to it, Hunter paused as he considered a new thought.

'Taking a break already?' Garcia asked.

'Not exactly,' Hunter replied, flipping the page back to where he had started.

Garcia watched attentively as his partner placed the tips of his fingers on the page and slowly began moving them from left to right, along the text line – as though he were reading Braille. Hunter moved from line to line until he got to the end of the page.

'Anything?' Garcia asked.

'Not yet.'

'This is starting to look like *National Treasure*,' Garcia joked. 'Maybe we should try some lemons and heat next.'

Hunter had begun running his fingers over the reverse of the first page. '*National Treasure*?'

'Oh, sorry,' Garcia apologized, pulling a face. 'I forgot that you barely watch any films. Yes, *National Treasure* is an old movie starring Nicolas Cage,' he explained. 'They're looking for a secret treasure and one of the clues is hidden on the reverse of the Declaration of Independence. In the film, they use lemon juice and some heat to—'

'Reveal invisible ink?' Hunter got there first.

Garcia was truly impressed. 'No way. You've seen that film?'

'Yes, I've seen that film,' Hunter admitted. 'But that information is wrong. Lemon juice is *used* as invisible ink. Not to reveal it. You never had fun writing secret codes using invisible ink when you were a kid?'

Garcia's lips stretched into a comical smile. 'You and I indeed have very different concepts of what fun is.'

'I guess we do,' Hunter accepted. 'Anyway, we won't

need lemon juice and heat. This killer hasn't used invisible ink on this.'

'How do you know?'

'Because you only use lemon juice and heat when you're a kid and you don't have the right equipment.'

Garcia's expression remained blank.

'The best prop to reveal invisible ink is UV light, Carlos,' Hunter explained. 'The same light used by forensics agents when searching for fingerprints. According to Dr. Slater, every page in this diary has already been tested for prints. If this killer had used invisible ink, someone in the FSD lab would've found it.'

'Point taken,' Garcia agreed, before returning to the text on his computer screen.

Hunter moved along to the next page, the one that had the first Polaroid photograph stapled to it. He started with the photo, but once again, he found nothing out of the ordinary – no markings, no impressions, no dents, nothing anywhere on that photo that could've suggested some sort of hidden code or information.

Hunter got to the end of the page and minutes later to the end of the entry – absolutely nothing.

Before moving on to the next diary entry, Hunter checked his watch. As the seconds rushed toward that five o'clock deadline, they seemed to be ticking faster and faster, while he seemed to be working slower and slower.

'Where are you in the diary?' he asked Garcia.

'About to start with the fourth entry, you?'

'About to begin the second one again.'

'Anything that's got you wondering? Even remotely?'

'Not yet, but it's still early in the game. There are still a lot of pages to go. What worries me is our timeframe, and the fact that I have no idea of what we're searching for here, or even if there is ...' Hunter paused and tilted his head slightly right then left, as he studied the diary from different angles.

'Everything all right?' Garcia asked.

'Yes,' Hunter replied. 'But I just had a ... crazy idea.'

Garcia chuckled. 'As if that was a first. What new crazy idea would that be?'

'Maybe there's a way that we can get to him, even if we don't find what's so important about this diary.'

Now Garcia was intrigued. 'And which way is that?'

'The diary itself,' Hunter said before clarifying. 'Maybe there's a way that we can hide some sort of tracker in this book. Maybe if we can get inside the cover without damaging it. Something that he wouldn't notice, at least not straight away.'

Garcia's entire face lit up with excitement. 'So the idea here is – at five o'clock, you follow his instructions and return the diary to him, but there's no need for a SWAT or an SIS team to tail you too closely, maybe even not at all. Then, when he thinks he's home safe ... BOOM ... we crash this sicko's party.'

'Something like that, yes,' Hunter agreed.

'Do we have any sort of tracker that we can fit into a book without it being obvious?' Garcia asked.

'Only one way to find out,' Hunter said, already reaching for the phone on his desk.

Fifty-One

The Los Angeles Police Department Electronics Unit was one of the four specialized units that comprised the LAPD Technical Investigation Division (TID). The unit's function was to provide technical investigative support for the Police Department by means of electronic surveillance devices. The vast majority of those devices were designed, constructed and modified in-house to match the nature of the investigation they were supporting, which meant that even if they didn't have a tracker device small and discreet enough to fit into the killer's diary, they could probably create one. The only problem they would have, Hunter thought, would be the ticking clock.

It had just gone ten in the morning when Vince Keller's phone rang on his desk.

The five-foot five, thirty-two-year-old head engineer for the LAPD Electronics Unit was as intelligent as he was short. With a Computer Engineering degree from UCLA and a PhD in Electrical Engineering and Computer Science from MIT, Keller had already won several awards for his electronic creations by the time he was offered the position with the Electronics Unit.

He was twenty-six back then, making him the youngest ever person to take on that role.

'Keller,' he said, as he answered his phone. 'LAPD Electronics Unit.'

'Vince, it's Detective Robert Hunter from the UVC Unit.'

Hunter and Keller had worked together on only one case, about one and a half years ago, but for some reason, which Garcia called 'the geek factor', they had become good friends.

'Hey, Robert,' Keller said in a silvery voice that sounded like it should've belonged to someone at least twenty years older. 'What's up? How have you been?'

'I'm fine,' Hunter replied. *'But I need your help with something.'* Hunter's tone was firm, which didn't bother Keller, as he knew that was the detective's style. It was the urgency in Hunter's voice that made Keller put his cup of coffee down.

'What's going on? What can I do for you?'

Hunter was brief with his explanation.

'So you need a tracker that can be hidden somewhere inside a leather-bound book?' Keller asked, once Hunter was done explaining. 'How thick would you say that the book cover is?'

'Two, maybe three millimeters, no more.'

'I don't think that will be a problem, Robert,' Keller said, reaching for his coffee once again. 'Even if we don't have something that slim and slick, we can create one. How long do we have?'

'My deadline is five o'clock this afternoon.'

'Piece of cake,' Keller said, giving himself a shrug. 'A simple tracker, one that simply sends out a location beacon, isn't a very complicated gadget to make, especially with how advanced

GPS is nowadays. If you bring the book over to me now.' He instinctively checked his watch. 'I'm sure that we can have this tracker fitted and tested by lunchtime.'

'*I'm on my way.*'

Fifty-Two

Though some field services operated out of Van Nuys Community Police Station, most of the units that comprised the LAPD Technical Investigation Division, including the Electronics Unit, operated out of the C. Erwin Piper Technical Center (Piper Tech), which was a mere four-minute drive from the Police Administration Building. Hunter and Garcia got there five and a half minutes after Hunter had disconnected from the call.

Architecturally speaking, the main building of the C. Erwin Piper Technical Center wasn't anything special to look at – an enormous, redbrick, windowless, three-story rectangular structure, considered by many to be a monstrosity, due to its uncanny resemblance to a self-storage facility. Its flat roof housed eighteen helicopter spaces and two helipads, from where the LAPD Air Support Division operated. Just past the large heliport, still on the roof of the main Piper Tech building, and accessible through a ramp on the north side of it, there was an even larger parking lot – for visitors and employees. Garcia parked his car there.

At the main building's reception lobby, despite displaying their badges, Hunter and Garcia were made to wait while one of the receptionists placed an internal call to the Electronics Unit. Even after getting the all-clear from Keller himself, the two detectives still had to wait for the head engineer to come down to get them.

The offices and labs of the TID's Electronics Unit were located on the second floor, which they reached via one of the five elevators in a squared foyer to the right of the semi-circular reception desk. After the customary greetings and the short elevator ride, Keller guided the two detectives down a wide corridor and into a room that was about half of the size of Hunter and Garcia's office, with a desk, a water dispenser, a wall-wide, floor-to-ceiling bookcase and not much else. Three large interconnected monitors took practically all of the space on the desktop. The bookcase looked like it was about to buckle under the weight of so many items – half of it was taken by books and the other half by brown cardboard boxes, the contents of which were clearly described on white labels.

'So let's have a look at this book you've told me about,' Keller said, closing the office door behind him and indicating the desk. He quickly walked over to it and moved the computer keyboard out of the way to create a little more space.

Hunter retrieved the diary from the opaque evidence bag and placed it on the desk, where the keyboard had been.

From the desk's top drawer, Keller grabbed a pair of latex gloves, slipped them on, and flipped open the diary cover. He pushed his black-framed glasses up his freckled nose and studied it through magnified eyes that were rounded with interest.

'You were right,' he said to Hunter, after a few deliberating seconds. 'The cover seems to be around three millimeters thick, no more.'

'Can it be done?' Garcia asked. 'Do you guys have a tracker that thin?'

'The tracker isn't the problem here,' Keller replied, now analyzing the inside of the cover, which was lined by a thin leather sheet instead of paper.

His professionalism was second to none. While examining the inside of the cover, not once did his eyes even peek at the diary's first page. He was asked to check if he could hide a tracker inside the book's cover. The rest of the pages and its contents were none of his or the Electronic Unit's concern.

'The problem is pulling this leather sheet from the cover and then carving out just enough room to slip in a tracker. All of that in such a way that it won't alter the look and feel of the cover.'

'Shit,' Garcia said. 'How thin a tracker do you have?'

'That depends,' Keller replied. 'How long do you need the tracker to transmit the location beacon for? Is it over twenty-four hours?'

'No, not at all.' Garcia firmly shook his head. 'We'll have a SWAT team ready to move in as soon as he's in possession of the book again.'

'Then it gets a little easier,' Keller explained. 'If the tracker doesn't need an activation button or a sizeable battery, we can come up with one that's practically paper thin. We've done it before, but the best thing for me to do right now is to try to remove this leather sheet and have a look at the flipside of the front cover. Some leather-bound books already have a hollow cover. If that's the case here and everything else goes as planned, then I'll probably be able to get everything done in two hours, maybe less.'

'Everything else goes as planned?' Garcia again. 'What everything else?'

'You said that your deadline is five o'clock this afternoon, right?'

'That's correct.'

A quick check of the watch before studying the inside of the cover once again. This time, he ran his fingers over the whole of the leather sheet.

'The internal leather sheet is glued not stitched to the cover.' Keller indicated while he spoke. 'And it looks like the glue has only been applied to the edges of the sheet, not the whole thing. If I'm right, it will make things a lot less complicated to insert a tracker. Maybe a thin but steady vapor jet will be able to melt the glue without leaving any marks on the actual cover or on the leather sheet itself. If that works, regluing the sheet back onto the cover shouldn't really pose a problem. I'll get started straight away.'

'All right,' Hunter agreed, nodding at Garcia. 'We still have quite a lot of reading to do, so we'll shoot back to the PAB. Give me a call if you run into any problems, or when you're done.'

'I certainly will.'

Fifty-Three

While Hunter and Garcia saw themselves out of the Piper Tech main building, Vince Keller took the diary down another corridor and into Electronics Lab number two. In there, he placed the book on a large wood workbench and once again flipped the front cover open. He still had his latex gloves on.

From a dispenser on the wall, he ripped a sheet of a special type of protective cling film, large enough to cover the first page of the diary. He carefully placed the cling film over the page and the rest of the book, leaving only the reverse of the front cover exposed.

From the third shelf of a metal cabinet, Keller retrieved a cordless, handheld steam gun that looked like a small kettle, with a long funnel nose and a thumb trigger.

In the bathroom, which was halfway down the corridor he had come from, Keller filled the steam gun with water and returned to the lab. In there, he placed the gun back on its cradle and switched it on before turning his attention back to the diary on the workbench. He swapped his glasses for a pair of watchmaker's magnifying glasses and had a long look at the edges of the leather sheet on the reverse of the front cover. Unless the glue used was some sort of special, hardcore, steam-resistant superglue, Keller didn't think that removing the leather sheet without damaging it would really be a problem, but he didn't want to take any chances. He ripped another piece of special cling film and placed it over the reverse of the book's front cover, this time leaving only the top edge of the leather sheet exposed.

Keller returned to the metal cabinet and picked up a medical scalpel. Behind him, the steam gun beeped on its cradle, indicating that the device was ready. Keller picked it up, repositioned himself around the workbench and brought the tip of the gun nozzle to the leftmost corner of the exposed leather sheet edge. He held it about half an inch away and slowly pressed the gun's trigger. A steady jet of steam launched out of the nozzle, heating the edge of the leather sheet and, consequently, the glue underneath it. As the glue began to dissolve, Keller very cautiously began pushing the tip of the scalpel between the sheet and the book cover. To his surprise, it took only a couple of seconds for the scalpel to penetrate.

Keller let go of the trigger, put down the steam gun, used a tissue to wipe away the condensation, and checked the leather sheet – no damage. He checked the book cover – no damage.

Maybe this would go even more smoothly than he had anticipated.

Keller returned to the steam gun and the scalpel and went back to work. Slowly and very delicately, he restarted the steam jet/scalpel process again. As the glue continued to dissolve and the scalpel penetrated between the sheet and the book cover, he edged left, millimeter by millimeter, without rushing. Three and a half minutes later, Keller had reached the spine of the book. The whole top edge of the leather sheet was now loose.

He had been correct; the diary manufacturers had used glue only at the edges of the sheet.

Keller put down the steam gun and the scalpel and wiped down the condensation from the leather sheet before removing the cling film and repositioning it, leaving only the outside edge exposed. With the steam gun and the scalpel back in his hands, he restarted the process once again, moving from the top of the book cover toward the bottom of it. In some places, the glue showed a little more resistance, so it took Keller a little longer to reach the bottom edge – six minutes and twelve seconds, to be precise.

Now Keller only had to repeat the process one more time – with the bottom edge of the leather sheet – and he would be able to flip the leather sheet open as if it were a page in the diary. He started the process once again, moving from the bottom outside edge to the inside, toward the spine of the book. Three minutes later he was done.

Keller put down the scalpel and the steam gun, wiped away the condensation and swapped his watchmaker's magnifying glasses for his regular ones.

'Now let's see if we can insert a tracker somewhere in here,' he whispered to himself, removing the special cling film from the flipside of the front cover.

As he flipped the leather sheet over, he paused and frowned.

His stare stayed on the now naked flipside of the book's front cover for several long seconds.

'What – the fuck – is this?'

Fifty-Four

Hunter and Garcia had just got back to their office when Captain Blake appeared at their door.

'It's all settled,' she said, addressing Hunter. 'A SWAT team, together with an SIS one, will be following your every move once you get the call from this freakshow. Not to mention air support. I'm not taking any chances here. Did you get the diary back from the FSD lab?'

'Yes,' Hunter replied.

'Where is it?' The captain stepped into the office and closed the door behind her.

'With the TID Electronics Unit,' came the reply from Garcia.

'The Electronics Unit?' Captain Blake's head jerked back in surprise. 'Why?'

Garcia gave her a quick explanation.

'They have a tracker thin enough to fit into the cover of a book?'

'Sounds crazy, doesn't it?' Garcia accepted it. 'Not that long ago, the only place where you would see something like that would be in the movies, in a Bond film.'

Right then Hunter's phone rang inside his jacket pocket.

'Detective Hunter,' he said as he brought the phone to his right ear. 'Ultra Violent Crimes Unit.'

'Robert, it's Vince. Are you guys back at the PAB?'

Worry immediately colored Hunter's face. It had only been around twenty minutes since they'd left the Technical Investigation Division at Piper Tech. Twenty minutes was certainly not enough time for the tracker to have already been put in place.

'Just got here, Vince. Why? Do we have a problem?'

Garcia paused what he was doing and turned to face Hunter. 'What happened?' he mouthed the words. 'What's going on?'

Hunter gestured for him to give him a second.

'I'm not sure,' Keller replied. *'But you guys need to get back here.'*

'Why?'

'Because the two of you need to come see this.'

Fifty-Five

This time, Captain Blake joined Hunter and Garcia as they rushed back to the Piper Tech building. During the short ride, Garcia told her about what they'd read in the killer's diary, the meaning of BFOA, and that, after Hunter's phone conversation with Mr. Wilson, they were now pretty confident that this killer was indeed ex-military.

'Jesus!' the captain gasped. 'That will complicate things a hell of a lot.'

'My words exactly,' Garcia replied.

At the Piper Tech building, they had to go through the same security check as before.

'We were here less than half an hour ago,' Garcia argued, his tone revealing his annoyance. 'You remember us, don't you?'

'I do,' the receptionist confirmed, as she returned her desk phone to its cradle. She was a large woman, with arms as thick as Garcia's neck. Her menacing eyes sat behind round-framed glasses. 'But those are my orders. No exceptions.' Her voice was calm and controlled. 'I'm sure as detectives you understand the importance of protocol, right? I can lose my job if I don't follow it.'

Captain Blake was about to pull rank and put an end to the argument when Vince Keller rushed out of the elevator foyer to meet them at reception. Hunter quickly introduced him to Captain Blake before Keller got them through with visitor passes.

This time, the group took the stairs instead of the lift.

'So what have you got?' Garcia asked, as they cleared the first flight of stairs up to the second floor.

'It's much easier to show you than to explain,' Keller replied, taking the steps two at a time.

As they got to the second floor, Keller guided everyone through the same corridor they'd been through before, past the small room where they'd had their meeting and into Electronics Lab number two.

As they closed the door behind them, Hunter and Garcia saw the diary sitting on top of a workbench, located toward the end of the room. Its cover was flipped open, exposing its insides together with the diary's first page. The leather sheet on the inside of the cover was still in place.

'As I've explained before,' Keller began, as everyone rounded the workbench, 'what I wanted to do was use a steam gun to melt the glue that held the leather sheet in place, so I could check how difficult it would be to insert a tracker into the cover. That part went smoothly. Within twenty minutes the job was done.'

'OK, and . . .?' Garcia asked.

Keller paused and his head angled slightly right. 'And I guess that I wasn't really expecting to find anything once I removed the leather sheet. But that wasn't quite the case.' He flipped the leather sheet, exposing the naked flipside of the front cover.

Hunter and Garcia stared at it with confused eyes.

'What the fuck?' Garcia craned his neck to get a better view.

Handwritten onto the inside of the front cover, previously hidden by the leather sheet, were four lines of text, all of them showing a strange combination of letters and numbers. The handwriting was identical to that in the diary pages.

3g2uptkl78pq6kufa9m
DOPS1207102375
122001FOBRhino
15052004MNF-I

'What the hell are those?' Garcia asked.

'That's the million-dollar question,' Keller replied, leaning shoulder-first against the wall.

'Those aren't coordinates again, are they?' Captain Blake asked Hunter, who shook his head decisively.

'Coordinates?' Keller asked, skeptically.

'Something that had come up as part of this investigation,' Hunter replied, not wanting to share too many details.

'So what do you think these are?' Captain Blake pushed, the question now thrown at everyone.

Garcia was the first to shake his head and shrug.

The captain fixed Hunter with one of her laser stares.

'If I had to venture a guess,' he said, the look on his face lacking confidence, 'I'd say that they're codes to something, but that's not really the point here. Whatever these are – this is it.' He stabbed his index finger onto the workbench. 'This is the reason why this killer wants his diary back so badly. He needs these. Whatever it is that they are – code words, passwords, coordinates, or whatever – he needs them back.'

While everyone's attention returned to the four mysterious lines of text, Hunter took out his smartphone and snapped a photo of them.

'Hold on a second,' Keller said, lifting his right index finger. 'Do you mind if I try something?'

'Try what?' Captain Blake questioned.

'The very first line,' Keller explained, 'is distinctively different from the other three.'

Once again, everyone reconsidered the cryptic text.

'It only uses lowercase letters,' Keller clarified. 'And it's also the only one out of the four lines of text where the numbers appear to split a letter sequence.' He quickly grabbed a pad of paper and copied the first line.

'OK, I see what you mean,' Captain Blake agreed. 'But what is it that you want to try?'

'Well,' Keller replied, urging everyone to follow him. 'This is a long shot . . .'

He led the group back out into the corridor before guiding everyone into the small room he, Hunter, and Garcia were in before.

'I've seen and used similar text lines before,' Keller said, positioning himself behind the desk and hitting the spacebar on the keyboard to wake up all three monitors.

'Where?' This time the question came from Hunter.

'On the Internet,' Keller replied, as he waited for an application to load onto the screens. 'This line right here . . .' He placed the notepad on the desk. '. . . could very well be a web address. All it's missing is a suffix.'

'A web address?' Garcia's puzzled eyes jumped from Keller to Hunter to Captain Blake and then back to Keller. 'Aren't there supposed to be a few dots somewhere in there?'

'No,' Keller countered. 'This wouldn't be your regular web address. Not your regular Internet.'

'The Dark Web,' Hunter said as a Tor browser appeared on Keller's computer screen.

'That's exactly right,' Keller agreed.

He turned to address the captain. 'And that's what I want to try. All I have to do is copy that line of text to the address bar and add a "dot onion" to the end of it. It's the suffix used by the darknet. Instead of dot com, or dot org, or whatever, they use dot onion.'

They all watched as Keller entered the first line of text that he had copied from the diary's cover into the address bar. He then added the known Dark Web suffix to it and hit the 'enter' key.

It took the Tor browser considerably longer than a regular one to load a web page onto the three interconnected monitors on Keller's desk, but it did.

'Bingo,' Keller said with a smile. 'It is a Dark Web page.'

Immediately as the site loaded, a pop-up appeared over it, asking for a login password.

Everyone exchanged concerned looks.

'Let me see that photo you took,' Keller addressed Hunter.

Hunter pulled out his phone and showed Keller the photo.

'Maybe one of these is the password,' Keller suggested.

'Maybe,' Hunter agreed. 'But to what?'

'It could be anything,' Keller replied with a quick shrug. 'A database ... a private forum ... who knows?'

'Only one way to find out,' Captain Blake joined in.

'Shall I give it a try?' Keller asked Hunter.

Hunter pondered over it for just a second. 'Sure.'

Keller typed in the second of the four lines of text into the password text-field.

'DOPS1207102375'

As soon as he hit the 'enter' button, an egg-timer icon appeared over the pop-up. A second later, a message was displayed – 'login successful'.

'We're in,' Keller announced, sounding half-surprised.

The pop-up disappeared from the screen, revealing the Dark Web site behind it.

All four of them paused, trying to understand what they were really looking at.

'What the hell is this?' Captain Blake asked the question that everyone was thinking.

'I'm not really sure,' Hunter replied.

It took him a couple more seconds to realize what he was really looking at.

That was when something new appeared on the left side of the screen.

'You have got to be kidding me.' The words dribbled out of Hunter's lips. 'This can't be real.'

Then something else appeared on the screen, also on the left side.

Garcia's arms dropped to his sides and he felt his heart sink to the bottom of his stomach.

'Oh . . . fuck!'

Fifty-Six

The man had no doubt that his plan would work. No more preparation was needed, and that was why he could afford to spend the morning sitting in front of the large wall monitor, inside the control room in the basement of the old building in Santa Clarita. For the past hour and a half, he'd done nothing but observe the three subjects he had locked up in the cells just down the corridor from where he was sitting. He could quite easily spend days studying whomever he had in those cells, as if he was bingeing on some addictive real-life TV series.

The man typed a command into the keyboard on the control desk in front of him and the image on the screen switched from cell 1 to cell 2.

It didn't take an expert to see that the male subject in cell 2 was beginning to get agitated again. He had moved out of his prayer position, a position that he had held for almost forty minutes, and begun pacing his cell.

Pacing the cells was something that every subject eventually did. Sometimes they did it for exercise, sometimes out of fear, and sometimes out of anger and frustration. For the man, recognizing the difference between the three pacing styles was easy.

A subject pacing for exercise walked with a steady and determined step. There were no distractions ... no interruptions. The subject either moved from the cell door to the bed, or from wall to wall, always in a continuous loop, until the subject had had enough. Some could do it for hours. Push-ups, sit-ups and squats were also common.

A subject pacing the cell out of fear walked with a very unsteady rhythm. The steps were tentative and the walking loop would be constantly interrupted, most of the time by tears.

Finally, a subject pacing out of anger and frustration followed a more distinct pattern, the steps were a lot heavier. The loop was also inconsistent, full of interruptions. Some subjects would, every now and then, punch and kick either the walls or the bed. Some would also scream at the top of their lungs, but they would do that only once and then never again. The cells were equipped with a noise meter. If the noise inside any cell went beyond sixty decibels (about as loud as two people having a conversation), two ceiling sprinklers would drench the cell, and consequently the subject, in ice-cold water.

The subject in cell number two was pacing it with heavy, angry steps, while murmuring something to himself.

The subject had been there for only two days, but he hadn't been abducted because the voices had commanded the man to do so. No, he had been abducted because the man needed him for his plan.

The man sat back in his chair, swung his feet onto the control desk, and interlaced his fingers behind his head. He enjoyed watching his subjects' reactions.

'Humans are so predictable,' he said out loud, as the subject punched the pillow on the bed a few times.

All of a sudden, a beep came from the metal cabinet to the right of the control desk.

The man's eyes shot to it and he frowned. A second later, his feet came back to the ground and he dragged his chair closer to the unit.

The beep continued.

The man hit the spacebar on the laptop on the second shelf of the unit to wake it up.

The beep persisted.

The laptop screen came to life and the man stared at it for several long seconds before an animated smile stretched his lips.

'Well, hello there,' he said in a lively voice. 'I was wondering when you would show up again.' The man checked the computer screen, waiting for the information to load. As it did, his smile became laughter.

Fifty-Seven

Inside Vince Keller's office, four pairs of eyes were completely glued to the three screens on his desk.

The look on Hunter and Garcia's faces were a combination of astonishment and perhaps a little fear.

'You all know what this is, right?' Keller asked, his gaze moving from face to face inside the room. He got no reply. 'It's a chat room. One of those old-style ones. Remember ICQ? AOL? This is pretty much the same, the only real difference here is that this one is a private chat room.'

Keller was right. What had appeared on his computer screens looked exactly like an old-style chat room, displaying two panels. The large one on the right would display the contents of the conversation between the chat-room participants. The one on the left displayed the names, or in this case the aliases, of said participants. As the chat room loaded onto Keller's screens, only one alias appeared at the top of the left-hand panel – Miles Sitrom – which represented them, but almost immediately two new participants joined the chat. The aliases for those were – 'Voice 1' and 'Voice 2'.

Hunter's stomach knotted. He had been right about the

voices. They were real people and not the distorted creation of a schizophrenic mind.

His and Garcia's eyes stayed on the screen.

'Are you guys all right?' Keller asked. 'You look like you've seen a couple of ghosts.'

All of a sudden, a line of text appeared at the top of the right-side panel.

Voice 1 – This is a surprise, Miles Sitrom. Wasn't expecting to hear from you so soon. Not for a few days, at least. Have you already acquired the subject we've requested?

'Fuck, fuck, fuck.' That was all Garcia could come up with right then. His eyes shot to Hunter, whose stare was still on the screens.

A new line of text appeared in the right-hand panel.

Voice 2 – Miles Sitrom? Are you there?

'Oh shit,' Garcia said, his hand cupping over his nose and mouth. 'What do we do?' he asked Hunter.

Hunter knew that if they didn't reply, whoever 'Voice 1' and 'Voice 2' were would immediately know that they weren't talking to the real Miles Sitrom. The consequences of that were unknown to him, but it didn't take a clairvoyant to predict that they wouldn't be good.

Hunter's thought process went from zero to sixty in half a second. His hands shot toward the keyboard on the desk.

'You're going to reply?' Garcia asked, his eyes the size of two giant marbles.

Hunter paused for a second before his fingers began typing. He could feel his heart hammering against the inside of his chest.

Yes, I'm here, he typed. *And no, I haven't acquired the subject yet.*

Everyone read Hunter's reply on the screen before their full attention moved to him.

Hunter had to think fast. He knew that he couldn't just leave it there. He needed to explain himself before the next question came.

'Can this computer be traced?' he asked Keller, who frowned at him. 'The IP address of this computer,' Hunter explained. 'Can it be traced from their side?'

'No,' Keller replied. 'Our firewalls scramble the IP address. And we're also using the Dark Web. No chance of tracing.'

That was exactly what Hunter needed to hear. He began typing again.

My original computer has been damaged. I have a new machine and I'm just reinstalling software, like the Tor browser. This was just a trial run to make sure that everything is running smoothly.

Garcia's head tilted slightly right as he nodded. 'Good thinking.'

'But will they buy it?' Hunter said, his tone nervous.

He was about to type something else and then disconnect when a new line of text appeared on the screen.

Voice 1 – What happened to your computer?

All eyes moved back to Hunter.

Water damage, he typed. *No coming back from it.*

There was a two-second gap before Hunter's fingers began moving on the keyboard again.

I'll be back in touch soon.

Hunter looked at Keller. 'How do I log out of the chat room?'

Keller's hands shot toward the keyboard and he simply shut down the Tor browser.

'That's it,' he said. 'We've disconnected.'

Captain Blake looked at Keller with a question in her eyes.

'The Tor browser does not retain a browsing history,' Keller explained. 'And it automatically erases every cookie that might've been placed in the computer throughout the session, which is also terminated as soon as we close the browser.'

Hunter's arms dropped heavily to his sides, as if all of his energy had just been sucked out of him.

'This is totally insane,' Garcia said, taking a step back.

'Hold on,' Captain Blake said, lifting a finger. 'Does this mean—'

'It means that we were wrong, Captain,' Hunter cut her short.

'Wrong about what?'

'Almost everything,' Hunter replied. 'Our killer is certainly a psychopath, but he's not schizophrenic, like we first believed.' Despite the chat room not being on the screens anymore, Hunter pointed to them. 'He's not hearing voices in his head. He's talking to them via a Dark Web chat room. The voices he refers to in his diary are actually other people.' He paused, as if he needed time to recompose himself and his thoughts. 'Other people who are requesting murders . . . specific murders. Our killer isn't crazy, or delusional. He's a mercenary . . . a death salesman. And the voices – they aren't a manifestation of his subconscious mind. They are buyers. They are his online customers.'

'Buying what exactly?' Captain Blake asked. 'It's not like this killer delivers the victims to these buyers, so what is he delivering?'

That was when another piece of the new puzzle finally slot into place for Hunter. 'Images.'

Everyone turned to face him.

'The camera we found inside the coffin in Deukmejian Wilderness Park,' he said, mainly addressing Garcia and the captain. 'The killer wasn't filming it for himself. He was streaming it live so that the people behind the voices, however many there were, could watch. That's what he does. That's what he's selling. That's what he's delivering – live streams of torture and death. The people behind the voices are ordering their specific sick pleasures online. They tell him what the victim should look like, how the victim should be dressed and what-have-you. They tell him what they would like him to do to them – how to torture them and, ultimately, how to murder them. And who better to deliver these people their torturous, sadistic fantasies than a ...' Hunter paused again. 'Sonofabitch!' He shook his head and let out a humorless chuckle. 'But of course,' he said as realization settled in. 'The alias.' He turned to face Keller. 'Do you have a piece of paper and a pen?'

'Sure,' Keller quickly handed Hunter both.

Hunter wrote the alias down before explaining. 'Miles Sitrom – the first word isn't pronounced Miles, it's pronounced "me-les". Hunter's pronunciation changed completely. 'And the second word – Sitrom – it's "mortis" spelled backwards. It's Latin. Miles Mortis means "Soldier of Death".'

Fifty-Eight

The air inside Vince Keller's already claustrophobic office seemed to have become even heavier and harder to breathe. Garcia and Captain Blake's eyes stayed on Hunter as they mulled over his words.

'You can't really be serious?' Captain Blake asked, her eyes wide.

'He's correct,' Keller confirmed, nodding ever so slightly. 'Miles Mortis does mean "Soldier of Death" in Latin.'

'Sonofabitch!' Garcia spit the word out. 'I guess this confirms the ex-military question once and for all.'

Keller frowned at him, but kept the question at the tip of his tongue to himself.

'How about the other two lines of text on the diary's cover,' Captain Blake asked. 'Are they also Dark Web sites?'

'I don't believe they are,' Keller replied. 'The configuration of letters and numbers seems wrong.'

'Well,' the captain pushed. 'Can we give it a spin just to be sure?'

'Of course.' Keller confirmed. He addressed Hunter. 'Can I see that photo you took of the cover again?'

Hunter handed his phone to Keller, who reopened his Tor

browser and quickly typed the third line of text from the diary's cover into the browser's address bar. He added a '.onion' suffix to the end of it and hit the 'enter' key.

This time the new page loaded in the blink of an eye. It was an error page.

'Unable to connect'.

'Nope,' Keller said before repeating what he'd just done, now using the fourth and last line of text from the diary's cover.

The same error page reloaded onto his screen.

'Unable to connect'.

'Like I thought,' Keller said. 'These aren't web addresses.'

'So what the hell are they?' Captain Blake asked. The irritation in her voice was undeniable.

Hunter turned to face Keller as, all of a sudden, a new piece of the puzzle fell into place.

'On the Dark Web,' he said, 'the currency used is Bitcoins, right?'

'Yes, that's correct,' Keller confirmed.

Hunter's eyes moved to his cellphone, which was still on Keller's desk.

Keller's stare followed Hunter's and his face lit up. He knew exactly what Hunter was about to suggest.

'Those two lines of text,' he asked. 'Could they be Bitcoin accounts? Or passwords to accounts?'

'They certainly could,' Keller confirmed, a ghost of a smile dancing around his lips. 'And if your theory about this guy selling murders on the Dark Web is right, it does make a hell of a lot of sense.'

'Can we track them?' Captain Blake asked. 'These Bitcoin accounts?'

'Not at all,' Keller replied. 'If these are passwords to access an account or accounts, there's no way we can track those accounts. Even if these were account numbers, we still wouldn't be able to do anything. The whole reason for the Dark Web is anonymity. We could have his account and password, we could log in to it and we still wouldn't get a name. Bitcoin accounts are not regular bank accounts.'

Captain Blake was about to ask something else when Hunter stopped her with a hand gesture.

'Captain,' he said, his voice urgent but non-aggressive. 'We can go over all this and whatever else you like once we get back to the PAB, but right now we need to figure out what to do about the diary. Yes, we have found out why this killer wants his diary back so badly, but that doesn't change the fact that he'll still call me at five o'clock today with instructions on how to deliver the book back to him.'

'The tracker is still a good idea,' Keller said, bringing everyone's eyes to him. 'I'm sorry.' His hands signaled surrender. 'I know I'm not part of the investigation, but if I may say so . . . if we can fit a tracker into his diary, which I think I can, I do believe that you stand a great chance of getting this guy . . . whoever he is. Nothing really changes from the original plan, except that instead of placing a tracker inside the front cover, I'll do it to the back one.'

No one in that room really needed any convincing.

'I'm fine with that,' Captain Blake said.

'I agree,' Hunter joined in. 'We have no reason to change our plan, unless—'

'Unless we find something else hidden in the back cover,' Garcia said, anticipating what Hunter was about to say.

'Let's go find out, shall we?' Keller said, gesturing toward the door.

Fifty-Nine

All four of them rushed back to Electronics Lab number two. In there, Keller carefully set the internal leather sheet of the front cover back to its original place, without reapplying any glue. He would do that later. Right then, his main concern was to have a look at the back cover. He removed the cling film sheet that was covering the diary and flipped the book to the last page, exposing the inside of the back cover and an identical leather sheet to the one he'd just dealt with. He switched the steam gun back on and, while he waited for it to heat up, he covered the body of the diary with another sheet of protective cling film.

'This could take about twenty minutes,' he announced to the group. 'Maybe more.'

'Anything we can do to help?' Hunter asked.

'Unfortunately no, not really.'

'Well, I'm staying,' Garcia said, rounding the workbench to the other side. 'This back-and-forth fuss between here and the PAB is tedious, and though I do want to go through all the entries in the diary, the rush to find why this killer wanted his diary back so badly is over.'

Hunter agreed with a nod.

'Is there a coffee machine somewhere around here?' Captain Blake asked.

'Yes, sure,' Keller replied, as he once again swapped his glasses for the watchmaker's magnifying ones. 'Go to the end of the corridor and turn right. You'll see it.'

'I'll help,' Garcia said, as Captain Blake got to the door. 'You want anything?' he asked Hunter, who shook his head. 'Vince?'

'I'm fine, thanks.'

As Garcia and Captain Blake left the room, the steam gun beeped behind Keller. He reached for it, grabbed the scalpel and started with the top right-hand corner of the leather sheet – the outside corner.

'Do you think they bought it?' Keller asked Hunter. 'I mean, the story about the water damage and reinstalling software?'

'I don't know,' Hunter replied. 'But I could think of nothing else.'

'It was a good response,' Keller agreed. 'But my concern is . . . and once again, I'm sorry for butting into something that I probably shouldn't, but what if they, whoever the "voices" are, try to contact Miles Sitrom, whoever he is, just for confirmation?'

'It's a risk,' Hunter admitted it. 'But I don't think they would.'

'How come?'

'I'm willing to bet that that chat room is the only way they can contact each other,' Hunter explained. 'Because it's in the interest of both parties to remain completely anonymous.'

'That's true,' Keller agreed.

'Once we logged in,' Hunter continued. 'The voices did say that they weren't expecting to hear from our killer yet, probably because they understand that their request, whatever that was, will take the killer a few days to acquire.'

'What kind of request?'

Hunter breathed out. 'Victims that match a specific profile.'

Keller paused and looked at Hunter through over-magnified eyes.

'The real killer himself is busy not only searching for this new subject, but he also has the lost diary problem to deal with, so I'm pretty sure that he won't be contacting the voices for a few days.'

'And if this tracker trick works,' Keller said. 'You won't need a few days.'

'That's the hope,' Hunter agreed.

Garcia and Captain Blake came back into the lab. By then, Keller had managed to melt just about an inch and a half of glue.

'So how's it going?' Captain Blake asked.

'I don't think that we're going to find any secret hidden in the back cover,' Keller replied, without looking up.

'Why is that?' Garcia asked, approaching the workbench.

'The glue on the front cover,' Keller confirmed. 'It dissolved a lot faster than this one, which did get me wondering earlier. What it tells me is that the glue on the front cover was tampered with before, as we now know it has, but the sheet on the back cover is showing a lot more resistance, indicating that it's still factory standard. It hasn't been messed with.'

'That's a good thing, right?' Captain Blake asked.

'Presumably. Let's wait and see.'

It took Keller twenty-nine minutes to finally dissolve the glue that held the leather sheet to the back cover. When he at last flipped the sheet over, everyone breathed out a sigh of relief. Just like Keller had predicted, there was nothing on the back cover.

In silence, Keller studied the cover for a full minute.

Everyone waited.

'I don't think we're going to have a problem,' Keller finally announced. 'I just need to carve a sliver off the cover and I'm very confident that I can insert an activated twenty-four-hour tracker in here seamlessly. You'd be able to run your hand over the inside of the back cover and you wouldn't notice a thing.'

'How long do you need?' Captain Blake asked.

'About half an hour to create the tracker,' Keller replied. 'Then maybe another half an hour to re-glue both cover sheets back in place, but . . .' He lifted a finger, halting everyone. 'For this tracker to be paper-thin, it needs to not have an activation button, or a battery that needs to hold power for more than twenty-four hours.' Keller nodded at Hunter and Garcia.

'Yes, sure,' Garcia agreed.

'Also,' Keller continued. 'Due to how thin this tracker will be, it will have limited strength. If whoever you're tracking takes the Metro, or enters a building and goes underground more than one sublevel, the signal will be interrupted.'

'Understood,' Hunter said.

'So,' Keller carried on. 'If there's no other urgent need for the diary right now and this killer will only give you instructions on how to hand it back to him at five o'clock this afternoon, may I suggest that we wait until maybe three or four before activating the tracker.' He checked his watch. It was coming up to 1:00 p.m. 'If we activate it in an hour's time, when I'm done creating the tracker, we'll be throwing a few precious hours away.'

'Good point,' Captain Blake agreed.

'I can re-glue the sheet to the front cover now to gain time,' Keller said. 'As well as start on the tracker, but maybe I should wait until four this afternoon to activate it, put it in place and seal the cover.'

'It's your call, Robert,' Captain Blake said. 'You're the one who's going to have to take his call and deal with this piece of shit's instructions.'

'Are you sure that if you activate the tracker around four this afternoon, you'll have enough time to seal it in place seamlessly?' Hunter asked Keller.

'I'm positive.'

'All right. Do what you need to do.'

Sixty

Once they all got back to the Police Administration Building, Captain Blake returned to her office and Hunter and Garcia went back to their desks and the diary entries.

Though there seemed to be no more need to search for the reason why this killer wanted his diary back so badly, Hunter continued to read everything in the diary slowly and very carefully, still trying to read between the lines. Maybe they now knew why the diary was so important to him, but the text entries could still reveal valuable information concerning the killer's identity, a location, or maybe even who 'the voices' were.

The seconds ticked away, and the more they read, the more shocked they became. All those murders – the barbarism, the sadism, the grotesqueness of everything ... all of it – wasn't down to a psychopathic maniac on a serial murder rampage. This was barbarism, unimaginable pain, sadism and grotesqueness on demand. These victims were being murdered simply because some people wanted to see it happen ... because they wanted their sick fantasies to become a reality.

'Do you know what?' Garcia said from his desk, interrupting Hunter's angry thoughts. 'I don't even know who I'd like to get my hands on the most right now. I don't know if it's this sack-of-shit mercenary killer or if it's the waste-of-space, spineless assholes who request and pay for these murders to happen. So these weird fucks have these sick fantasies in their heads, but they don't even have the guts to live them themselves. They pay someone else to do their dirty work for them and then sit at home in front of a computer screen, watching the result and probably playing with themselves.'

'Maybe you're right,' Hunter agreed. 'Maybe that's why they do it, or maybe they're just being smart and covering their tracks. They are not taking any risks here. If anybody is going to get caught, it will be the killer himself, not them. They're ghosts in cyberspace, Carlos. Unidentifiable. Probably not even the killer knows who they are.'

Garcia breathed out anger.

'Or maybe their fetish,' Hunter continued, '. . . their fantasy, really is to just watch, not to take part. Believe it or not, that is a thing.'

'Still,' Garcia said, with an irritated shake of the head. 'They are just as guilty as the killer.'

'There's no doubt about that,' Hunter agreed.

Garcia slumped back into his seat, his posture defeated. 'This world has lost its head. It has lost its sense . . . its dignity.' He shook his head dismissively. 'This isn't a videogame, you know? This is real life . . . real people.'

Hunter stayed quiet, but he couldn't disagree with his partner. The only difference was, he had come to the conclusion that humanity had lost its sense a long time ago.

After a short break, both detectives went back to the diary. To Hunter, it seemed that with each new entry he read the level of violence and sadism went up a step. This killer's victims had been subjected to some of the most horrific torture methods and deaths imaginable. There were mutilations, decapitations, ancient torture techniques and instruments – which the killer had to craft out of wood and metal himself – dismemberments, burned alive, eaten by hungry rats, and more. Just like with the first two entries, most of the new ones ended with specific longitude and latitude coordinates to where the victim's remains had been buried. With two of them, their remains had been dropped into the ocean and would no doubt be lost forever. A third victim, a twenty-two-year-old student from UCLA, had her remains cremated and the ashes flushed down a toilet. Hunter and Garcia would have to inform her parents of that.

'I feel sick,' Garcia said, as he finished reading another entry. 'I literally feel sick to my stomach.' He stood up and placed a hand against the top of his chest while wincing. 'Which entry are you on?'

'Just finished number ten,' he replied. 'Six more to go. You?'

'One less than you. Did you find anything?' Garcia asked, knowing that Hunter had been doing his 'reading between the lines' thing. 'Any hint of a clue that could point us in any direction?'

Hunter's shake of the head was slow and considered. 'Nothing. If the people behind the voices in that chat room covered their tracks by being totally anonymous, the killer has covered his tracks by being extremely careful with what he wrote.'

'This thing with the tracker in the diary,' Garcia said, now massaging his chest. 'It's got to work. We need to stop this guy.'

Hunter nodded in silence, because he feared the same thing. If their plan with the tracker in the diary didn't work, Hunter was sure that they would never hear from this killer again. He and the voices would certainly dissolve the Dark Web chat room they saw earlier and simply create another one with a different web address – problem solved. The killer could also change cities – go to another metropolis like Chicago, New York, Dallas, wherever, because the city in which he operated had no bearing on the final result of what he did. He could find victims anywhere.

'I need to go get something with sugar in it,' Garcia said, still struggling with the sick feeling crawling up his throat. 'A Dr. Pepper or something. Would you like anything?'

'I'm OK,' Hunter replied. 'Thank you.'

As if on cue, just as Garcia stepped out of the office, Hunter's cellphone rang inside his jacket pocket.

'Detective Hunter,' he said, bringing the phone to his ear. 'UVC Unit.'

'*Hey there,*' a young female voice said. '*How's it going?*'

It took Hunter's brain a couple of seconds for it to finally match the voice to a face. As he did, worry came over him like a shroud.

'Angela?' he asked, his voice full of apprehension.

'*Yes, who did you think it was?*' Angela's voice, on the other hand, sounded bored. '*I just wanted to check what time you'll be dropping by with the tablet you promised me?*'

'Hold on a second. How are you calling me?' Hunter asked. 'Whose phone are you using?

'*Well . . . mine, of course.*'

'How are you using your phone when you gave me your SIM card?' On reflex, Hunter's hand shot into his right jacket pocket. It found nothing.

'*Well . . . I did hand it to you . . . but I took it back.*'

'What? When?' His fingers were still rummaging his pocket for the SIM card.

'*When we were sitting outside in the backyard. I was smoking a cigarette, remember?*'

Hunter could barely believe what he was hearing.

'Why would you do that? Didn't you hear or understand why I asked you for your SIM card? This killer could be tracking you right now. You need to end this call, and you need to do it now.' Hunter paused for a second. He knew he should've taken the phone instead of the SIM card. He cursed himself under his breath.

'*Yes, of course I understood why you did it, but c'mon, we talked about this. This guy isn't 007. Tracking a stranger's phone isn't that simple. Plus, I'm being guarded by "the best of the best" – your words, not mine – and I don't think this guy has a death wish or the desire to rot in prison. He's not going to simply turn up at an LAPD safehouse just like that, is he? Anyway, take a chill pill; I haven't been on the phone for long. I just needed a couple of songs to help me start the day. I need my motivational music or I don't even get out of bed.*'

'Music?' Hunter jumped to his feet. 'Angela, when did you put your SIM card back into your phone?'

'*Earlier this morning. Once I woke up. And it was to listen to just two songs. Not even ten minutes of streaming.*'

'Jesus Christ, Angela.'

'All right. All right. I'll take the SIM card out again. Just don't forget the tablet, will you?'

Right then, just before Angela disconnected, a distant sound came through on Hunter's earpiece that sent horror tumbling down his spine. It sounded like a doorbell.

'What was that?' Hunter asked, worry coating every word – but it was too late. The next thing he heard was the sound of the line going dead.

Sixty-One

Garcia pulled open the door to the UVC Unit office just a fraction of a second before Angela had disconnected from her call to Hunter. As he entered the room, he brought his can of Dr. Pepper to his lips and had another long sip.

'No don't hang up ...' Hunter almost shouted down his phone. 'Angela ...? Angela ...?' He looked at the display screen again. The call had ended.

'You were calling Angela?' Garcia asked, chuckling as he got to his desk. 'She's still giving you attitude, huh? That girl needs to learn some manners.'

Garcia's words hit a wall on Hunter. He was way too busy going into his recent calls list and pressing the call-back button. He brought the phone back to his ear and waited.

'*The person you have called is temporarily unavailable,*' a recorded voice said, indicating that Angela had turned off her phone.

Hunter quickly searched his contacts for the phone numbers of the two SIS agents. He called Martin first. The phone rang once ... twice ... five times before Martin's voice mail picked it up. Hunter left an urgent 'call me back' message and disconnected. Then he dialed Jordan's number and got exactly the same result.

'You have got to be kidding me,' he said, before once again leaving an urgent 'call me back' message.

'What the hell is going on, Robert?' Garcia asked.

Hunter quickly explained the conversation he'd just had with Angela.

'Are you sure that what you heard was a doorbell?' Garcia asked.

'That's what it sounded like.'

'But it could've been something else?' Garcia pushed.

'Yes,' Hunter replied. 'It could've, but then why isn't anyone answering their phones?'

Garcia had no answer.

Hunter tried Angela's phone one more time and got the same recorded message as before.

Martin's phone – voicemail

Jordan's phone – voicemail.

Again, all three – same result.

'This can't be happening,' he said, as he checked his watch – it was nearly one thirty in the afternoon. He reached for his jacket.

'Where are you going?' Garcia asked.

'To the safe house.'

Garcia checked his watch. 'Where is the safe house again? Calabasas?'

'Yes.'

'If we're lucky with traffic, that's about an hour's drive each way,' Garcia said. 'That means we might only be getting back here for around four o'clock. Don't you think that's cutting it a little too fine? We can call the Sheriff's Department in Malibu and ask them to dispatch a unit to the house. They can be there in ten, fifteen minutes.'

'I know,' Hunter replied, moving toward the door and already calling Shannon Hatcher. 'We're doing that too.'

Sixty-Two

Hunter knew Garcia was right. A simple call to the Sheriff's Department in Malibu, whose jurisdiction the incorporated city of Calabasas fell under, would get a black-and-white unit immediately dispatched to the safe house. With traffic in Calabasas being nothing compared to LA, the unit wouldn't take longer than ten minutes to make the journey. That meant that Hunter would have a reply in fifteen minutes, tops, but he was trying to be as practical as possible. Those fifteen minutes could be spent either sitting inside the office, waiting in agonizing anticipation, or gaining time by making a move toward the safe house in case his worst fears were confirmed.

The fact that neither SIS agent had answered their phones in the past five minutes sent fear into every atom of Hunter's body. The SIS Witness Protection Protocol Rulebook was clear – the agent or agents guarding a witness needed to be reachable 24/7. If they failed to answer a call at any time of day or night, alarm bells would start ringing everywhere. In the case of both agents in a two-strong team failing to pick up their cellphones more than once, those alarm bells would ring louder than a bomb-attack siren.

As he left his office, Hunter called dispatch and asked them to connect him to the Sheriff's Department in Malibu. He spoke directly to the Deputy Sheriff, asking him to please send a patrol car to the safehouse address for a Code 3 and a possible Code 6 – Emergency Call, coupled with a possible Out-of-car Investigation.

As Hunter jumped into the passenger's seat of Garcia's car, he tried calling the SIS agents one more time.

'Still nothing?' Garcia asked.

Hunter gave him a single shake of the head.

Something was wrong. Something was very wrong.

Sixty-Three

Sergeant David Brooks and Corporal Sergio Rivera had just finished devouring a large Toscana Spicy pizza when the call came through on their radio for an LAPD Assist. The request was for an extreme cautious Code 6 at an address that was less than six minutes away from their current location.

'Dispatch,' Sergeant Brooks said into the radio's mouthpiece. 'This is unit two-three-eight. We're about five minutes away. We'll take it.'

As Brooks and Rivera jumped back into their Ford Escape, dispatch gave the sergeant all the necessary information. With sirens blasting, Corporal Rivera, who had taken the wheel, swerved right into Paul Revere Drive and stepped on the gas, bringing the black-and-white SUV to 65mph in a 35mph residential area. At that speed and with their sirens clearing the way, they covered the short distance between the pizza parlor and the safe-house address in less than four minutes. As they reached the top of the road, Corporal Rivera slowed his car down to a crawl and switched off the siren.

The dead-end road that they found themselves in wasn't long – four houses in total, three on the left-hand side and one on the right. The house they were looking for was the last one on the left. Right from the top of the road, they could see a black Cadillac ATS parked directly in front of the house.

'That's the SIS agents' car,' Sergeant Brooks said, indicating with his left hand. 'Which means that they should be in.'

'Which means that they should have answered their phones,' Corporal Rivera replied.

The sergeant nodded his agreement.

The corporal parked his vehicle right behind the agents' car, but he did it in such a way that it partially blocked the Cadillac's escape route, should it need one.

'OK,' Sergeant Brooks said. 'Let's go check the house.'

Both officers stepped out of the car and very cautiously approached the house. As they walked past the agents' car, the corporal cupped a hand against the driver's window and looked inside. Everything seemed to be in order.

From the driveway, Sergeant Brooks studied the front of the house. The single front window was almost completely obstructed by the tall foliage from the front garden, but he could still tell that the curtains were drawn shut. That was when he noticed the front door. It was ajar.

'Door is open,' he announced, immediately unclipping the security belt on his weapon holster.

That's never a good sign, Corporal Rivera thought, following suit.

Both officers drew their weapons and approached the front door. Sergeant Brooks took position to the left of it and Corporal Rivera to the right.

The sergeant rang the doorbell before shouting from the outside. 'Is there anybody in the house? This is the Sheriff's Department.'

No reply.

He rang the doorbell one more time and called again. 'Hello . . . is there anybody in this house? This is the Sheriff's Department.'

No reply.

The sergeant slowly pushed the door open. Dispatch had given him the names of both SIS agents.

'SIS Agents James Martin and Darnel Jordan,' he called, his voice loud and firm. 'This is the Malibu Sheriff's Department. We are entering the house. Please acknowledge if any of you are inside.'

Dead silence.

Sergeant Brooks nodded at Corporal Rivera who, in a very well-rehearsed move, fast-rotated his body 180 degrees to the right, placing him at the open door. His arms were extended in front of him and his Smith & Wesson M&P9 pistol held in a firm double-hand grip. His eyes, which guided his aim, immediately moved right.

A fraction of a second later, Sergeant Brooks repeated the same 180 degrees rotation, his body rotating left. His weapon, a Glock 21 Gen 3, also held in a double grip, followed his eyes and aimed left, both officers searching for any signs of danger.

They didn't find danger.

They found something a lot worse.

Sixty-Four

By the time Hunter and Garcia got to the green-fronted house in Calabasas, forty-nine minutes after they'd left their office, the street was already crawling with Sheriff's Department personnel. Four new cruisers had arrived and a perimeter had already been established at the top of the road.

A young corporal lifted the black and yellow crime-scene tape to allow Garcia to drive into the street and park on the right. Just a few seconds after Garcia had parked, two other cruisers appeared at the top of the road.

Hunter and Garcia stepped out of Garcia's Honda Civic and instinctively their gaze moved up and down the road. There were so many officers walking about, it looked like a Sheriff's Department conference was taking place somewhere.

Without wasting another second, both detectives rushed toward the last house on the left. Hunter's facial expression showed the anger that he felt inside.

As they got to the internal perimeter, which had been set up at the house's porch, they were met by a stocky police officer with a thick peppery moustache and a receding hairline.

'You guys must be the UVC detectives,' Sergeant Brooks said.

'That's correct,' Garcia confirmed. He and Hunter

quickly displayed their credentials. 'Were you the first at the scene?'

The sergeant gave the detectives a head nod. 'Yes, me and Corporal Rivera over there.' He indicated another officer who was standing by the cruiser parked directly behind the black Cadillac ATS. 'We got the call from dispatch just after one-thirty in the afternoon. We got here less than five minutes after that.'

They began walking toward the front door.

'As we approached the house,' the sergeant continued, 'we noticed that the front door was ajar. We followed standard protocol. After getting no reply ...' As all three of them got to the door, Sergeant Brooks paused them for just a second. ' ...We entered the premises – and this is what we found.' He motioned for the two detectives to enter the house.

Hunter was the first to step through the door. The anger that he felt inside intensified tenfold as it collided headfirst with sadness.

Garcia stepped into the living room a split second after Hunter. As he did, his right hand cupped over his mouth while, under his breath, he cursed everything and everyone.

On the floor, about four paces from the door, SIS Agent Darnel Jordan lay on his back in a pool of his own blood. He had been shot twice in the chest and once in the head. His 9mm pistol lay about three and a half feet from his right hand.

On the red corner sofa, to the right of the front door, Agent James Martin was sprawled against the sofa's backrest. He too had been shot twice in the chest and once in the head. His pistol sat just by his right hand.

Hunter took a second, his right hand clenching into a fist by the side of his body. 'How about the girl?' he asked Sergeant

Brooks, moving past the two bodies and heading toward the bedrooms.

'There's no sign of her whatsoever,' the sergeant replied, as his mouth twisted awkwardly to one side. 'But there's a message.'

Those words halted Hunter and Garcia in their tracks.

'There's a message?' Garcia asked.

Sergeant Brooks nodded, as his right index finger pointed toward the bathroom. The door was already open. 'In there. You can't miss it.'

The two detectives entered the bathroom and their attention was immediately dragged toward the large wall mirror above the washbasin. In big letters, written once again in red lipstick, was a single phrase.

I told you that you wouldn't be able to protect her.

Garcia closed his eyes, while allowing his head to slump forward, his chin almost touching his chest.

Hunter, on the other hand, kept his eyes wide open and on the message. Right then, two destructive feelings took over his body, making him shiver – guilt and failure. He breathed out, trying to compose himself. It didn't work. Without saying a word, he turned and walked out of the bathroom and into the room that Angela had occupied. There was no blood anywhere. There was no sign of a struggle either.

'Do you think she's dead?' Garcia asked, pausing by the unmade bed.

'No, not yet,' Hunter replied, his voice steady but beaten. 'He still hasn't got his diary back, so he'll use her as leverage. Plus, her things are gone,' he said, checking the wardrobe. 'If his intention was to kill her straight away, what would be the point in grabbing her things before taking her with him?'

'How is this even possible?' Garcia asked, as they returned to the living room, his voice shaking with anger. 'These guys were SIS agents. They're highly trained and the best of the best at what they do. This guy right here,' he indicated Darnel Jordan's body on the floor, 'was clearly the one who answered the door.' He skipped over the body and the pool of blood, and approached the agent's 9mm pistol – a HK VP9 tactical semi-automatic. From his jacket pocket, Garcia retrieved a pen, hooked the weapon through its trigger guard and brought it up to his nose before shaking his head at Hunter. 'No gunpowder smell. He didn't even get to fire a shot.' He walked over to the sofa and did the same to James Martin's weapon. 'Same thing here. So how do two, highly trained LAPD Special Investigation Section agents get executed in this way?'

Sergeant Brooks had no answer, but he looked like he would be very interested to hear one.

'They obviously weren't caught by surprise,' Garcia continued. 'Because this guy . . .' He once again indicated Darnel Jordan's body on the floor. '. . . came over to the door to open it up. Yet, neither agent managed to squeeze a single shot at their assailant. How?'

'Because our killer is also highly skilled and probably an expert in tactical close-quarters combat,' Hunter replied, walking over to the front door. 'So the killer knocks on the door.' He allowed his mind to picture the scene. 'I'm sure that he had a very believable story already cooked up. Something like, "I'm so sorry to bother you, but I'm looking for my daughter, or my daughter's dog. Have you, by any chance, seen her/it?"'

Sergeant Brooks scratched the side of his head.

'He could've very well had a photograph with him to strengthen his story,' Hunter said. 'The agent who answered the door, Darnel Jordan, probably followed protocol, dismissing the question and trying to get rid of the stranger as fast as possible, but the stranger pushes. He's got tears in his eyes, or whatever, insisting for the agent to have a look at the photo, telling him that she's just five years old or something. The agent gives in and looks at it, even if only for a split second. That's all the time the killer needs. His gun was probably ready, hidden behind the photo.' Hunter used his hands to demonstrate the position. 'Bang. Bang. Double-tap straight to the chest. The agent stumbles backwards and the killer takes a single step into the house.'

As Hunter re-enacted the scene, Garcia and Sergeant Brooks turned to look at the sofa.

'The front door opens to the left, if you're standing inside the house,' Hunter explained. 'And to the right, if you're standing outside. So from the door, the killer could see the portion of the living room to the left of it. He knew that there was no one there, so as he steps into the house, his body rotates right, looking for a target. He finds agent number two, James Martin, sitting on the sofa. The agent sees his partner stumbling backwards and reaches for his gun, but it's way too late. The killer is already inside, with his weapon ready to fire. Bang. Bang. Another double-tap to the chest. Have you checked the bullet wounds?'

Garcia nodded. 'Both shots to the heart and barely fractions from each other.'

'Which tells us that he's also an expert marksman,' Hunter concluded. 'So the killer knows that both agents are dead, but it doesn't matter to him because he's trained to take no chances – two to the chest and one follow-up shot to the head. This is a close-quarter tactical kill method known as "The Mozambique Drill", or "The Failure Drill".'

'War technique?' Garcia asked.

'And assassins,' Hunter confirmed. 'So, after putting two rounds into their hearts, our killer walks up to agent number one.' Hunter walked up to Darnel Jordan's body on the floor. 'And bang, delivers the follow-up shot straight to the brain. He walks over to agent number two and does the same.'

'Silencer?' Garcia again.

'I have no doubt,' Hunter agreed.

'So Angela didn't hear any of this, other than the doorbell?' Garcia supposed.

'Probably not,' Hunter confirmed. 'The rest is easy. He goes over to her bedroom, knocks on the door and sedates her. Game over for us.'

Sixty-Five

Hunter was right. Angela never got a chance to fight.

'I've got to go,' she said to Hunter over the phone and, without giving him a chance to say anything back, she disconnected from the call. A split second before she did, she heard the front doorbell ring.

Angela knew that Hunter would probably try to call her back straight away, so she immediately pressed and held down the power button on her phone to switch it off. That done, she used the paper clip she had used earlier to extract her SIM card and put it away.

DING, DONG.

The doorbell again.

Angela checked the time. It was nearly one thirty in the afternoon.

'Did those two order some food without asking me if I wanted in on it?' she said out loud, while reaching under the bed for her tennis shoes. She didn't like walking around the house barefooted. 'Motherfuckers. I could really do with some pizza right about now . . . or maybe some fried chicken.'

Angela tied her shoelaces and got to her feet, ready to go

give Martin and Jordan an earful for not having asked her for her order, but she didn't even get a chance to leave the room. As she approached the bedroom door, she heard three knocks.

'Oh, now you come ask me if I want some,' she whispered to herself, pulling the door open.

It took Angela's brain a full second to realize that the tall man standing there was neither of the two SIS agents.

That was a full second too late.

As she locked eyes with the man, the syringe in his right hand was already halfway to her neck. The needle pierced her skin, embedding its tip into the muscle, and dispersing two milligrams of the fast-acting sedative, Flunitrazepam.

Angela didn't even have time to react.

'Easy now,' the man said, while using his left hand to hold the back of her head. 'It will all be over soon . . . very soon.'

Sixty-Six

On their way back to the PAB, neither Hunter nor Garcia said a word. Their expressions were solemn, their eyes distraught.

By the time they got back to the LAPD Headquarters, Hunter was feeling sick to his stomach, so while Garcia went straight back into the UVC Unit's office, Hunter took a bathroom detour. He splashed some cold water over his face before staring straight into his reflection in the mirror. His eyes looked tired, drained of light. He was about to say something to the man looking back at him in the mirror when his cellphone rang in his pocket. He answered it without checking the display screen.

'Detective Hunter, UVC Unit.'

'*Robert, it's Vince. Everything is set and ready to go. The tracker is ready and in place. All I need to do is switch it on and seal it in, which shouldn't take me any longer than twenty minutes. The front cover has been restored to what it was before and it looks pretty flawless, if I may say so.*'

'Great,' Hunter replied. 'You said that the tracker will be able to transmit for twenty-four hours, right?'

'*That's correct.*'

'OK,' Hunter checked his watch. It was past four in the afternoon. 'Let's do this.'

'*I'm on it,*' Keller replied. He was just about to disconnect from the call when Hunter stopped him. A new idea had just popped into his head. It was a bold idea, but it could provide him with an odd type of insurance.

'Vince, hold on a second,' Hunter said. 'I need something else.'

'*Sure.*'

'A contingency plan.'

'*OK? What do you have in mind?*'

Hunter told him his idea.

For the next few seconds, Keller went totally quiet. Finally, he spoke.

'*Are you sure about this, Robert?*'

'Not one hundred percent,' Hunter admitted. 'But I still want to go ahead with it. It might save a life. Taking Angela was his insurance. This is mine.'

'*Taking who?*'

'Never mind.' Hunter dismissed the question. 'Can you do it? Do we have enough time?'

'*Sure. No problem. I'll get on it right away.*'

'I'll be over at twenty to five to pick up the diary.'

'*All right, I'll see you then. Oh, and don't forget to bring your cellphone with you. I'll give you a tablet with the tracker application, but I can also install it onto your phone.*'

'Don't worry. I'll have it with me.'

Sixty-Seven

At exactly twenty to five, Hunter and Garcia were once again at the reception desk inside the Piper Tech building. This time he didn't have to wait, as Keller had left specific instructions with all the receptionists to buzz both detectives in as soon as they got there.

On the second floor, Keller had just finished his task, when Hunter and Garcia appeared at the door to Electronics Lab number two.

'Wow,' Keller said. 'Talk about perfect timing. I just finished sealing the back cover less than a minute ago.' He ushered them into the lab with a hand gesture. 'Here, have a look.'

Both detectives approached Keller's workbench. He handed the diary to Hunter with the back cover flipped open.

'Run your finger over the leather sheet and let me know if you're able to notice anything.'

Hunter ran his finger over the leather. There were no bumps, or lumps, nothing to indicate that it had been tampered with. He checked the edges of the leather sheet, where Keller had reapplied the glue. Perfect. Hunter watched Garcia also run his fingers over the sheet before flipping the diary to the front cover. Another perfect job.

'This is excellent,' Hunter said, closing the diary.

'Thank you.' Keller looked very proud of the good job he had done. He turned back toward the workbench and picked up two tablets that were to the right of where the diary had been. 'I remember your captain saying that you would have a SWAT and an SIS team tracking you, so I've installed the tracking app on these two tablets.'

Keller turned both tablets on. The tracking app was already loaded and opened on the screens. It showed a blinking red dot on a map.

'As I've said before, the signal that the tracker emits isn't terribly strong, and it works using cell towers. That means that this is as effective as a cellphone. So in locations where a phone would lose its signal, so will this.'

'We understand,' Hunter said.

'Do you have your cellphones?' Keller asked. 'It takes less than a minute to install the app.'

'Sure.'

Hunter and Garcia handed them to Keller. He guided both detectives to his small and crammed office, connected the phones to the computer on his desk and loaded the tracking application onto them.

'There you go,' he said, returning the phones to their respective owners. 'All done and ready to go.'

'Thanks, Vince.'

'Robert,' Keller called as Hunter and Garcia were leaving his office. Hunter turned to face him again. 'Good luck. I hope the plan works.'

'So do I,' Hunter said before closing the door behind him.

Sixty-Eight

Hunter and Garcia got back to the Police Administration Building at 4:53 p.m. – seven minutes before the killer was due to call Hunter again. Captain Blake was waiting for them in their office, but this time she wasn't alone.

'Detective Hunter, Detective Garcia,' she said, as both detectives entered the room. 'This is Agent Terrance Shaffer, SWAT team leader . . .' She indicated a very tall and slim man with a three-day stubble, who was standing to her left. ' . . . And this is Agent Trevor Silva, SIS team leader.' She indicated the person to her right – a six-foot-one, dark-haired, broad-shouldered, muscular man who could easily be mistaken for a professional linebacker. 'They're each leading a six-man strong team that will be following you throughout whatever this murderous piece of trash comes up with when he calls.'

'Both of our teams are locked and loaded and ready to go as soon as you are, Detective,' Agent Silva said, as he and Agent Shaffer shook Hunter's hand.

The anger that burned inside their eyes traveled down their arms and into their handgrips, which with just a few more pounds of pressure could've probably crushed bones.

The news that two LAPD SIS officers had been murdered

earlier in the day had spread like wildfire throughout the entire Los Angeles Police Department. Yes, it was true that certain units inside the department didn't really get along. Rivalry between some divisions was even considered normal. But every single division, every single unit inside the LAPD would drop any beef and come together as one when a fellow law enforcement officer lost their life in the line of duty. Rivalry did exist, but so did respect.

'Thank you,' Hunter replied, before handing each team leader one of the tablets that Keller had given him just minutes earlier. As he did, he explained the limitations of the tracker.

'Both teams will be using unmarked cars,' Agent Silva said, acknowledging Hunter's explanation. 'Two agents in each car, or on foot, whatever the case may be, spread across possible routes according to your position.' He tapped his index finger against his tablet screen. 'All of it from a safe enough distance. But in case his plan is to run into a subway or the sublevels of a building somewhere, I can guarantee you that one of the vehicles with a two-man team can get to said location in thirty seconds or less. The others will be right behind. Air support will also be hovering in the sky nearby, ready to engage if needed.'

'There's also this,' Agent Shaffer said, handing Hunter a small, kidney-shaped earpiece. 'It should sit comfortably inside your ear. It will allow us to hear you and you to hear us.'

Hunter adjusted the earpiece into his left ear.

'How does it feel?' Agent Shaffer asked.

'Comfortable.'

'As always,' Captain Blake took over, 'a tracer will be immediately run against any calls you might receive on both of your cellphones – personal and work. Not that we're really

expecting him to be stupid enough to give us a location, but . . .'
She gave Hunter a 'you never really know' kind of shrug.

'I really hope he does,' Agent Silva said.

Hunter locked eyes with him for a long moment. The anger
there, if anything, seemed to be intensifying.

'Trust me, no one wants to get their hands on this killer
more than I do, but I must stress that whatever happens, no
lethal force is to be used. He has a hostage – Angela Woods,
twenty-one years old. Until we're certain that she's safe, this
killer, whoever he is, holds all the cards and we have to play
by his rules.'

Agent Silva didn't shy away from Hunter's stare.

'James and Darnel weren't just SIS agents,' he said, his
voice full of pain but firm, nevertheless. His heavy-lidded eyes
gave him a dim-witted look, which was deceiving because
Trevor Silva was one of the brightest minds inside the Special
Investigation Section of the LAPD. 'They were friends . . . close
friends . . . my close friends. They both had families: . . . kids
who'll never see their father again . . . wives who'll never sleep
by their husband again.' He paused, doing his best to contain his
anger. 'Do you have a family, Detective Hunter? A wife? Kids?'

'No, I don't.'

Agent Silva nodded back, slowly. 'So you cannot possibly
begin to understand—'

'Look,' Captain Blake intervened, addressing Agent Silva.
'I understand that they were SIS agents, and maybe we didn't
know them as well as you did, but they were still LAPD
officers, which makes this personal to all of us. All of us have
sworn an oath, which is "to protect and to serve". Detective
Hunter is right. First and foremost, our duty is to protect the
life of an innocent civilian and that means that no lethal force

is to be used until we have confirmation that the hostage is safe and well. Is that understood?'

The captain's eyes widened and her brow deeply furrowed. Her stare threatened to decapitate the SIS team leader.

He held her stare, but hesitated.

'Is that understood, Agent Silva?' Her voice was thunderous.

'Yes.'

Captain Blake's eyes moved to Agent Shaffer.

'Yes, ma'am.'

'Once we have confirmation that she's safe and well . . .' The captain shrugged unconcerned. 'Then all gloves are off.'

'We better end this pointless conversation and right quick,' Garcia said, consulting his watch. 'It's four fifty-nine. We've got one minute.'

At that exact moment, a knock came on Hunter and Garcia's office door.

'Come in,' Hunter called.

The door was pushed open by a young uniformed officer carrying a small FedEx envelope.

'Detective Hunter?' he asked from the door.

'Yes,' Hunter replied.

'This just came for you, sir.' The officer stepped inside and handed Hunter the envelope. 'It says "Urgent".'

Hunter frowned. He wasn't expecting any deliveries.

'For me? What, just now?'

'That's correct, sir.'

Hunter's stare rounded the room.

Despite the same quizzical look in everyone's eyes, they all knew that that wasn't a coincidence.

Hunter took the envelope, ripped it open and tipped the contents into his right hand.

A smartphone.

Five o'clock.

The phone rang in Hunter's hand.

Sixty-Nine

No one had to ask. Everyone inside Hunter and Garcia's office knew who the caller at the other end of the line would be, even before Hunter had accepted the call. The display screen read 'unknown number'.

'You didn't have to kill them,' Hunter said, accepting the call and immediately switching it to speakerphone. He managed to keep all his anger out of his tone.

Everyone gathered around.

Hunter held the phone in front of his face, just a couple of inches from his mouth.

'*Detective Hunter,*' the male voice said. It was the same husky, toneless voice that Hunter had heard on the phone the day before. '*I did tell you that you wouldn't be able to protect her, didn't I?*'

'You didn't have to kill them.' Hunter said it again.

'*Really?*' the voice replied. '*So what should I have done? Asked them to hand the girl over to me? Somehow I don't think that would've worked.*'

From the corner of his eyes, Hunter saw the look on Agent Silva's face change. He instantly lifted a hand at the agent to stop him from saying anything.

Agent Shaffer placed a warning hand on Agent Silva's shoulder.

'*So now that you know what the bargain is,*' the caller continued, '*let's talk about what really matters. Do you have it?*'

Hunter's head dropped to his chest and he refilled his lungs with air. 'I do,' he replied.

'*OK.*'

The line went dead.

Hunter looked at the display screen in confusion. The caller had disconnected.

'What the hell?' Hunter said, with a quick shake of the head.

'What happened?' Garcia beat everyone to the question.

'He disconnected,' Hunter replied.

'He what?' Captain Blake looked dismayed. 'Why?'

'I don't . . .' Hunter started his reply, but he was interrupted by a new phone ring. The melody to this ring was significantly different from the first one.

Hunter checked the display screen again.

Video call.

Hunter's stare once again circled the room.

As if rehearsed, everyone nodded at him to take the call.

Hunter slid his thumb across the screen to accept it. The display immediately changed into a live camera feed. At the very top of the screen, a tiny green light lit up to indicate that the phone camera that faced Hunter had been activated.

On the screen, the lighting at the other end wasn't great, making the picture dark and brittle. All Hunter could see was a crude, white wall. It looked like a basement.

Everyone quickly repositioned themselves directly behind

Hunter to peek at the small screen, but Hunter quickly swung away from everyone. He pointed the phone away from his face for a quick second, as he shook his head at them.

Garcia and Agent Silva both lifted their hands to show their understanding.

Hunter aimed the phone back at him.

'*Show me,*' the caller said.

Hunter was still looking at a wall.

'Show it to you?' he asked.

'*Yes. You just told me that you have it. So show me my diary. Do it now.*'

Hunter once again pointed the phone away from his face. He took one step to his right and collected the diary from his desk. He held it at around chest height and aimed the camera at the book.

On the small screen, despite the odd angle, Hunter could see movement. Then, someone wearing a rubber werewolf mask came into view.

'*Flip it open,*' the Werewolf said.

'Any particular page?' Hunter asked.

'*Surprise me.*'

Hunter opened the diary to a random page, somewhere around halfway.

The Werewolf examined it for five seconds.

'*Flip it again,*' he commanded.

Hunter did. Further forward.

Another five seconds examining it.

'*Funny how having something – or someone – to use as a bargaining tool can make things happen a lot faster, isn't it?*'

'I already had the diary,' Hunter shot back. 'You didn't have to kill them. You didn't have to take Angela.'

'*But now you also know not to try anything,*' the Werewolf replied. '*Which brings us to the real reason for this call. First, let's start with the rules. One — I say, you follow. No questions. No buts. If you question anything I say, the thieving bitch dies.*' A short pause. '*Two — I'm going to put you through a number of tasks. Every one of them will come with a time limit. If you are even a second late accomplishing any of them, the thieving bitch dies.*'

Everyone in the room exchanged a worried look.

'*Three,*' the Werewolf continued. '*I know that you'll have people following you. I would be stupid if I believed that you wouldn't have. I don't mind it, but if anyone interferes with any of the tasks I give you, the thieving bitch dies.*' Another short pause. '*That's it. Three simple rules. Are those rules understood, Detective Hunter?*'

'Yes.'

Agent Silva scratched an itch at the back of his head.

'*So here comes your first task. Are you ready?*' The Werewolf didn't give Hunter a chance to reply. '*Do you know where the Downtown Independent Theater is?*'

Hunter's eyes narrowed slightly at his phone screen. 'Yes, of course. It's just around the corner.'

'*That's right, it is,*' the Werewolf agreed. '*Take the diary, make your way there on foot, buy a ticket for the film that will start in ten minutes and grab seat K16 on the last row.*'

'What if there's somebody already sitting in seat K16?' Hunter asked.

'*Then you ask that somebody to move,*' the Werewolf replied. '*And, Detective, don't be a dick and flash your badge at the ticket office. Buy a ticket like a regular person.*'

Hunter nodded at his screen. 'OK.'

'*You have five minutes to make it. Those five minutes are starting ... now.*'

The line went dead.

Seventy

As soon as the Werewolf disconnected from the call with Hunter, both agents, Shaffer and Silva, got on their radios and immediately instructed their teams to take position near the Downtown Independent Theater.

'Robert,' Captain Blake said. 'You've got five minutes. Go. Now.'

Hunter turned on the balls of his feet and reached for the diary on his desk. As he did, the phone in his hand rang again, stopping everyone dead.

'What the hell?' Garcia said.

Hunter checked the screen – another video call request.

He took the call.

As the screen came alive again, the image of the Werewolf materialized once more.

'*One last thing, Detective Hunter. There's something else I want to show you.*'

'And what is that?' Hunter asked.

'*Just keep your eyes on the screen.*'

Hunter did so and a second later the image began to slowly pan right, dragging along the crude white wall for about three to five seconds before it finally paused again. Hunter looked at the screen in such a way that made everyone in the room frown at him.

'What's going on?' Garcia mouthed the words.

With his index finger, Hunter ushered everyone to come closer again.

They all bunched up behind Hunter and in a flash their frowns quickly morphed into dismay.

'What the fuck?' Agent Shaffer said under his breath.

What they were all looking at was a young man who appeared to be around twenty-one years old, twenty-two at a push. His features would've been attractive, if not for the state he was in. His longish, black hair was dirty and disheveled. His fringe, drenched in sweat, was glued to his forehead, with part of it falling over his left eye. His eyes, very dark in color, were now an ugly shade of pink and the dark circles under them, together with how puffy they looked, indicated that he hadn't slept for days or had been crying for days, or a combination of both. The stubble on his face was a consequence of at least three days without shaving. His lips were severely dried, with a couple of cracks at the edges.

'Who the hell is this?' Captain Blake whispered in Hunter's ear.

Hunter's shrug was followed by a subtle shake of the head.

The camera panned out just enough to reveal that the young man was sitting on a heavy metal chair. His arms were bound together behind his body, securing him to the chair's backrest. His bare feet were tied to the chair's leg by his ankles. The white T-shirt he had on, just like his hair, was dirty and soaked with sweat.

'*Look up.*' They all heard the Werewolf command the young man. '*Look into the camera.*'

Slowly, the man did as he was told.

The Werewolf zoomed in to focus solely on his face. The man's eyes were filled with absolute terror.

'*Don't be shy,*' the Werewolf said. '*Introduce yourself to the detective.*'

Just like that, the young man's eyes were completely over-taken by tears, but on hearing the word 'detective', Hunter also saw something else appear in them – hope.

'*Please, help me,*' the man said in a barely audible voice that was strangled by tears.

'Stay calm,' Hunter said in return, his voice steady. 'We'll get to you. Trust me.'

'"*Please help me" isn't your name, is it?*' the Werewolf said.

The man's terrified eyes wavered just a little, before refocus-ing on the camera.

'*Tell him your name,*' the Werewolf commanded again, this time with anger.

'*My name is Clay ...*' the man said, amid more tears. '*Clay Heath.*'

Immediately, Garcia took down the name.

'*Tell them your address,*' the Werewolf ordered. '*Where do you live?*'

'*I ... I live with my parents at ...*' Clay paused for an instant, as if he had forgotten his own address. '*Apartment 15, 2098 Butler Avenue, West LA.*'

Garcia noted down the address.

'*Now tell them what you do.*'

'*What I do?*' Clay looked confused.

'*Yes,*' the Werewolf confirmed. '*What do you do for work?*'

Clay shook his head at his captor. '*I don't have a job. I'm a ... full-time student at UCLA.*'

'*Tell the camera, not me.*'

Clay looked at the camera and repeated what he'd just said.

'Clay,' Hunter said. 'Try to stay cal—'

'*Shut the fuck up, Detective.*' The Werewolf cut Hunter short. '*This isn't a dialogue. This isn't a conversation. This is a lesson.*'

'A lesson?' Hunter asked.

The frown on everyone's faces intensified.

'*Yes, a lesson, so do pay attention.*' The Werewolf addressed Clay again. '*Tell them what you study at UCLA.*'

'*Umm . . .*' Clay looked lost again. '*My major is . . .*' It took him a couple of seconds to remember. '*Chemistry.*' Tears returned to his eyes and his voice sounded suffocated. '*Help me . . . please . . . help me.*'

Right then, the picture shook for an instant, followed by a clicking sound, then the picture stabilized again.

The Werewolf had placed the phone on a holder.

On Hunter's small screen, they all saw Clay's eyes look up before his head began slowly moving left. Hunter immediately read the movement as Clay's gaze following the Werewolf as he moved from behind the phone.

In a flash, Hunter swung away from everyone else in the office, once again trying to keep the other room occupants from being spotted by the Werewolf.

Hunter was right. All of a sudden, the Werewolf appeared behind Clay's chair. Since the phone camera was focusing on Clay's face, all Hunter could see of the Werewolf was part of his torso. Whoever he really was, he was, without a doubt, a very fit and strong individual.

'*All right,*' the Werewolf said. '*Let's get back to our lesson, shall we?*' Three silent seconds went by. '*I'm sure that you've*

*understood the rules that I've put to you. I'm also sure that you
understand the consequences, should you break any of them
or fail to accomplish them in time.'*

'I have, yes,' Hunter replied, as he checked his watch. He
now had less than four minutes to get to the Downtown
Independent Theater.

*'So the lesson right here is ... don't fuck with me, Detective
Hunter. If you do, this will happen to the thieving bitch.'*

The Werewolf's gloved left hand grabbed hold of Clay's hair,
pulling his head back and exposing his naked neck. A fraction
of a second later, the Werewolf's right hand appeared in the
picture. Firm in its grasp was a shining, stainless-steel hunter's
knife. Its razor-sharp blade connected with the flesh on Clay's
throat so fast, Hunter almost missed it.

'No,' he yelled, but it was all too late. In the blink of an eye,
the blade sliced Clay's throat from left to right as if it were
going through nothing but thin air. A river of blood spurted
out of the gaping wound and began running down the young
man's body.

Hunter saw Clay's eyes roll up in surprise and horror, as all
hope vanished from them in a split second.

No one was coming to help him.

No one was coming to save him.

Clay knew that now.

His mouth dropped open as his body began to instinctively
fight for survival. He gasped for air, emitting a gurgling shriek
that sent goosebumps up and down everyone's spine, but his
fight – his desperation – made no difference. Oxygen would
not reach his lungs anymore, as his windpipe had been severed
by the shining blade.

The Werewolf held Clay's head back, displaying the large

open wound on the young man's throat. Blood continued to cascade down his torso like a slow-running, red and viscous waterfall.

Clay's eyes blinked slowly – once . . . twice . . . three times . . . and then no more.

His body gave up fighting.

His throat stopped gasping.

Life left the young man forever.

'You sonofabitch,' Agent Silva yelled. At that moment, he couldn't care less if the Werewolf knew he was there or not. But the Werewolf also didn't seem bothered by the fact that there were others listening in.

'*Lesson concluded,*' the Werewolf said, letting go of Clay's head, his voice arctic.

Clay's lifeless body slumped forward on the chair. Blood still poured down his torso like a live crimson shroud.

'*You have . . . two minutes and forty-eight seconds to accomplish the first task*.' The Werewolf added, '*If I were you, I'd get going.*'

The killer disconnected.

Seventy-One

Despite Hunter's rage and total dismay at what he'd just witnessed, he knew that he needed to run to make it to the Independent Theater in time. There was no time to be angry or disgusted.

Hunter grabbed the diary, jammed the smartphone that the Werewolf had sent him into his pocket and rushed out of his office.

It took him thirty-nine seconds to cross the detectives' floor and fly down six flights of stairs to the PAB ground floor.

Two minutes and nine seconds left.

Instead of running out the main entrance door, which would drop him on West First Street, Hunter ran past the large reception desk and up a new set of stairs on the east side of the building. Those stairs took him to an outside garden that overlooked South Main Street.

One minute and forty-four seconds left.

Hunter shot through the garden, disregarding the 'please stay off the grass' sign, and made his way to the outside staircase that would take him to the street below. Seventeen seconds later, he had landed on South Main Street, just past a Mexican restaurant called Señor Fish.

One minute and twenty-seven seconds left.

From where Hunter had landed, it was a straight line to the Downtown Independent Theater, 170 yards ahead of him. Without even catching his breath, he took off like an Olympic sprinter. As he crossed West Second Street on a red pedestrian light, Hunter forced a motorbike to swerve hard left, almost causing an accident.

'What the fuck is wrong with you?' he heard the bike rider yell, as he got to the sidewalk on the other side.

One hundred yards to go.

One minute and sixteen seconds left.

The sidewalk wasn't at all crowded, which made things easier. Hunter covered the remaining one hundred yards in sixteen seconds, leaving him exactly one minute to purchase a ticket, get into the theater and find seat K16.

Hunter was lucky. As he got to the ticket office there were only two people in front of him, a young couple who looked to be in their early twenties. The film showing was *Send Me to the Clouds*.

The young couple purchased their tickets and went inside.

'One please,' Hunter said in an urgent voice, as he got to the ticket office. 'Are there assigned seats to the show?'

The cashier, a slim gentleman in his mid-sixties, looked back at Hunter with tired eyes.

'There are indeed,' he replied, swerving his computer monitor around so Hunter could see the seating plan. 'The seats in blue are free,' the old man said. His voice sounded like he'd been smoking and singing the blues for most of his life. 'The ones in red are taken.'

'Seat K16 is taken?' Hunter asked, blinking at the seating plan.

'Is it red?' the old man asked.

'Yes,' Hunter replied.

'So it's taken.'

The next available seat on row K was seat number fourteen.

'OK, I'll take K14 then,' Hunter said, checking his watch – thirty-eight seconds left.

'That will be sixteen thirty-five, please.'

Hunter gave the old man a twenty-dollar bill. 'Keep the change.'

Twenty-nine seconds left.

Hunter practically threw his ticket at the attendant as he passed him.

'Sir,' the young boy called 'You need the stub for the seat.'

But Hunter wasn't listening anymore. He had already turned the corner into a short corridor. Two seconds later, he pushed open the doors to the theater where *Send Me to the Clouds* was showing.

Twenty-four seconds left.

The film hadn't started yet.

Hunter ran up the stairs to the last row of seats – row K. From the door, it took him four seconds to reach his assigned seat – K14. He didn't take the seat. Instead he addressed the lady sitting on K16.

'I'm sorry,' he said, displaying his credentials. 'LAPD, I need that seat.'

'Excuse me?' the man who was sitting in seat K15 said, frowning at Hunter.

'I'm so sorry, but I need seat K16,' Hunter explained. 'This is official business.'

Seventeen seconds left.

'You need my girlfriend's seat on official business?' the man said, getting to his feet. Some odd quirkiness found its way into his tone.

Fourteen seconds left.

'That's correct,' Hunter replied.

'Oh, OK,' the man continued. 'And what official business might that be?'

Eleven seconds left.

Hunter didn't have time for any of that. Instead of giving the man an answer, he pulled open the left side of his jacket to show him his weapon holster.

'I really do need that seat, sir.'

Eight seconds left.

The man lifted his hands in surrender. His girlfriend, on the other hand, let out a loud yelp as she catapulted from her seat.

Every head inside the theater turned to look at the commotion happening on the last row of seats.

'It's OK,' Hunter reassured them.

Two seconds left.

'I'm not staying here,' the woman puffed at her boyfriend, as she squeezed past Hunter.

The boyfriend tried to look Hunter in the eye.

'I need your name,' he said. 'I'm going to make an . . .'

Time was up.

All of a sudden, they all heard a cellphone ring, which prompted everyone to stop and look around, trying to identify where the sound was coming from.

It rang again.

They all looked down.

Hunter pushed past the boyfriend and bent down to have a look at seat K16.

It rang again.

Hunter reached under the seat. Taped against the underside of it was a new cellphone. Hunter ripped the phone from the tape and looked at its screen – video call request.

Hunter accepted it and the Werewolf's image materialized on the small screen once again.

'*Hello, Detective,*' the Werewolf said. '*I'm glad you managed to get to the movie theater in time.*'

'What the fuck?' the boyfriend said, pulling a face at Hunter.

With one finger, Hunter motioned him to be quiet. The gesture was so firm and authoritative that the man shut up immediately.

'*If you still have the cellphone I had delivered to you a few minutes ago,*' the Werewolf continued, '*you can get rid of it now.*'

Hunter retrieved the phone from his jacket pocket and dropped it on the seat.

'All right,' he said. 'Now what?'

'*Do you still have the diary?*'

'Of course,' Hunter replied, lifting the leather-bound book so that the Werewolf could see it.

'*Excellent.*' A very quick pause. '*Ready for task number two, Detective?*' There was no need for a reply. '*I want you to use the emergency exit at the front of the room to leave the theater.*'

Instinctively, Hunter looked up to check where exactly the emergency exit was – to the left of the screen.

'OK, and where do I go?'

'*Do you know where the Grand Central Market is?*'

'Yes. South Broadway Street. Two blocks from here.'

'*That's right,*' the Werewolf confirmed. '*The male bathroom at the far end of the market. The last cubicle on the left. You have two and a half minutes to get there.'* The Werewolf pressed a button on his wristwatch. 'Go.'

The line went dead.

Seventy-Two

As Hunter rushed down in the direction of the emergency exit, he heard Agent Shaffer's voice come loud and clear into his left ear.

'*Roger those instructions, Detective Hunter. Teams are already on their way.*'

'Tell them to keep their distance,' Hunter replied. 'And not to approach the bathroom at the far end of the market.'

'*Of course.*'

Under the watchful eyes of everyone inside the theater, Hunter flew down the stairs like a rocket. From row K, it took him nine seconds to reach the emergency exit by the screen.

Two minutes and twenty-one seconds left.

The theater's emergency exit opened to a back alleyway that led to the building's parking lot. Hunter had to zigzag between several cars to reach its west end, where he encountered his first problem – the iron-mesh gate that connected the parking lot to South Spring Street was chain-locked.

'Shit!' Hunter gasped, tugging at the chain as hard as he could.

'*What?*' Agent Shaffer's voice exploded in Hunter's left ear once again. '*What's shit? What's going on, Detective?*'

'The gate at the back of the parking lot is chained. That's why he wanted me to use the emergency exit. He knew that from there, this would be the fastest way to get to the Grand Central Market.'

Two minutes and seven seconds left.

'*Can you climb it?*' Agent Shaffer asked.

'I could,' Hunter replied. 'But this is easier and faster.'

He reached inside his jacket for his Mark 23 pistol, took a step back from the gate, aimed at the padlock and pulled the trigger. The shot thundered down the alleyway and through the neighboring streets as if a bomb had gone off, but the .45-caliber bullet that exited the barrel of Hunter's semi-automatic weapon practically disintegrated the padlock. The impact was so destructive that it also shattered a couple of loops from the chain, making the whole thing fall to the ground with a clatter. Hunter used the heel of his right boot to kick the gate open.

'*What the hell was that?*' Agent Shaffer asked in Hunter's ear. '*Did you just shoot the gate open?*'

'Yep,' Hunter replied, already sprinting down South Spring Street in the direction of West Third Street. 'Pretty much.'

Hunter heard Agent Shaffer yell a 'stand down' order to his SWAT teams.

One minute and fifty seconds left.

Hunter got to the corner of South Spring Street and West Third and swung right, still sprinting west. He was a block and a half away from the Grand Central Market.

One minute and thirty-nine seconds left.

Hunter covered the next fifty yards with enough ease, but his heart was starting to thunder inside his chest. He could feel his nostrils beginning to struggle to suck in enough oxygen to feed his lungs. He could feel sweat running down his neck and back, the build-up of lactic acid in his muscles.

I'm definitely getting too old for this kind of shit, he thought, as he looked over his shoulder to check traffic conditions. At that time – end of office hours – traffic was chaotic.

Hunter needed to get across West Third Street and fast. He paused at the edge of the sidewalk and waited – one second . . . two . . . three . . .

Too long, he thought.

Four seconds . . . five . . .

One minute and twenty-one seconds left.

'Fuck it,' Hunter said out loud, and went for it.

His right foot touched the road and if the driver of the blue Mazda 6 that was coming toward him hadn't been alert and slammed on the brakes as hard as he could, Hunter would probably have ended up with two broken legs.

The loud screeching of tires against the asphalt made every passer-by turn and look in Hunter's direction. The fright made Hunter's heart skip a couple of beats and his stomach perform an Olympic somersault. His hand intuitively came up to protect his body from the impact, making him almost drop the diary. The Mazda 6 managed to come to a full stop two inches from Hunter.

'Are you out of your fucking mind, you fucking suicidal prick?' the driver yelled out his window.

The car to the left of the Mazda – a white Kia Optima – also braked hard, but it had moved about a yard and a half past the Mazda, blocking Hunter's path. His answer was to jump on and slide all the way across the Kia's hood – *Dukes of Hazzard* style – which made the Kia driver's jaw drop.

Hood-slide done, Hunter landed on a lucky one-car gap.

He took two steps forward and waited for the van on the last lane of traffic to go past before finally reaching the curb on the other side. He was now only fifty yards from the Grand Central Market.

One minute and two seconds left.

But Hunter now had another problem. To get to the Grand Central Market, he also needed to get to the other side of South Broadway, a much busier road than the one he'd just crossed.

Hunter checked the display for the crosswalk – twenty-two seconds to the green 'walk' man.

'Nope,' he said to himself, before once again stepping off the curb – but this time he waited for a gap. It came two seconds later, between a red Jeep Cherokee and a black Ford Fusion. He extended his right hand, signaling the driver of the Ford Fusion to slow down.

The driver did, but he also angrily rammed the horn while cursing from behind the wheel.

Fifty-six seconds left.

Hunter moved forward to the second lane of traffic, and from then on it was like an old videogame where a crazy chicken was trying to cross a busy road. While looking for the right gap to move into, Hunter jigged his body left, right, left, in an almost comical way. He had to allow two vehicles to go past before he was able to clear the second lane.

Forty-nine seconds left.

Hunter got to the third lane and once again did his little body jig before managing to squeeze himself between a white van and a motorbike.

The fourth lane was the easiest to clear, as it was a single lane of traffic flowing in the opposite direction. In central Los Angeles, at rush hour, a single lane of traffic meant bumper-to-bumper vehicles. Hunter quickly rounded a green Chrysler 200 before finally getting to the other side of South Broadway.

Forty-three seconds left.

Hunter covered the distance from his position to the entrance to the Grand Central Market in seven seconds.

New problem – it was two weeks until Christmas and the market was jammed with people. The bathroom was at the very back of the market.

'How am I doing for time?' Hunter asked.

'*You have thirty-six seconds left,*' Agent Shaffer replied.

Hunter had no time to stop and think. He had no time to pause for breath either.

'This is going to be ugly,' he said, as he reached the market entrance at almost full speed.

Hunter managed to swerve around the couple with two toddlers that was exiting the market, but from then on it became a push-and-shove festival. He had thirty-three seconds to get to the last cubicle inside the male bathroom right at the back of the market, and a crowd of Christmas shoppers wasn't about to stop Hunter from getting there in time.

'Sorry,' he began calling out, his voice urgent and firm. 'LAPD, coming through . . . LAPD, coming through.'

As he shouted those words in a never-ending loop, Hunter zigzagged, turned, danced a jiggle and did his best to avoid colliding with as many shoppers as he possibly could. The ones he failed to avoid ended up being thrust out of his path in whichever way possible. Some ended up on the ground. Some were pushed onto others, who then ended up on the ground.

As Hunter practically plowed his way through the crowd, he could hear members of the public shouting abuse and words of indignation back at him. Some yelled the most famous of American phrases – 'I'm going to sue your ass for this shit.'

The pushing, the shoving, the jiggles, the turns . . . all of it ate at his time. It took him twenty-one seconds to get to the male bathroom at the back of the market.

'Time?' he asked. 'How much time do I have?'

'*Twelve seconds,*' Agent Shaffer informed him.

Hunter stormed into the bathroom like a wrecking ball. Once he went past the urinals, he found two rows of four cubicles – one on the left, one on the right. The two last cubicles on the left had their doors shut.

Hunter rushed to the last one and tried the door – locked.

'Busy,' a high-pitched male voice called from behind the door.

But of course it would be, Hunter thought.

Nine seconds left.

'Sir, LAPD, this is official business. I need to get in there.'

'Official business?' the man replied, incredulous. 'You need to take an official dump, is that it?'

Three seconds left.

'Sir, this isn't a joke.'

Time was up.

All of a sudden, Hunter heard a sort of muffled cellphone ringtone coming from inside the cubicle.

'What the hell?' he also heard the man exclaim from inside.

No more explaining himself to anyone.

Hunter took a step back and, just like he'd done to the gate at the theater's parking lot minutes earlier, he sent the heel of his right boot onto the cubicle door with all the power he had. The flimsy lock burst immediately. The door swung back as if it had been hit by the shockwave of an explosion, slamming into the cubicle occupant's knees.

'What the fuck?' he jumped up.

Hunter stepped inside to see a half-frightened, half-surprised, overweight man sitting on the toilet with his trousers down to his ankles. In his right hand he had a bunch of crumpled-up toilet paper.

'What the fuck is wrong with you?' the man shouted.

The phone rang again.

Hunter looked around, searching for where the ring was coming from.

The man on the toilet continued to shout abuse at Hunter.

'Be quiet,' Hunter commanded, pointing a finger at the man.

The man shut up.

The phone rang again.

Hunter looked at the man.

The ringing seemed to be coming from behind him.

Hunter angled his body left to look past the large man.

The muffled ringtone came again.

It was coming from inside the toilet's water tank.

'Excuse me,' Hunter ordered, stepping to the left of the toilet, forcing the man to angle his body the other way. Hunter lifted the water tank lid to find a new smartphone taped to the underside of it. He untaped it and checked the screen.

Video call request.

Hunter accepted it, aiming the phone at himself.

'*I was about to hang up,*' the Werewolf said, as his face materialized on the small screen.

'Well, here I am,' Hunter replied, a little out of breath.

'What the hell is going on?' the man on the toilet asked. 'Are you playing a game?'

'*Oh,*' the Werewolf sounded surprised. '*Is there someone there with you?*'

'I was here first,' the man said out loud.

'*C'mon, Detective Hunter, pan the phone around. Let me meet our new friend.*'

'Sorry,' Hunter said to the man, before doing as requested.

The man immediately blushed, but the Werewolf didn't get to see his face, as he lifted his right hand to cover it.

'What the hell, man,' he said, his voice angry. 'I'm on the fucking john here. I don't want to be part of your kinky toilet-stall game.'

The Werewolf laughed animatedly.

Hunter aimed the phone back at him. 'Now what?'

'*Do you still have the diary?*'

Hunter frowned at the screen. 'Of course I have the diary, or did you think I've dropped it in the past two and a half minutes?'

'*Show it to me.*'

Hunter did.

'Do you have to have this conversation in here?' the man on the toilet asked. 'I really need to go and I'm holding on as hard as I can right now, but I'm about to lose the battle.'

'Sorry,' Hunter said, his tone sincere. 'I apologize again for barging in on you like this.'

'Dude, just go, please.'

Hunter exited the cubicle, closing the now busted door behind him.

'*That was fun, huh?*'

'Yes, hilarious,' Hunter replied, his voice lacking all humor. 'So what do you want me to do now?'

'*Discard the old phone.*'

Hunter reached into his pocket for the phone, showed it to the Werewolf and then dropped it into the bathroom's wastebasket.

'OK, and?'

'*The Westin Bonaventure Hotel, do you know it?*'

'The one in South Figueroa Street?'

'*That's exactly the one. Five and a half blocks from where you are. Get to the thirty-fourth floor and find suite 3452. Go on foot. When you get to the hotel, use the stairs, not the elevator. You have twelve minutes. Go.*'

The Werewolf disconnected from the call.

Seventy-Three

The Westin Bonaventure Hotel and Suites was the largest hotel in the city of Los Angeles – 35 stories high, with 1,358 rooms and 135 suites. The hotel also offered its guests fine-dining restaurants, luxury spa services, swimming pools and a revolving restaurant and bar on the top floor that presented spectacular views over the City of Angels.

'*Twelve minutes to cover five and a half blocks on foot.*' This time it was Garcia's voice that came to Hunter's ear. He was obviously riding with SWAT Agent Shaffer. '*Then thirty-four floors up through the stairs? That's just nuts.*'

'There's not much I can do about it,' Hunter replied, already exiting the bathroom at speed.

'*If you exit the market through the back doors,*' Garcia said, '*it will drop you on South Hill Street. Go right, not left. Take West Third Street, then it's a straight run for four blocks until you hit South Flower Street. Go left for another block and you'll get to the hotel back entrance, which is two levels below the main lobby on South Figueroa Street, but faster to get to.*'

'Good thinking,' Hunter said, bursting through the emergency exit door at the back of the market. That saved him from having to plow through the crowd once again.

Eleven minutes and forty-one seconds left.

Just as Garcia had suggested, Hunter swung right on South Hill Street, in the direction of West Third Street. He covered the half-block distance in seventeen seconds.

Eleven minutes and twenty-four seconds left.

Once Hunter got to West Third Street, just like Garcia had informed him, it was a straight, four-block run until South Flower Street.

Crossing the roads posed a little bit of a problem, but not as much as Hunter had expected. In total, the crossings cost him an extra twenty-three seconds. Hunter's new problem was his boots, cowboy-style and fake leather but with a one-and-a-half-inch heel. Definitely not made for running.

His feet had already started to hurt by the time he got to the Grand Central Market. By the time he had covered two blocks on West Third Street, they were begging for mercy and his pace was beginning to slow down.

'I should've thought of changing my shoes before I left,' he gasped.

By the time he finally covered four blocks and arrived at the corner of West Third and South Flower Street, he could feel that his boots had claimed skin and quite a bit of it. His pace had also seriously deteriorated. Altogether, from the market to his current position, including the extra twenty-three seconds at the road crossings, Hunter had used six minutes and twenty-nine seconds out of what was left of the twelve minutes.

Four minutes and thirty-two seconds left. To climb thirty-five stories.

From the street corner where Hunter was standing, there was still a block and a half to go until he reached the Westin

Bonaventure Hotel, but right then, his feet were screaming at him: 'Please, no more.'

'Screw this,' he said to himself.

'*Screw what?*' A worried Agent Shaffer asked in his ear.

'My boots,' Hunter replied, as he quickly leaned against the side of a building, took both of them off and left them on the sidewalk. That cost him another seven seconds. 'Ask someone to please pick them up. They're right at the corner of West Third and South Flower.'

'*What do you mean – "pick them up"?*' Agent Shaffer asked. '*You left your boots behind?*'

'Yep,' Hunter replied, as he took off down the road, wearing only socks on his feet. 'They were killing me.'

His pace improved a little, but it still wasn't his best. His boots had already caused the kind of damage that would force anyone to hobble as they walked, let alone run.

Hunter disregarded the pain as best he could and, in an awkward, half-limping sprint, covered the final block and a half in thirty-one seconds.

'I'm at the hotel,' Hunter said, his voice labored. 'Time?'

'*You have three minutes and fifty-four seconds left,*' Agent Shaffer replied.

'Awesome,' Hunter said, zooming past the hotel valet and the porter before entering the back lobby.

There was absolutely no way that the hotel porter wouldn't notice a hobbling-running man entering the hotel in his socks, which by then had already ripped to shreds.

'Sir,' the porter called in a loud voice, taking off after Hunter.

'Police business,' Hunter shouted back, without looking over his shoulders.

Before the porter could get through the doors, he was

approached by a slim dark-haired woman, who placed a strong hand on his shoulder, stopping him. She, very stealthily, showed him the badge that she was holding in her left hand, while whispering a few words into his left ear.

The porter looked down at the badge and first frowned at her words before his eyes widened in surprise.

A second later, the woman disappeared into the hotel.

By the time the woman entered the back lobby, Hunter had already climbed four flights of stairs, which only got him to the main hotel lobby on South Figueroa Street, two levels up.

There were two zigzagging flights of stairs per level. Hunter took the steps two, sometimes three at a time. At that pace, he would cover a whole flight of stairs – fourteen steps – in about four to five seconds.

'Time,' Hunter asked again, as he climbed the stairs past the main lobby.

'*Three minutes twenty-seven seconds left.*' Garcia this time.

'Not great,' Hunter said, getting to the first floor. 'Not great at all.' He carried on climbing two, three steps at a time, but he could already tell that he wouldn't be able to make it to the thirty-fourth floor in time.

By the time Hunter reached the sixth floor, his legs were starting to hurt. The muscle burn from the lactic acid build-up was also weakening him.

Two minutes and forty-two seconds left.

From the ninth floor onwards, Hunter had to use the handrail to help his aching legs.

'Time?' Hunter asked through heavy breathing, as he hit the tenth floor.

'*You have exactly two minutes, Robert,*' Garcia told him. '*Which floor are you on?*'

'Moving on to the eleventh,'

'Shit!' Garcia exclaimed.

'That's helpful,' Hunter came back. 'Thank you.'

Hunter knew that even if he could climb ten floors in one minute flat, he still wouldn't make it to the thirty-fourth floor in time. Despite that knowledge, he would give it his best shot.

The next ten floors felt like a marathon. Somehow Hunter found the energy from somewhere deep within him and he managed to cover them in one minute and eleven seconds.

Forty-nine seconds left.

Thirteen floors to go.

Begging his legs not to give up, Hunter was now covering a floor in about eleven seconds.

Floor twenty-two – thirty-eight seconds left.

Floor twenty-three – twenty-seven seconds left.

Floor twenty-four – sixteen seconds left.

Floor twenty-five – five seconds left.

Hunter's legs were starting to shake. His heart sounded like a rave.

Four ... three ... two ... one ...

Hunter was halfway between floors twenty-five and twenty-six when the phone in his pocket rang. It was the phone he had taken from the toilet water tank inside the bathroom at the Grand Central Market.

With a trembling hand, he reached for the phone, but he could already imagine what the Werewolf was about to say to him.

Hunter accepted the request for a new video call.

'*Tsk, tsk,*' the Werewolf said with a shake of the head, as soon as his face materialized on the phone's screen. '*Please tell me it ain't so, Detective. It looks to me that you haven't really made it to the thirty-fourth floor in time.'*

Hunter never stopped climbing. The phone in his right hand shook from left to right, as he carried on taking two to three steps up at a time.

'That was an . . .' Hunter said, completely out of breath. He had reached floor twenty-six and was busy moving on to floor twenty-seven. 'Impossible task . . . and you know it.'

'Are you still going for it?'

Hunter said nothing in return.

Floor twenty-seven reached, on to floor twenty-eight.

'Wow, I must admit, I do admire your commitment.'

Floor twenty-eight.

'Do you . . . still want . . . your diary?' Hunter half asked, half coughed the words.

Floor twenty-nine.

'Ha-ha-ha-ha.' The Werewolf laughed a humorless laugh. *'Please, Detective, don't tell me that you're trying to bargain with me.'*

Floor thirty.

'Well . . . if you still . . . want it . . . I . . . still . . . got it.'

Floor thirty-one.

'I like you, Detective Hunter. You're not the type that gives up on a fight, no matter how much that fight seems to already be lost.'

Floor thirty-two.

'I respect that in people. Which floor are you on right now?'

'Thirty-three . . .' Hunter's voice was a whisper.

'What, really?'

Hunter coughed, trying to drag some more oxygen into his lungs. He could feel his legs turning to jelly under him and he grabbed onto the wall for balance.

'No,' he replied. 'Not thirty-three ... I'm on floor ... thirty-four.'

Hunter aimed the phone in his hand at the number on the wall by the door – 34.

Seventy-Four

Hunter paused by the door that connected the stairs to the thirty-fourth floor. His chest was heaving so heavily, he actually thought that a heart attack was on its way. He coughed again. This time he tasted bile in his mouth.

'*Are you all right, Detective?*' the Werewolf asked. '*You don't sound too good.*'

'Never better,' Hunter replied, spit flying from his mouth. He finally found the strength to push open the door and step onto the landing on floor thirty-four. 'So . . . I'm here . . .'

'*Really?*'

'Yes . . . floor thirty-four . . .'

'*But you didn't make it in time, Detective.*'

'C'mon . . .' Hunter pleaded, oxygen at last traveling a little more freely into his nostrils. 'I'm here.'

'*Here where?*'

'On the thirty-fourth floor.'

'*OK, but are you anywhere near room 3452?*'

Hunter had been so concerned with getting to the thirty-fourth floor of the hotel that he had forgotten that he also needed to get to a specific room. He lifted his head to look down the long and brightly lit corridor that ran left and right from where he was standing. Both sides seemed to go on for-ever before rounding the corner. His eyes moved to the plate on the wall that indicated which rooms were to which side. Room 3452 was to his left. He took in another lung full of air and took off down the corridor, as fast as his aching legs could move.

Guest rooms lined both sides of the corridor. The first room Hunter passed on his right was numbered 3426. Room 3452 was not that far ahead.

'*You're running again, Detective?*'

It took Hunter just a few seconds to reach room 3452.

'I'm here. Look,' Hunter said, aiming the phone at the number on the door. 'Room thirty-four fifty-two. I'm here.'

'*Yes, I can see that,*' the Werewolf said. '*But like I've said, you didn't make it in time. You do remember rule number two, don't you, Detective Hunter? "If you are even a second late accomplishing any of the tasks you are given, the thieving bitch dies." And by my watch, you were late.*'

'C'mon,' Hunter pleaded again. 'No one would've made it from the market here and then up sixty-eight flights of stairs in twelve minutes. That was an impossible task.'

'*You're wrong, Detective. That was in no way an impossible task. I can think of a handful of guys that would've made it there with time to spare.*'

Hunter refilled his lungs with air.

'Let me guess . . .' he said, and almost stopped himself, but he figured that right then, he didn't really have much to lose. 'You're talking about some of your buddies from the military.'

The Werewolf paused and even through the small screen on the smartphone in his hand, Hunter could see the focus in the killer's eyes intensify.

Hunter wondered if he had made a fatal mistake.

'*I'm impressed,*' the Werewolf said after several long silent seconds. '*And yes, some of my buddies from the military would've accomplished that task in ten minutes or less. So you've failed, Detective Hunter. The bitch has to die.*'

'If you kill her, you're never going to see this diary again. Do you understand me?'

'*Are you threatening me, Detective?*'

'It's not a threat. It's reality. You want the diary. We want the girl. It's a simple exchange. I'm here now, just outside room thirty-four fifty-two. So let's cut the crap and do this.'

Right at that moment, from the corner of his eye, Hunter saw the first two-man-strong team emerge from the same stairwell door that he had come through moments earlier. An instant later, a second team appeared, this time coming out of the elevator. With the same hand that was holding the diary, Hunter used his right index finger to signal both teams that they should stand down. The Werewolf wasn't an idiot. He wouldn't have boxed himself inside a room on the thirty-fourth floor of a hotel. Behind that door, Hunter would probably find his next task.

'*You're right, Detective,*' the Werewolf finally replied. '*I do want my diary back. And since you didn't give up on the stairs when the time was up, since you pushed yourself to complete the task despite everything, I will cut the crap. Let's do this.*' A new pause, this time a little longer. '*To the right of room 3452 there is an unnumbered door. Do you see it?*'

'Yes.'

'*It's unlocked. I want you to open it. Keep the camera aimed at your actions.*'

Hunter aimed the phone at the unnumbered door, extended his hand and twisted the doorknob. The door opened inwards.

'*Good,*' the Werewolf told him. '*The light switch is to the right of the door.*'

Hunter reached for it and switched it on. He found himself staring into a medium-sized room where three large laundry trolleys took most of the space inside. All three trolleys were empty.

'*This is the floor's laundry room,*' the Werewolf informed Hunter. '*On the far wall you'll see a large hatch. That's the laundry chute. Open it and drop the diary down it. Do it now.*'

'*Shit!*' Hunter heard Agent Shaffer's voice in his ear. '*He's down in the fucking laundry room. All teams get to the laundry room NOW.*'

Clever misdirection, Hunter thought.

'*Now, Detective,*' the Werewolf commanded again.

'How about Angela?' Hunter asked. 'The deal was the diary for Angela.'

'*The deal also was for you to accomplish every task in the time given. We're not having a discussion, Detective. The diary in the chute and you'll get the girl. You have my word. Otherwise, I promise you that you'll get a new piece of that little bitch delivered to your door every day for the next two months, do you hear me? You've got three seconds. One ... two ...*'

Hunter had no way of stalling anymore. He would not risk Angela's life for the diary, plus, he did have a contingency plan in place. He rushed over to the wall hatch, opened it and dropped the diary down the chute.

'*Nice doing business with you, Detective Hunter,*' the Werewolf said before terminating the call.

Seventy-Five

'Shit!'

Through their radios, all three two-man SWAT teams heard their leader, Agent Terrance Shaffer, shout the expletive.

'*He's down in the fucking laundry room. All teams get to the laundry room – NOW.*'

The three SIS teams got the exact same order from their leader, Agent Trevor Silva. The problem was, two of the six teams had positioned themselves by the elevator and the stairs on the thirty-fourth floor. One other team had positioned itself one floor below and another one floor above, in case the Werewolf had some crazy escape plan in mind. The final two teams were downstairs, guarding the front and back exits to the hotel.

The laundry room for the Westin Bonaventure Hotel was located on sublevel one. It would take the four teams on floors thirty-three, thirty-four and thirty-five way too long to get down to the basement. The two teams on the ground floor stood the best chance, and as they received the command from their leaders, all four agents rushed through the large and luxuriously decorated lobby in the direction of the stairwell, but they only managed to travel a total of five paces before they were interrupted by the screaming sound of a fire alarm.

The reception lobby was reasonably busy at that time of the day. There were guests arriving and checking in, guests checking out, guests trying to ask for directions or information and people just sitting around, chatting.

In the busy lobby, the fire alarm immediately caused a cacophony of movement just about everywhere. All of the guests began looking around in wonder, their hands going up in the air to indicate that they didn't really know what was going on. At first, the staff mimicked the guests' movement – wondering stares and confused looks – but in mere seconds, as they all realized that what was happening wasn't a drill, training kicked in. The bellboys, the concierges, the receptionists, the security guards, the hotel manager . . . all of them began rushing around, trying to coordinate the guests into exiting the building in an orderly fashion. To avoid a bottleneck at the hotel doors, the porters held them all wide open while the guests, some of them dragging their cases with them, flooded through.

That initial operation – guests who were already in the lobby – ran considerably smoothly, but still to come were the guests who had been inside their rooms. Out of the 1,358 rooms inside the Westin Bonaventure Hotel, 1,202 were taken. Out of the 135 suites, 101 were taken. Not all guests were in their rooms at that time, but the ones that were, were enough to fill a medium-sized concert hall.

Within fifteen seconds of the alarm going off, the long corridors in every single floor became a busy highway of guests dressed in all different sorts of clothes. Their concerned voices also joined forces with the loud alarm and, just like that, the entire building became a beehive of buzzing and somewhat anxious noise.

Though they knew they had no chance of getting to the laundry room fast enough, the four teams on floors thirty-three, thirty-four and thirty-five rushed to the stairwell, only to find a traffic jam of guests.

Fire regulations in California specified that elevators are not to be used during a fire evacuation – stairs only – and so the Westin Bonaventure Hotel fire alarm was programmed to automatically deactivate all the elevators.

Back down in the reception lobby, as they tried to rush into the hotel to reach the stairwell access door, the two ground-level teams were greeted by a wall of people traveling in the opposite direction. The more people they got past, the more people they encountered, as new guests started pouring into the lobby from the floors above.

'The target could be anyone exiting the hotel right now,' SWAT Agent Karl Hudson, leader of one of the two teams, said into his radio.

'And that's why we have a tracker hidden inside the diary that he's now carrying,' Agent Shaffer replied into Agent Hudson's ear. *'I'm coming into the lobby right now with the tracker app.'*

Agent Hudson and his team partner immediately turned around to check the lobby's main entrance.

Standing six-foot four inches tall, Agent Shaffer towered above most of the guests trying to exit the hotel. Garcia, who was six-foot two, was right next to him. It took the two-man SWAT team no time at all to spot them. Right on their heels was SIS Agent Trevor Silva. The second two-man team on the ground floor belonged to him.

All seven of them met by the long reception desk.

'Excuse me, gentlemen,' a short and plump man said, as

he emerged from behind the counter. 'Could you please make your way outside the building. The fire assembly point is just across the road, by the Enterprise car park.' He indicated with his right hand. The badge on his suit jacket read 'Luis Tornado, Concierge'.

'LAPD,' Garcia said, displaying his badge. He thought about telling the concierge that the alarm was actually a diversion, created by the person they were after, but he quickly thought better of it. Instead, all he said was: 'We're staying.'

All six other members of the police group looked at the hotel employee sternly.

'Suit yourselves,' he said, lifting both of his hands and quickly turning to assist others.

The lobby was starting to look like Walmart on a Black Friday, as more and more guests emerged from the stairwells.

Agents Silva and Shaffer placed their tablets on the reception counter to check the progress of the blinking red dot.

There was no red dot at all on the map.

'Where the fuck is it?' Agent Silva asked. 'Is this shit working?' His eyes sought Garcia's.

'Maybe he's still down in sublevel one,' Garcia replied. 'It's not a very strong tracker. It won't transmit from underground.'

'So let's go down and box him in,' Agent Shaffer suggested. 'You two.' He pointed at his two SIS agents. 'You go . . .' But before he was able to say anything else, a red dot suddenly appeared on the electronic map and started blinking.

Seventy-Six

'*What's going on?*' All seven in the group heard Hunter's voice come loud and clear through their earpieces. '*Where is he?*'

'The tracker just began transmitting,' Garcia told his partner.

'*OK, and where in the hotel is he?*'

Garcia joined the rest of the group, as everyone attentively stared at the map on the tablets' screen.

'He's not in the hotel.' This time the answer came from Agent Silva. 'Not anymore. He's just exited it, using a staff exit somewhere at the back of the hotel.'

They all exchanged concerned looks.

'He's on South Flower Street,' Agent Shaffer told Hunter. 'Same entrance you used.'

Another exchange of looks, only this time a little more urgent.

A split second later, all seven of them took off as fast as they could toward the hotel second entrance, the one that faced South Flower Street. The congestion of bodies in the hotel lobby was a problem and they dealt with it the only way they could – like a wide receiver going for a touchdown, pushing and shoving guests out of their way. It took them around forty seconds to make it to the door.

'Where?' Garcia asked, as they finally got outside.

Agents Shaffer and Silva consulted their maps. As they did, the expressions on their faces became anxious.

'He's on West Fourth Street,' Agent Shaffer announced. 'It looks like he's rounding the hotel, all the way to the main entrance on the other side.'

'He's going to join the crowd of guests,' Garcia said, figuring out the Werewolf's plan. 'What better way to disappear than among so many bodies?'

They could all hear the sound of fire engines somewhere in the distance.

'Let's go,' Agent Silva said, leading the group on a hectic sprint up to West Fourth Street, then left for an entire block. As they got to the corner of West Fourth and South Figueroa, they checked their maps again.

'You're right,' Agent Shaffer addressed Garcia. 'He's crossed the road and joined the crowd.'

'Let's split up and flank him,' Agent Silva suggested, before turning to address his agents. 'You two come with me.' He faced Agent Shaffer. 'We'll go down South Figueroa and approach from the left. You guys cross right here and take the right. That will give him only two escape routes – he either crosses the road again, coming back to the hotel main entrance, or he enters the Enterprise building across the road. Either way we've got him.'

'Roger that,' Agent Shaffer replied before getting on his radio again. 'Teams one and two, where are you?'

'*We're coming down as fast as we can.*' The reply came back immediately. '*But the stairs are mayhem.*'

Agent Shaffer could hear the buzzing of voices coming through his agent's radio.

'*We're on floor thirteen,*' the agent informed his leader.

'Do better,' Agent Shaffer replied. 'I need you guys down here pronto.'

Agent Silva and his SIS two-man team had already crossed South Figueroa Street and were approaching the crowd from the other side.

Agent Shaffer had another look at the map. 'Let's go,' he commanded, leading Garcia and his two-man team across the road.

The crowd standing in front of the Enterprise building was a large one, getting larger by the second, as more and more guests exited the hotel and crossed the road.

The fire engines were getting closer.

'So where is he?' Garcia asked.

Agent Shaffer checked the map. 'He's smart. He got himself right in the middle of the crowd.'

'Let's move,' Garcia said.

All four of them began making their way through.

'*How close are you?*' everyone heard Agent Silva ask though their earpieces.

'We're about forty yards from the target,' Agent Shaffer replied. 'How about you?'

'*We're a little closer – about twenty-five yards.*'

'OK,' Garcia took over. 'Get to about ten yards and hold. Spread your team up to block his escape routes in case he tries to run. We'll approach from this side to make the arrest.'

'*Please let me face him,*' Agent Silva asked. '*He killed two of my men.*'

'This isn't a revenge exercise,' Garcia replied, his tone solid. 'This is still a UVC Unit investigation. We're making the arrest. Hold at ten yards and spread your team to block his escape routes, is that understood?'

'*Understood.*' Agent Silva didn't sound pleased.

Garcia and the three SWAT agents continued to make progress through the crowd.

Thirty yards.

Twenty yards.

Ten yards.

'*We're in position,*' Agent Silva's voice came through in their ears.

Five yards.

They checked the map on the tablet one more time. The red dot was blinking just ahead of Garcia, in a straight line.

'I can't see any smoke,' said a short woman in a white bathrobe, who was standing to Garcia's right. 'If there's a fire, where's the smoke?'

Garcia disregarded the woman and took another step forward. There was no mistaking who they were looking for. Standing in the middle of the crowd, looking back at the hotel, was a broad-shouldered, six-foot-three man. His physique could've belonged to a professional boxer. The man had a worried look on his face. His eyes kept on scanning the crowd anxiously. The man was wearing blue jeans, a black T-shirt and an LA Dodgers baseball jacket. Hanging from his shoulder and by the right side of his hip was a small black and white gym bag.

Agent Shaffer ordered his men to go left and right, creating a circle around their target.

Garcia's right hand moved to the inside of his jacket. He unclipped his gun holster and allowed his fingers to wrap around the grip of his Sig Sauer X-Five Legion 9mm pistol. He thumbed the safety, but kept the weapon hidden under his jacket. He took another step forward and that was when he and the target locked eyes for just an instant. The man narrowed his eyes at Garcia, as if he had somehow recognized him.

To Garcia, the next couple of seconds moved in slow motion. He saw the man's right hand seek his gym bag, which was already unzipped. The man blinked once and his hand disappeared into the bag.

Garcia couldn't see what the man had reached for because the man's body blocked Garcia's view.

The man's eyes returned to Garcia and his body rotated slightly left in the detective's direction. He was repositioning himself.

What Garcia didn't know was that SWAT Agent Terrance Shaffer had positioned himself behind the target, keeping him in a direct line of view. Agent Shaffer had also witnessed the man's movements. Once he saw the man's hand move into his gym bag, Agent Shaffer made his move, and he moved fast. By the time the man began rotating his body in the direction of Garcia, Agent Shaffer was already flying through the air.

The man never saw him coming.

The tackle, if in a football game, would've probably won 'play of the year'.

While in midair, Agent Shaffer collided with the man's body with incredible precision, grabbing him by the waist. The man was, without a doubt, a lot heavier than Agent Shaffer, but Agent Shaffer's momentum, together with him suddenly appearing out of a standing crowd, gave him the advantage.

The heavy impact of body against body catapulted the man forward and into two other hotel guests. All four of them fell to the ground, which immediately prompted a chorus of loud voices to come from the crowd.

Standing just a few feet away, Garcia already had his weapon drawn, as did the two other SWAT agents that had circled the man. Their sights locked onto the man's head.

'Freeze,' Garcia yelled. 'LAPD.'

The man had hit the ground hard ... very hard. First his left shoulder, then his head. His unzipped gym bag tumbled against his hip as he fell and most of its contents spilled onto the sidewalk.

Though his full attention was centered on the man on the ground, Garcia's eyes flickered to the items that had just spilled out of the man's bag. One of the items ended up almost at Garcia's feet. He looked down at it, blinked once ... twice ... then froze.

'What the fuck?'

Seventy-Seven

Five minutes earlier – laundry room, sublevel one of the Westin Bonaventure Hotel.

'This is the floor's laundry room,' through his video call, the Werewolf informed Hunter. 'On the far wall you'll see a large hatch. That's the laundry chute. Open it and drop the diary down it. Do it now.'

...

'Now, Detective,' the Werewolf commanded again.

'*How about Angela?*' Hunter asked. '*The deal was the diary for Angela.*'

'The deal also was for you to accomplish every task in the time given. We're not having a discussion, Detective. The diary in the chute and you'll get the girl. You have my word. Otherwise, I promise you that you'll get a new piece of that little bitch delivered to your door every day for the next two months, do you hear me? You've got three seconds. One ... two ...'

He watched Hunter rush over to the wall hatch, open it and drop the diary down the chute.

Just a few seconds later the Werewolf watched as the

diary fell from the chute onto a pile of dirty clothes, inside a large cart.

'Nice doing business with you, Detective Hunter,' he said before disconnecting from the call.

On the floor, by his feet, the Werewolf had an unzipped gym bag. He retrieved the diary from the pile of dirty clothes and pulled the Werewolf mask from over his head before reaching into the bag for an electronic device that looked a little like a handheld metal detector – the kind used by airport security. He switched the device on and brought it to the diary's front cover.

The needle on the device didn't move. There was no sound either.

The man flipped the diary over and brought the device to about half an inch from its back cover. As soon as he did, the device began beeping loudly while the needle on the meter kicked all the way to the right.

'Oh, Detective Hunter,' the Werewolf said to himself with a shake of the head. 'You disappoint me. A tracker? Really?' He reached back into the gym bag. This time, he retrieved a heavy-duty box cutter. 'OK, then. Let's have some fun, shall we?'

After flipping open the back cover, he used the cutter to slice the whole of the back cover off the diary. It took him only a couple of seconds to do it. He placed the diary inside his gym bag before walking over to the fire alarm button on the wall by the door to the laundry room and activating it.

In a flash, all thirty-five floors inside the Westin Bonaventure Hotel were taken up by the desperate screams of the fire alarm. A few seconds later, worried guests and hotel employees started pouring into the corridors and stairwells. Confusion and disorientation took over the crowd in no time at all, which was exactly what the Werewolf was after.

He grabbed his gym bag, together with the diary's back cover, pulled his hood over his head and quickly stepped out of the laundry room. The corridors of sublevel one were already busy with people. Guests and employees alike were coming out of the gym, the spa, and one of the kitchens, all located on the same level.

The Werewolf joined the crowd, which was already being guided by a hotel employee, telling everyone to use one of the emergency fire exits, instead of using the stairs to go up to the ground floor. As the man joined the crowd, he couldn't believe his luck. Only a few paces in front of him, a tall and well-built hotel guest had just exited the gym. The guest was wearing blue jeans, a black T-shirt and an LA Dodgers jacket. Hanging from his shoulder was a small black and white gym bag, which the Werewolf noticed was unzipped.

'Perfect,' he whispered to himself.

He hurried to catch up with the hotel guest. With everyone so close to each other, the man had absolutely no problem slipping the torn diary cover into the guest's gym bag.

'This should be fun,' he thought. As the group of people exited the building and turned left in the direction of West Fourth Street, the Werewolf turned back on himself and re-entered the hotel.

There was still something he needed to do.

Seventy-Eight

Outside, as the contents of the man's gym bag spilled onto the ground, Garcia's eyes flickered to the one item that had ended up just by his feet.

He blinked once – doubt muddled his thoughts.

Twice – that was when he finally realized what he was actually looking at – the torn back cover of the killer's diary.

'What the fuck?'

The other two SWAT agents, who also had their weapons drawn, had already moved forward to help Agent Shaffer. It took them just a blink of an eye to get to him. In no time at all, they had immobilized the man on the ground, holding his head tight against the sidewalk and handcuffing his hands behind his back.

'You're under arrest on suspicion of murder,' Agent Shaffer said, as he started to read the man his Miranda warning. 'You have the right to remain silent . . .'

'What?' the man on the ground yelled back. 'What the hell is going on here?' The expression on his face was a mixture of anger, surprise and terror. 'Suspicion of murder? What murder?'

Agent Shaffer disregarded the man's cries and carried on with the warning. 'Anything you say can and will be used . . .'

Agent Silva, together with his two SIS Agents, had seen the hurried movement of people, as Agent Shaffer tackled the man to the ground. They too moved in to assist the SWAT agent.

Garcia quickly retrieved a paper tissue from his pocket, bent down and picked up the torn back cover by his feet. He flipped it one way then the other, studying it.

'*What's going on out there?*' he heard Hunter ask through his earpiece. '*Do we have him?*'

'Yes, we have the scumbag,' Agent Silva replied. He had got to the man and was helping the SWAT agents get him back on his feet. As he held the man by his arms and pulled him up, he moved his lips to less than half an inch from the man's ear and whispered. 'Please try to run so I have an excuse to blow your brains out right here . . . right now.' He let go of the man. 'C'mon . . . run. You can do this.'

'Robert,' Garcia finally said. He was still staring at the torn back cover. 'I think that we might have a problem here.'

'*What sort of problem?*'

Garcia saw Agents Shaffer and Silva, who had also heard Hunter's question and Garcia's reply in their earpieces, move their attention from the handcuffed man to him. Both of them had that same question floating around inside their eyes: *What sort of problem?*

Garcia lifted the cover to show Agents Shaffer and Silva. 'It looks like Werewolf man has anticipated our move,' Garcia replied to Hunter.

'*Which move is that?*' Hunter asked.

'The tracker,' Garcia explained. 'Someone tore it off.'

'*What do you mean, "tore it off"?*'

'Someone tore off the whole of the diary's back cover, Robert. That's what the suspect we just bagged had with him – the torn-off back cover, which contained the tracker we planted into the diary.'

Agent Shaffer immediately let go of the man, reaching for his gym bag. He rifled through whatever was left inside it for a few seconds before throwing the bag back on the ground. 'No diary,' he announced. 'Fuck!'

The two SWAT agents had already patted the man down. He had no concealed weapons with him, but they did find a wallet with $112 in cash, three credit cards, a driver's license and a photo of a smiling dark-haired woman next to a little boy that looked to be about three years old. The name on the license matched the one on the credit cards – Gabriel Quinn.

By then, the crowd at that particular spot had moved back considerably, clearing a large space around the man and the LAPD officers. Ninety-eight percent of the crowd that formed the large human circle had their cellphones out and were filming everything.

Agent Shaffer walked over to Garcia and handed him the man's wallet.

'Apparently,' Garcia started telling Hunter, but he was forced to pause, as the fire engines finally started arriving on South Figueroa Street – six in total. 'Hold on ...' He waited for almost a minute until they had all parked and switched off their sirens. 'OK, apparently the person we've just arrested is one Gabriel Quinn – thirty-eight years old, from Palo Alto.'

'What the hell do you mean – "apparently"?' the man shouted back, his eyes wide open in shock. 'That's who I am.'

'This could all be a trick,' Agent Silva said, staring the man down. 'We all know how clever this guy is.'

This time the man didn't shy away from the agent's stare. 'Oh, you better get ready for the lawsuit of the century,' he told

Silva, his tone defiant. 'Just have a look around you, buddy. Can you see all the phone cameras pointing your way? Well, that's called evidence and that's exactly what I'm going to use to fuck you up.'

'Mr. Quinn,' Garcia said, coming up to the man. His tone was calm and a little apologetic. 'I'm Detective Carlos Garcia with the LAPD's Ultra Violent Crimes Unit. You're right, this might all be a misunderstanding, and if you could please come with me to one of our patrol cars, we can clear all this up in a few minutes.' He paused and looked at the man's gym bag on the floor. 'We might also need your help.'

Seventy-Nine

From when Hunter last spoke to Garcia over the radio, it took him another fourteen minutes to clear the last few flights of stairs and finally get all the way down to the hotel's reception lobby. It took him another minute and a half to get through the crowds and find the patrol car to which Garcia had taken Gabriel Quinn.

Garcia was just coming off a call to Shannon Hatcher when he saw Hunter appear barefoot from the crowd.

'I've just got off the phone to Shannon,' Garcia said, as Hunter got to him. 'Everything checks out. The guy in the back seat ...' his chin jerked in the direction of the patrol car and the tall man sitting inside it, '... really is Gabriel Quinn from Palo Alto. He's a web developer. He's in LA for a convention, which is actually happening right here at the Westin Hotel.'

Hunter already knew that the man's identity would check out.

'He was just coming out of the hotel gym on sublevel one,' Garcia continued, 'when the alarm went off.'

'Did you ask him if he remembers seeing anyone coming out of the laundry room right about that time?' Hunter asked.

'I didn't ask him about the laundry room,' Garcia admitted.

'But I did ask him if he remembers anyone trying to strike up a conversation with him while he was exiting the hotel, or if anyone bumped into him or anything . . .' Garcia shrugged. 'Mr. Quinn laughed. He said that everyone was bumping into everyone . . . everybody was talking to everyone.'

Hunter nodded, disappointment making the edges of his mouth droop.

Garcia shook his head. 'How the hell did Werewolf man know about the tracker?'

'He didn't,' Hunter came back. 'But he probably suspected that we would've tried something. My guess is that he had some sort of device with him that picked up airwave transmissions. That's how he found the tracker so fast.'

'Fuck!' Garcia whispered under his breath. 'Now what?'

Hunter knew that there was nothing that they or anyone else could do.

The fire brigade had finally established that there was no fire. It'd been a false alarm, triggered from the laundry room on sublevel one.

Hunter paused and looked back at the crowd that was at last being allowed to go back into the hotel. He wondered if the Werewolf was still around, hanging in the crowd just for the fun of it. Hunter wouldn't be surprised if he was.

He was about to go to speak to Gabriel Quinn himself when he felt a phone vibrate inside his outside jacket pocket. He frowned at Garcia before reaching for it. As he retrieved the phone, Hunter's frown morphed into a questioning look. He didn't recognize the phone. It was neither his own nor the one that he had been carrying with him since he left the Grand Central Market. This time, it wasn't a smartphone. What Hunter had in his hand was a Motorola Doro 6520.

He looked up and searched the crowd again. Obviously, the
Werewolf had somehow slipped the phone into his pocket
as he was leaving the hotel, which meant that he probably
was somewhere close. Probably somewhere where he could
see Hunter at that exact moment. The problem was, at that
exact moment, most people in the crowd had a phone in
their hands.

Half a second was all it took for Garcia to figure out what
was going on. His eyebrows arched at Hunter.

'Are you joking?' he asked. 'It's him again?'

Agents Shaffer and Silva quickly joined the two detectives.

Hunter flipped the phone open – unknown number.

He took the call.

'Hello?'

'*A tracker, Detective Hunter?*' the Werewolf asked. '*Really?
How much of an amateur do you think I am? You did have
a look at the diary, right? Did I come across as an amateur to you?*'

Hunter didn't really know how to reply.

'*All I can tell you right now, Detective, is that your little
trick . . . your little tracker, has sealed the girl's fate.*'

'Don't,' Hunter tried. 'You have your diary back. That
was the agreement – you get the diary, we get Angela. Just let
her go . . . please. Taking her life will not achieve anything.
Let her go.'

'*Oh no, Detective Hunter, it sounds to me like you're
begging. Is that what you're doing? You're begging a killer
not to kill?*'

Hunter took in a deep breath. 'Yes. I am begging you. Please.
Let her go. Let her live.'

'*That would indeed look very bad on your record, wouldn't*

*it? Your "tracker" plan goes wrong and it costs the life of a
civilian hostage. That can't be good.'*

'This is not about me,' Hunter said. 'I really couldn't care
less about my record. This is about a young woman's life. A
woman who made a mistake when she took your bag. That was
all. She doesn't deserve to die for that.'

*'Well, Detective Hunter, since you're begging, let me
see you beg.'*

'What?'

*'I want to see you beg me not to kill her. I want to see you
get down on your knees and beg.'*

Hunter's gaze went back to the crowd, which was then considerably thinner than moments ago. The only way in which
the Werewolf would be able to see him beg was if he did indeed
have eyes on him.

Despite the thinning crowd, Hunter could not identify
anyone as a likely suspect.

'I'm waiting, Detective. On your knees.'

Hunter didn't move.

'Get on your knees ... NOW.'

Slowly, Hunter got down on both knees.

Garcia, Agent Shaffer and Agent Silva took a step back and
all three of them looked back at Hunter sideways.

'What are you doing?' Garcia asked.

'Now beg.'

'Please,' Hunter said, still holding the phone to his right ear.
'I'm begging you. Let Angela live.'

The penny dropped for Garcia and the two agents. It was
their turn to scan the crowd.

'Motherfucker,' Agent Silva gasped, as he signaled his agents
to get back into the crowd and start looking.

'Who are we looking for?' one of the agents asked.

'Anyone suspicious,' Agent Silva replied, motioning them to scatter into the crowd.

'*I'm sure you can do better than that, Detective. Say it louder.*'

Hunter repeated the same seven words of seconds ago. This time louder.

'*No, no, Detective. I want you to shout it as if your lungs were on fire. Let the world know that you want the girl to live.*'

Hunter powered his lungs with as much oxygen as he could breathe in.

'PLEASE, I'M BEGGING YOU, LET ANGELA LIVE.'

Absolutely everyone around turned to look at the seemingly crazy man, down on his knees, yelling his guts out.

'*One more time.*'

Hunter yelled it again.

'*And again.*'

Hunter complied.

'*You have a powerful voice, Detective.*'

There was a short pause, as if the Werewolf was thinking about his answer.

'No,' he finally announced. '*The bitch dies. But I'll call you again to let you know where you can go pick up her body . . . or whatever is left of it.*'

The Werewolf terminated the call.

Hunter got back to his feet, and his gaze went back to the few guests still hanging around outside the hotel.

The Werewolf's words kept ringing in Hunter's ears. He didn't know who or where the killer was, but there was one thing that he knew for sure – the Werewolf was wrong. He would call Hunter before that.

Eighty

Back at the PAB, Hunter and Garcia were immediately summoned into Captain Blake's office.

'What a fantastic shit-show this was,' she said from behind her desk, as soon as Hunter gave her a rundown of what had happened, including the final phone call.

'He was much better prepared to deal with us,' Garcia said, 'than we were to deal with him.'

'Oh, you think?' Sarcasm oozed from Captain Blake's every pore. 'He ran laps around the two of you, the LAPD SWAT and the SIS.'

Hunter kept his mouth shut and kept his eyes down on the floor.

'Goddamn it,' the captain continued, getting to her feet. 'We're talking about a very prolific serial killer here ... and he was going up against one of the most prolific serial killer hunters this country has ever seen, and said serial killer has played you like a fiddle.'

Hunter's eyes moved from the floor to meet Captain Blake's.

'You're making this sound as if this is about reputations, Captain,' Hunter came back, his voice showing annoyance.

'No, I'm not. I'm making this sound like disappointment. How could this have happened so easily?'

'Because he was calling the shots,' Hunter replied. 'We had to play by his rules and follow his commands. He always had the advantage because he knew what was coming ... he knew what the next step would be because he was the one who created each step.'

Captain Blake closed her eyes and used the tip of her index finger to gently massage between her eyebrows. 'So that poor girl – Angela Wood – she's as good as dead.'

Garcia looked down at the floor in anger, accepting Captain Blake's statement, but Hunter didn't look so convinced.

'Maybe not,' he said.

'What do you mean?' the captain asked.

'We'll have to wait for his call.'

'Oh, you mean the one where he gives you the location of where we can find her body,' the captain said. 'That was what he told you he would do, was it not?'

'Yes,' Hunter agreed. 'But I have a ...' He gave his captain an almost imperceptible shrug. 'A ...hunch that he's not done with us yet.'

'Great!' Captain Blake replied, throwing her hands in the air. 'You and your goddamn hunches will end up giving me an ulcer, Robert.'

Eighty-One

After leaving Captain Blake's office, Hunter spent the next hour sieving through the CCTV footage they had obtained from the camera on sublevel one of the Westin Bonaventure Hotel. He checked the images from before and after the fire alarm went off and on both occasions – as he entered and then as he exited the laundry room – the camera had caught who they believed was the man they called the Werewolf. The problem was, the man had clearly done his homework. He knew exactly where the CCTV camera was located, because all that Hunter and Garcia could see was a tall figure wearing a hood that had been pulled well over his head. Not once did the man look up, or even in the direction of the camera.

As Hunter parked his old Buick in the designated spot for his apartment, he took a moment to appreciate the Christmas decorations that graced some of his neighbors' windows. There were flickering lights, fake snow, colorful stars, reindeers, Santa Clauses, Baby Jesuses, the three kings and even a full-sized Homer Simpson in a Santa outfit hanging out of a window on the fifth floor. Hunter's window, on the third floor, was completely bare. He never really celebrated Christmas.

Not now. He had when he was a kid, but after his mother was taken by cancer near Christmas, his father couldn't bring himself to celebrate it anymore. Hunter grew up without the splendor of Christmas – no trees, no decorations, no lights. But his father would always buy him a gift and tell him that it had come from his mother.

Hunter breathed the memories away and checked his cellphone – no messages, no missed calls. He checked his watch – 8:55 p.m.

He felt exhausted. His feet hurt and his body ached from all the physical effort from earlier on. He closed his eyes, leaned back against the headrest and did the best he could to fight the awful feeling that was threatening to suffocate him, because he simply couldn't stop thinking of Angela and the probable consequences of what he had done.

Was she really already dead?

Would the Werewolf have acted on impulse instead of checking his diary first?

Hunter had refused to believe that, but as the clock ticked away, certainty had turned to doubt, and doubt was now beginning to give way to fear.

He had been so lost in his thoughts, so concerned in fighting away the fear, that Hunter barely heard the back door on the passenger's side being pulled open.

By the time he twisted his body to check what was happening, it was too late.

Eighty-Two

One minute earlier

From across the road, the man had been waiting patiently behind the wheel of his van. When he finally saw Hunter's Buick turn left onto Seville Avenue, he smiled, pulled his beanie a little lower down on his forehead, readjusted the leather gloves on his hands and stepped out of his vehicle.

Using the night as cover, the man moved quickly and stealthily, crossing the road and keeping himself in the shadows. By the time Hunter had parked and shut off his engine, the man was already crouching down behind a blue SUV, two spaces to Hunter's right. From the small of his back, he pulled out a 9mm semi-automatic pistol and got ready to make his move.

The man had expected Hunter to get out of the car straight away, but instead, the LAPD detective sat at the wheel with his eyes fixed on the building in front of him.

Stooping down, the man inched closer to hide behind Hunter's car. He waited another couple of seconds, but still there was no movement from Hunter.

'C'mon, c'mon. Get out of the car, Detective,' he urged Hunter under his breath.

The man was absolutely sure that Hunter hadn't spotted him. He was too good, too experienced, too professional to have made a mistake.

Quick change of plans.

If he's not coming out, I'm going in.

The man moved right toward the passenger's side, got his pistol ready and reached for the handle on the back door. He gave himself a count of one.

In a movement that was almost too fast to comprehend, the man pulled the door open and slipped into the backseat like a spider.

Hunter never saw him coming.

Game over.

Eighty-Three

Pure reflex kicked in and Hunter twisted his body right, in the direction of the noise.

Too late.

Before he could blink, Hunter found himself staring down the barrel of a 9mm semi-automatic pistol equipped with a sound suppressor.

'Detective Hunter,' the man said in his usual monotone voice. 'So nice to finally make your acquaintance.'

Hunter's gaze left the man's weapon and settled on his face.

So this is the man behind the werewolf mask, Hunter thought. *The man who sells his murders over the Dark Web.*

The man Hunter was looking at was in his early forties, wearing a black beanie that had been pulled down low on his forehead. His eyes, as dark as a starless night, were so cold that they could've belonged to a cadaver. He had a jagged scar traveling right across the bridge of his nose – a nose that had certainly been broken before – but that wasn't the only scar that graced the man's face. On his chin, a half-moon shape started at the left edge of his bottom lip and curved right, ending at the tip of his mandible. That particular scar hadn't healed nicely, the skin was thick and leathery. The man's face was square, his lips fleshy, his eyebrows thick and his jaw strong. His frame was muscular, but not the kind of muscle one got from working out at the gym. No, this was the kind of lean muscle you got from hard physical work. He wore midnight-black combat fatigues and black army boots.

Right then, Hunter thought that the man sitting on his backseat looked like an action hero. All that was missing was the five-day stubble.

'OK,' the man continued. 'This is what I need you to do, Detective – I need you to turn around and face front. Then I need you to put both of your hands behind your seat, one on each side, as if you were giving your seat a backwards hug. Do it now.'

Hunter held the man's eyes for a second.

The man chambered a round.

'Now, Detective.'

Hunter turned around to face his apartment building once again before doing exactly as he was told.

In a breath and with incredible dexterity, the man zip-tied Hunter's hands together.

'OK,' Hunter said. 'So now what?'

Instead of replying, the man got out of the car through the driver's side and opened Hunter's door.

Hunter looked up at him, intrigued.

Still taking aim at Hunter's face, the man reached into Hunter's jacket to retrieve his weapon, his cellphone, his badge and his handcuffs.

'Wow,' he commented as he eyed Hunter's piece. 'A Heckler and Koch Mark 23 pistol? I can see you know your stuff, Detective.' The man nodded at Hunter. 'I like it. Old school and the preferred offensive weapon of the US Special

Operations Command.' The man secured Hunter's gun against the small of his back. 'Back-up weapons?' he asked.

'No,' Hunter replied. 'None.'

'Well,' the man shrugged. 'I'll check anyway.'

The man patted-down Hunter's torso, legs and ankles. He found nothing.

'Happy?' Hunter asked.

The man smiled a cold smile. 'I don't even know what that word means anymore.'

Those words made the psychologist in Hunter stand to attention.

The man dropped Hunter's handcuffs onto Hunter's lap before reaching into one of his pockets to retrieve a large combat knife.

'You and I are going for a little ride, Detective,' the man said, as he used the knife to slice off the zip-tie and free Hunter's hands. His pistol was once again aimed at Hunter's head.

Hunter locked eyes with the man while massaging his wrists.

'Now,' the man continued, as he took a step back. 'Grab those handcuffs and handcuff your hands behind your back. No need to get out of the car. Just lean forward a little. Do it now and do it slowly.'

Hunter followed the man's instructions.

'A ride?' he questioned. 'Where are we going?'

'We're going to go see your little friend, the thieving bitch,' the man replied, now motioning Hunter to get out of the car.

Hunter did so.

'Walk in front of me,' the man commanded, jerking his chin in the direction of the road. 'See that dark van just across the road there? That's where we're going. You make one wrong move and it will be the last thing you'll ever do in this life. Are we clear?'

'Crystal.'

They walked slowly and in silence until they reached the van. Once they did, the man slid the side door open.

'Now face the van,' the man ordered.

Hunter did.

The man noisily sucked his teeth as he shook his head. 'You shouldn't have done what you did, Detective. Now, because of your stupid little trick, I'll have to show you what I'm capable of. I don't only want you to see what I'm going to do to that little bitch. I want you to be there. I want you to smell her fear. I want you to hear her screams. I want you to taste her blood. But most of all, I want you to pick up her pieces.'

The man slammed his pistol's grip onto the back of Hunter's head.

Lights out.

Eighty-Four

As Angela Wood woke up with a start from a dreamless sleep, confusion set in almost immediately. She looked around the room frantically, her head moving jerkily, like a chicken searching for food, but darkness was all around her – dense and solid, enough to make her think that her eyes were closed when she knew that they were wide open. All of a sudden her body began shivering – a combination of fear and cold. She hugged herself to try to produce some heat, rubbing the goose-bumpy skin on her arms as vigorously as she could. She wasn't naked, but she could feel that her clothes were a little damp. She grabbed the collar of her T-shirt and brought it to her nose. It didn't smell like sweat.

'Where the fuck am I?'

As soon as she uttered those words, Angela's throat exploded in agonizing pain, making her cringe. Reflexively, her hand shot to her neck. That was when she finally remembered – the safe house, the knock on her bedroom door, the man, the painful prick in her neck.

Angela sat still for a long while, her breathing labored, her shivering intensifying. She pulled her legs towards her chest and made herself small, hoping for more heat. It was then that it finally occurred to her that she wasn't restrained. She was cold and her clothes were damp, but other than the pain in her throat, she felt fine. She didn't even feel dizzy. She extended her legs and then brought them back against her body again. Definitely no pain. She did the same with her arms – they felt fine.

Angela forced herself up into a sitting position and waited. No wooziness. No headache. She took a deep breath and tried to think.

The first thing she needed to do was figure out where she was. Her body felt a little stiff from lying on the hard, uncomfortable surface. She inspected it with her hands, feeling every inch around her – a metal-framed single bed fitted with a thin mattress.

Angela swung her legs over and sat at the edge of the bed, her bare toes touching the cold cement floor.

For a moment she hesitated – her fear battling with her desire to get the hell out of there.

Desire won.

She got to her feet but stood still for a second.

No dizziness.

Her legs didn't feel weak.

Like a blind woman on a bad acid trip, her arms shot out in all directions, searching for something. She touched nothing but empty space. She turned to her right and took small steps, walking in a straight line. She counted her steps as she took them. Eight paces later, she came to a bare wall.

Angela extended her arms right, until she found a corner. That done, she faced left. She kept her right arm on the wall and with her left one she carried on feeling the way in front of her. Eight more paces and she hit a second wall. She faced left again and moved forward. This time she took only three steps. The wall went from bare cinderblock to solid metal – a door – but as soon as her hand touched it, for a fraction of a second, the whole room was lit by a blinding sparkle of light, as if a camera flash had gone off right in front of her. The sparkle was coupled with a loud popping noise. The electricity discharge was so surprising that Angela's reflexes catapulted her back onto the bed. Pain exploded through her, making her whole arm feel as if it were on fire and her brain finally realize that escaping that room was downright impossible.

Eighty-Five

Hunter was brought back into consciousness by a bucket of icy water to the face. In a fright, he lifted his head from his chest and immediately began coughing, gasping for air. The sudden head movement made Hunter focus on a headache that could've raised the dead. It started at the back of his skull and traveled forward, enveloping his entire head, his eyes, nose and mouth.

'Wakey, wakey.'

Hunter was sitting down on some sort of sturdy metal chair – thick and heavy. His hands had been zip-tied together by the wrists behind the chair's backrest. Each hand had then been zip-tied again to the backrest itself. His ankles had been zip-tied together in an 'X' shape, then each ankle had been individually zip-tied to the chair's legs. No matter how much strength Hunter had left in him, he knew that he would never be able to free himself without a sharp instrument to cut them off.

The room he was in was wide and square, and the walls were made out of solid cinderblock.

Hunter lifted his chin up just a little to check the ceiling. Eight halogen-bulbs bathed the room in bright light. Across the room from the chair he had been zip-tied to, he could see a control desk with a large monitor mounted on the wall directly above it. To the right of the desk there was a tall metal cabinet filled with electronics and computer equipment. There was a second cabinet, to the right of that, which looked to be locked. To the left of the control desk there was a metal door. Leaning against it was the man who Hunter knew as the Werewolf. By his feet Hunter could see an empty metal bucket.

Hunter coughed again before shaking his head to try to get rid of some of the water that kept dripping from his wet hair into his eyes. The movement gave his headache a new surge of power.

The Werewolf lifted his right hand to show Hunter his diary. The back cover was missing.

'I need the information that you've crossed out,' he said. His voice was still monotone, but his anger was clear.

He flipped open the diary to reveal that the thin leather sheet that lined the inside of the front cover had been removed. All four lines of handwritten text that Vince Keller had discovered that same morning back in the Electronics Unit lab had been crossed out with a thick black marker. The information was impossible to read.

This was Hunter's contingency plan.

That afternoon, once he'd heard the news that the Werewolf had murdered both SIS Agents at the safe house just to get to Angela, Hunter had called Keller and asked him to go back to the cover, note down all the information and then cross everything out. Keller had been skeptical about it. It was indeed a risky plan, but Hunter knew that the information on the flipside of the diary's front cover was the only reason why Angela was still alive, and he had a hunch that the Werewolf would throw some sort of surprise at him at the exchange, if there was to be one at all. Hiding a tracker in the diary's cover had been a good idea, but Hunter couldn't risk going into the exchange without some sort of backup plan, no matter how desperate that plan might be.

Hunter had committed the information to memory, but he also had the photo saved on his phone.

'I need it now,' the Werewolf commanded.

'I know you do,' Hunter said, trying his best to sound as calm as possible. His wet clothes chilled his body, making him shiver. 'That's the real reason why you brought me here. You need that information.'

The Werewolf studied the detective tied to the metal chair for several long seconds.

'Oh, I see,' he finally said, taking a couple of steps forward. 'You think that what you did – crossing out the information, keeping it in some safe place ...' The Werewolf paused as his eyes narrowed at Hunter before a sparkle of realization lit them up again. He gave Hunter a cold smile. 'Let me guess, that safe place is your head, right? You memorized it all, didn't you?'

Hunter stayed quiet.

'But of course you did.' Another smile from the Werewolf, this one without the slightest hint of humor. 'So you think that that would give you what, Detective Hunter, some sort of bargaining power?'

Once again, Hunter stayed quiet.

'Please, allow me another guess here,' the Werewolf continued, placing his diary on the control desk. 'You want to exchange the information in your head for the little bitch, am I right?'

'I'm just trying to stick to our original deal,' Hunter replied.

Every word he spoke made more fireworks of pain explode in his skull. 'The diary for Angela, remember? I had a hunch that you wouldn't stick to your side of the bargain, so I improvised.'

The Werewolf chuckled, sarcastically.

'Says the man who inserted a tracker into the back cover of my diary,' he said. 'You broke the rules first, Detective. Not me. You would've gotten the girl. I gave you my word on that.'

'And I was simply supposed to trust you?' Hunter questioned.

The Werewolf's gaze met Hunter's. 'Yes, you were.'

Right then, Hunter heard and saw something in the Werewolf's voice and eyes that he wasn't expecting – a sincerity that almost convinced him that he was telling the truth.

Hunter decided to test his opponent.

'Trust needs to be earned,' he said. 'You should know that. It's one of the first things they teach you in the military.'

This remark caught the Werewolf by surprise and he once again locked eyes with Hunter.

'Are you sure you want to go there, Detective?' he asked, his body becoming more tense. 'What would you know about the military, anyway? You've never served. You've never toured. You've never seen combat.'

From the Werewolf's tone of voice, Hunter could tell that he had hit a nerve. He had to make a split-second decision to either push it further or simply let it go.

Hunter chose to push it.

'The police academy teaches many of the same principles as the military,' he replied. 'And you're wrong. Every investigation I've been a part of is a tour of duty. Every time I had to face a criminal – any sort of criminal – is combat. We have both served our country, but we've done it in different capacities, that's all.'

'Oh, is that what you believe, Detective? Really? That we are equals?'

'Oh no, I don't believe that we are equals,' Hunter replied. 'There's a huge difference between you and me. I didn't turn rogue. I didn't betray my country's trust, or the "to protect and to serve" vow I made years ago. I didn't start murdering people for money and selling the footage on the Dark Web.'

As he said those words, Hunter saw something change inside the Werewolf's eyes.

That was when he knew that he'd made the wrong decision. He shouldn't have pushed.

Eighty-Six

A well-placed blow to the solar plexus – a complex network of nerves located in the abdomen – can cause the diaphragm to spasm, momentarily sending it into paralysis. When that happens, the lungs deflate fast, giving the person the sensation that the wind has been knocked out of them. Breathing becomes difficult and the heart struggles to regain its pace.

Hunter's last few words to the Werewolf seemed to have that same effect, almost making him gasp for air. Their eyes were locked. It didn't take an expert to see that anger burned red within the ex-soldier.

Hunter immediately regretted what he'd just said. Maybe he should've waited a little longer before playing that card, but it was too late to backpedal now. Hunter decided that his best move was to keep going.

'Yes,' he admitted, his voice firm, his tone unexcited. 'We figured out what those lines of text meant. We found the Dark Web chat room. We found the "voices".'

For a heartbeat, the Werewolf looked like he was about to lose control.

'Did you log in?' he asked in a voice heavy with rage.

Instead of replying, Hunter studied the man before him.

'Did – you – log – in?' the Werewolf asked again, this time through clenched teeth.

'Yes,' Hunter finally admitted. 'I did. Clever handle, by the way – Miles Sitrom – Latin. Sounds like a common American name. Second word, backwards – Mortis. Put them together and boom – *Miles Mortis*.' Hunter's Latin pronunciation was right on the money. 'Soldier of Death. Is that how you see yourself?'

The Werewolf stood still.

'Did any of the voices come into the room?' he asked. 'Did you chat with anyone?'

Once again, instead of replying, Hunter studied the man before him.

'You better answer me, Detective, or I swear to God that little bitch in there dies, right here, right now.' The Werewolf's head tilted in the direction of the metal door behind him.

'Yes,' Hunter said, giving him a single nod. 'Voice one and two. They joined the chat just seconds after I logged in.'

That was Hunter's second blow to the Werewolf's mental solar plexus. He could see the killer's eyes glow with fury.

'Now listen up and listen carefully, Detective. I need you to think back to the chat. I need to know what was said, and I mean the exact words you typed . . . the exact words the voices used. The little bitch's life depends on it.'

'Not much was said,' Hunter told him.

'I don't give a flying fuck how much was said. But I do need to know exactly *what* was said. As much, or as little as it was. And I need to know now.'

The stress levels in the Werewolf's tone of voice were beginning to change.

'OK,' Hunter said, before slowly recounting exactly what

had happened inside Vince Keller's office that same morning. He could recall every word.

Once Hunter told him about the water-damaged computer story that he had cooked up as an excuse to why he'd logged into the chat room, the Werewolf closed his eyes as if he were in pain.

'The voices would've traced your computer,' the Werewolf said. 'Their technology is state of the art. They would've known it wasn't me.'

'No, they wouldn't,' Hunter countered. 'Because so is ours. The firewalls protecting the computers at the Technical Investigation Division scramble the IP address and reroute the connection several times over. We were logged in for less than two minutes. Even if they had the technology to unscramble the address, there wasn't enough time to do it. Not to mention that the connection was made over the Dark Web. Maybe they could trace it in a movie, but not in real life.'

'Still, you shouldn't have done that, Detective. You really shouldn't have logged in. And for that, you will have to pay.'

The Werewolf reached for the weapon on the control desk and pointed it at Hunter's head. The silencer was gone.

'You said that the police academy teaches you the same principles as they do in the military, right?' he asked.

Hunter's entire body went rigid.

The ex-soldier didn't give Hunter a chance to reply.

'Well, let me ask you something else, Detective – did they teach you to shoot like this?'

The Werewolf squeezed the trigger twice in quick succession. The famous 'double-tap'.

Eighty-Seven

Angela Wood sat in the dark, her back against the cold and rough cinderblock wall, her arms hugging her legs, her head down, tucked in between her knees. Her hand still hurt from the electric shock she'd received earlier. Her eyes were puffy and red from crying.

She had had forgotten how exhausting crying really was. She'd forgotten how much energy it took – physically, mentally and emotionally. After her brother's death, Angela had spent months at the mercy of tears. Those crying months had drained so much energy out of her that she would pass out from seemingly no reason at all.

Right then, sitting in that dark and cold cell, Angela felt as shattered as she had felt back in those dreadful months.

Physically, at that moment, she knew she wouldn't be able to outrun a ten-year-old. She was so frightened that just about anything – a noise from outside her door, the light being turned on, even the sound of a fly buzzing past her ear –would trigger more tears and make her body start shivering uncontrollably.

The darkness that she'd been sitting in, coupled with her crippling emotional state, meant she'd lost track of time. She really couldn't tell if she'd been locked in that cell for hours, days, or even weeks. Her mind wasn't processing things as it should anymore. All she could do was to concentrate on her breathing – in, out, in, out – but fear turned even breathing into an uphill struggle.

Angela had just blown a third warm breath into her cupped hands to try to warm them up when all of a sudden . . .

BANG! . . . BANG!

Two blasts that sounded like an explosion. So loud that they made her cell door vibrate, almost activating the sprinklers on the ceiling.

In the blink of an eye, Angela's heartbeat went from resting pace to tachycardia, because she knew exactly what that sound was. She'd heard it a few times, before.

It was the sound of shots being fired.

Eighty-Eight

Inside the underground control room, the sound of the Werewolf's unsuppressed 9mm pistol going off rivaled that of a cannon, bouncing off the walls like a crazy pinball.

Smoke and the unmistakable smell of gunpowder filled the air inside the room, which made the Werewolf smile. He loved that smell. All of a sudden, he broke into a loud laughter.

On the metal chair, about eight paces in front of the ex-soldier, Hunter sat absolutely still, his unblinking eyes glued to the weapon still held firmly by the Werewolf, his chest rising and falling in an odd rhythm.

'You should see your face,' the Werewolf said. 'Oh wow, that was funny.'

From how hard the Werewolf was laughing, Hunter could tell that his mind had been severely fractured.

It took the Werewolf almost a minute to compose himself. 'Anyway, my question still stands, Detective – did they teach you to shoot like that at the police academy?'

The Werewolf's accuracy had been unerring. Hunter had not only heard both rounds flying past him, but he had also felt the bullets' air displacement. The first round zoomed by less than an inch from his right ear and the second less than an inch from his left.

Hunter refilled his lungs with air to try to calm his nerves and stop his body from shivering. His heart seemed to have tumbled upwards, lodging itself somewhere in his throat.

He waited a moment to see if he felt any pain – nothing. He then finally moved his head, first right, then left, his eyes moving everywhere, checking his body for blood – nothing.

'You see, Detective Hunter, what you don't realize is that I am the best there is.' Pride coated the Werewolf's words. 'With a reliable 9mm pistol like this one . . .' He showed Hunter his Sig Sauer P228. 'I can hit a moving target the size of a basketball from two hundred yards away. A still target with favorable wind conditions?' He shrugged. 'Three hundred yards – maybe a little more. I've done it before. Give me a sniper's rifle and I'll drop a mark from a mile away. That's what the US military has taught me to do, Detective.'

Hunter noticed that some of the tension in the Werewolf's voice and demeanor had begun to dissipate, and he had a pretty good idea why.

He had been in similar situations before – face-to-face with a killer – where the killer had had the upper hand and could've ended Hunter's life in a blink of an eye, but instead of doing so, the killer had talked.

Without any exceptions, there was always a reason behind why each and every serial killer killed. That reason, or reasons, might not make much sense to anyone else but the killer, but there was always a reason; and deep down, they all felt an almost uncontrollable need to explain themselves . . . They wanted others to understand why they were doing what they were doing . . . they wanted others, even if only for an instant, to see life through their eyes, no matter how distorted that vision might be. But most of all, they wanted the world to understand that they didn't consider themselves to be crazy.

In the case of someone like the Werewolf, that desire to be understood – to explain himself – would be multiplied exponentially and it wasn't difficult to understand why.

The Werewolf was an ex-soldier. More so, he was a veteran – someone with at least one tour of duty under his belt. He had fought for his country, he had killed for his country and he had been prepared to die for his country. That meant that he had spent a part of his life living under one of the strictest codes of conduct there ever was – the US military code of conduct – which, if put in layman's terms, could be summarized into one simple word: honor.

Hunter understood that there would have to be a very strong reason for why someone who had been prepared to live, kill and die in the name of honor had undergone such a huge U-turn from what he once so wholeheartedly believed. And the Werewolf would want Hunter to know what that reason was. Such a huge U-turn in someone's personality, especially when that someone had once sworn to protect the oppressed, would also bring on two of the most psychologically destructive feelings there ever were – guilt and shame.

Hunter was experienced enough to know that if a killer wanted to talk, then his best move was to let him.

'That's right, Detective,' the Werewolf continued. 'The military taught me how to kill people – with weapons, with my bare hands . . . and I was good at what I did . . .' He paused, as if he was rethinking his words. 'No, actually, I was *great* at what I did. I was the best.'

Hunter expected the ex-soldier to carry on, but he went quiet again. Hunter was also experienced enough to know that that was *not* a good sign. He pushed.

'Were you Special Forces?' he asked.

The Werewolf laughed, sarcastically.

'Compared to what we did, Detective, Special Forces was an amateur unit.'

As he held Hunter's stare for several long seconds, the ex-soldier's posture relaxed some more. All of a sudden, he gave Hunter a careless shrug, as if saying, 'Oh, what the hell.'

'We were a clandestine outfit,' the Werewolf explained. 'A kill team ... an assassination squad ... call it whatever you like.' He placed his weapon on the control desk once again.

That was definitely a good sign.

'What did *you* call it?' Hunter asked, his interest genuine.

The Werewolf smiled. 'Officially, we never had a title.' He shrugged again. 'Officially, we never existed. You won't find any paperwork or electronic records on us. How can you find anything on an outfit with no name? Where do you look? What do you search for? They didn't even use our real names. We were enlisted with false names for the protection of the unit. But as a joke, we sometimes referred to ourselves as "Mission Impossible", because we were told from the start that if any of our operations were ever unsuccessful ... if any of the members in our squad were taken or killed in action, our government would disavow all knowledge of us.' He paused for a beat. 'Mission Impossible, get it?'

Hunter's eyebrows arched in response.

'We were never deployed anywhere to keep the peace,' the Werewolf continued, 'or to aid the needy, to protect the weak, to survey hostile terrain, to search for weapons of mass destruction, or any of the other pile of bullshit our government tends to feed the press and the public every time our troops join a conflict. If we were deployed anywhere, that was the end of the line ... sometimes for a single individual, sometimes for a whole group. We didn't take hostages and we didn't negotiate. What we did was put a final stop to a situation that had somehow gotten out of control. And we were as final as it got.'

Once again, the Werewolf went quiet. Once again, Hunter re-engaged, but this time he didn't beat around the bush.

'So what happened?'

The Werewolf looked back at Hunter with a blank expression on his face. 'What do you mean?'

'What I mean is, how does someone who was trained to kill or die for his country – someone who was part of an elite military squad ... someone who lived by a very strict code of conduct – how does that someone start selling murders over the Dark Web?'

The Werewolf laughed again. This time it wasn't a sarcastic laugh, it was a disillusioned one.

'Because as it turns out, Detective,' he replied, 'the press and the public aren't the only ones who get lied to by our government.' He allowed his eyes to meet Hunter's once again and Hunter saw something change in them. He just didn't know exactly what it was.

The Werewolf ran a hand over his mouth, a gesture that seemed a little anxious; as if the ex-soldier was deliberating whether he should elaborate on what he'd just said, or simply let it go.

'Fuck it,' he finally said, throwing his hands up in an

apathetic way. 'Would you like to know the truth, Detective ... the real truth?'

'Yes.'

'OK. I hope you're sitting comfortably.' He laughed at his own joke.

Eighty-Nine

Looking calm and completely unperturbed, the Werewolf leaned against the control desk and folded his arms over his chest.

'Our unit was handpicked,' he began. 'But I don't mean handpicked from existing soldiers, or Marine recruits, or Army cadets, or Navy Seals, or anyone else already involved with any of our military forces. I'm talking handpicked from the lost.'

Hunter frowned. 'The lost?'

'That's what we all were,' the ex-soldier replied. 'Lost and very, very angry. We all had nothing to lose and a score to settle with the world.'

Hunter still looked unsure.

'I was recruited at the age of fourteen,' the Werewolf revealed. 'From juvie.' He laughed. 'I bet you didn't know that our military did that, did you?'

Hunter shook his head. 'I wasn't aware of that. No.'

'My mother struggled with drug and alcohol addiction for as long as I can remember.' Anger and sadness collided inside the Werewolf's eyes. 'So, to support her addiction, not her family – and by "her family" I mean me – she turned to prostitution. Most of her clients came to the shoebox of an apartment we lived in in Edison. That's in Fresno, where I'm from. Anyway, I *hated* being home. I hated seeing all those men coming and going. I hated seeing their smiling faces. I hated hearing the noises that came out of my mother's bedroom, I hated everything about that life ... about that place, so I spent most of my time and did most of my growing up in the streets, in one of the most dangerous neighborhoods in Fresno, and let me tell you, Detective, I was one angry kid.' He paused and ran his hand over his mouth once again. 'My first encounter with the police came at the age of twelve.' He shrugged again. 'Well, eleven and a half, but who really cares, right? I was picked up for shoplifting. From then on, I was in and out of juvenile halls as if they were candy stores.'

'How about your father?' Hunter ventured.

'Never met him. Never knew who he was. I don't think even my mother knew for certain.' Those words were delivered bluntly, with zero emotion.

'Brothers?' Hunter asked. 'Sisters?'

'Nope.' The Werewolf pointed at himself. 'One humongous mistake was enough for my stupid mother.'

Hunter tried to readjust his position, but with his arms tied behind the chair's backrest and his ankles to the chair's legs, his range of motion was very limited.

'At the age of fourteen,' the Werewolf continued, 'while serving a short stint in juvie again, I got a visit from someone who I'd never seen before.' He chuckled. 'He called himself Atlas. That was it. No last name. Big, muscly guy with an ugly moustache and crude black eyes that could see into your soul. First thing he told me was that he had met hundreds of kids like me – angry kids, pissed off at life, abandoned by those who should've loved them the most. Kids full of life but with no life to fill. Kids either with no family, or a family that didn't want them. Kids who always ended up in juvenile halls. He told me that nine out of ten of those kids would inevitably grow up to be hardcore criminals and that by the age of twenty-five, they would either be in prison for life, or six feet underground.'

Hunter knew that to be very true.

'He then asked me if I wanted to become another statistic, or if I wanted to do something about my shitty life – something that would help others and save lives . . ., something that would transform me from a nobody into a somebody . . . something that would give me a family, the family that I always wanted, but never had.'

Hunter picked up on a new tone in the Werewolf's voice. Something like pride.

'Well,' the Werewolf carried on. 'Atlas was a good speaker. A very convincing one. He knew how to press all the right buttons. He knew how to make a fourteen-year-old kid who was slowly digging his own grave feel like he wasn't just another reject. That day, it was the first day in my life that I felt like I mattered . . . I felt like I wasn't a mistake. So I fell for it. I bought Atlas's bullshit speech and was sent to a special training camp the next day – the same day he got me out of juvie.'

Angry fire still burned in the Werewolf's eyes, but it was a different sort of anger now – this time full of hurt.

'The problem with me was,' he clarified, 'I threw myself into that crazy training because I liked what they were teaching me.' He paused and lifted an apologetic hand. 'No, that's not right. I *loved* what they were teaching me – how to hurt people . . . how to kill people. I loved the way it made me feel. I loved the power that it gave me.' He paused again, this time for effect. 'We were also trained in counterespionage, computers, explosives, surveillance, interrogations . . . you name it. For almost five full years they worked us to the bone. Not a day's rest. Seven days a week. Fifty-two weeks a year. Sixteen hours every day. They wouldn't give anyone a break – ever – not even on Christmas. Five years later, I was a well-oiled and obedient killing machine. Then the missions started – Kuwait, Iran, Iraq, Somalia, Haiti . . . pretty much everywhere. We were even sent on kill missions to countries that we were not in conflict with. I bet you didn't know that either, did you Detective?'

Hunter shook his head once again.

The Werewolf used his right hand to massage the back of his neck.

'For years,' he told Hunter, 'none of us questioned any of our orders. We were trained not to. We were brainwashed from day one to believe that if we were sent into any country, any territory, it was to eliminate a very real threat to our national security. The funny thing was that right from the start, some of it just felt wrong. Why did we have to eliminate entire families? That just didn't seem right, but we never asked why. "Why" wasn't part of our vocabulary, until during one of our missions, I was practically ordered to rape a woman.'

For the first time since the Werewolf began telling Hunter his story, he broke eye contact with the detective.

'That order, or, how can I put it? "Strong suggestion", somehow broke through the shield I had created surrounding questioning orders. That was when I finally asked: "Why" . . .'

The Werewolf went quiet once again. It was obvious that the memory of that particular incident struck a nerve with the ex-soldier.

'Did you get an answer?' Hunter asked.

The Werewolf laughed. 'Yeah. I was told that we needed to

teach them a lesson. "They do it to us, we do it to them" kind of thing.'

Hunter's brow furrowed almost unconsciously.

'Yeah, I know,' the Werewolf said, reading Hunter's expression. 'So my follow-up question was: "When did an Iranian soldier rape an American citizen?" For that I got no answer, except that I should not be questioning my commands.'

'But you still refused to follow that command,' Hunter said.

The Werewolf paused again and regarded the LAPD detective one more time. 'You read the passage in the diary,' he said with a bleak smile.

Hunter nodded once.

'Yes,' the Werewolf confirmed. 'I refused.' He paused for a second and his stare became distant. 'Funny how childhood traumas work on your mind, isn't it? I can murder people without even blinking. I can gut them, behead them, torture them in ways you probably never even heard of, I can hurt them to a hair away from death, but still keep them alive ... but I will *not rape* anyone.'

Five silent seconds went by before the Werewolf managed to shake the memory away.

'Anyway, some might say that that was when the problems began – with my refusal to comply – but other members of our crew were already waking up to some of the things we were ordered to do during some of our missions. Things that just didn't feel right. Things that just didn't fit into the context of "something that would make a difference ... something that would help others and save lives".' He lifted another excusing hand. 'Don't get me wrong, Detective. I know for a fact that we have saved our country and defended the safety of our citizens countless times, but I also know for a fact that some of our missions were a lie . . . and a big one. We weren't acting in the interest of our country, or our national security. We were acting in the interest of individuals, or political parties, or enterprises, or whatever . . . It really didn't make a difference, because at the top of that chain was the greatest of all American gods. The only god that matters to most – the god Money. But we had all been well trained – or should I say, well, lobotomized – because through so many of our missions, we simply failed to see the signs. And trust me, Detective, the signs were there. But hey, better late than never, right?' He laughed.

Hunter stayed quiet, so the Werewolf carried on.

'Pretty soon after we started having doubts about some of our individual orders, we began having doubts about entire missions, and that was the beginning of the end. Ten months later, our unit was terminated and dismembered. It didn't matter that we had successfully executed over three hundred and fifty missions with only two casualties on our side. It didn't matter that all of us were prepared to bleed for our country . . . to kill for our country . . . to give our lives for our country. None of that mattered because the well-oiled and obedient killing machines didn't seem to be that well-oiled anymore, and our obedience was starting to show some cracks. The effect of our unit being terminated was devastating to all of us. Not because we loved what we did so much, but because we were a clandestine outfit. Mission Impossible, remember?'

Hunter could already guess what was coming next.

Ninety

The Werewolf looked away for a second, his eyes unfocused.

'So,' he said, bringing his attention back to Hunter. 'With the end of our unit, we returned to American soil to find ourselves in the same position we were in when we were recruited at the age of fourteen – discarded, rejected, abandoned, betrayed – this time, by the family that we were all promised on that first day.'

Hunter heard real pain in the ex-soldier's voice.

'Once you're off the frontline, strange things start happening to you . . . to your mind.'

The Werewolf used his right index finger to tap the right side of his cranium, but he did it so hard it looked like he was stabbing his own head.

'Throughout our missions, we did and saw things that no one on this earth is really prepared for, and let me tell you, Detective . . . those images, those smells, those sounds, those textures, all of it . . . they all have a very special way of fucking with your head, a special way of scarring your mind, your soul.'

The Werewolf paused for breath before continuing.

'Within months of us being back in the land of the free, those mental scars began showing, and they were much, much deeper than what anyone would've anticipated. All of us ... we were all broken. We just didn't know we were broken.'

Hunter could hardly imagine what years of being in the frontline with an assassination squad could do to the human mind.

'Very soon,' the Werewolf said, 'all of our lives began fracturing, together with the state of our mental health. We all began showing symptoms of PTSD. Out of the blue, my memory began deteriorating, mainly my short to mid-term memory – the past five to seven years.' He used his index finger to tap his head once again, not so hard this time. 'I forget things ... important things. I also forget people ... and faces, but it's not a coherent loss of memory. For example, I can remember certain things from ... let's say three years ago, but other things, from the exact same period, have been completely erased. But when compared to the rest of my squad, I had it easy.'

Hunter's question was asked with a simple tilt of the head.

'Josh developed psychotic depression and severe anxiety,' the Werewolf explained. 'Milo developed chronic depression and some sort of panic disorder. Stu also developed acute depression and paranoia. Darren – bipolar one. You know what that is, right.'

Hunter nodded.

'The others I can't remember.' The ex-soldier shook his head in anger. 'I mean, I can't remember who they are. I can't remember their faces. I can't remember anything about them.' He took a second to compose himself. 'We didn't ask for much, you know? All we wanted was for our government – our military – to take care of their own ... like they should. After everything we did for this country ... after putting our lives on the line time and time again, all we wanted was not to be abandoned, but we were a ghost outfit. Our unit never really existed, remember? We, as individuals, never really existed.'

The Werewolf exhaled angrily.

'So we got back to the country that we were prepared to die for and we had nothing: no job . . . no money . . . no health insurance . . . no help . . . no assistance . . . nothing.' He began pacing the space in front of Hunter's chair. 'Like I've said, Detective, we were all broken . . . our minds scarred and fractured from inflicting and seeing so much death, so much hurt, so much pain. We were all ticking bombs just waiting to go off. They knew it. Our government knew it, but they did not give a rat's ass about any of us. It was cheaper and easier for them to just let us implode.'

Anger was now clear in the Werewolf's movements as well – clenched fists, lip biting, face rubbing.

'All we wanted was some help in dealing with the fucking demons in here.' He once again stabbed his head with his index finger. 'And there are hundreds of them. And they keep on coming at you every second of every day . . . non-stop.'

'No one from the military you could've talked to?' Hunter asked. 'How about the Atlas guy?'

The Werewolf laughed. 'None of us had seen him in years. We don't even know if he's still alive or not. We never got to know his real name either.'

'Isn't there anyone else?'

'Nope. And believe me, Detective, we've tried. Mission Impossible, remember? Officially, we were never even part of the armed forces. There are no records of us.' The Werewolf shrugged. 'With no help from our government and no money to help ourselves, we began cracking.'

He paused and swallowed dry.

'Josh and Milo blew their own heads off. Stu lost his marriage because of his mental-health deterioration. He couldn't get a job. He couldn't afford to feed his family. How degrading and humiliating is that, Detective? Not being able to feed your own family.'

Hunter didn't voice a reply, but his expression gave away how he felt.

'A week after his wife left him, Stu hanged himself.'

It was Hunter's turn to breathe out heavily.

'I also came this close to ending my life a few times.' The ex-soldier used his thumb and forefinger to show Hunter a gap no larger than a strand of hair. 'The day that I came the closest, I was interrupted by a knock on my door. It was Darren. I know that he saw the anguish . . . the hopelessness inside my eyes. That was when he suggested the Dark Web. At first, I thought that he was joking. Then he showed me a couple of sites on there where you could purchase photographs and videos of people dying. Some due to disease, some during war, some in their hospital beds, some filmed or photographed by chance like being run over by a car, or a train, or falling off a cliff, or whatever. You know what I mean, right?'

Hunter had never seen any of those sites, but in today's world, he wasn't surprised that they existed.

The Werewolf chuckled. 'People out there are paying money to see other people die and they're paying good money. How fucked up is that, Detective? I admit, I was shocked, and that was when Darren looked at me and said, "What if we tailor-made deaths?"'

Right then, Hunter felt as if an arctic blast had blown into the back of his neck and run down his spine. 'WE'. 'What if *we* tailor-made deaths?' The Werewolf wasn't acting alone. There was someone else with him – Darren.

'And he was serious about it,' the Werewolf continued. 'Very serious.' He lifted both hands in an 'I give up' gesture. 'At first I thought that that was total madness. "I can't go around killing American citizens for money," I told Darren. I had sworn to protect them, not terminate them. I was trained to give my life for them, not take theirs away. But Darren's answer to my argument was a very compelling one. He told me that so was he and everyone else in our squad. And that that was exactly what we did ... for years. Like I told you, Detective – over three hundred and fifty successful missions. Darren kept on telling me a lot of stuff, which I can't remember anymore, but he insisted that we had done our part. We had done what we were trained to do. We protected this country and we protected its citizens, and he was right, Detective. The number of lives we've saved is incalculable. There are thousands upon thousands of American citizens sleeping in their beds tonight, making love to their partners, kissing their kids, laughing with their friends and loved ones ... basically living their lives without even knowing that the reason why they are able to do all of those things is because we did our job, and we did it well. And just look at what doing our jobs and doing it well has got us, Detective. Look at what saving all those lives has brought us – Josh and Milo and Stu ... dead. Not killed by our enemies, but by their own hands because they couldn't handle it anymore.' The Werewolf yelled those last few words. 'You didn't know him, Detective, but Stu was the sort of person who wasn't afraid of anyone, or anything. He would've gone head to head with a rhino and probably kicked its ass. We're talking about the funniest guy I've ever known and he hanged himself because he couldn't afford to buy a loaf of bread to feed his kids. Where's the justice in that?'

It was not the first time that Hunter had heard similar stories about ex-soldiers who were ignored and treated like outcasts by the country they had been prepared to die for.

'Darren and I,' the Werewolf continued, 'we were already traveling down the same road as Josh, Milo and Stu. I know that because I also saw the desperation in his eyes . . . just as intense as it was in mine. He was battling with the same dark thoughts as I was.' The Werewolf paused and took a breath. 'Then Darren said something like . . . we had two choices – get busy living or get busy dying – and that got me thinking, Detective. We did save thousands of American lives, so what if we took a few of them back as payment? We'd earned it. They owe us. This country owes us. What do they expect us to do when our own government betrays us?'

The Werewolf paused and cracked his knuckles against the palms of each hand. The look in his eyes became distant.

'That day,' he carried on, 'just before Darren came to my door. The reason why I had decided to end my life was because I was wandering the streets in downtown LA and I saw this veteran sitting at a corner – unwashed, ripped clothes, hungry. He had a piece of cardboard in his hands that said something like: "Homeless veteran. Just trying to survive out here. Please help me out. Anything you can give is very much appreciated. Please don't discard me like my government did. God bless you." That day I came home and the thought in my head was – what's the point? I would rather dead than end up like that . . . and I would be, if Darren hadn't turned up at my door.' The Werewolf shrugged at Hunter. 'It wasn't like I had to do something I had never done before. Killing is what I was trained to do ... what I was programmed to do ... and what I do best. When you're that good at something – I mean, *really good* at something – then you just keep doing it. And I was great at it.'

Hunter saw pride and ego flare up in the ex-soldier's eyes like Christmas lights – the narcissistic side of the psychopath inside him making itself known.

'Darren had a lot more experience with the Dark Web than I did,' the Werewolf continued. 'We used one of the sites he showed me that first day to very subtly put out a "suggestion" about his idea.' He used his finger to draw quotation marks in the air. 'Within a day we got contacted by someone. The creation of a very private chat room was suggested.'

'The voices,' Hunter said.

'The voices,' the Werewolf confirmed. 'In one week, we had ten of them. I should have started the diary then, when we got the first request from one of the voices, but for some reason all that escaped me back then.'

'How many were there?' Hunter asked. 'Before you started the diary ... how many subjects were there?'

The Werewolf sniggered. 'Do you really believe I'll be able to remember it?' He shook his head. 'I have no idea. A few for sure. But there's one thing I can tell you, Detective – throughout our military missions, I thought that I had seen the kind of evil that beggars belief. Every sort of torture ... every sort of degradation and humiliation possible ... but I was wrong. Some of the things the voices ask for blow anything I have seen or done in the frontline straight out of the water ... hands down.'

'Do you have any idea who the people behind the voices are?'

The Werewolf laughed. 'You do understand the concept behind the Dark Web, don't you, Detective? These are anonymous people, very rich and powerful anonymous people spread all around the globe. We'll never find out who they are, unless they want us to find out, and trust me, Detective, they don't. But what I can tell you is that Darren was wrong. Being able to afford a loaf of bread ... being able to feed himself and his family ... none of that was able to save him. A year and a half ago, during one of his most severe depressive episodes, he stepped off the top of a building in downtown LA.'

Right then, Hunter was hit by two different emotions – relief from knowing that there wasn't a second killer on the loose, and sadness from learning that yet another ex-soldier had taken his own life because the government had failed to give him the help he so desperately needed and deserved.

'As far as I know,' the Werewolf said, 'I'm the only one left out of my squad. They're all gone. Killed not by an enemy, but by the country we defended so many times. '

The room went quiet for a moment. Hunter had no response.

'So now that you know the truth about who I am, and about why I kill, we need to get back to business, Detective. The codes. I need them, and I need them now.'

Hunter shook his head. 'Let Angela go and I'll give you the codes. Not before.'

The Werewolf looked at Hunter in disbelief.

'Just because we had a little chitchat you think that you can now negotiate with me? Really?' He picked up the semi-automatic weapon he had left on the control desk.

'Let her go, and I'll give you the codes,' Hunter said. 'You have my word.'

'OK.' The Werewolf nodded at Hunter, a little sarcastically. 'The codes for her life. Sounds like a fair trade. We can do that. But first, do me a favor, will you? Have a look at this.'

He reached for a switch on the console and flipped it on.

Ninety-One

The large computer monitor mounted on the wall directly above the control desk came alive. It took less than a second for an image to appear on the screen.

Hunter's eyes moved to it and he felt his hands clam up behind his back as a hollow cavity filled his chest.

The image showed the view of a small room. Just like the one he was in, the walls were made of cinderblock and the floor of solid concrete. Pushed up against one of the walls was a metal-framed single bed.

On the bed, curled up into a human ball with her head tucked into her arms, hugging her legs, was Angela Wood. Hunter didn't need to see her face to know it was her.

As the image materialized on the screen, Hunter saw Angela's body jerk ever so slightly before stiffening. Her head lifted from her arms in a half-surprised gesture, before she blinked a few times and looked around the room for a couple of seconds. After that, she looked up and directly into the camera. Her eyes were cherry red and puffy. From the way she'd looked around the room and then up at the camera, Hunter was able to arrive at two conclusions: one; the room had probably been in the dark until then, and two; she knew exactly where the surveillance camera was inside her cell.

'She's just through that door,' the Werewolf told Hunter, his thumb thrown over his right shoulder to indicate the door behind him.

'I'll give you the codes,' Hunter said again. 'But you need to let her go. You have no use for her. She's only twenty-one years old. She's just trying to rebuild her life after losing her little brother.'

Hunter paused because he saw the surprise in the Werewolf's eyes. He didn't know about that. That could be the angle Hunter needed – at least for Angela.

'Angela's brother, Shawn, was only eleven years old when he was abducted, raped and murdered.'

Hunter used names instead of pronouns – it humanized them. If there was still any humanity left inside the Werewolf, Hunter needed to appeal to it, especially because the Werewolf seemed to have a suggestion of a moral code around rape. That was made clear by the story he'd told Hunter.

'Shawn's savagely mutilated body was found five weeks later,' he explained. 'It destroyed Angela. It destroyed Angela's family as well. Angela is really just trying to pick up the pieces of her mind. She's a broken soul who is desperately trying to fix herself. Just like you and the soldiers from your squad. Give her a chance to do so.'

'She's trying to fix herself by becoming a thief?' the Werewolf countered. 'A pickpocket? That's great.'

Says the guy who sells murders online for a living, Hunter thought, but kept it to himself.

'People make mistakes,' he said instead. 'We all do. We're humans. When the mind has been darkened by grief, rational thought sometimes loses the battle and people make mistakes. No one can escape it. It's part of the healing process. It's part of us trying to get back on our feet after a loss that has thrown us down. Please give her a chance and she will realize that she's made a mistake. She's a good person, but right now she feels lost and in pieces. She feels broken, but I know that she'll find her path. Please . . . I'll give you the codes, just let her go. Give her a chance.'

The Werewolf's gaze intensified as he studied Hunter again.

'Since you're so concerned for her life,' he said, 'let me ask you something, Detective. Would you give your life for hers?'

It was Hunter's turn to study the man in front of him. Was he serious?

'Would you die for her, Detective?' the Werewolf asked again, as he looked at the gun in his hand. 'If right now I offered you the chance to exchange your life for hers, fuck the codes, fuck everything else . . . would you do it? Would you die for her, right here, right now?'

It was the determined look in the ex-soldier's eyes that told Hunter that he could not have been more serious.

'Would you die for her, Detective?' the ex-soldier pushed.

'Yes,' Hunter replied, his voice firm, his tone assertive. 'I would.'

The Werewolf paused and scratched his left cheek with the barrel of his semi-automatic. 'You would? Are you sure?'

'If you're serious about exchanging my life for hers . . . then yes,' Hunter reiterated his reply.

'So if I set her free,' the Werewolf said, 'I can shoot you in the face right now?' He extended his arm and aimed his weapon at Hunter's face. 'I can blow your head off?'

'If you let her go first and I have your word that you won't go after her ever again, then yes, I would swap my life for hers.'

The Werewolf's eyes narrowed at Hunter. Two seconds later, his weapon arm relaxed and sank back to the side of his body.

'Why?' the Werewolf asked. 'Why would you give your life for someone who you barely even know? I'm curious, Detective.' His concern sounded sincere.

Hunter tried without success to shake off some of the tension, which had traveled up from his bound arms and legs, to gather in a knot at the base of his neck.

'Because I swore to protect and to serve,' he explained. 'Because I've been in this world much longer than she has and I've lived my life. I've fought my demons. With some I've won the battle, with some I've lost. Angela is still young. She has so much to live for ... so much to see ... so much to experience. She deserves a chance at life. I spend my days dealing with death, and pain, and suffering, and evil ... and all that is bad, in a world that isn't getting any better. A world that isn't getting any more compassionate or understanding. Maybe I've had enough. And if the bargain is to save the life of someone who has a lot more to live for than I do, then I consider that a good exchange.'

The sincerity in Hunter's tone surprised the Werewolf.

'That's very noble, Detective.'

'Not that different from you, really,' Hunter added. 'You were prepared to give your life for the citizens of this country. People you don't know. People who you've never met. People who you've never even seen.' Hunter shook his head. 'You were miles ahead of me there.'

The Werewolf nodded as he mulled over Hunter's words. 'Great speech, Detective, and I can completely sympathize with the bit about having "had enough". But if you were really prepared to die for that thieving bitch, then I have a surprise for you.' He turned and typed a command into the keyboard on the control desk.

Instinctively, Hunter's eyes moved to the monitor on the wall and what he saw made the hairs on the back of his neck stand on end.

The picture on the monitor changed into a four-way split – two images on the top row and two on the bottom, each occupying a quarter of the screen.

The pictures on the top row showed two women who Hunter had never seen before. They were imprisoned in cells identical to the one that Angela was in.

The woman in the first image – top left – looked to be around twenty-five years old, with longish blonde hair that had been tied in a loose chignon. She was sitting with her back pressed hard against the cinderblock wall and her knees pressed against her chest.

The second image – top right – showed a woman with short, curly black hair, Betty Boop style, who looked to be a few years older than the one in the first image. Just like Angela's, the woman's eyes looked red and raw.

The two images on the bottom row showed an empty confinement cell – bottom left – and the scene from Angela's cell – bottom right.

'Who are those two women?' Hunter asked, his attention playing tennis between the Werewolf and the monitor.

'Who they are isn't important. What's important is that you understand that they're all going to die if you don't give me those codes.' The Werewolf's arm came back up, once again aiming his weapon at Hunter's head. 'Now, Detective.'

Hunter was surprised at the Werewolf's mistake. He should've showed him those images after Hunter had given him the codes, not before.

'No,' he said, holding the Werewolf's stare.

The ex-soldier blinked in disbelief. 'I'm sorry?'

'You're not listening to me. I'll swap the codes for their lives,' Hunter said. 'Let them all go and I'll give you your codes . . . and . . . you'll still have me.'

The Werewolf chuckled. 'You are one stubborn sonofabitch, aren't you?' He scratched his chin, as he considered Hunter's proposal. 'OK,' he said after a long moment of deliberation. 'You wait here. I'll be right back.' He turned and exited the control room through the metal door behind him.

Ninety-Two

Just before leaving the control room, the Werewolf typed another command into the keyboard on the control desk and the image on the monitor changed again. It went from the four-split screen back to a single image, but it didn't show Angela Wood. This time, the entire screen was filled with images from the CCTV camera inside confinement cell number 1 – the blonde woman.

On the screen, Hunter saw the woman use her hand to protect her eyes from the bright light before looking around the room like a small bird that had just perceived danger, her head moving in snatches. Her eyes filled with tears and she curled herself up into a ball by the head of the bed, clasping both hands together as if in prayer. A couple of seconds went by before her eyes shot in the direction of the cell door. An instant later, the door was pushed open and the Werewolf entered the scene.

The woman looked up at him with fearful eyes, but as she noticed the gun that he was holding in his right hand, fear morphed into terror.

The Werewolf pinned the woman down with an ice-cold

stare, but said nothing – no explanation, no angry words, no merciful ones either. He simply lifted his weapon, aimed it at the woman's head and squeezed the trigger.

Through the screen in the control room, Hunter saw the woman's head practically explode, as the bullet hit inch-perfect at the center of her forehead. Blood misted the air as if the Werewolf had shot a can of red spray paint. The wall directly behind the woman was stained with blood, bone fragments, skin, hair, and brain matter. Her body went instantly limp. Her arms, still held together by her clasped hands, dropped down to her lap.

'No,' Hunter shouted at the top of his voice. 'You mother-fucker. *No.*'

The Werewolf stepped back from the cell door, closed it behind him and returned to the control room. In there, he typed a new command into the control-desk keyboard and the image on the large wall monitor changed once again. This time, the screen was split into only two – left and right. The picture on the left showed the woman with the Betty Boop hairstyle. The one on the right showed Angela Wood.

'Why did you have to kill her?' Hunter shouted at the Werewolf. 'Why?'

The Werewolf replied with a cynical smirk.

Hunter took a deep breath and did something he usually never did – he allowed anger to propagate through his body.

'Why did you have to kill her?' he said again, his voice shaking with rage.

'Because you insist on trying to bargain with me, Detective.' The Werewolf's voice, on the other hand, sounded calm and calculated. 'You seem to refuse to understand that you have no power here. Maybe this will convince you.' He paused and placed his weapon on the control desk once again. 'So, let's try this again, shall we? The codes, Detective.'

Hunter squeezed his eyes tight as he tried to get control of himself. 'You didn't have to kill her. Who was she?'

'There you go again,' the Werewolf said. 'I need you to focus, Detective. Forget about the blonde woman. Forget about who she was or how old she was. She's gone.' He pointed to the screen. 'And the same will happen to those two if you don't give me those codes.'

Hunter was playing a loser's game and he knew it, but the cop in him still wouldn't let go. He needed to try and save Angela and the dark-haired woman.

'OK,' he said. 'The codes and my life for those two.'

The Werewolf looked like he couldn't believe what he'd just heard. 'Jesus Christ, you're still trying to bargain with me. Are you nuts? Do you actually *want* them dead? Because that's fine by me.' He turned, picked up his weapon and took a step toward the metal door.

'No, wait,' Hunter pleaded. 'Please hear me out. It's a fair trade. One for one – the codes for the dark-haired woman, my life for Angela's.'

The ex-soldier's eyebrows arched awkwardly.

'You can't ask for a bigger compromise than that,' Hunter added. He knew that he had to appeal to something that the Werewolf could relate to, something that he understood . . . the sort of honor that the ex-soldier once believed in. 'I'm willing to end my life for this. It's the same sort of compromise you made for this country years ago. It's the ultimate sacrifice. A life for a life. You would've given your life for this country . . . for the citizens of this country. I'm giving my life for hers. And you'll still get the codes.'

The Werewolf's lips drew a thin line while he scratched his chin with the barrel of his gun.

'All right,' he finally agreed. 'Give me the codes and you have my word that I'll set both of them free.'

'No,' Hunter countered. 'It doesn't work like that. You set them free first and then you get the codes.'

'The problem with that, Detective,' the Werewolf retorted, 'is that you don't know where you are. So let me put you in the picture here. We're in the middle of absolutely nowhere. If I simply open the door and let them out, they won't go far because there's nowhere to go from here. The only way for them to get out of here is for me to sedate them and drop them somewhere where they can find their way back. Now, you have my word as a soldier that I will do that. That's the best I can do. That's the only deal you're going to get. I told you that you should've trusted me before when I said that I would release the thieving bitch once I got my diary back, and I would have. My word is the only thing I have left. I won't go back on it and I always, always honor it.'

There was a mixture of sincerity and emotional pain in the Werewolf's words.

Hunter weighed his options – in truth he had only one.

'That's the deal,' the Werewolf pushed. 'If you don't take it, I'm going back through that door and I'll blow the dark-haired woman's head off. You can watch it all from the comfort of your seat.' He gestured toward the wall monitor. 'Then I'll come back here and we can try this whole thing one last time.'

Hunter's attention moved back to the two women on the screen. He had no doubt that the Werewolf wasn't bluffing. If Hunter didn't give him the codes, he would kill the dark-haired woman without hesitation. From there, the next logical move would be to kill Angela and then Hunter.

The Werewolf also had Hunter's cellphone. After Hunter was dead, it stood to reason that the Werewolf would break into Hunter's phone just to see what he could find, and he would find the photo with the codes.

'The codes, Detective.'

Hunter held his breath for a second.

'I have your word that they'll be freed and you'll never go after them again.'

The Werewolf looked Hunter dead in the eye. 'You have my word.'

Given Hunter's predicament, there was absolutely nothing else he could do. Whichever way he thought about it, it looked like game over for him.

Hunter took a deep breath and, as he spoke, his voice almost faltered. 'The Dark Web address is—' he began, but the Werewolf interrupted him.

'The web address and log-in I still have them,' the Werewolf said, moving back to the computer on the control desk and opening up either a program or a website. Hunter couldn't tell from where he was sitting. 'I use them regularly. The other two codes are my—' He thought about it for a quick second. 'Special kind of insurance, I could say. And I need them now, Detective.'

Hunter closed his eyes as he dictated. 'The first one is – 122001FOBRhino.

The Werewolf wrote it down before typing it into the keyboard. A couple of seconds later he smiled at thin air. 'Fantastic. Next.'

'15052004MNF-I,' Hunter said.

Once again, the Werewolf wrote it down before typing it into the keyboard. Another satisfied smile.

'Now let them go,' Hunter said. 'You gave me your word.'

'I did,' the Werewolf agreed. 'And I will honor it, but first, you have to die. That was the deal, wasn't it? The codes for the dark-haired woman and your life for the thieving bitch.'

Hunter stayed silent.

The Werewolf picked up his weapon.

'You're a good man, Detective. You have honor and integrity, something quite rare these days. You should've joined the military. You would've made an excellent soldier. Unfortunately, this time you came up against someone who is better than you ... much better than you, actually, and in this shit world we live in, it's survival of the fittest.' The Werewolf extended his arm and aimed at Hunter's forehead. 'Goodbye, Detective.'

Everything inside Hunter's body got tangled into a suffocating knot, but he still held the ex-soldier's stare. He would not close his eyes and wait for his death. He would not give the Werewolf that satisfaction.

Hunter saw the Werewolf's finger tighten on the trigger of his P228 and all of a sudden his subconscious picked up on something that he had overlooked – *this time you came up against someone who is better than you ... much better than you, actually.*

There it was again – the ex-soldier's ego ... the narcissistic side of the psychopath in him screaming from somewhere inside.

Hunter had studied and dealt with many similar cases before. He understood how the mind of a narcissistic person worked. He knew how to push it.

Hunter's next words left his lips almost involuntarily, as his subconscious simply spat them out.

'Yes, they did,' he said. 'Even better.'

Ninety-Three

Gun in hand, aimed at Hunter's head, the Werewolf frowned as the detective's words reached his ears.

'What was that?'

'Earlier on you asked me if the police academy had taught me to shoot the way you do. Do you remember that?'

'Yes,' the ex-soldier's grip on the trigger relaxed just a tad.

'Well, that's my answer,' Hunter said. 'Yes, they did. Even better than you.'

A broad smile spread across the Werewolf's lips. 'Don't do this, Detective. It's embarrassing.'

'What is?'

'You, clutching at straws. That *is* embarrassing. You know you're going to die. You know that you have no way out of this. What are you trying to do, prolong the inevitable? Why?'

'Believe whatever you want to believe,' Hunter said back. 'But with a handgun, I'm a better marksman than you are.'

The Werewolf's laughter was sincere. 'That's a very bold statement, Detective. You saw me shooting, right?'

'Yes, I did,' Hunter replied. 'You *are* good. No doubt about that. But I'm better. Give me a gun and I'll show you.'

Another animated laugh. 'But of course, let me just pass you a gun. Hold on a sec.'

The Werewolf lowered his weapon, turned around and made as if he were going to the locked cabinet in the corner, but stopped after two steps.

'Oh yeah, sorry, I forgot. I can't hand you a gun because you might *shoot me*. C'mon, Detective, stop embarrassing yourself. Don't beg. What's the point in delaying this any longer? Like you've said – you've been in this world much longer than that bitch has. You've lived your life. You've fought your demons. You won some, you lost some. Today, this demon won.' The Werewolf's thumb pointed at himself.

Hunter had no real idea where he was going with this. No one was coming for him, but he understood what he needed to do.

The most basic, animalistic instinct humans possess is the instinct for survival. When the body realizes that it's about to lose its fight for life, it enters a sort of hyper mode. Rational thought goes out the window and the brain starts sending desperate 'fight harder' signals everywhere – muscles, lungs, heart, brain. Those signals have a partner – adrenalin – which superpowers everything. Muscles become stronger, lungs can take in more oxygen than normal . . . and so on. The body, as a living organism, wants to live, no matter what. Well, Hunter's body was tied down, so his brain did the fighting.

'I think you're the one who is scared of embarrassing yourself,' Hunter said. 'You keep on saying that you're the best at this, the best at that . . . but the truth is that you're scared of being proven wrong, aren't you?'

'Oh, is that what you think?'

'It's quite obvious, isn't it? And in this case, I know I can shoot better than you.'

The Werewolf smiled at Hunter. 'And how would you like to prove that, Detective? Shall I just drive us down to the shooting range?'

'I'm OK with that,' Hunter said. 'Or we can just go outside and shoot at cans, beer bottles, whatever you like. Whatever you choose, I'll still beat you.'

Hunter's brain was getting desperate.

'Or we can shoot at each other, if you prefer.' Hunter's suggestion surprised even himself, but he kept a steady poker face.

The suggestion halted the ex-soldier. The smile vanished from his lips and his gaze scrutinized the detective in front of him.

Hunter knew that that sounded like a crazy idea, but as everything stood, he would die anyway. Might as well die fighting.

'Old West duel style,' he added. Once again, desperation outweighed rational thought. 'A single round each. Winner takes all.'

From the expression in his eyes, Hunter could tell that the narcissist inside the Werewolf was seriously toying with the idea. He pushed again.

'Are you scared to put your life on the line?'

The Werewolf exhaled and narrowed his eyes at Hunter. 'We do this and the deal is off. After I kill you – because that's what's going to happen – I will not set them free.' He indicated the monitor once again. 'I will either kill them right after I've killed you, or sell them to the voices, where they'll die screaming and in agony. Are you OK with that?'

Hunter felt the pit in his stomach expand to a black hole.

'I kill you now,' the Werewolf continued, 'they go free as I've promised. You'll be dead, but you would have saved two lives. A very dignified last act as an LAPD detective. I kill you in a "duel" and they both die. Are you sure you want to murder them as well, Detective? Because this won't be a gamble. You don't stand a chance in a face-to-face shootout with me.'

The Werewolf had a point – save two lives or gamble all three. The problem, Hunter thought, was that in his mind, *both* sides of the equation were a gamble. He had no guarantees that the Werewolf would set them free, other than the ex-soldier giving him his 'word'. Which could mean absolutely nothing at all, but even if it did, even if the Werewolf stayed true to his promise and did release Angela and the other hostage, even if he never went after any of them again . . . he would still go after other people, abduct them and then sell them to the voices. In the long run, this was a bad deal, no matter which way Hunter looked at it.

He decided to trust himself..

'I guess we'll see about that,' Hunter replied.

With another broad smile on his lips, the Werewolf walked over to the metal cabinet to the right of the control desk and unlocked it, using a key he'd retrieved from his pocket.

Hunter saw the Werewolf reaching for something inside the cabinet, but he couldn't tell what it was, as the Werewolf's body was blocking his view.

'I like you, Detective Hunter. I like the fact that you want to go down fighting. I can't blame you. I would do the same. Like I said, you really should've been in the military.'

As the ex-soldier turned to face Hunter, he was finally able to see what the Werewolf had retrieved from the locked cabinet – a Ruger SR22 pistol.

'And I know just how we can do this.'

The Werewolf placed the new weapon on the control desk

and returned to the cabinet, where he reached for something else. This time he picked up a Kevlar ballistic vest, which he put on.

Hunter's whole face became one huge question mark.

Once the ex-soldier had put on the vest, he reached for the pistol on the control desk. The SR22 was a lot more compact than the 9mm Sig Sauer P228 that he was holding earlier.

'This is a Ruger SR22,' he explained. 'I'm sure you've seen it before.' He pressed a button on the weapon and released its magazine. 'Ten rounds.'

With his thumb, he began extracting all the bullets from the clip. He extracted nine of them and then stopped, leaving only one in place. He made sure Hunter had seen what he was doing. He then slotted the magazine back into the weapon and chambered that single round.

'I'm sure that I don't need to explain that the sort of damage that a 22-caliber bullet inflicts is minimal, especially when compared to something like this.' The Werewolf once again showed Hunter his P228. 'Unlike a 9mm round, a 22-caliber one will not halt an enemy coming at you, it's not powerful enough . . . unless that round perfectly strikes a vital organ.'

He used his index finger to first point to his heart, then to his forehead.

'Well,' the Werewolf continued. 'As you can see, my heart is protected by a ballistic vest, so my only exposed vital body part is my head.' He pointed to it again. 'So this is how this is going to go down, Detective. I will untie one of your hands – your shooting hand – and I will hand you the Ruger SR22. As you saw, there's only one bullet in the chamber, none in the magazine, which gives you one chance and one chance only to hit the target. Right here.' His index finger pointed to the center of his forehead one more time. 'This is the only way you will stop me, Detective. A 22-caliber bullet through my brain will halt me. A 22-caliber bullet anywhere else on my body . . .' He shrugged.

Hunter had certainly not anticipated the ballistic vest.

'So, continuing with the rules of the game. You'll have the Ruger SR22 with a single chambered bullet and I'll have my own 9mm Sig Sauer P228.' The Werewolf once again showed Hunter his weapon. 'Now, what you need to know is that my clip contains expanding rounds. That's why the blonde woman's head exploded like a watermelon.'

Hunter breathed out.

Expanding rounds were bullets that were designed to expand on impact, sometimes to twice the original diameter. When that happened, the bullet slowed down and more of its kinetic energy was transferred to the target, producing a much larger wound and consequently a lot more damage than a regular round. Expanding rounds were the most lethal type of ammunition available on the market.

'So,' the Werewolf continued with the rules of the game. 'Arms down by the sides of our bodies.' He demonstrated. 'I'll give us a count of three. To even things out, I promise you that I will sit as still as possible. At the count, we shoot.'

'Am I supposed to trust you that you won't shoot before the count?' Hunter asked.

'Am I supposed to trust *you* that *you* won't shoot before the count?' The Werewolf threw the question right back at Hunter. 'You'll also be holding a gun, Detective.'

Hunter stayed quiet.

'Remember,' the Werewolf carried on. 'You've got a single round in your weapon and you're tied to a pretty heavy chair, so don't go thinking about injuring me and then calling for help.' He shook his head carelessly. 'Not going to happen. A 22-caliber bullet won't stop me.'

The Werewolf placed the Heckler and Koch Mark 23 pistol he had taken from Hunter on the control desk. Too far for Hunter to get to, but just an arm's reach from him.

'This is so you don't get any ideas, Detective, and try to shoot the gun out of my hand,' he continued. 'Remember, you're tied to that chair. Only your shooting arm will be free. Wounded or not, I'll still be able to reach for your gun and finish the job way before you get to me. And yes, I can shoot with both hands. If you choose to shoot to wound, that's your prerogative, but at the count of three, I promise you that I'll shoot to kill and this time, I *will* blow your head clean off your body. After that, like I've said, I'll either kill those two in there, or I'll sell them to the voices.'

He paused and smiled at Hunter.

'So, are we really doing this?'

Hunter knew he couldn't go back now.

Ninety-Four

Calmly, the Werewolf returned to the same cabinet from where he had retrieved the SR22 and the ballistic vest; he picked up a sharp, stainless-steel knife, and walked over to Hunter's chair.

'I will now free your shooting arm and hand you the weapon,' he said to a silent and tense Hunter. 'We'll sit facing each other with our weapons down by the side of our chairs. At the count of three, we lift our arms and we shoot. That's it. Simple. Like you said – an Old West-style duel.' He lifted the front of Hunter's shirt.

'Hey, what are you doing?' Hunter asked, his eyes wide in surprise.

'Relax, Detective. You're not my type.' The Werewolf slid the Ruger SR22 pistol into the front of Hunter's trousers. 'You have my word that I will not shoot before the count of three. I trust you'll do the same, but I'm quick and my eyes are very sharp, so if I notice the slightest movement from your arm before the count is over, I'll shoot.' From the small of his back, the Werewolf retrieved his Sig Sauer P228 and showed Hunter. 'Let's do this like gentlemen, shall we?'

Hunter could barely believe that the Werewolf was referring to himself as a gentleman.

The Werewolf went round to the back of the chair.

SNICK.

He cut the zip-tie that held Hunter's right arm to the chair.

SNICK.

He cut the zip-tie that secured Hunter's right wrist to his left one. His left arm was still zip-tied to the chair, as were both of his legs. As his right arm was freed, Hunter extended and curled it several times to get the blood circulation back to normal. He did the same with his fingers.

'Yeah,' the ex-soldier said, as he rounded the chair again to face Hunter, his P228 held firmly in his right hand and aiming at the LAPD Detective. 'Move it around a little. Get that blood pumping. I'll wait.'

With his weapon still aimed at Hunter, he walked backwards until he reached his chair, about eight paces away.

'Are you ready, Detective?' he asked after several minutes.

Hunter breathed out as adrenalin flooded his brain and body. Ready or not, he knew that the Werewolf wouldn't wait any longer.

They locked eyes once again.

'You can reach for your weapon now,' the Werewolf said.

Hunter lifted his shirt and wrapped his fingers around the grip of the Ruger SR22.

'Easy now, Detective. No sudden movements. You don't want me to read it wrong and shoot you before the right time, do you?'

Slowly, Hunter retrieved the gun and felt the weight of it in his hand. The empty magazine made it quite light.

'Good, now just let your arm fall to the side of the chair. The round is already chambered, remember?'

Hunter's arm dropped to the side of the chair and his index

finger curled over the weapon's trigger. Inside his chest, his heart began its own drum solo while a kaleidoscope of butterflies was released inside his stomach.

The Werewolf nodded and allowed his arm to drop to the side of his chair.

'This is it, Detective Hunter,' he said. His voice was peaceful, accepting.

Hunter kept his gaze cemented on the Werewolf's face. And it surprised him. The ex-soldier had no discernable expression. No anger ... no pity ... no remorse ... nothing. Hunter was looking at a man who would either die or kill someone in the next few seconds and he was treating it as if he was just about to pour himself a bowl of cornflakes. He also seemed to have no psychological response to danger. His pupil dilation, skin tone and breathing remained exactly the same.

'OK,' the Werewolf said, giving Hunter a single nod. 'Let's do this.'

A second drum set joined the one already inside Hunter's chest.

'On three. And I'll show you who is the best.'

Hunter breathed in through his nose, trying to take in as much oxygen as he could without making too sudden a movement. His eyes would not leave the ex-soldier.

'One.'

The Werewolf's facial expression was absolutely still, his arm was like a dead limb by the side of his chair.

Hunter wondered if the ex-soldier would really stick to his word, or if he would fire his weapon on the count of two instead of three. The anticipation threatened to send a shiver down Hunter's arm, but he fought it with all he had. A shaky arm would be the last thing he needed right then.

'Two.'

Absolutely no movement whatsoever from the Werewolf. He didn't even seem to be breathing.

Hunter's finger made itself comfortable around the SR22 trigger. He relaxed his shoulders and breathed out through his mouth just as the count reached 'three'.

In a flash, both of their shooting arms came up.

Only one of them managed to fire his weapon.

Ninety-Five

A few minutes earlier.

After hearing the two gunshots that to her sounded like two explosions, Angela Wood had begun pacing the small cell.

'What the hell is going on out there?' she asked in a voice loud enough to reverberate off the cinderblock walls, but quiet enough not to activate the ceiling sprinklers.

Angela could feel her whole body shivering under her. Her mouth went desert-dry and she struggled to breathe. To her, it felt as if the cell walls were wrapping themselves around her like fingers closing into a fist. She knew exactly what was coming because she had felt like that a few times before – they were the telltale signs of a panic attack.

'No ... please don't,' she begged her body and her brain. 'I don't need this now. I really don't need this now.'

She squeezed her eyes tight and did her best to concentrate on her breathing, trying to calm it down before it got completely out of control.

'Breathe, Angie,' she whispered to herself. 'Long, deep breaths, not short bursts.'

That was what a doctor once told her to do.

It took Angela a several minutes, but the exercise worked and she managed to get her breathing under control and halt the panic attack before it could take her over.

As her breathing stabilized, she heard the sound of a door closing somewhere outside her cell, followed by footsteps.

'What the fuck?' she whispered, before approaching the door to her cell. She knew much better than to put her ear against it, though that was exactly what she wanted to do.

'Hello?' she called out in a tentative voice. 'Is anyone there?'

She got no reply.

'Hello?' she tried again.

Nothing.

Angela got as close to the door as she possibly could without touching it. She was about to call out one more time, when something beat her to the punch.

BANG!

A third gunshot, but this time it sounded like it had come from a lot closer than the previous two. Practically, just outside her door. The sound was so loud, ice-cold water started raining from her ceiling.

Fear hit Angela like a speed train and she quickly stepped back from the door.

'Something's wrong,' she thought. 'Something's seriously wrong here.'

That was when a whole new train of thought entered her mind, making her heart almost stall.

What if I'm not the only one? What if he's got other hostages locked into cells just like this one? What if he's angry and he's going around killing them one by one? What if I'm next?

Angela tried to think, but her confused brain kept on misfiring.

The ceiling sprinklers finally came to a stop, but just as they did ...

BANG!

A fourth shot.

This one did not reactivate the ceiling sprinklers, but did send Angela's heart back into overdrive.

'Fucked if I'm going to just sit here and wait for this psycho to come and kill me,' Angela said to herself, as she walked back to the bed. 'I'm not going out like that. If I'm going down, I'm going down with a fucking fight.'

Facing the door, Angela got into a linebacker position – body bent forward, left leg in front, right leg behind, ready to push her whole body forward with all the strength she had left in her.

'The only way that you're getting in here is through that door, you sick sonofabitch,' she said in a murmur, taking deep breaths to psych herself up. 'And as soon as that door opens, I'm coming at you like the fucking thunder. You might kill me, but I'm going to break your fucking ribs before I go.'

Through the tiny gap between the door and the cement floor, Angela saw two dark shadows appear – feet. Someone had walked up to her cell.

'Here we go.'

A key was inserted into the lock.

Angela clenched her fingers into a fist.

The door unlocked and Angela shot forward like a human cannon ball.

Ninety-Six

Seven tenths of a second – that was how long the duel between Hunter and the Werewolf lasted.

Both of their arms shot up like rockets, but even before the countdown began, the Werewolf already knew that he would win.

Hunter's weapon was a lot lighter than his and the Werewolf knew that that gave Hunter an advantage, but still, the power of his 9mm against Hunter's 22-caliber pistol gave him a much bigger edge.

Just like the Werewolf had explained, the only way in which Hunter would be able to stop him would be if Hunter's single bullet hit him right on the forehead. The projectile had to pierce his skull and then his brain to bring him to a stop ... and that was the problem. Even from a distance of eight paces, Hunter would have to aim to hit his target, while the Werewolf didn't necessarily have to. His expanding round would cause enormous damage wherever it hit – stomach, chest, arm, leg, head ... it didn't really matter. As long as the Werewolf's round hit Hunter, it was pretty much the end for the detective. Even if the Werewolf hit him on the leg, the pain of shattered bone and ruptured muscle and nerves would be so intense, Hunter would immediately drop his weapon.

Game over.

If the Werewolf's first bullet didn't kill him, the second one, fired against a wounded Hunter, would blow his head off.

'This is way too fucking easy,' the Werewolf thought before counting to three.

On 'three', he knew that Hunter was as good as dead, and so were the two hostages in the confinement cells.

Ninety-Seven

'Three.'

Both of their arms shot up like rockets, but only one of them managed to fire his weapon.

Just like the Werewolf, Hunter was an excellent shot, one of the best in the whole of the LAPD, but he also knew for a fact that the Werewolf was a much better marksman than he was ... much more accurate. The ex-soldier had proven that by missing Hunter's head by no more than an inch, twice, in a double-tap discharge. Hunter was good, but not that good. He knew that.

What he also knew was that their duel would not be won on accuracy. From a distance of about eight paces, he was sure that both of them could bullseye a target, even under pressure, but worse of all, Hunter knew that he was really the only one who needed to hit the target – the Werewolf's forehead. The Werewolf's bullet could hit him just about anywhere on his body and the destruction power of the 9mm expanding round would do the rest. So Hunter knew that the only way he would be able to win that duel would be if he either cheated or came up with some sort of magic trick.

Magic it was.

As soon as the Werewolf handed Hunter the SR22 pistol, his analytical brain began calculating the odds.

The first factor he took into consideration was the weight of their weapons.

The SR22, with a full clip, weighed around 1.4lb, but the magazine in Hunter's gun was empty. All he had was a chambered round. With an empty clip, the SR22 weighed only around 1lb, which wasn't the case for the P228. Unloaded, the P228 weighed around 1.85lb. Its magazine was bigger and the rounds larger and heavier than the SR22, and the Werewolf's magazine was almost full. Hunter guessed that the ex-soldier's weapon would weigh well over a pound more than his.

The second factor that entered Hunter's calculations was the amount of pressure each trigger required to activate and release the hammer. Being a much smaller and lighter weapon, the SR22 required around 3.5lb of pressure on the trigger to activate the hammer. A straight-from-the-factory Sig P228 required around 12lb of pressure on the trigger. Many professionals customized their weapons, making the trigger lighter for faster action, but even if that was the case with the Werewolf's P228, the reduction on the trigger pressure would be around 4–4.5lb, no more. Customized or not, Hunter's SR22 would have a much faster trigger action than the Werewolf's P228.

Those two factors alone – the Werewolf's weapon being over a pound heavier than Hunter's and the considerably higher trigger pressure needed to activate and release its hammer – would give Hunter a couple of fractions of a second advantage in a game that they both knew wouldn't last more than a second. That tiny advantage was exactly what Hunter needed to make his magic trick work, because his trick was in his arm movement.

On three, the Werewolf's *entire* arm shot up, searching for a fire position.

Hunter, on the other hand, decided that on the count of three, instead of moving his whole arm from a resting position into a shooting one, he would simply bend his elbow and fire. That would allow him to fire from waist height – a position that he was extremely comfortable firing from – and that was where his trick lay, because it angled his shot.

The Werewolf wasn't lying when he told Hunter that the only way to stop him would be to put a bullet in his brain, which meant that in normal circumstances – a bullet traveling horizontally – Hunter would have to hit the Werewolf square on his forehead, but Hunter's round was traveling at an upward angle, starting at waist height, and that meant that his bullet could now hit the Werewolf practically anywhere on his face.

And that was exactly what happened.

Hunter's round struck the Werewolf just below his nose. Despite being a small bullet, from such a short distance the 22-caliber round was still powerful enough to rupture through bone, muscle tissue, and cartilage, reaching the Werewolf's brain through the bottom of his eye socket. In the brain, the bullet ripped through the mesencephalon and the pituitary gland, before finally losing momentum and terminating its journey at the top of the Werewolf's parietal lobe.

The destruction was severe and irreversible and the ex-soldier's brain ceased functioning way before it could send his finger a signal to squeeze the trigger on his weapon.

Hunter saw his round hit the Werewolf in the face. The entry wound was minimal – practically the size of a nostril, maybe a little smaller – but due to the bullet's upward traveling angle, Hunter knew that it would reach the ex-soldier's brain matter. In there, its destructive power would be lethal.

As the round hit the Werewolf, a restricted blood mist sprayed up from the wound, coloring the air directly in front of the ex-soldier's face. His head jerked back violently and his torso slammed against his chair's backrest. His arm, which was about a quarter of the way up, carried on with its momentum, but his hand lost all its grip on the P228, releasing it into the air. The weapon flew from his hand in Hunter's direction, almost hitting him in the head.

Momentum gone, the Werewolf's arm collapsed back down by his limp and already lifeless body. His head tilted a little to the left. His eyes, still wide open, were staring straight at Hunter. The look in them was cold and determined.

Blood cascaded from his nose-wound down to his mouth and chin, before dripping onto his chest. His legs shook awkwardly for a couple of seconds, before coming to a full stop. Life, for the Werewolf, had finally been extinguished.

It took Hunter another full minute to properly catch his breath and feel his heart slowing down inside of him.

He was still tied down to his chair. Only his right arm was free, but the Werewolf was gone.

Hunter took another deep breath and threw the whole weight of his body forward, throwing himself and the chair to the floor. He used his free arm to break the fall, then to drag himself across the concrete floor until he got to the control desk. Sweat dripped from his forehead. He still couldn't believe that he had somehow managed to cheat death one more time.

Hunter caught his breath once again and reached for the

stainless-steel knife that the Werewolf had used to cut the zip-ties minutes earlier. He had left it on the control desk.

It took Hunter no time to completely free himself from the chair.

Hanging from the Werewolf's belt, Hunter found the keys to the confinement cells. He grabbed them and walked through the metal door to the left of the control desk, which the Werewolf had left unlocked. The dimly lit corridor that he saw as he walked through the door was a lot longer than he had expected. In fact, it seemed to go on forever before it curved left in an 'L' shape. There were only two doors on the left wall, separated by a gap of about twenty yards.

Hunter checked the keys in his hands. From the monitor inside the control room, he knew that Angela was in cell number three. He followed the corridor to the end and then around to the left. Confinement cell number three was just ahead of him.

Hunter got to it and unlocked it. As he pushed the door open he was tackled so hard, he heard one of his ribs crack.

Ninety-Eight

Police Administration Building – Sunday, December 13th.

'So,' Captain Blake asked, as Hunter and Garcia stepped into her office and closed the door behind them. She had called for an early meeting in anticipation of her afternoon briefing with the Chief of Police and the Mayor of Los Angeles. 'Are you guys and forensics finally done with that hell house?'

The Werewolf's hideout location turned out to be a large and dilapidated structure at the edge of some woodland in Santa Clarita. The building, they learned, was an abandoned retirement home. It had been left to decay for over a decade. For the past two days, Hunter, Garcia and a small team of forensics agents had been scrutinizing every inch of it.

'Well, *we* are,' Garcia replied. His eyes peeked at Hunter before moving back to Captain Blake. 'Forensics will still be there for a while. Hell knows how many different samples of DNA they'll be able to collect in there.'

'Fair enough,' the captain acknowledged, sipping on her coffee. 'So what have you guys come up with so far?'

Garcia chuckled. 'What *haven't* we come up with, Captain?' His eyes moved to Hunter again, who took over.

'The killer's real name was Dean Turner,' he began. 'He was forty-two years old, originally from Fresno. He came to LA after his "kill team" was disbanded.'

Hunter had already briefed Garcia and Captain Blake on the back-story that the Werewolf had told him.

'But we still have no real confirmation that this "kill team" really existed, do we?' the captain asked. 'No confirmation that this freak was really in the military.'

'No,' Hunter replied. 'And we'll never have that confirmation, Captain. Like I've explained – it was a clandestine team. No code name ... no call sign ... nothing. For total secrecy, all team members were enlisted under false names. This is the kind of outfit that our government, our military, doesn't want anyone to know exists.'

Captain Blake sat back on her chair and laced her fingers together.

'Do we at least know how many people he's murdered since he came to LA?' she asked. 'Do we even know *when* he first came to LA?'

'I did ask him how many subjects there were before he started his diary,' Hunter said. 'But he couldn't remember. All he said was that he was sure that there had been a few.'

'Fuck!' the captain cursed under her breath. 'So definitely more than sixteen?'

'No doubt,' Hunter agreed.

'The mayor will love that,' the captain said, sarcastically. 'How about the hostages at the hideout?'

Hunter's eyes darkened, as vivid images of the Werewolf entering the blonde woman's cell and shooting her in the face came crashing back to him.

'The one he murdered while I was there was Alexandra Berger,' he said. 'Twenty-four years of age from Santa Monica. We found her handbag with her driver's license and house keys stashed in one of the rooms. She shared an apartment, also in Santa Monica, with her boyfriend, Luke Bradford. I gave him the news yesterday.'

Captain Blake shook her head while her eyebrows arched. She knew only too well how tough the job of passing on that sort of news was. 'How about the other one?'

'Her name is Silvia Hinton from Garland in Texas. Twenty-six years old. Her parents flew in to stay with her. Not surprisingly, she's still in shock, so we haven't had a chance to get a full statement from her.'

'Do we know when she was abducted?'

'Five days ago,' Hunter confirmed. 'Miss Hinton is a nurse at the Children's Hospital in Sunset Boulevard. Apparently she was taken as she got into her car after finishing an evening shift.'

'And how is she doing?'

'Healthwise, she's OK – a little malnourished, but OK. Psychologically? She'll definitely be traumatized. How much? Only time will tell.'

'How about Angela Wood?'

'She's a little shook up,' Hunter confirmed. 'But she's fine. She's being discharged from hospital this morning. After I leave here, I'm picking her up and giving her a ride back to her place.'

'Also,' Garcia added. 'Clay Heath's body was discovered inside sublevel one of the "under refurbishment" multi-story car park, just across the road from the Westin Bonaventure Hotel. Work had been interrupted a couple of weeks ago – something to do with the budget – that's why the body was only found last night by a group of teenagers.'

'So the killer sliced the poor kid's throat,' the captain said. 'And then calmly crossed the road into the hotel to wait for Robert and the diary.'

'Precisely,' Garcia agreed.

Captain Blake finished her coffee and got to her feet. The look on her face was concerned.

'That chat room we saw on the Dark Web?' she asked. 'The "voices", can we track those people down? Get the FBI or Interpol after them?'

'No, we can't,' Hunter replied. 'That's the appeal of the Dark Web, Captain. It's untraceable. They can buy or sell whatever they like in there, safe in the knowledge that they will never be identified.'

Captain Blake paused by her office window and stared at the sky outside for an instant – her stare distant and lost.

'It's a sad and very dark world we live in,' Garcia commented, 'when people can not only sell those things over the Internet, but there are hundreds ... thousands of people out there willing to buy them and there's nothing we can do about it. It pisses me off.'

'We can't save the whole world, Carlos,' Hunter said. 'We can't save everybody. You know that. All we can do is keep doing what we're doing – giving our best to the job, saving the ones we can save, protecting the ones we can protect ... putting the people we catch behind bars.'

'Robert is right, Carlos,' Captain Blake said, turning to face her detectives. 'All you can do is keep on doing what you're doing – giving your best to the job, and I couldn't ask any more of you two. So shake that goddamn frown off your faces, go have a couple of donuts and a glass of milk, and go do what you do best.'

'You mean – look this good all day long?' Garcia asked.

'Get out,' the captain demanded, pointing at her door.

Ninety-Nine

While Garcia went back to their office, Hunter took a drive down to the Good Samaritan Hospital on Wilshire Boulevard. Angela Wood was waiting for him at the reception, together with a nurse.

'How are you feeling?' Hunter asked, after he signed the release papers. He had used his health insurance to cover her hospital stay.

'I'm fine,' Angela replied, as they made their way to his car. 'I'm just glad to be out of here. Hospital food is a joke.'

'Do you want to go grab something to eat?' Hunter asked.

'No, I'm OK. Thank you.' She paused as Hunter unlocked the passenger door to his Buick. 'Look, you don't have to drive me to my place. I can walk or get the bus. I would've left hours ago, but they won't discharge you if you don't have someone to come pick you up.'

'Just get in, will you?'

Reluctantly, Angela got into the passenger seat. 'You really need to think about getting a new car. This ... thing, is falling to pieces ... and it smells in here.'

'No, it doesn't,' Hunter countered, looking a little offended. 'Smells like what?'

'Old,' Angela replied. 'It smells like old.'

Hunter said nothing back, but he winced as he veered left.

'How's the rib?' Angela asked in a tone a lot more gentle than usual.

'Black and blue,' Hunter replied. 'And it hurts like hell, but I'll live. They've patched me up nicely.'

'I *am* really sorry about that,' Angela sounded sincere. 'The tackle was not meant for you.'

'I know that.'

'Why didn't you call out my name before opening the door? I really thought that that door would open and it would be "goodbye Angie".'

'Yeah, I should have,' Hunter admitted.

'Yes, you should.'

'Anyway,' Hunter said with a smile. 'It was a damn good tackle.'

Angela smiled back. 'Just so you know,' she said, as Hunter turned right on West 6th Street. 'I'm quitting the game. I'm quitting being a pickpocket.'

'Really?' Hunter looked pleased, but not surprised.

'Yeah. I promised myself that if I ever made it out of that stinking hellhole, I would quit. I stick to my promises.'

'That's fantastic,' Hunter said with a smile. 'Do you have a plan? Do you know what you would like to do?'

'Not yet, but I will.'

Hunter reached into his pocket and retrieved a small piece of paper. 'Here.' He handed it to Angela.

'What's this?' she asked, as she unfolded the note. It contained a name and a phone number. 'Who's Richard Cole?'

'He's a friend of mine, who happens to be the Los Angeles head of security for the Bloomingdale's group. I told him about you and he would love if you could give him a call so he can set up an interview with you.'

'An interview? An interview for what?'

'For a job.'

Angela looked at Hunter, a little confused.

'The way they see it,' he explained, 'it's much better to have someone with your skills on their side instead of against them. I'm sure that you could teach them a few things, like what and who to look out for.'

Angela's stare stayed on Hunter, but the look in her eyes softened a little.

'It's a good job and the pay isn't bad at all,' Hunter added. 'I'm sure you'll be great at it. Give him a call. He's a really nice guy too.'

Angela placed the note in her pocket and sat quietly for the next ten minutes.

'Can I ask you something?' she finally said.

'Sure.'

'Why are you being so nice to me?'

Hunter blinked and looked back at Angela, as if trying to figure her out.

'What I mean is . . . I know I've been a bitch to you. I know that because I'm a bitch to everyone. I don't trust people, so being a bitch is kind of my defense mechanism. But this time being a bitch has cost two agents their lives, and I'm so, so sorry about that.' Angela's eyes welled up and her voice faltered. 'I was stupid, I was selfish . . . I was much more than just a bitch . . . and now they're dead.' Tears began streaming down her face. 'I'll never forgive myself for that for as long as I live. I am so sorry.'

The deep remorse in Angela's voice filled Hunter's car with emotion.

'I'm not a bad person,' she continued, as she wiped away the tears. 'At least I didn't used to be. Please believe that.'

'I do,' Hunter said in return.

'I want to go back to the person I used to be. I want to start again. I don't want to be this way anymore.'

'That's great,' Hunter agreed. 'And a new, legit job can be the new beginning you're looking for. Give Richard a call.'

Angela tried to catch Hunter's eyes, but he kept them securely on the road.

'You didn't answer my question,' she pushed. 'Why are you being so nice to me?'

'Because I know a lot of people like you, Angela,' Hunter finally replied. '*I* was once like you, and all of us, no matter how tough or strong we think we are . . . we all make mistakes, and we all need a little help every once in a while, because none of us can be tough and strong one hundred percent of the time. I know it, because I've tried it before and I've failed.'

Tears came back to Angela's eyes.

'I'm not really doing anything out of the ordinary here,' Hunter said in a tender voice. 'I'm just trying to help a friend get back on her feet, that's all. I'm just being human.'

Angela paused. 'You're a much nicer human than most of the ones I've met. Trust me on that.'

They went quiet again for another minute.

'Do you really mean what you said just now?' Angela asked, as she dried her tears once again.

'About the job?' Hunter replied. 'Of course I—'

'No, not about the job,' Angela interrupted Hunter. 'About helping a *friend*. Do you consider me a friend?'

This time it was Hunter who sought Angela's eyes. 'I do. I was hoping that maybe you would feel the same.'

Angela smiled a shy smile.

'I'd like that. I'd like that very much.'

Hunter pulled up in front of Angela's apartment building and turned off the engine. 'So, will you give Richard a call?'

'I think I might. Yes.'

'Great. By the way, your door has been fixed.' Hunter handed Angela the keys to the new lock.

'About time.' She took the keys, paused, then quickly leaned over and gave Hunter a kiss on the cheek. 'Thank you . . . for everything.'

Hunter smiled and watched Angela run into her building's entry lobby and up the stairs.

He turned the ignition key, and his engine misfired.

He tried again.

Nothing.

One more time.

Nothing.

'Goddamn it.' He sat back in his seat. 'Maybe I should really get a new car.'

Acknowledgements

Unfortunately, during the process of writing this novel, I suffered a loss that shattered my universe, bringing with it the sort of personal darkness I hoped I would never have to face again. If not for the amazing help and companionship of some of the most special people I've ever met, this novel would've never been finished, and I probably wouldn't be here anymore.

Helen Mulder, Jair and Lisa Pelegrina, Uwe Lippold, Andru and Tracy Kalker, Lynne Marie Campbell.

From the bottom of my heart, I thank you all. You guys have saved my life and you mean a lot more to me than you'll ever know.

Thank you for being there for me.

On a professional level, my heartfelt thanks goes to a few special people – my agent, Darley Anderson, for being the best agent an author could have. Darley's Angels – Mary Darby, Kristina Egan, Georgia Fuller and the whole team at the agency, for simply being amazing. My new editors at Simon & Schuster – Anne Perry and Bethan Jones – who have worked tirelessly to fix all the problems in this book.

Thank you also to all the readers and everyone out there who have so fantastically supported me and my novels from the start. Without your support, I wouldn't be writing.

Do you want more Robert Hunter?
Then don't miss

Lucien Folter, the most dangerous serial killer
the FBI has ever known, has just escaped. Now, he's
looking for Detective Robert Hunter – and he's
going to make him pay . . .

Keep reading to enjoy an extract now.

SIMON &
SCHUSTER

One

That morning, due to a broken-down truck partially blocking one of the slip roads on US Route 58, it took Jordan Weaver exactly twenty-eight minutes and thirty-one seconds to drive the almost nine miles between his house and his work place; about twelve minutes longer than usual. Parking and the walk from his car to the staff entry door cost him another one minute and twenty-two seconds. Security check, clocking in, dumping his bag in his locker and a quick trip to the bathroom added another eight minutes and forty-nine seconds to his time. Grabbing a quick cup of coffee at the staff cafeteria and the final walk down the long, L-shaped, west-wing corridor that led to his station – one minute and twenty-seven seconds, which meant that in total it took Jordan Weaver, an infirmary control-room guard at Lee high-security federal prison in Virginia, exactly forty minutes and nine seconds to go from his front door to the worst day of his life.

As he rounded the hallway corner and his eyes settled on the squared control station just ahead of him, Weaver felt his throat constrict and his heart pick up speed inside his chest. The station, which was encased in large bulletproof-glass windows, was never, ever left unattended, but from where he was standing Weaver could see no one inside the control room, which was worrying fact number one. Worrying fact number two was that the room's assault-proof door had been left wide open, an absolute no-no according to the rulebook, but what really sent a shiver of fear down Weaver's spine, making him drop his cup of coffee and pray to God that this was just a horrible dream, were the blood splatters and smears that he could see running down the inside of the windows.

'No, no, no . . .'

Weaver's voice got louder as he went from walking to the fastest sprint he'd ever done. With each step, the large ball of keys that hung from his belt bounced loudly against his right hip. He reached the control-room door in four seconds flat and nightmare became reality.

On the floor, inside the bulletproof enclosure, the bodies of Guards Vargas and Bates lay in one massive pool of blood, both of their heads twisted back awkwardly, revealing the extent of the injuries to their throats – thick, crude lacerations that ran the width of their entire necks, slicing through the internal jugular vein, the common carotid artery and even the thyroid cartilage.

'Fuck!'

Across the room from the two guards was Nurse Frank Wilson – a 24-year-old Asian American who had recently graduated from Old Dominion University in Norfolk. His body was draped out of shape over a swivel chair. His throat had been slashed so ferociously, it was a miracle he hadn't been decapitated, but unlike Vargas and Bates, Wilson's eyes were still wide open and full of terror. Oddly, given the angle in which his head had fallen, Wilson seemed to be staring straight back at Weaver, as if even after death he was still begging for help. All three bodies had been stripped of all their clothes, with the exception of their underwear. The guards' weapons were also missing.

'Jesus H. Christ! What the hell happened here?'

Confused and shaken, Weaver had to step over Vargas's body to reach the main control console and the alarm button. As he slammed his right palm against it, the entire complex was instantly enveloped by the deafening screams of sirens.

The facility's west-wing infirmary housed eight individual medical cells and according to the daily manifest, only one prisoner had stayed overnight – the prisoner in medical cell number one. Weaver's eyes immediately moved to the blood-splattered monitors just above the central console, more specifically to the one on the far left – cell one.

The cell was empty, its door wide open.

'Shit! Shit! Shit!'

Weaver felt his legs weaken under him. He'd been an infirmary guard at Lee federal prison for nine long years and in that time, not a single prisoner had ever escaped.

'Shit!' Weaver yelled at the top of his voice. 'How the hell did this happen?'

His gaze rounded the control room one more time. Weaver had never seen that much blood before and despite the perils of being a maximum-security prison guard, he'd never lost a colleague to the job.

'Shiiiiiiiiiit!'

Suddenly Weaver paused, his brain at last registering something that it had somehow missed until then.

A blinking faint white light that was coming from inside a semi-open drawer.

'What the hell?'

FIND OUT MORE ABOUT
CHRIS CARTER

Chris Carter writes highly addictive thrillers
featuring Detective Robert Hunter

To find out more about Chris and his writing,
visit his website at

www.chriscarterbooks.com

or follow Chris on

f @ChrisCarterBooksOfficial

All of Chris Carter's novels are available
in print and eBook, and are available to
download in eAudio

Once again, Weaver had to step over Vargas's body to get to where he needed to go. As his right foot touched the ground, the thick film of blood that lay between his sole and the linoleum floor caused his foot to slip. Instinctively, Weaver's hands shot forward, desperately searching for something to hold on to. His left hand found nothing, but his right one managed to grab hold of the semi-open drawer, where the blinking light was coming from,. As he tried to steady himself, his foot slipped again. As a consequence, his grip tightened on the drawer, fully pulling it open.

Even through the loud shriek of sirens, Weaver heard the odd 'click' that came as the drawer was pulled open.

It was the last sound he ever heard before his entire head exploded into a mess of blood, bone and gray matter.